Becoming Helen

Becoming Helen

A novel about
Love, Lies, and Treason.

GILLIAN LONG

Becoming Helen

GILLIAN LONG © 2022

Cover design by: John Russell, Qld. Australia.
Cover photograph: © Keith Mendel, Atlanta. USA.
Library of Congress Control Number: 2018675309

First Published, 2022
ISBN 978-0-6455760-0-9
Millaa House Publishing
PO Box 89
Millaa Millaa
Queensland 4886.

Becoming Helen is dedicated to
Margaret Latta Illingworth nee Landale,
1915 – 1983,
whose memories of the Second World War
inspired this story.

Contents

New York 1943..0

1. Bavaria 1935...1

2. Gertrud...5

3. Munich 1937...16

4. Dachau Barracks 26

5. Church of the Holy Cross 33

6. Munich to Brussels 47

7. A Convent near Leuven 55

8. The Spanish War 1938 63

9. Brussels, Autumn 1939...70

10. Fleeing Belgium 83

11. France, May 1940 92

12. Surrey 1941 104

13. Occupied France 117

14. Paris 127

15. Undone 136

16. Spain...147

17. Sardou...153

18. Violetta 158

19. Madrid 168

20. Gibraltar..180

21. Baker Street London 1942..198

22. Death, loss, and leaving 206

23. La Belle Hélène 214

24. Autumn Propaganda..232

25. North Atlantic Crossing 1943..242

26. The Concert..251

New York 1943 266

About the Author..268

New York 1943

Fifth Avenue, Office of Strategic Services

The Brigadier General sitting across the desk was about 60 years old, once blond, but now greying hair parted on the side. His intense blue gaze appraised me as I explained my mission.

"I'm sorry you have come all this way Major Guilford, but I cannot allow it. I have heard of your bravery, your skills with language and your extraordinary voice. Of course, we would value your input into training and translations, but not anything operational, especially not behind the lines."

I took a steadying breath, and continued speaking, perhaps a little more forcefully that I intended. "You only say that because you have no idea of my previous work—particularly the journey I took before becoming Major Helen Guilford. The British have given permission for my collaboration, and agree I am to hold nothing back. I admit I am no expert, but I have succeeded where others have failed. I am certainly not brave, and yet my own innate cowardice has served to preserve me throughout all my assigned missions. But I am getting ahead of myself, for in order for you to understand my capability, as well as make sense of what happened, and why I make this request, I will need to go back and tell you a story that began before this war.

To give you an overall picture, I need to explain how I became Helen, and that story goes back to my adoption in 1933, just before my fourteenth birthday. Old for adoption I know but bear with me and you will see why. That was the moment that set me upon my life's path. A journey, I might add, for which I asked no part."

He looked a little taken aback at my forthrightness, or I might have imagined it, but undeterred I forged on. "You must understand that until that time, I had been protected and secluded, brought up in a Berlin Catholic orphanage and schooled under the rigid discipline of Dominican nuns. I knew right from wrong, but only in a concrete and unilluminated way. That was until an SS officer and his wife, people of high social standing in Berlin, adopted me and cast me into the abyss."

I felt my jaw thrust and set, and the man frowned. I tried to gauge what he was feeling, but his gaze reverted to its former blandness with only a remnant shadow hovering in his eyes. He was like an immovable object, a granite statue, albeit fashionably tailored in his uniform. His arms were folded, leaning on the desk. His gaze was penetrating but entirely devoid of any discernible compassion. I took another breath to calm my thrashing pulse. To hell with him and all my puppet masters! They were the same the world over. I had not yet succumbed to any of them, and I would not now.

I leaned back in my chair, a challenge forming in my expression, one that I found hard to remove. I felt it compressing my mouth into an ugly line. "How much do you think I should have known at that age? How much, as a well-educated and intelligent young girl, should I have guessed?"

The man didn't respond. He was better at this game than me. I shook my head and continued. "No, I can't answer that question either, except to explain how I made the decisions I did, and how those choices led me to you here in New York.

At the end of it you will understand why, despite everything that has happened to me, I have requested to return to Germany. It is not bravery, but necessity.

When you hear my story, you may judge me harshly for what I did to survive. Nevertheless, I will tell it all as I remember it because ultimately I believe I have been of service to the Allied cause and am owed some small indulgence for myself. While I can understand your mistrust, I can also assure you I will be faithful to your service. I too want to help end this war and will serve you steadfastly in whatever capacity you may see fit. But if I transfer to American intelligence, it is only on the condition I can return to Germany. With your permission, I will begin…"

1. BAVARIA 1935

Although I had lived in Berlin all my life, the last two years with my adoptive parents, the story about how I betrayed my country, and, against my will, became Helen, really started my first night in Bavaria. That was when I came to realise that all was not as I believed. The world is not a certain place. Not even my world view was a fixed thing, and from that moment to this, chaos has forged me like the birthing of a new cosmos.

That September evening in 1935, as I listened to the screech of amplified sound that told me Dr Ley made his introductions to the Reich Party Congress of Freedom, the roar of an adoring crowd carried from the Luitpoldarena across Nuremberg and through my open window. I admit, when the blue rays shot through the night sky to form a cathedral of light to honour our beloved Führer, my chest puffed out. Yet already I was aware that another sensation hid beneath; one which, despite everything, made me breathless with foreboding.

In the street below the hotel, people and cars swarmed like ants towards the arena, and as I watched them I imagined my new father, Papi Karl, smart in his black uniform and shiny boots. He would be there already, perhaps with his arm held out stiffly. He was to be singled-out for his loyalty.

1

I could only imagine because I could not attend the Party rally. Karl said I was too young and should stay behind in the hotel room, although he took Frau Hoffermann. I curtseyed to my reflection in the window glass, pretending I was at Karl's side, delighting our Führer, and earning Karl further honours with my Aryan perfection and pending motherhood. Then I turned away, angry they had left me alone. Yet, I also knew I shouldn't sulk, for that was mere self-pity. Even so, that night I cried myself to sleep.

Just before dawn the next morning I felt nauseous, but as the hours passed the sickness retreated and hunger made saliva quicken under my tongue. I expected to stop at the next village for something to eat, for we had left Nuremberg before dawn. We were now driving through the autumn-hued Bavarian morning, heading for a destination unknown to me. It was where I was to stay for the next few months with Frau Hoffermann as we prepared for the birth of my child, a shame that must be hidden from truth.

Eventually, we arrived at a village, its signpost announcing we had reached Steinhöring. I glanced in the wing mirror, seeing the reflection of my beloved Karl's sleep-slackened face. His head rested on the seatback, eyes closed, mouth a little open, causing the loose skin of his neck to fold over the stiff collar of his emblazoned uniform. How could I bear being without him for the months ahead? I hungered for the moments we had alone, his fleeting touch, his careless caress, but lately, he did not come to me, and I wondered what I had done to drive him away.

Perhaps he merely tired of me. Night after night, I had racked my brain for something witty to say. Something that would make him smile. Something that would cause him to stroke my arm and kiss my neck, but I found myself dumb in his presence. All the words and conversation I practiced in his absence fled as he opened the door to my little room each night. But as my belly swelled and my breasts became tender, he stopped coming, and I, in my childish fantasy, did not blame Karl. Instead, I blamed Frau Hoffermann, whom I could not bring myself to call mother.

A few kilometres further on, the car slowed and turned into a driveway, alongside which stood a large white two-storey building, its black flag proudly displaying the SS of the twin runic lightning bolts of the Schutzstaffel. The sky had grown as dark as gunmetal, and leaves thrashed on the trees bordering a grassy area alongside the building. A nurse in apron and cap, scurried to rescue her tiny charges, wheeling in the little white lace-skirted cots before the storm broke.

The car pulled up before the front entrance of the building, above which a bold sign announced the name HIGHLAND HOUSE. The driver opened the door for Karl, who in turn walked around the car to help Frau Hoffermann. Together, they walked towards the entrance, her hand clutching his arm. Only then did the driver open my door. He left the two suitcases for me to carry while he remained with the car. A rain drop wet my cheek, and I bent to pick up the bags, immediately feeling pressure on my bladder. My face burned, and I avoided looking into his knowing eyes.

The reception hall was decorated with scrolled cornices, pressed ceilings, a chandelier, mirrors, and wall hangings. I imagined a ballroom could not have been as grand. I placed the bags at my feet and gazed around in awe.

Karl spoke quietly to a beaked-nosed man in a white coat whom he called Gregor. I later came to know him as the doctor who would deliver my baby, Dr Ebner. Frau Hoffermann stood across the room reading a framed print hanging on the wall, her billowing maternity wear camouflaging a withered womb. Karl handed documents to the Doctor, who flicked through them before placing them on the lacquered reception desk and shaking Karl's hand.

Then the doctor walked over to circle me, inspecting every detail of my demeanour. He addressed Karl while recording the marks of breeding, my high narrow brow, the light blue colour of my eyes, the paleness of my hair and the smooth ivory tone of my skin. Without speaking to me, he turned to Frau Hoffermann, taking her elbow as he guided her towards a set of large doors. His hand signalled me to follow, but I, like the old donkey at my school, refused to budge.

Karl followed Frau Hoffermann to the door, taking her in his arms and kissing her cheek as he said farewell. The heaviness of despair weighed on me until I thought I might collapse. If I fell to the ground, would Karl pick me up? Would he kiss my cheek one last time? If I fell, would I feel his arms once more? If he would only look at me like he looked at her, I could find the courage to beg him not to leave me here, but I have always been a coward.

Frau Hoffermann and the doctor walked through the double doors, and Karl left the building. Thunder cracked overhead and for a moment I was alone in the reception with just the tock, tock, of the clock on the wall. Then Frau Hoffermann's voice floated distantly from beyond the doorway, "Magdalena keep-up! Always dawdling. It's so exasperating Doctor. You have no idea what I must put up with."

Outside, Karl's car wheels crunched on the gravel as he drove out of my life. I dragged myself after Frau Hoffermann, my heart filled with Nightshade. As I passed the reception desk, I spotted my Ahnenpass on top of the identity documents Karl had handed to the Doctor. In a spark that foreshadowed my later insurrection, I slipped the documents under my coat before following Frau Hoffermann along the dimly lit hallway.

2. GERTRUD

I began to question my judgement when I met Gertrud although I was preoccupied, and it took a while for me to learn the right lessons. As the first weeks at Highland House slipped by, and autumn lost its hues to the grey of winter, I became accustomed to the rhythm of my surroundings. People came and went, babies were born, cried, and were fed, and there was little with which to occupy my time, except to read.

I was unused to idleness, but when I tried to help look after the babies, the nurses shooed me away. I remained in indolence, a book from the library opened on my lap as I struggled with my poor schoolgirl Spanish.

At the time I was attempting to decipher Miguel de Unamuno's novel about a modern-day Cain and Able, a parable about the passion of envy. The ideas it brought to my attention had never before concerned me, but by the time I was halfway through, I recognised what my life would become if I lived through the hatred by which I was consumed.

Each day I tried to unpick the behaviour, likening it both to my own actions and to that of others. That is until someone saw the title of the book and complained to Matron, who demanded I burn it, saying, "Such books should not survive in modern-day Germany."

If that was the case, someone should have thought about cataloguing the House library before now. After that incident, I spent hours in my room reading. Hiding the books in case they were also subversive material that had avoided detection. I read avidly to escape boredom. Books in French and Spanish were my preference because they were difficult to translate and occupied my mind.

Sometimes, I pretended my darling Anna was with me. We would sit with our heads together at our old classroom desk in the convent, discussing our small world. In my imagination, I explained my growing concern about envy, demanding her advice on quelling its appetite. Of course, there was no answer. Anna was gone, along with everything from my old life.

While I missed many things from my past, what I missed most was Anna for she would know what to make of it all, being so much wiser than I. At night, alone in my bed, I whispered to her as if she were still with me, remembering our clandestine conversations at the orphanage.

We would hide beneath the bed covers, alert for sounds of Sister Immaculata doing her evening rounds. Talking after lights-out was forbidden as too was being caught in another girl's bed. Such a thing was transgression multiplied, unhygienic and immodest, a sin of Magdalena proportions. I was never sure why my name was used to describe all things sinful, except that it was somehow connected to the nature of our Saint Mary Magdalene, for whom I was named.

I loved Anna as I imagined one might love a sister. Torn between excitement at my adoption and sadness, I begged Sister to persuade my new parents to take Anna also, but Sister just frowned and bade me speak only when addressed. My adoption was an unusual event for one so old, almost fourteen years, and although I was full of gratitude, I did not wish to leave Anna behind.

When it came time to leave the orphanage, Anna was gone. I searched for her in all our usual hiding places, but I could not find her. In the time it took me to collect my things, taking them to Sister for checking and packing into a small wooden trunk, Anna had vanished. I searched frantically, knowing there were only minutes before I was to go to the reception parlour where my new parents waited. I asked Sister and the other girls, but no one seemed to know where Anna had gone.

I hung back, dragging my feet as Sister hurried me to the parlour, saying I had changed my mind about being adopted. Sister was angry at my ungratefulness and told me Anna had already gone from the orphanage and would not be coming back. I could not believe she had left and did not say goodbye—not Anna. But all that was before I lived with my new parents, Papi Karl and his wife Frau Hoffermann.

Now in Highland House I had no one, for I was not welcome to spend time with Frau Hoffermann and the other married women, who sat together in the cosy sitting room, knitting by the warm fire. Sometimes, I left off reading to hide at the top of the stairs in a secluded niche. From my hiding place, I could covertly observe the sitting room below.

I spied on the fat, ugly matrons, whom I could see through the double doors, and the cancer of my envy grew. Sometimes, I felt such emptiness—I wanted to hurt myself, to feel pain, to know that I was still alive. My nails sank deep into the fleshy parts of my arms until the skin broke and bled, and then I returned to my room to read again. I spent my days like this until Gertrud arrived.

Gertrud was a plump, dimpled, smiling woman with fluffy blonde hair, at least ten years senior to my sixteen years. At first, I misjudged her demeanour, for which I blame my cloistered life. She had the art of appearing soft and compassionate, which I craved beyond life. It drew me to her, and so attracted was I by her warm charm, I did not realise until too late that it hid the empathy of a stone. Yet, I marvelled at her ability to change her face to the world with such ease, and I coveted her talent. She taught me willingly, making me practice deception in the mirror to see how it felt and scolding me when the tell-tale blood flooded my cheeks.

Gertrud was an actress and a dancer she had announced proudly. I suppose that was why she shifted so easily into other roles and moods and did not have the same distress that I harboured in the face of exposure at deceit. Before coming to Highland House, she had many small parts in films and theatre, although she was finding it harder and harder to secure work since so many of the theatres had closed for their un-German ways.

As a faithful Berliner, Gertrud was also a passionate advocate for our Führer, talking grandly about Germany's future, painting a vision of the spread of our great leader's status and power, and the rightful place of a strong, successful German nation leading the world.

Much of what she said I had heard before on the wireless or read in newspapers. It was not news to me, although I cannot honestly say I understood all of it then, or that I even cared. I never doubted the truth of her statements, but my life was a small thing concerned only with itself, and not about spreading Nationalsozialist politics.

Gertrud boasted of things such as the German discipline of hard work. To me, this sounded as though Herr Hitler went to the same convent in which I was schooled, but when I asked Gertrud what she meant by the cleansing of the German spirit, I found she did not like questions. Later, when she talked about our Führer refocusing the German people on moral purity, I did not ask her how moral purity and our stay in this place, unmarried and pregnant, could be reconciled.

Rather than politics, I loved the stories she told me of her life in Berlin, especially the romance of the night she met her lover Manfred. I saw the event through her eyes. It was a starless night. Streets lit by bonfires. Smoke obscuring the sky. People revelled along boulevards, drunk on beer, patriotism, and the exhilaration of crowds as they ransacked libraries and shops for material to feed the fires that would purify Germany.

Books were the favoured fuel that fanned the euphoric flame of a cleansing hope for the future. Imagining so many books burning made me feel sad, but when I asked why books, Gertrud scolded me, so I learned to keep my mouth shut. As she described the joy in the streets, my mind filled with images of people, running, laughing with gaping pink mouths, moving as one multi-legged organism from building to building, the merriment fanning the blaze in their eyes.

I saw the reflections: flickering orange flames licking at dark shadows. I saw the brown-shirts orchestrating the masses. I saw fervent women flirting, hips swinging, bosoms bouncing as they skipped gaily, a slim arm around a manly waist. I saw Gertrud's abandonment to her officer in his smart black uniform, holding her thrust against a wall in the alley that led to the back of her theatre. What then for a few books?

As Gertrud spoke, her eyes shone with memory, and at that moment, I felt the ardour she had for her lover. Words tumbled from her mouth as if in a torrent. Sometimes I could not follow her. Some things she said I do not now remember. Sometimes exhausted by her fervour, I let the meaning wash over me in a melody of passion, with envy its only conductor.

Despite my mean spirit, Gertrud eased my loneliness, and we became friends of a sort because the matrons of the fireplace rejected us both. When the married women passed us in corridors or public places, they did so with pursed lips, sweeping their skirts aside as if contact with us was contagious. Gertrud laughed and lunged, calling them old hags, jealous of our youthful beauty. I was grateful for her friendship, for I do not think I could have withstood their condemnation alone.

She also asserted that, as the proud mistress of an officer in the SS, she bore a child as her patriotic duty, explaining it was our role to save the Aryan race from extinction. Perhaps naively, I asked her why Manfred did not marry her. After that, she refused to speak with me for days, so I learned to accept her ideas uncritically, agreeing with her even when I didn't know what she was talking about.

Often Gertrud made me laugh at her stories and mockery of the matrons. It wasn't the way I laughed with Anna, for Gertrud's coarse humour and rough language lacked Anna's needle pointed wit. Sometimes, in laughing with Gertrud, particularly as she made gestures with her fingers at the matrons, I felt unwholesome. Even so, I laughed, for if I did not, she would exact revenge by refusing to speak with me and I would do anything necessary to return to her favour.

Then Gertrud discovered my talent for singing. As a child, I had sung in the school choir and at Mass every morning, but I had not sung since leaving the orphanage and did not realise how much I missed it. Singing made me whole. It was a healing balm in a world of hurt. Despite my love of singing, and the priest's assertions that my voice was a gift from God, it never occurred to me that it was any more special than that possessed by the next person.

Yet, Gertrud demanded I train because she said we could make money with my singing and her dancing. That she took an interest made my chest swell, although she was a relentless taskmaster. Singing practice was not for joy, but for Gertrud, it was all business, and I was to become her ticket out of there.

For some reason, as my voice strengthened Gertrud's enthusiasm waned, although now the fire had been lit, my hollow soul filled with music, which in turn withered my blossoming envy. My strength grew until each morning I would awaken, impatient to sing. I practised and practised, never satisfied, always demanding my voice do more. Every day, I begged Gertrud to play a little longer, but always she lowered the lid of the piano saying, enough!

At night I sang the words in my head, examining them for meaning and nuance, grasping their emotion and trying new timbers and tones that might match the emotion. The next morning, I would try it out. I always knew if I had done it right because Gertrud would not notice. If I got it wrong, Gertrud would turn on me, saying, "Pay attention, Magdalena! That is not what I taught you." More unfairly, she would accuse me of laziness.

Her prophecy came to pass. It was late in November when I found I lacked the will to get up from my bed.

Gertrud came into my room chanting, "Later, later, not today, all the lazy people say."

I struggled to sit up but had no will of my own. Instead, obeying her sharp commands, I slid my heavy feet to the cold floor, my ankles swollen and puffy as I struggled into my clothes. I plodded behind her as we walked to the music room.

She had eaten breakfast, and I was uninterested in food, but neither could I raise the energy to sing, and Gertrud eventually gave up. She slammed closed the piano and marched out of the room saying, "You must see the doctor. You look so ugly and puffy; I can't look at you anymore."

The doctor took my blood pressure and tasted my urine, saying nothing to me, but murmuring to the nurse, who gave me an injection. Later, the pain came, and I clamped my teeth in case I disgraced myself by screaming.

The agony grew and grew until it seared and twisted and racked my body. I fought the nurses for I wanted to pace, but they held me fast to the bed. In my muddled mind, I believed I was in purgatory and determined that stoic suffering for my sins might gain me absolution.

I remember little else over the next day except the pain and the darkness and the undignified mess my body gave into. I was beyond caring. Like an animal, I bore the midwife's murmuring ministrations in cowering agony, slippery with sweat and other bodily excretions. My struggle waned with exhaustion, and I attempted to lull my mind into a torpor, taking myself to a place where pain might not reach, but still it seized my entrails, finally wringing out the slithering body that was my baby.

11

Immediately after she was born, they whipped her away and placed her in an Isolette. I heard one nurse say they did not expect her to live, and I cried alone in the dark where no one would hear. Yet, the next time I saw her, she seemed fully recovered from the ordeal of her early birth, even if I was not.

A few weeks later, from my secret vantage point at the top of the stairs, I peered through the bannisters to the matron's sitting-room, crowded now with people, mostly SS officers and their wives. There, in Frau Hoffermann's arms, I saw my delicate daughter in a beautiful naming dress, trailing white lace and satin. It swaddled her entire body, and a frilly white bonnet obscured her face. The only part of her I could see exposed was the fingers of one tiny hand, but I didn't need to see her face to know.

I didn't need to hear Gertrud's voice explaining what was to happen next to know that she was my baby. Frau Hoffermann, barren in her maternity wear, had stolen my baby. Karl, my Papi, my lover, stood proudly beside her, beaming with pride at his wizened wife and the baby girl she held.

It should have been me! My mind wailed. She's a thief.

Despite the torture of seeing her so close, and yet beyond reach, I continued to watch. Men in black uniforms stood about smoking, and chatting, while women, stylish in furs and hats sat with their silken legs crossed and looked on as they celebrated the naming of my daughter. A name of which I was to remain ignorant.

My breasts stung with the throb of suppressed milk, and I welcomed the pain, once more craving its distraction, but it was not enough.

Gertrud dragged me away from my viewing place, her tone scolding. "You must forget. She is not yours and nothing can come of moping."

"How can I forget?" I wailed.

Gertrud slapped me, and in shock, I did as she bid, burying my hurt deep.

Karl took Frau Hoffermann and my baby away without a word. Matron told me to pack my belongings as I should move to the staff quarters. I was no longer an honoured Lebensborn guest producing good Aryan offspring for the officers. I must now work for my keep.

A month later, Gertrud delivered a boy but there was something wrong with his head. He was taken away and neither Gertrud nor I knew what happened to him. But by then Highland House had begun to fill up. Most of the married women had given birth and left and a new kind of tenant was moving in.

Young women arrived and filled the house although they were not pregnant. They were checked for health and fertility, their bodies measured from head to toe, examined, and prodded before being declared fit and admitted. Some were sent away, weeping, and ashamed.

The House became like some sort of feminised military training camp with guards stationed outside the grounds, not to keep the inmates in, but to keep intruders out. The women were not treated like we had been, nor were they treated like the matrons of the fireplace. Instead, they undertook compulsory exercise every morning in the cold, snow-covered grounds.

Gertrud, now that her birthing was over, joined me in the servants' quarters where we shared a room. As we worked, I speculated about the women and their role until one spring evening it became clear.

A ceremony, like a mass wedding, took place in the quadrangle outside the main house. It was a strange sight as SS officers in dress uniforms, lined up in military formation, opposite the young women of the House. They exchanged wedding bands and then each couple broke off to walk beneath a beribboned arch to enter the building.

Gertrud exclaimed with pride that we were the first of these patriotic women. They were answering the Führer's call to populate the country with a new type of racially superior children, fathered by members of the SS.

Gertrud's boasting got on my nerves. Spitefully I said, "No, you were abandoned just like me."

A pang of guilt stopped my sarcastic retort going further as I thought of Gertrud's baby boy and his misshapen head. It was too late. Gertrud rounded on me, her eyes flashing, her face deathly pale, her mouth pinched with rage. The words she flung at me cut through the cold air, and like ice shards they stabbed into my being with a force that struck the breath from me.

"At least I was not raped by a child molester."

For weeks Gertrud's words rang in my head. I retreated into myself, nursing my fragility like an ailing animal. To function daily I buried my betrayal deep, but it ate away at my soul. I felt its poison flowing in my blood as I slowly sloughed off the childish skin of unmet hope to grow a new shape. I was like the butterfly emerging from its cocoon, its jewelled beauty sparkling as it trembled, drying its wings in the sunlight. But one always knows, that beneath and behind such beauty lies the ugliness of a worm.

The months passed without notice as I carried out my daily duties, something I had done my entire life. Sweeping, polishing, cleaning, and washing. Thumping the weighty iron on heavier sheets. Gertrud sat about watching me, complaining that they over-worked her for the pittance she earned. She chafed to be gone, back to the bright lights of the stage and boasted she was saving to return to Berlin.

As I ironed, she recounted stories of the life of the dancer. How hard they worked, but what rewards were to be had as the curtain fell to thunderous applause. Young men waited in line at the back door of the stage to beseech a smile, and for those bolder, or wealthier, a date or a kiss.

Meanly I thought, *and a quick grope in a dark alley,* but I said nothing, and in my mind, images formed of the people, restaurants, streets, nightclubs, and theatres. This was the city of my childhood and even though I had lived a secluded life in the orphanage, many of the landmarks were familiar.

From Gertrud, I began to gain an inkling of what I was yet to learn about treachery, passion, and love, although sometimes envy's petals would unfurl, and I found myself listless and longing for such glamour and excitement. But immediately my cynicism would seek to stomp all over her dreams, and I must bite my tongue in order not to snap at her. In any case, much of what she told me I did not believe, and I tried to let her words wash over me without comment. I had retreated into my natural cowardice, afraid to challenge, secretive in scepticism.

When she complained and whined, I found excuses to work away from her, but when she dreamed her dreams of returning to the stage and being discovered, handpicked by Dr Goebbels to play the lead in one of his new films, I humoured her. Her crazy dreams reminded me of Anna, and sometimes I would allow myself to wallow in those dreams, only to realise what I was doing and jerk myself back to the reality of my existence.

As the months passed, my heart healed. A puckered scar formed over the fissure that held my baby, and the jagged rupture to my childhood that I had mistaken for love of Karl. I learned to live in a fog of mundane reality as my dreams changed and my breast ached less for want of my baby.

Slowly my body strengthened and became whole again, but I felt the dark void always beneath the surface. I worried that it would one day swallow me, sucking me down to drown in screaming profanity. Every step and decision became purposeful and calculated. I breathed, worked, and ate only to survive, plodding through each day after each day in a kind of torpor, not thinking beyond the moment in which I existed. All the time I saved every Pfennig I earned.

It wasn't until May Day 1937 that an opportunity arose for Gertrud to escape the monotony of servitude, and I with her.

We were to have the day off to attend the national workers holiday celebrations in Munich. At first, I hadn't wanted to go although we were expected to march in the parade in our uniforms. I probably would have got away with not going if Gertrud hadn't made such a fuss.

So excited was she by the prospect of the celebration, she raved on about the soldiers who would attend. She dreamed of her officer and wrote begging him to come. Gertrud had written to him before, but to my knowledge he never responded. For some reason, this time she believed he would. She described him coming across her as she marched with the workers, head held high, patriotic, and proud. He would fall in love with her all over again, and in an anguish of regret he would draw her from the crowd, falling to his knees pleading for Gertrud to marry him, and then he would whisk her back to Berlin.

She promised I could go too, and her excitement became infectious, embroiling the other staff in her myth although I was not so gullible, not any longer. Perhaps I was growing up. Afterall I was now eighteen years old, but despite my misgivings, I began to believe through the fog of my own cynicism. I packed a small linen sack in anticipation, forcing exhilaration into the locked pessimism of my emotions.

The sack had once been a laundry bag until it perished and instead of throwing it out as I was instructed, I had salvaged the good linen, making a small drawstring bag. It contained my meagre savings and my most precious items, including the papers I had secreted on my first day in Highland House. The other treasure it held was a small piece of quartz.

Anna had given me the quartz in atonement for pulling my hair that first day we met. Before I could exact revenge, she offered her apology in the form of a smooth pebble, almost clear. With a furtive glance to see who was watching she said, it's a diamond from the great Kimberly mine in Africa. You must keep it to remember me forever. I had never heard of the great Kimberly mine, but as I was to find out, this was Anna's way of pretending the reality of her life did not exist.

May Day dawned with a promise of summer in the air. After breakfast we assembled on the driveway, dressed neatly in our workers uniforms, waiting for the House bus that was to transport us to the city. Gertrud clung to my arm and was strangely withdrawn, her face pale. I could not find out from what affliction she suffered but found myself defending her against the onslaught of questions from the others.

Matron came over, her long face stern, and ordered silence. As the bus drew up, she gave instructions for us to form an orderly queue to board. Gertrud and I found a seat towards the rear, and as the bus pulled away from the House, I turned to gaze out of the back window. Memories of my arrival flooded my mind. I recalled the imposing buildings of my impending incarceration, the neatly squared gardens, manicured hedges, and unruly blossoms, and I was not fully convinced that it was the last time that I should gaze upon it.

3. MUNICH 1937

I crossed the street, leaving the city park, which was full of picnicking families. My legs were tired from marching, my head ached from brass bands and speeches, and I searched for somewhere quiet to rest. I just wanted to go back to Highland House, and I knew no matter how many men Gertrud accosted, she would never find her officer although she had begged every soldier she saw for news.

A Scharführer from the Deutschland Regiment, had appeared confounded by her questions, and asked why, when our Führer addresses his people in the Lustgarten, would he come from Berlin to this backwater? I couldn't help but agree with him, but Gertrud had walked off in a fury although I knew she would soon be back.

I also knew she would have no money. She never did. It slipped through her fingers on fripperies and delicacies that she simply must have. I leaned against a wall and closed my eyes, contemplating the expense of a bus fare for both Gertrud and I to get back to Highland House. I had become so caught up in her fantasy I persuaded myself to believe, and now the House bus had returned without us. To get back to Highland House we would have to pay for a regular bus trip.

Resentment closed my throat, but I had only one person to blame and berated myself for a fool. What had I been thinking? What would I do in Berlin anyway? I had so wanted to believe Gertrud when she told me that my voice would be my fortune that I became caught up in her lies as she painted pictures of Dr Goebbels in raptures, when he heard me sing. She had lulled me into her world of fiction until I believed in her fairy tales.

"Dummes mädchen–stupid, stupid girl, why would you do this to yourself?"

The cough of gunfire jerked me from brooding. I pushed myself away from the warmth of the sundrenched wall, just as a boy or rather a skinny young man, flew around the corner. His emaciated arms flailed as he stumbled but quickly righted himself. For a second I stared into his gaunt face, but his hesitation lasted only until he saw that I would not try to stop him, and he ran on.

Paralysed by surprise, I could not have moved even if it had occurred to me to try to stop him. He ducked around the next corner into a dark alley that I had passed earlier that day, just twenty meters from where I now stood. But I felt his terror. It was like the stench of a wounded animal, contracting my skin as icy tingles passed through me. For a second I recognised, in his misery, my own rejected and abandoned soul.

Two Schutzpolizei raced around the corner before slowing when they saw me.

One of the SchuPo said, "Did you see a man, a prisoner?"

He was holding a rifle, his pink face lathered in sweat, his blond hair plastered to his skull under his shako.

I felt vacancy infuse my face and shrugged.

"Which way did he go?"

I pointed down the road towards the park entrance.

The two policemen looked towards the park a mere hundred meters away, then looked back at me in disbelief. While trees lined the entrance to the park, the lawns otherwise stretched into the distance, interspersed only with low shrubbery. People milled about between the trees or sat at picnic celebrations on the grass. There were no obvious places to hide.

Pink face nodded to his companion, and then loped off towards the park. The other man, dark haired and heavily built, walked closer, examining me intently.

"Papers please, Fräulein."

He was in his early twenties, his broad shoulders giving him a maturity that did not extend to his face. With dark hair cut short under his shako, he reminded me of Papi Karl. He was handsome in his uniform. The scent of apple blossom wafted on the air. Was it real or imagined? I shuddered as I remembered Karl's pomade as it lingered in the room after he had left.

My stomach constricted, and vomit rose in my throat as I looked into the policeman's brown eyes. I forced it down and tried to regain my composure, fumbling with the tied string at the neck of the bag, conscious of his eyes examining every aspect of me as he cradled his gun in his arms, almost like a baby.

An image of Frau Hoffermann holding my baby rose before my eyes. Tears came unbidden, reddening my nose. My hands shook so that I could not undo the knot, and the bag slipped from my grasp.

"What's wrong with you?" His voice was hoarse with suspicion.

"I'm sorry, the gun frightens me." It was a lie. I was more afraid of handing him my papers.

He lowered the barrel, pushing it down by his side on its leather shoulder strap so that it pointed to the ground. His face took on a self-conscious sheepishness and I could see he was not as confident as I had first thought.

"Pick up your bag," he said.

I remained immobile. They were my papers, but I had taken them unauthorised. I was terrified in case he recalled some report a year ago about stolen papers.

"Here." He retrieved the bag from the pavement and handed it to me.

My hands trembled as I tried again to unpick the knot, and his impatience got the better of him.

"Let me."

I watched his deft fingers loosening the knot, and I felt Karl's hands, caressing, probing, and intimate.

He handed the open bag to me and stepped back. Then he said again, "Papers, please *Fräulein*."

I forced my panic and nausea down as I scrabbled in my bag, drawing out the papers I had stolen from the desk on my entry to Highland House.

He merely flicked through them, turning the photo in my identification book upright, examining it and then searching my face.

"The photo does not do you justice." He handed the ID back before opening the booklet from my days in the BDM, the German maiden's league. He nodded, the eagle and swastika badge on his shako winking in the light, as he counted the stamps at the back. Jerking his thumb at his chest, he said, "SS-Junkerschules at Bad Tölz, til last month," and smiled showing stained teeth.

His gaze flickered down my body, resting for a moment on my breasts as he opened the Ahnenpass, outlining my heritage. "Impressive, but I don't need papers to tell me you are the perfect Aryan maiden. I only need to open my eyes."

My neck mottled as the blood rose. He was so sure of himself, so sure of me, but he mistook the volcanic glow in my cheeks for maidenly shyness.

"You work at the Highland House?" His gaze rested on the badge on my uniform pocket.

Blood throbbed in my temples, but he seemed not to notice my revulsion.

"I can see I will have to find some business in that direction soon." Then clicking his heels in old-fashioned courtesy, he smiled as he turned to follow his partner, flipping his gun back to the cradle of his arm as he sauntered off.

I watched, knowing he knew I watched him swagger across the road. He assumed I watched in admiration, but only I knew murder was in my heart. At that moment, he represented everything that had led to my betrayal, every abuse and neglect I had suffered; my every sorrow mocked by his broad chest, his smooth skinned handsomeness, his cupid red mouth, his short dark hair, his deep brown eyes—I hated him, hated Karl and my heart's blood darkened.

He disappeared among the shrubbery in the park before I cautiously walked to the alley entrance where the fugitive had disappeared. He was slumped behind rubbish bins, trying to staunch the blood oozing from a gash across his upper arm.

"You're bleeding."

He ignored me and I didn't blame him. It was obvious he was bleeding. After a few moments of silence, I turned to leave.

He said, "I saw what you did."

I stopped.

"Why did you do it?" he asked.

I turned back to him. "I don't know."

He looked puzzled. "Do you know who I am?"

"No." I waited.

He shook his head and stood up, leaning heavily against the wall, grimacing from the pain as fresh blood oozed from the gash. "You should go. You don't want to be tainted with a Jew's blood."

His words were laden with bitterness. I didn't move. I knew of the laws, of course I did, like I knew that the sun rose every day. How could I not know, but I never thought about them before. I remained mute, foolishly bereft of words to say.

His large eyes, recessed in the cavernous hollows of an emaciated face, burned with feverish intensity, the rims red and the whites yellow and bloodshot. He was young, in his early twenties, but his face sank into the hollows of an old man. He was taller than I was despite his frail physique. His dark hair, mere stubble on his shaved head, his clothes rotting on his skinny carcass. A tattered fragment of rag clung to his arm, grimy and stained with splattered blood but still distinguishable as the mark of David.

Despite his condition, his eyes mesmerised for they were like Anna's eyes. The Jew devil I had seen in the street posters had coal black eyes that burned with malevolent red light. This boy's eyes were green, the colour of bottle glass, with sooty lashes surrounding red rims and yellow corneas, but I could see the beauty of such eyes if the boy had health. Surely this person was not a devil, sent in conspiracy to enslave all the peoples of the world as the posters said. For in his eyes there was something soft, tender, something that reflected the yearning of my soul.

"Go!" He hissed at me so that I backed away.

I turned towards the sunshine in the street, glancing back to see him collapse into a huddled bundle of rags among the rubbish.

I hurried back to him. "Please, you are hurt."

A sound like a grunt emanated from the rags, and I stayed where I was. I couldn't leave another human to die, but I didn't know what else to do. He was a Jew, the enemy of the State, a person not even human, perhaps one of the Communist traitors escaped from the prison at nearby Dachau. Should I call the SchuPo? At least then he would get medical help.

Why should I tell them? They are trying to kill him. They can't be trusted. But he is a traitor—but he is a poor hurt and starving boy, a sick animal like me, abused, abandoned and alone.

He didn't move. I couldn't even see the rise and fall of breathing. Perhaps he was dead. I couldn't stand it and fled from the alley running across the road to the park, looking for

Gertrud. I had to get out of this place, back to the safety of the House, back to the safety of drudgery. Fear and ignorance of the world gave impetus to my natural cowardice, and I fled.

I found Gertrud standing amidst a group of officers, playing the gracious prima donna with her face pink and beaming. Her laughter repulsed me, so I took a detour and crossed the park, seeking somewhere to sit, somewhere away from the people, the noisy children, and the happiness of family contentment. I was an outsider in this place and did not deserve to be where families thrived.

In the distance, a church spire rose above the trees. I hadn't been into a church since I had left the orphanage, but it was familiar territory to me. I imagined the cool dimness and quiet of its vaulted nave and longed to shelter in its seclusion, feeling the hard kneeler beneath my knees, feeling the calm presence of acceptance.

I entered the vestibule cautiously, dipping my hand automatically in the holy water font, genuflecting in the aisle as I entered the empty church. I sat immobile in the long pew, knowing I should kneel and pray, but instead remaining seated, thinking about the boy.

He needed help. I should have done my duty, found the SchuPo and they would have taken him to the hospital, but instead I had overreacted. After all, the policeman had been kind, undoing the string on my bag so that I could get out my papers. I berated myself for my irrational emotions. The nuns at school told us that to put emotions aside, and seek wisdom, was to find favour with God and although all my life I had coveted wisdom, all I seemed to find was foolish emotion. God had abandoned me.

Yet, if I confessed now, what would the police say when they found I had misdirected them? Would the policeman who untied my bag think I was harbouring the fugitive? He would arrest me as a Jewish sympathiser, and I knew from the wireless that Dachau was where the evil Jewish Communists and their supporters were imprisoned. I hardly knew what a

Communist was except that they were traitors and enemies of the Fatherland, but one thing was for certain, I did not want to be thought of as one of them.

The sound of booted footfalls in the vestibule startled me and I sank to my knees, covering my face with clasped hands as if in prayer. The footsteps neared and stopped, yet I could feel the presence behind me. Slowly I turned my head to see who it was that stood so still in the silence.

The two SchuPo's stood side by side cradling their guns staring at me as if I were a species unknown to them.

"You, again!" The SchuPo who had untied the string of my linen bag said, "What are you doing in here? Surely, you are not a Catholic!" He spat the word out as if it offended him to have it pass his lips.

His companion's pink face became animated, and he looked interested in his friend's reaction. His pale eyes flicked back and forth, and a smile of anticipation broke across his face. He licked his lips and muttered, but the brown-eyed policeman shook his head.

Then another figure loomed tall behind the two policemen, black cassock flapping about ankles as the man stepped around them. He took in the scene, but I am not sure what he saw for he walked purposely towards me, bending to kiss my cheek.

"Ah, my little niece you have come to see your old uncle again. Welcome child." He laid his hand, dry and cool on my brow and looked meaningfully into my eyes. "How are you today my dear? Fully recovered I hope."

I remained dumb but unresisting, not knowing how to respond.

He covered my confusion by turning to the SchuPo and saying, "My niece is recovering from mumps."

The policemen took two steps back, their guns raised a little in my direction as if they needed bullets to keep me from infecting them.

"There is no need for guns in the church my good friends. God's house is a place of peace."

The pink-faced blond haired SchuPo sneered at the priest and spat on the floor saying, "You cannot be faithful to two masters, priest. Either you revere our Führer, or you serve your idols, in which case you are an enemy of the State."

The priest did not watch the spittle descend to splatter on the stone. Instead, he kept his eyes fixed on the face of the blond SchuPo saying in a voice that remained mild and even, "We are not enemies of the State, but if you will excuse me, I must take my niece for refreshment and rest. Please gentlemen make yourselves at home in God's house."

He took my arm, pulling me upright and walked me towards the Alter, guiding me as one would an invalid. We genuflected and turned to walk along a corridor to his sacristy and out through a back door.

It wasn't until we were standing under the trees behind the church that he turned to me. "Will you be alright now my child?"

I nodded, unsure what had happened or why I was standing here with this stranger who called me his niece. It seems he had saved me from something although from what I was not sure. I nodded again then a thought popped into my mind. If he saved me, perhaps he could save the man in the alley.

I shook my head. "Father, I need help."

He looked startled as if I had shocked him by asking for help. Why had he whisked me away before? What did he think he was saving me from? Then it dawned on me. It was their unwanted amorous intentions, not from any real danger. Now I was unsure if I should tell him about the hurt man in the alley.

"What is it?" He looked around and I could see he was nervous.

The uniforms of the SchuPo were visible through the trees. They were on the road, heading back to the park.

"Wait, it is not safe to talk here. Come, my house is not far, behind that shrubbery only. The Schutzpolizei will be expecting me to take you to my house and we should fulfil their expectations." A small smile began in his eyes and his lips twitched in sympathetic humour as he once more took my arm to guide me along a path to his house.

His housekeeper brought tea and petite fours. She fussed about Father, pouring tea, while I sat waiting demurely upright in my chair, hands folded, ankles crossed as the nuns had taught me. My back was ramrod straight in memory of Sister's yard ruler that might be, at any moment, shoved down the back of my uniform if she found me slumping. It was hard to maintain such posture on the soft chair, and I was relieved when the housekeeper vacated the room and Father invited me to relax.

He smiled. "I can see you have been brought up a good Catholic. Please relax there are no nuns in this house."

His eyes danced with mischief, but I was wary as there was something odd about his accent. His German was impeccable, but still I sensed a foreignness, which I found hard to place. It could be French, I supposed. At school I had learned a little French, Latin, English, and Spanish, but my teachers all spoke with heavy German accents, no matter the languages they taught.

"Now my child what can possibly be troubling you?" He handed me a cup of tea and asked if I would like a dollop of cream. To my amazement, he poured milk into his own tea, but I was easily distracted by the proffered plate of petite fours, which made my mouth water. I had eaten nothing since breakfast.

I stared into my lap wondering what I could tell him. Could I say that a fugitive, a Jew , a Communist, needed his help? Would a priest help a Jew the killers of Christ, or even a Communist who denied the existence of God? It was a mistake coming here for his help, but I had to do something. I couldn't just leave a man in a rubbish pile to die.

I saw the priest watching me, his face composed, his eyes gentle yet curious and I knew he waited for me to collect my courage to speak. His fair hair was a translucent silver and glowed in the light from the window behind him--like a halo. I took it as a sign.

"It's a man. He's in the alley. He's hurt, dying I think. Those SchuPo were after him." My words fell over each other as I blurted the information, adding, "He's a Jew!"

The priest's eyes did not waver as I spoke, only continued to watch my face, reading my intent, my motivation, as I knew I would do in his place.

Eventually he said to me. "Go now in peace and love the lord your God. Speak to no one of our encounter and to no one of your folly." He stood up, his amusement gone and his face stern.

The blood rushed to my face, and shaking, I placed my teacup on the table leaving the uneaten cake on the saucer, the remnants of icing sticky on my fingers. I stood clutching my linen bag wondering if he now looked at me as a traitor, a Jew lover, an enemy of the State.

As I walked toward the door he said softly. "What would you have me do my child?"

I glanced back at him before dropping my eyes to hide my fear. "Don't hurt him Father. He's just a boy."

The priest paused and then said, "Stay and finish your tea. Tell me who you are. Why you are here."

"I am sorry Father I should not have come. I must go. My friend will be wondering where I am."

I left the priest, stumbling on the uneven paving of the pathway that led to his house, returning to where I last saw Gertrud. I knew I must hurry and find her because the last city bus was leaving soon, and we needed to be on it if we were to get back before dark.

Gertrud came towards me, waving her arms. "Where have you been Magdalena? I have been searching for you everywhere. Hurry or they will go without us."

"We'll miss the bus."

"What are you talking about?" Gertrud grabbed my arm pulling me back along the path from where she arrived.

"It's the last bus. If we miss it, we won't be able to get back." I panted as I tried to keep up with her.

"Silly! I told you we are not going back. They will take us to Berlin. We leave tomorrow. Wilhelm is driving and he has room in his car. He promised. We can stay at the barracks tonight. They said we can sleep in the visitor's quarters but hurry or they will leave without us."

"You're hurting my arm." It didn't feel right. Something wasn't what it appeared, and all my protective antennae were shrieking their alarm, but Gertrud was on a mission and my protests were ignored. I allowed her to drag me along to where an army bus waited. Several officers stood around smoking and chatting, waiting for us. Gertrud pushed me onto the bus and as I sat down I saw the priest across the road, watching. Had he followed me?

4. Dachau Barracks

When we alighted from the bus at Dachau barracks, Gertrud led me to the guest's cloakroom. She offered to hold my bag while I went to the lavatory, but when I came out again she was gone. I retraced our steps and then heard the murmur of people.

Along a corridor was a recreation room, where she was standing at the bar with two of the officers from the bus. I strode over to her and yanked my bag from her wrist.

She must have understood my annoyance because she whispered, "I needed it to show your papers."

One of the men was staring at me and I looked away, but he said, "Would you like a drink Fräulein?"

I shook my head and Gertrud, turning her back on me, said, "Oh, don't bother with her, she's sulking."

The large common room was furnished with snooker tables, small groups of chairs around occasional tables, some with men poring over chess, cards or reading newspapers. An upright piano sat off to one side of the bar and at the opposite end of the room, a tall window overlooked the grounds and the driveway.

I walked over and sat at the table by the window, my back to Gertrud and the bar, furious with her but also angry at my inability to resist. More men came into the room, and I slumped lower in my chair, hoping they wouldn't notice me.

From the window I could see across the driveway, to where lawns and gardens petered out at another fence, beyond which sat a huddle of low buildings. Was that the place from where the Jew had escaped? I could not get the memory of his eyes out of my head, but I should not have lied to the police. That made me complicit.

Whatever else, he was an escaped prisoner, and I should have told the police where to find him. Why did I lie? I could not fathom my own motivation, and every time I tried I would follow the same pattern of circular logic. First, I convinced myself I had acted as a good Christian with charity and kindness. Then I would reach the point where I could not get past the fact that I had protected an escaped prisoner, an enemy of the State, perhaps even a murderer, a Communist, an evil Jew. For the second time in my life, I had committed a deliberate act in violation of the law. The first stealing my papers from my legal guardian, and now this. A voice interrupted my reverie.

"So Fräulein, you will be famous soon, working with Harry Piel our very own SS patron. Did you see him play in *His Greatest Bluff* with Marlene Dietrich? Ah, what a true Aryan beauty she is."

I flinched as if my thoughts could be overheard and looked up at the giant hovering over me. He blocked out what light streamed in the window and continued talking as if he knew me. I remain silent, but he behaved as if my silence was his cue.

"I saw that film in '27 or '28, I forget now. It was when I was in my final year at school; it must have been '27. Mein Gott, but I was in love." He paused. "Like I am now, looking at your beauty."

The black and white patterns on the floor became fascinating as I waited for him to go away.

31

"Ah so, did you know you have the same name as our Marlene. She was also Magdalena - Marie Magdalena at birth." He stroked his chin. "Yet, at least you are here, as she should be." He pulled up a chair and sat down sighing. "Why must she live in America when we make such illuminating films here?" He shook his great head. "It is un-German for her to live in America, don't you think?"

He paused again and when I did not reply, he said, "I am Lothar. I know your name already. It is the name on all the officers' lips, the beautiful younger sister of the famous Gertrud. Ah, I have made you blush. Please accept my apologies. I am a clod, Lothar the clod. Will you forgive me my little Ice Maiden? Please speak to me."

I scanned the room for Gertrud. What had she told the officers about us? I interrupted Lothar and stood up. "Excuse me I must speak with Gertrud."

Before Lothar could answer, I made my way through the crush of men, and tugged Gertrud's jacket to get her attention. She swung around. "Ah ha, speak of the devil. Come Magda sing for these lovely men, show them your talent."

I hated her calling me Magda and scowled but complaining was pointless. She did as she pleased.

"Yes sing, sing," The men called. Lothar joined them, grinning from ear to ear as he lifted his beer in salute. He joined the chant of, "Sing Fräulein, sing."

I shook my head. "Gertrud, I need to talk to you."

"Magdalena, Magdalena must sing for her supper." She slapped the bar counter.

She was tipsy, and I had no idea what deal she made with these men and no inkling about where we were to sleep. It was late and we were in a barracks in the grounds of a prison camp far from Highland House. It had taken the bus more than an hour to drive across Munich to get here, too far to walk back, and it would soon be dusk?

I needed to know what she told them, and what plans she was making. But I was too late. Gertrud slid off her stool and swung her hips across to the piano. She plonked down on the stool and began playing one of the tunes we had practiced so many times.

Men rapped on the bar with their knuckles, and it seemed I had little choice. I walked over to join Gertrud and a little breathlessly, I began to sing, *Adieu, mein kleiner Gardeoffizier.*

Soon the officers were keeping time, tapping their feet, and nodding their heads. My confidence returned and my throat opened to give full voice to the song. I sang until I was horse, sipping the beer offered to wet my throat. Perhaps it was the beer, perhaps the singing, but I began to enjoy myself. I felt alive and free for the first time since I was a child. I tried songs from The Black Forest Girl, *Mein Herr Marquis* from die Fledermaus, although I was not sure if it was quite correct to sing anything by Johan Strauss anymore. I had forgotten the lists of unacceptable composers who were not quite German enough.

With a belly full of beer on an empty stomach I became emboldened to try an American song. My English was poor, and I stumbled over the words of *Stormy Weather*. I was not sure if it was the poor rendition that drew the frowns or the English words, until one of the men nearest me turned his back saying disgustedly, "Negermusik."

Hurriedly, I turned to Verdi's *Drinking Song* and the men cheered. More beer was brought out, and Gertrud began missing keys, fingers stumbling as she played. Laughing, she closed the piano, saying, "Enough! More beer." She raised her tankard.

The officers applauded as she walked unsteadily to the bar. I felt an arm slip around my waist and found Lothar at my side. "You are truly amazing." He pressed me into his chest. An enormous ham-like hand slid up from my waist to squeeze my breast, and his beery breath wafted over me in a wave of fetid neglect.

I forced a laugh, wriggling out of his grasp as I said in what I thought sounded like a cheery voice, "You always catch me at the most inconvenient times Lothar. I must go to the cloakroom."

This time I pushed past the men standing around Gertrud, and grabbed her arm saying, "Gertrud come with me now!" I dragged her forcibly away and marched her out the door not knowing where I was going, although I was determined to get out of there before an increasingly drunk Lothar bedded me against my will. Once safely inside the cloakroom I pushed her hard against a wall, primarily because without something to lean against she might fall over.

"What now Gertrud, what is your plan? What have you told these men about us? When did I become your sister?"

Her beery breath sloshed across my face. "Oh, you have to be my little sister because you lost my papers like a silly girl. How do you think we got in here, me without papers? They looked at yours and I said we are from the same family. I told them you left my papers in the House where we work as nurses."

"Nurses!"

She ignored my incredulity. "I told them Matron will forward them to our uncle's place in Berlin. You know Uncle Karl! Shut your mouth little Magda, or you will catch flies." Laughing at her own joke, she threw her head back, baring small teeth in pink gums. "Anyway Uncle Karl loves his little nieces and my dear, did you know that your lovely Karl has now joined the Geheime Staatspolize—promoted to Obersturmbannführer, or should I say Oberstleutnant, now he is in the Staatspolizei. That is where the political power is. You should know these things! What kind of niece are you, who cannot follow the career of our beloved uncle?"

My head felt like it would explode. She used what she knew of my past to weave her own future, used my adopted father's position, my beloved Karl, who had stolen my baby, who had abused and abandoned me and whom I hated. My outrage turned inward, so full of beer I couldn't think straight. I decided to ignore what she's said, and asked instead, "How do we get out of here? I'm hungry." My voice whined and I took a breath. This was serious and complaining of hunger would not make Gertrud focus. She laughed and I knew I had lost.

"Oh Magda, wasn't that wonderful. They loved us. We will be stars together in Berlin just you wait. In the meantime, I am sure Lothar will find you a sausage to fill your belly. Lothar the Lothario." She sang, and laughing at her crude joke, she pushed herself away from the wall and walked unsteadily out the door, leaving me alone with no answers as I stood looking at myself in the tin mirror on the wall.

The next morning, I awoke with Lothar shaking my shoulders, telling me to get up if I was to catch the bus leaving for Munich. It was barely light, and I was cold. My head hurt from the beer I had consumed. I was unaccustomed to drinking alcohol. Groggily I sat up feeling my nakedness, seeing my clothes strewn across the floor. I felt sick at what I'd done merely for a bed and shelter for the night and pulled the sheet around me like a toga. I could remember nothing after returning to the bar last night, accepting yet another beer thrust at me by Gertrud. How low had I stooped?

I ducked my head as Lothar's thick lips sought mine.

"One last kiss Fräulein, before you go."

I put my hand to my mouth as if I were going to be sick and stood up, eyes wide. "Bathroom?" I gasped.

Lothar stood back affronted, pointing the way to the bathroom. When I came back my clothes were laid in a neat pile on the made bed, the room empty of Lothar. I dressed quickly wondering how I would find Gertrud and what Lothar meant by catching the bus for Munich. I looked about the room. My bag, I couldn't see it. What had I done with it? I looked under the bed, nothing at all.

The room was sparsely furnished with a trouser press, shoe rack, tallboy, and wardrobe. Under the window was a small desk with a chair lodged beneath it. Aside from the tallboy and the wardrobe there was nowhere else for the bag to be. I decided to search the wardrobe first. There was nothing in it but Lothar's clothing, another uniform, and a greatcoat. Lothar came back into the room as I closed the wardrobe door.

"What are you doing?" His face was suffused in suspicion.

"I'm looking for my bag."

"Your bag, what bag?"

"The linen bag I brought with me yesterday. It isn't here. I thought you had put it away somewhere safe. It has all my money in it." I tried to soften his aggression. "I was a little tipsy last night and you looked after me so well." I walked up to him and ran my finger down his tunic buttons.

He softened, leaning forward his arms wrapping me into his embrace. He leaned to kiss me, and I steeled myself, holding my breath while I pecked his lips before turning to bury my face against his chest.

"Your sister took the bag last night when Willie drove her to your hotel in Munich. She said she would see you this morning. See, your sister knows how to look after you. Yes," He nodded his big head. "It was what you said to her in the women's room last night, how you longed for me and begged her to let you stay, but you should not drink so much. I had to carry you here last night after you fell asleep on the bar counter. But tonight, I will show you what it is to be loved by Lothar."

I pulled back from his embrace looking up into his face to see if he was laughing at me. This must be a horrible joke, but his face was placid. He kissed me on the forehead as he misinterpreted my dismay.

"My poor little Knuddelmaus. You must go now. We are not supposed to have women in our rooms, and I must smuggle you out before anyone finds you. I have arranged for Franz to take you back to Munich on his run this morning, and

I will come and see you tonight if I can get leave. Süße come, we must hurry but be quiet."

"But I will need my papers."

"You will get them when you see your sister. No one will stop you for papers while you are accompanied by a uniformed officer of the SS-Totenkopfverband."

"Don't I need my papers to leave the barracks?"

Lothar threw back his head laughing so that his chest wobbled. "My Liebchen, Liebelein. Why would you need papers to get out when you didn't need papers to get in? Now my silly little cabbage, we must go."

5. Church of the Holy Cross

The exhaust fumes clouded my view as the bus left me standing on the pavement in central Munich. Where could I go without money, without papers and with no means of getting back to the House where I could beg for my job back? The bus driver had stopped only long enough for me to get off, before pulling away, in a hurry to get to where he was supposed to be. We had driven into the city in silence, me alone in the back of the bus and he alone in the front.

My head was still fuzzy, and I struggled to gather my woolly thoughts, racking my memory for mention of a hotel. I could not believe what Gertrud had done or perhaps we made some plan that I had forgotten after she had pressed that last beer on me, telling me to drink to ease the hunger pangs. It might have been then she mentioned the hotel where we would meet. Maybe I had misunderstood her when she said we needed papers to get into the barracks. The past evening was a hazy blancmange as if I had taken a drug, not just beer.

Think Magdalena, think! What did Gertrud say? What have you forgotten? Nothing more came to me, and I looked around wondering where I should go, what I should do. The driver had dropped me back near where we met the officers at the bus yesterday. At least I knew where I was now, although that was not really much help as I had no idea where I was going, or how I would get there.

I walked toward the park for want of any other direction, remembering the man in the alley. I felt a macabre urge to see if he had died in the rubbish pile and if his body was still there mouldering in its rags. I hurried along the pavement and across the road, taking a shortcut across the park, seeing the church spire to the north as I headed east. Casting glances over my shoulder, I ducked into the alley.

The rubbish was gone. There was nothing except bins, empty and lined up neatly along the wall. There was no pile of rags slumped in the overflowing rubbish. There was no sign that anyone had been there at all other than to clean up the mess. I stepped closer, peering at the pavement to see if there was a sign of blood. A few meters beyond the bins, a door opened and a man in an apron stood at the top of the steps.

He looked startled to see me. "Can I help you Fräulein? Are you lost?"

"No, I thought I dropped something, but I must be mistaken. Thank you."

I hurried back along the alley, out into the open road, turning left, out of his line of sight, and crossed to the park, where I sat on a bench to catch my breath. My heart hammered in my throat, and I forced a sense of calm to get the pounding under control.

After my pulse slowed, I reflected on my predicament. I had nothing, no money, no job, no place to stay, no clothes except the ones on my back, the uniform of the House, and worse, I had no papers.

I put my head in my hands trying to clear the fuzziness from my brain. I should go to the police and report Gertrud. I imagined asking for the SchuPo I had spoken to yesterday. He knew I had papers; he saw them. He hadn't seen Gertrud, but I could describe her. Perhaps they would find her.

He would want to know why I hadn't stayed with my uncle at the church. He would want to know why I had gone to the barracks with Gertrud instead. He would want to know why I stayed overnight, and he would know what I did. He would accuse me of infecting the officers with mumps. I shook my head, surely not, but in any case, the SchuPo would have too many questions. There were too many lies from which I could not untangle myself.

An oddly accented voice broke through my fretting.

"Child, what are you doing here?"

I dropped my hands to my lap trying to compose my features. The priest from the day before stood before me clutching a large parcel wrapped in brown paper and string. It looked heavy for he stood holding it in both arms, leaning back slightly to counterbalance the weight.

"Hello Father," I tried to sound bright, but my voice was flat as if an iron had steamed the spark from me.

The priest walked towards me, laying his package on the bench. "That's a relief." He flexed his fingers and stretched his arms. "Do you mind if I sit with you to rest for a while."

In answer, I straightened my skirt as if to make room for him, which was an absurd gesture as the package filled more of the bench than I, but I could not overcome the manners the nuns had instilled in me.

"Please Father, rest." I wished he would go away and leave me to my muddled thinking. Instead, we sat in silence while my mind screamed for something polite to say.

"I love May in Bavaria, don't you?" he asked. "The sun shining, blossoms everywhere, bees humming and the smell of nectar."

I hadn't noticed the weather or the flowers, so caught up in my own problems, I hadn't time to look about me to appreciate the beauty everywhere. I nodded as tears welled in my eyes, and I looked away afraid he would notice, but if he saw, he had the good manners not to comment.

After a few more moments of silence, he said, "I don't think we introduced ourselves yesterday. I'm Father O'Bryan."

He held out a long thin hand. The hand of an ascetic.

I grasped its cool dryness and stumbled over my name. "I am Magdalena...Magdalena..." I stopped, not knowing what surname to use. Should I use the one on my papers? The one into which I was born. Or should I use Karl's name, my legal name given to me by my adoptive parents, Magdalena Hoffermann. I had not had cause to use my surname until now and I didn't know which name was proper to use. My papers were still in the name of my parents, von Herff, but I had no papers, not anymore.

"Magdalena Magdalena, that's a beautiful name if a little unusual to have a Christian name the same as a family name." The priest was mocking me, but his lips twitched into a kindly smile.

"No, not Magdalena Magdalena. It is... I am Magdalena von Herff."

In less than a second I had wiped the Hoffermann's from my history. I owed them nothing, but they owed me a life and a childhood.

"What kind of name is O'Bryan," I ventured? "Your accent is also...."

"Foreign?"

"Yes. I'm sorry. I do not wish to be impolite."

"Ha, but my dear, curiosity is often considered impolite, is it not? Of course, it all depends on one's perspective, whether one has something to hide or if one is an open book. But for the latter what point is curiosity? There is no challenge to reading an open book."

I couldn't follow him. Twisting my fingers in my lap, lacing them, and unlacing them in concentration, I tried to get onto conversationally safer ground. My stomach rumbled loudly and to my embarrassment he laughed again.

"It must be lunch time for I too am hungry. My dear Fräulein von Herff would you do me the honour of sharing a meal with me. Yesterday you did not even eat the cake my housekeeper is so fond of baking, and I am sure she was quite put out by your neglect. Today you may make amends and tell her what a wonderful cook she is."

He stood up and bent to pick up the parcel. I looked at his kind open face and realised I had no other options. If I didn't tell the priest, then in whom could I confide? Who else could help me? I got up to follow him, wondering how much I should disclose. Should I beg a confession so that I could cleanse myself of the sin of fornication, lust and even adultery? Would he still want me to have lunch with him if he knew that I had given birth out of wedlock then slept with a man I hardly knew just to have shelter for the night?

He would throw me out of his house. I was the Magdalene all right, the great harlot of the bible. Would he, like Jesus, forgive my sins? Unlikely. He was still a man. I couldn't risk it. I would eat lunch with him for I was hungry, then I would leave. My head was still woolly from the beer I had consumed although I was beginning to suspect it was more than beer that had made my head so fuzzy. It might help if I ate something.

Lunch was cabbage with potatoes and black bread. I was so hungry not having eaten in two days that I wolfed down my portion. I only noticed after I ate my fill that Father hardly touched his. He stirred the food around his plate while he made small pleasantries to which I responded with uncouth grunts.

As I wiped my mouth on the napkin, I caught him looking at me. There was something in his eyes that told me this was not a normal glance, not the look of someone merely looking at their companion over the lunch table. It was a shrewd look – calculating - as if trying to ascertain who I was, what was in my character. It struck me that he was wondering if I was who I said I was.

Not long before I had done the same thing, making up my mind in a second that I could not trust him. I realised I was wrong. For me it was not a case of him being untrustworthy. I could tell this was not so, for he was as trustworthy as any. It was about me—I could not trust him with my secrets, for in so doing I would be exposing myself. For that, I had not the courage.

I began to fidget, staring at my hands in my lap and picking at a small flap of skin that had come loose next to my thumb nail. I wanted to excuse myself and flee from this room. I began to feel that I had committed a dishonesty in repayment for the priest's kindness. It made me feel grubby. I opened my mouth to speak but he spoke first.

"I can see you are in trouble, my child. I would like to help you if I can."

He paused. The silenced stretched out. He seemed to have forgotten I was there as he looked down, fiddling with his knife.

He was waiting for my reply. My mind raced as I sat struck dumb by indecision.

His gaze showed me he was gathering courage to speak his mind.

"I too am in trouble and need your help." His pale blue eyes locked onto mine. "If we can rely on each other we can help each other. I will not judge you if you do not judge me."

It was as though he had read my mind. Remorse surged at my selfishness. I never imagined that he could need my help. My better nature stepped forward as I put my own problems from my mind.

"Father if it is in my power to help you, I will try, but as you said I am in trouble also. I have no money and no papers. I have no job and nowhere to live. I..."

The priest held up his hand to stem the rush of confessions. "None of that matters child. I need to know where your heart lies."

"My heart?" Gulping air, I tried to reply but no words came to my mind. What did he mean? I retreated. Did he want me to confess my adultery here at the lunch table? How did he know? My uniform told him I worked at the Highland House, but he must see that a uniform meant that I was a worker not a resident. At least my uniform disguised that shame from prying eyes.

"Yes, your heart. Yesterday you told me something that showed me that you had great compassion for other human beings. A kindness untainted by ideology. I also noted that the company you keep is not of that persuasion. Swans do not fly with geese my child."

My eyes stung as I heard myself described as such. I wanted to shout I am not like that. I am not one of them. I am not like Gertrud. I am not a military whore. But I could not speak for in my heart I knew I was just like Gertrud, and the priest was right. I may wish people to see me as a swan, but I knew what I was. Tears swelled and spilled over my lids. I ducked my head so he would not see my guilt.

His hand rested on my shoulder. "Come, I do not wish to upset you. We will take coffee in comfort, and we can talk more. Perhaps you will have room for my housekeeper's superb cakes. She was wounded when you did not eat yours yesterday. It is a slight to her great culinary skill."

He was smiling, giving me time to recover, and as we sat waiting for his housekeeper to bring coffee and cakes, he talked of his childhood. He talked in his gentle voice of rain, and mist, and cold and hunger, and joy. He talked of siblings, too many to count, of working in the field, praying for a good harvest to help their family survive, of blight, and of rivalries and hatred, of family joy and love and the desperation of survival. He said, "We are all merely God's creatures, and all desperate in our own endeavours to survive."

As I listened, I saw an image of him as a young man joining the seminary. I saw a fair man with pale golden freckles and pale skin, dressed in a black cassock flapping around his skinny legs. I saw him lying prostrate before the altar as he was taken into the priesthood. He talked about entering university, and resentment stabbed in my breast as he talked of his education being one of the greatest blessings God had showered upon him in his humble life.

He talked about how education opens one's mind and heart and how it had provided him with so many possibilities after the deprivations of his youth. I stopped listening. His words bathed me in acid as I battled down the unfurling petals of envy. I had always imagined that one day I would go to university but now I knew I never would. Bitterness filled my heart as I thought what could have been. In my mind I heard Sister Immaculata saying, "God places us all where he wants us to be child. To fight God's Will is to fight the wind."

I tried to bury my envy and turned my attention back to him, as he spoke of the lasting friendships he had made in university, and of the friend who was staying with him now. I saw no sign of a friend, but perhaps he was talking in metaphors.

I sat forward, and he paused, waiting for my question.

"Am I where God wants me to be, Father?"

He looked startled. "Where do you want to be child?"

I felt the tears bubbling up from my core. The long-held suppression of hurt, anger, and resentment spilled into confession. My orphaned loneliness, my lost friendship with Anna, my adoption, my adultery, my abandonment, my lies, the theft of my papers, their loss, and my destitution. Words so long buried, scrambled to get out. They tripped and fell over each other in their haste to see the afternoon light, where they mingled with the dancing sunbeams that slanted through the window.

The priest listened in silence, as I told him my history, from the moment of my birth, which is only hearsay and about which the nuns at the orphanage had said I exaggerated.

"I was born in 1919, during the early days of the Weimar Republic, when workers clashed with police in bloody street battles. Because of this, my life began in death." I paused. "My birthing came unexpectedly in a back street of Berlin while the fighting raged. My mother was killed moments after she pushed me into the world."

I glanced at the priest, but he remained silent, and I ran my hand across my mouth. The imagery of my birth was pieced together from what I had gleaned from old newspapers. The nuns had never allowed me to express it, and it was the first time I had spoken it aloud. I wasn't sure he would believe me.

With increasing conviction, I said, "I can imagine her now, lying in my father's arms as he watched the life leave her eyes. I can imagine him cradling me, a haven of love amid hate." I sighed and decided I needed to be truthful. "I can imagine a lot of things, but all I know is that the Sisters of Christian Charity found me naked and wrapped in a bloody greatcoat, my father's cold body slumped next to hers as he shielded me against that March bitterness."

Now I had begun, I could not stop, and the priest listened in silence as I confessed my sins. I spoke of envy and pride and the worst of all, abandoning Anna to seek my own joy in adoption, but instead, finding my purpose was other; to beget a child for a childless Schutzstaffel officer and his barren wife.

Only then did Father O'Bryan speak, slowly and with thought. "You have had a difficult life, but it is not of your making. You have been badly treated, and it should not have been so. Put away your guilt my child. The God of Heaven that I know, would not condemn you for what you have done."

Then he said what sounded like a prayer, or benediction.

"Seek redemption and it shall be yours. Pursue renewal and enlightenment. The past can only continue to hurt us if we give it permission. Reject hurt and grasp only faith and happiness into the future, for faith conquers fear. Trust that the unknown will become knowable as you pass through life and then you will have conquered guilt and become true only to your own conscience. Sublimate selfish desire to the service of others and you will find all you seek my child."

I tried to digest the meaning, but it was too much and said too quickly for me to comprehend. Still, I felt lighter. He did not condemn me but told me that I would have happiness if only I could grasp courage. Or I think that is what he meant.

That, and I should serve others. An idea began growing in my mind as I saw myself in wimple and scapula, books laden in my arms as I walked into a classroom.

Eventually he broke the silence saying, "But answer me one more question. How did you know those two policemen who were with you in the church yesterday?"

"The SchuPo!"

"Yes."

"But they were the ones the boy was fleeing from." Why did he change the subject? Did he think I had an assignation with the policemen in his church? Indignation made my words harsh. "They chased the boy I told you about. I told them he ran to the park, but he was in the alley like I told you. They were looking for him. They didn't know I...."

I stopped abruptly--caught out. Believing the priest benevolent, I had walked into his trap. I admitted I lied to the SchuPo; admitted I misled them by pointing to the park instead of the alley. The priest did not want to hear my confession about adultery at all. He wanted to catch me out lying about the boy in the alley. Was he an informant for the police? Had they found the boy and dragged him back to the prison, or worse, killed him. Now they were getting me to admit that I was a Communist collaborator, a Jew lover.

The priest stood up. Walking to the window he stood looking out into the garden. His back was to me, his shoulders stooped, his hands clasped behind him. "You care about that boy, the man in the alley. Why? Why lie for a Jew?"

I pressed my lips together firmly. I would not tell him anything more.

Turning back to face me, his gaze searched mine. "I have to be sure you see. I must know you are not lying. You are not one of them." Anguish furrowed the thin translucent skin of his freckled brow. "You see I need your help, but I must be sure I can trust you. Not for myself. I do not care for myself but for him, I must be sure."

Was he telling the truth or was this a trap? There was no way of knowing and I wasn't sure I could trust my judgement. Not anymore. I trusted before and look where it got me. If I trusted again and my trust was abused, what would become of me? This time I would be in serious trouble. This time I helped an escapee from the prison, a wanted man, but the priest already knows what I did. It was already too late. If he was going to give me up to the police, he had enough information to have me sent to prison.

"Father, what is it you want from me?"

The priest was once more looking out the window and did not reply but instead said, "Ah, he's here. I want you to meet someone. He is a friend from my English university days." He walked to the door, "Please excuse me one moment."

Minutes passed and I contemplated leaving, but where should I go? I hesitated and then the door opened. The priest introduced me to the man who stepped into the sitting room. He was about the same age as Father O'Bryan, mid-thirties, tall and stooped as he walked through the low doorway into the low-ceilinged sitting room.

"David, this is the young woman I spoke about. Fräulein von Herff." He turned to me. "Magdalena may I introduce my great friend David Asquith."

Herr Asquith raised one eyebrow. *"La Traviata's* Violetta?"

The priest frowned. "I sincerely hope not."

Asquith merely smiled. "Perhaps less tragic, but the name suits her, don't you think?"

They spoke too rapidly in English, and I could not follow everything although they spoke about Verdi's opera as if it had some relationship to me.

Herr Asquith shook my hand, and in German, he said, "My dear Miss. von Herff I have heard many good things about you."

I blushed. What could he know? Perhaps, he was merely being charming, but already he had turned to Father and again

48

spoke rapidly in English. I felt ignored like I was an interloper. I should leave as I had probably overstayed my welcome. I should not intrude on the time these old friends had together. As I opened my mouth to say I would go, the housekeeper came in with a tray of coffee and cakes, interrupting the conversation.

I had eaten so much, I did not think I could fit anything more in my stomach, but from politeness, I took one of her cakes. Besides, I knew there was nowhere for me to go, and the room was warm. I didn't want to think about what would happen to me tonight. Father would know of somewhere I could go or some sort of work I could obtain, but without papers it would be difficult. I would have to go to the police and report my missing papers. I hoped Father would go with me.

The pink and yellow icing was sticky as I held it in my fingers, holding my cup in my other hand. I placed the cake on the saucer. Immediately the icing melted against the hot porcelain. I was getting into a fine mess, but the two men paid no attention, instead they continued their conversation in English.

The English man's fair hair flopped into his blue eyes, and he pushed it back repeatedly. He was too tall for the low chair on which he sat, and his knees stood high above the floor, above the level of his chin as he leaned back, oblivious to the odd effect he created. I had never met an Englishman before, although Father O'Bryan had said he was originally from Ireland and that was somewhere near England.

As far as I could make out, they talked of inconsequential things like where Herr Asquith had been that morning, the plants he had noticed and the places he had seen. I wasn't sure if he was a botanist or an architect, but clearly, those were two of his passions. He was scouting for a place for some English Duke and his betrothed to stay after they married in the summer. He called the duke, *Bertie*, and his betrothed, *that dreadful woman,* so I knew he didn't like her much, despite his task to find them somewhere nice to stay.

My schoolgirl English, bolstered by American films and the occasional magazine, was rudimentary, and the concentration it required to follow such a boring conversation was exhausting so I gave up trying. Instead, I focused on Herr Asquith's tone, sounding in my head the rounded vowels, noting the difference between his clipped notes and the priest's lilting tenor.

The housekeeper finished fussing about Father and left the room. With relief I placed my cup and saucer on the table. I couldn't manage it all and I was afraid I would spill the coffee. As the housekeeper shut the door behind her I surreptitiously licked the icing off my fingers, wiping the last fragments on the hem of my uniform, but a sudden silence penetrated my concentration.

The men's conversation had stopped, and they were both looking at me. Mortified I tucked my sticky hands beneath my thighs and hung my head.

Herr Asquith said, "Tell me Fräulein von Herff do you speak English?

I shook my head.

"You obviously do speak some. Or you would not have understood the question."

"I speak a little only."

"I will speak in German then, but as you would have noticed my accent is pretty atrocious…out of practice, I suppose."

He was right, but I said nothing, trying to follow him until he said, "I knew a man called von Herff once. You wouldn't be related to him by any chance. His name was Georg, Doctor Georg von Herff. He was tragically killed many years ago."

An immense surge of excitement rushed through my veins. I had never met anyone who knew my real father, and exhilaration pushed me to the edge of my chair. "Yes, yes, my father's name was Georg, and he was a Doctor, a Medical Doctor. Did you meet my mother also?"

Herr Asquith smiled; his blue eyes lit with humour. "I am sorry to say I never had the pleasure of meeting your mother. I think you must resemble her because I cannot see anything of Georg in you. Life has dealt you a sorry hand. Father O'Bryan says you were raised in an orphanage and have no other relatives. Tragic, simply tragic. You must have been incredibly young when they were killed."

"I was just born." I said in English. "How did you meet my father?"

"I wouldn't say I met him exactly. I was a lad barely in long pants. My father was posted here after the war, and I attended school in Berlin for a few years. I saw Dr. von Herff speak at a rally. My senior schooling in Berlin was the reason I returned to do my master's degree at the Humboldt University. I was interested in the architectural ideas that were growing in Berlin at the time. Amazing results, particularly the Horseshoe Estate. Do you know it? Remarkable." He shook his head.

I shook my head too, unconsciously copying his mannerisms, willing him to talk of my father instead of stupid buildings. My mouth formed around his clipped tones and rounded vowels, and I said in English, "Please, tell me about my father."

"I say, Your English is splendid." He laughed, speaking rapidly. "Of course, that is what I would want to know if I was in your shoes."

I shook my head again. "Please, you speak too fast, I don't understand."

"Oh." He looked nonplussed but said more slowly. "I can't tell you much because I only saw him a couple of times. Our politics didn't really accord. He was a great supporter of Rosa Luxemburg before her dreadful death, and it was all too radical for me."

Herr Asquith smiled. His lips opened when he smiled showing one of his front teeth, slightly crooked, almost overlapping the edge of his other front tooth. It was like his mouth was too crowded to fit all his teeth.

"I wasn't as liberal then as I am growing to be. The older one gets, the wiser I suppose. Your father was far more modern than I. In fact, at the time he was a committed Communist."

I sucked in my breath and felt the blood drain from my face. My father was a Communist. What did that mean?

He looked at me with sympathy. "Sorry my dear, did you not know this?"

I shook my head in disbelief. My parents were Communists, enemies of the State. I became subdued and lapsed into silence, slumped in my chair, caught up in thoughts so deep I forgot my immediate surroundings, forgot my manners, and forgot to sit in the neat, and ladylike way the nuns had taught me. I noticed Father was watching me with concern, but I ignored him. He turned back to Herr Asquith, leaving me alone to brood.

I was in shock at the revelation. Far from having heroic parents, they were criminals opposing the legitimate authority of the State. What then did that make me? I needed time to think this through and understand what a Communist was, other than merely a criminal. All I knew about Communists is that they deny the very presence of God. The Communists in Russia killed the Tsar and his family and caused a bloody revolution.

Surely, my parents could not have been such monsters. Surely, I did not come from such stock. I always imagined I came from parents so romantic, so good and blessed that something so beautiful would be taken from this world, doomed for its purity and love; demanded by God to grace heaven. Now all I could think was that my parents would be in Hell or at best in Purgatory. How could this be, surely it was a lie.

Later that afternoon, Father suggested that I go with him to St Boniface's Abbey. He said the nuns would look after me, give me a bed and help me find my feet. I agreed passively, still brooding over the shocking news of my father's convictions. The excitement of finally meeting someone, who knew something of my parents, was just another burden to carry, like a stone in the shoe of history, and another folly I would need to conceal.

I longed to be someone else, someone of fantasy and goodness, clean and wholesome and decent. I forgot the Jew. I forgot Gertrud and Lothar. Instead, my head filled with an obsession to be clean, untainted by horror, untainted by sin and untainted by the burdens I carried. I certainly did not expect to meet the Jew again, nor did I expect what they asked of me next.

6. Munich to Brussels

The wheels screeched as the train slowed and then stopped
with a settling sigh at Aachen station. I was trying to
concentrate on the words before my eyes, and I looked up
from my prayer book, nerves vibrating like violin strings. The
compartment had seating for six people, three on one side and
three on the other although if the journey were not too long,
eight people could find comfort. I sat on the bench with my
charge, the Jewish boy, disguised now as an aging Sister
Marcellina. Across from us sat a family of three, mother,
father, and a young girl, around ten years old.

I fingered my rosary beads as I peered out the carriage
window, looking past the slumped and apparently comatose
Marcellina, to the countryside beyond. The sun was already
low, hidden behind bruised clouds on the western horizon.
Streetlamps reflected oily rainbows in glistening puddles.

There were soldiers everywhere, in cars, in trucks, walking
two by two, guns hitched over their shoulders. I watched two
border guards chatting as they sauntered along the train tracks,
but through the closed window I could not catch their words.

Fear clawed at my stomach and filled my throat, making it
hard for me to breathe. I fought it down. *Mother of God, have
mercy, save us, please save us.* Sister Marcellina, chin on

chest, appeared oblivious to our danger as he slept with his black veil rumpled, wimple askew. His mouth hung open with a small skein of spit caught in the corner, the skin of his cheeks flaked as if diseased. The greying eyebrows, thick but with the odd stray dark hair poking out. Rumpled wrinkles flaked under his eyes, as if he really was dying.

The family opposite clutched at each other's hands, their faces impassive, and staring out the window. They too saw the soldiers. I could feel their tension and wondered what sins they hid.

The train conductor passed our open door, calling out that we should stand in the corridor with our passports ready. I'd forgotten. My breathing came in shallow pants. Breathe I told myself. Think serenity. Imagine you are Sister Immaculata gardening at the Home, her straw hat perched on top of her veil, shading her face from the sun. Imagine you are she, tranquil and oblivious to the giggles of pointing children, so amused by the hat. *Jesus and Mother Mary help me.* I clutched the prayer book on my lap and hid my hands and the book within the folds of my scapular.

The passports! What was wrong with me? I had to have them ready. I jerked myself into action. They were in the bag in the overhead luggage rack with the papers, and I could not have prying eyes rest on those papers.

Oh, why hadn't I thought of it earlier? I must hurry. I could not open the bag in the guard's presence. He would see the papers and ask me what was in them. I had no idea, but I knew they were dangerous or why else the subterfuge. Why else had Herr Asquith not delivered them himself.

I heard the border guard speaking to passengers outside the next-door compartment and I fumbled with the bag, taking out our passports, snapping the bag shut just as he arrived at the compartment door.

"You must wait in the corridor," he said frowning.

My breath was rasping as he stepped into the compartment, and I held out the passports.

When he saw me, his attitude softened. His Nationalsozialist insignia winked and flashed at me as I made a move to wake Sister Marcellina.

He raised his hand to stop me. "It's a long journey for the elderly. Let her sleep."

His gaze followed my form from head to booted feet, taking in my white veil, the veil of the novice and his eyes lingered too long on my covered breasts before smiling at me.

Then turning to the father of the family standing opposite, all goodwill disappeared under the rapped command. "You must wait in the corridor."

They tried to get around him, but he didn't budge.

"It's my fault. I am so sorry, I held them up from leaving the compartment. I was in their way you see…getting my passport from my luggage."

"Ach, give me the papers!"

The father handed over three passports. His hands shook as he held them out towards the guard.

The guard scrutinised the family, studying their clothing, their faces, and their bags in the racks above, and then he thumbed through the passports.

"Jewish?" he asked.

"No," the father muttered glancing at his feet. His daughter began to whimper, and her mother placed her arm around her.

I stepped in again, foolishly. "I can vouch for them."

Incredulousness was written all over his face, but he addressed the father. "You have visas for the Netherlands."

"Yes." The man nodded.

"Don't bother coming back then. You won't be welcome."

He snapped the top passport shut, holding them out.

The father stepped closer to take them but as he stretched out his hand the guard dropped them to the floor. The father hesitated glancing from the guard to me. He remained still, his passports untended on the floor and then the guard placed his foot on them as he turned to me.

"Now Sister, I do not believe for one moment you can vouch for this scum, but I can see you have a soft heart." His eyes fell on my breasts again. I was grateful for the layers of woollen habit for they flattened my form. He asked. "You have your passports—good? What is the purpose of your visit to Belgium?"

Breathe, you have nothing to fear. You are two nuns on a journey. You have passports. But the passports were forgeries produced by some magic at Herr Asquith's disposal. In mine, I was twenty-two years old, beyond the need for parental approval to travel. Would he see through them, look at me knowing I was merely eighteen and not twenty-two, look at Marcellina and know that she was not an old woman.

My speech was breathless, for I could not get air into my constricted chest. I tried to hold the border guard's eyes but that too was difficult. I looked at the floor, the blood surging up my neck. He would see my guilt. The blush spread until my face was on fire. Was he suspicious?

I glanced at him from under my lashes, and the silence lengthened. Then I realised he was waiting for my response and blurted out my prepared story. "It's my duty to take her home." I inclined my head at Sister Marcellina. "She wishes to go back to Charleroi, to die there." I shrugged as if I felt nonchalant about the nun dying, hiding my lying eyes by looking at the floor.

"What's wrong with dying in Germany?"

The blood crept back before it had time to subside from the last lie.

He grinned at my discomfort and adjusted his shouldered rifle to take the proffered passports. "You are born in Munich?" He examined the photo in my fake passport, holding it to the light. "I too am from Munich. I also studied at St Boniface's." He smiled. "Such a waste. You should rethink your destiny Fräulein. You are too beautiful for the convent. When do you return from Charleroi? Tell me what train and I will try to be on duty that day."

"I don't yet have a return date, but it should be in July perhaps." I ducked my head, my fingers clutching the rosary beads hanging from my waist, twisting them into knots.

"Then I shall meet every train." He handed back the passports, caressing my fingers as he released them into my hands.

As he closed the compartment door, I sat down slowly, my legs shaking. Tears pricked my eyelids, and I bowed my head so as the family would not notice. Father O'Bryan was right, old women were invisible. No one noticed them. No one looked closely, and Marcellina's disguise held.

The family's passports lay on the floor near my feet. I bent to pick them up, handing them back to the father. I couldn't look at him, afraid he would condemn me for my feeble attempts to help him. The guard treated him so rudely and I stood by, concerned only with my own problems.

The way we were treated was marked by chilling contrast. I knew then with certainty that it was wrong, and what they said about the Jews, was wrong. They were just people like me. If they lied, who could blame them. They lived in fear of discovery as I did. If they were evil, then so too was I.

Passport control on the Belgium side was easy. The border guard, a pleasant elderly man, wished us welcome. When he had gone, I busied myself with returning our passports to the bag while I regained some control.

As I stood to heft the bag back onto the luggage rack again, I noticed a wet stain spreading across the floor of the carriage. It took me a moment to realise from where it originated. The young girl opposite me had wet herself. It seemed we were all lying, but she, poor mite, was terrified.

The mother had apology etched in her face. For a moment I forgot my fear, forgot I was an imposter. All I wanted to do was tell this woman I would not hurt her, but I could not think how to do that without betraying my own situation.

"God will take care of us," I said lamely. I had to believe that. Father O'Bryan had promised, and it was all the armour I had.

Sister Marcellina still appeared to be asleep. He did not open his eyes until the train began building up steam. When he eventually sat up, his bottle green eyes looked at me in silent communication. With a small nod of thanks, he turned to gaze out the window as we shunted away from the border.

We had been travelling all day, changing trains three times to get from Munich to Aachen, and yet I was unable to talk to him other than polite comments such as excuse me, or thank you. There was always someone around before whom we must maintain our charade. Soon we would be in Brussels, and I would know nothing about him except that he could act superbly as an old woman, bowed and crone-like with his walking stick.

The bullet that the SchuPo fired, had ripped flesh from the triceps of his left arm but otherwise did little damage. Sometimes, if someone brushed against him or jostled him, he winced, so I knew the wound hurt. His skin tone had improved with the food and medical treatment he received at the Abbey in the past few weeks, although I could not really see much of his flesh under the fake wrinkles and drooping chins.

Father would not tell me his name, nor he mine. He said it was safer; we could not make a mistake if we only knew each other by the names Sister Marcellina and Sister Ursula. Father arranged for us to travel to Brussels, where someone would meet us. That was all I knew, except that I would travel on to Leuven, to a convent where he promised that once I had completed my seclusion, I would be given training as a nurse. It wasn't university but at least I would learn something.

When I said I wanted to join the convent Father asked me to consider why I wished to do so. He said I should examine if it was because I loved God or if there was some other reason. I didn't know. At that stage I didn't care. I just knew that with the nuns I felt safe. I wanted to stay with them. They were kind to me, and the familiar smell of beeswax and incense made me nostalgic for my childhood.

The woman opposite me said something that I didn't catch. I looked up at her as she shyly held out a small piece of cake wrapped in a napkin. She nodded at me. "Please it is good, take it."

I looked at Marcellina who nodded imperceptibly. I took the cake, biting into it greedily as crumbs fell to my lap. Cinnamon flooded my senses, the fluffy sweetness of the cake melting as I pressed it against the roof of my mouth. I savoured it, nodding my thanks, and smiling at the girl who sat straight, shyly watching me. Her mother turned to Marcellina, offering him a small piece of cake also.

He sat up slowly taking her gift with both hands carefully as if in ceremony and then he turned to the window, placing small pieces between his lips, a faraway look in his eyes. A surge of pity engulfed me, for with certainty I knew he was thinking of some lost family.

I had never thought about him as a person with a family. In my mind, he was the escapee, the Communist, the Jew, the hurt boy in the alley. Instead, here he was as lonely as I, sitting on a train, leaving his country behind for whatever fate placed in his path.

The powder that greyed his eyelashes and eyebrows was wearing off, and I remembered the thick black lashes fringing his glass-green eyes, as he told me to go away in the alley that day. It seemed so long ago. Under his disguise he was beautiful, like the Angel Gabriel as he banished Adam and Eve from the garden, his eyes blazing with righteous wrath. His oval face was smooth, and olive skinned, but it was always his eyes I was drawn to, like the eyes of Anna, my beloved Anna.

Anna who told me there is no God. I could see her laughing at me. Her wide mouth would open, uninhibited as she laughed and teased me for my naivety, telling me that guilt was a wasted emotion, an emotion that the nuns encouraged to keep the children in check. She would say we are all just animals, monkeys trying to survive. Then she would add, "Except for the Nazis." She would spit every time she said the derogatory word for the Nationalsozialists. She taught me to call the party Nazi too, but only in private.

My eyes closed over my memories, our blood pact as we pricked our fingers, promising to stay together forever. I remembered Anna telling me that she too was a Jew although she said her family were all atheists and didn't practice any religion. She swore me to secrecy unto the grave. It dawned on me then that Anna's family were also Communists. Such a revelation was less shocking to me now than it would once have been.

I dozed off thinking of Anna and was jolted awake by the train stopping again. Groggily I looked out the window and saw the sign, Antwerpen. I stood up. My leg was full of pins and needles, and I waited until the tingling subsided. Sister Marcellina sat up, looking out the window with the first interest he had shown since we left Munich.

Someone was to meet us. I hoped we would know who it was. I went to pull down the bag from the luggage rack, but the father already had it down and handed it to me with a nod, his face still serious. I smiled my thanks and turned to heft the bag and myself out of the door, but Marcellina took the bag from me, his eyes catching mine with a small smile. I could see the relief in that smile. He was free. They could not get him now. There was no need to play the dying nun any longer and I was glad for him.

A priest stood on the platform. His long black cassock stretched over a stomach that seemed enormous on such short legs. When we alighted from the train he waddled over to us, swiftly taking the bag from Marcellina, and speaking rapidly in Flemish, gesturing for us to follow him.

Marcellina looked at me, "Do you understand Flemish," he asked?

I shook my head, but it wasn't too hard to pick up the gist of what he was saying. We followed the priest to a waiting car where we transferred Herr Asquith's papers to another bag. I sat in the back of the vehicle with Marcellina in the front with the priest. We pulled out of the station, and I looked about me with interest. The place was bustling, even this late in the evening, and streetlights showed buildings that looked different from those I was used to although I couldn't make out exactly what the differences were, just that they were foreign. Then I realised there were no banners with Nazi insignia, nor Nazi flags flying everywhere. A bolt hit me. I had left my country. I was a foreigner in a strange country, and I did not even speak their language.

It was late when we arrived at the convent thirty kilometres east of Brussels. Somewhere along the journey, we left Marcellina at another Abbey. When he alighted from the car Marcellina opened my door and took my hand in his, saying, "Thank you Ursula, you saved my life twice and I am forever in your debt," and then he was gone.

Dawn was lightening the sky to the east by the time the priest pulled up outside a red brick and sandstone building. Massive wooden doors blocked my entrance, and I placed my bag at my feet to pull a bell rope next to the gate. The priest was already driving away, taking with him Herr Asquith's secret papers, and leaving me alone in the shadowed street outside the convent wall.

I was just beginning to wonder if anyone could hear me or if they would let me in, when a gate further along the wall opened, and a head popped out, speaking rapidly to me in French. With relief, I realised she was asking if I was Sister Ursula from Antwerpen. I hurried towards the old nun nodding. At least I spoke a little French. She stood aside for me to pass and then closed and locked the gate. At that moment, the bells of the Angelus began to ring.

I followed her across a paved square towards a cloistered building. She gestured for me to keep up for I was dawdling as

I tried to take in my surroundings. In the centre of the paved area was an oval lawn on which stood a plinth with a statue of Mary, her bare feet resting on a globe. Stone children knelt looking up to her face as she held the baby Jesus, cradled in her arms. It was a similar statue to the one that had graced the entrance to the orphanage where I had been raised. My heart lifted. It was a sign that at last I had found my new home.

7. A Convent near Leuven

The three months of my seclusion passed and now I waited for Mother Superior's verdict on whether she would approve my application for nursing training. I stood in front of her desk, my hands behind my back as I was taught, and my eyes cast down in humility, or at least what I hoped passed for serenity.

Her eyes were rheumy behind thick lenses. "Your situation is unusual Sister Ursula, and you have a privilege extended to none of the other postulants. See that you honour us with your conduct. You will board with the Sisters of Charity of Jesus and Mary near the hospital in Brussels." The skin around her eyes was wizened with circles of age, her cheeks hung in dewlaps, gnarled hands, clawed with rheumatism, rested on the desk in front of her. "If you are so keen to nurse you may consider transferring to them in any event. I am not sure why Father O'Bryan sent you to us, except that he and Father van den Gheyn know one another." She muttered, "And what Father van den Gheyn wishes, must be obeyed." All the time she spoke, she tapped on the desk as if counting her impatience with the priests.

I was seething with joy but knew better than to show it. I should not speak until spoken to, as I had been instructed as soon as I entered the convent on that early morning, three months earlier. Now, I was to get out. Finally, I could move beyond the walls, to commence my training as a nurse. So many times, over the past months, I had thought this day would never come.

I tried to occupy my mind with God, as I went about my ceaseless chores, but I found I did not have the aptitude, and I earned many disapproving sniffs. When I was allowed to speak with the other postulants, I asked if they found it as difficult as I, but they seemed to think the question was an odd one.

Eventually, I hit on an idea. I would talk to God in French, Flemish or Dutch. That way I would become proficient in the languages of Belgium, and I could entertain my mind while my mouth was to remain shut. French was easy because I had studied it at school. Dutch was so close to my own language that I found it easy to understand although my pronunciation drifted to the German emphasis. Flemish was a mixture of them all, more a dialect.

Anyway, I spoke to God telling him about the minutiae of the day and recalling events in my past. I copied the accents of the nuns who spoke French, and paid special attention to the Dutch speakers' accents, rolling words around in my mouth as if they were marbles. In that way I learned, and when I became stuck for an expression or the correct grammar I would wait until recreation period to ask one of the others.

I only once confided what I was doing to another postulant, but I soon learned that I should keep such things to myself. When I explained I was talking to God in French and Dutch in order to learn the languages, she looked as if there might be something wrong in what I did. Her blotchy pink skin became furrowed between almost white eyebrows, making her look more rabbit-like than ever. She spoke to the postulate sister-in-charge about my confession because she thought it might be a blasphemy. After that I restricted my limited conversations to the banal.

My daily task, after Mass and before community rosary, was to clean the offices. The library was on the same floor, which meant I cleaned the library also. I was able to access books, which otherwise would not be permissible. I would *borrow* them, secreting them in my basket of dusters and beeswax polish, to read during the rest-period.

Sometimes, if the books were narrow I took risks, holding them in the centre of my bible or prayer book. Then I would continue to read in our recreation period after supper. This was a far greater hazard, and I would be as skittish as a wild animal when anyone came near me.

It never occurred to me that I had any other choice but to be in the convent. It never occurred to me that by breaking such rules it was clear I did not have a vocation. To me it was merely an extension of the Children's Home, where there were so many rules that it was inevitable that some must be broken, or one would go mad. It was my lot, what God had chosen for me, and I was content, so long as I could sing, read, and study.

As I stood before Mother's desk, I surged forward on my toes with excitement and Mother frowned. I planted my heels firmly back on the floor trying to contain my glee as I watched her in silence. My mind shrieked—I was to begin training as a nurse at the Bergmann Hospital. I had been accepted.

For the last six weeks I had prayed fervently that God would see fit to allow my studies. In moments of weakness, I worried about what I should do if He had other plans for me. I was not sure that a life of contemplation and worship was what I truly wanted. I fidgeted during prayers and was told off constantly for my distraction. I found it hard to be serene, humbling myself daily to the will of God. I often thought His Will was no more than the will of our Mother Superior.

The only place I seemed to fit was in choir. The first morning I arrived, I was shown to the chapel just before Mass began. They were singing a song so familiar that I joined in with delight. The part of the song that said *pray for the wonderer, pray for me* I felt was very personal, so I sung it with fervour. Voices around me faltered momentarily and then resumed as surreptitious glances were cast in my direction. I lowered my voice immediately, realising I was singing too loudly. Berating myself for my unthinking actions I saw that I had spent my life acting in haste without thought for my surroundings.

I heard Sister Immaculata's voice in my head. Empty vessels make most sound Magdalena. My memory flew back to the Children's Home, as Sister poked her head around the dormitory doorway, scolding me for making too much noise. I shivered at the memory. Now here I was again, forgetting myself. It wasn't a good start.

Thereafter, I was told to report to Sister Matthias, who directed the choir. Aside from the books I pilfered, Sister Matthias gave me my sanity. She came from a place close to the French border and conversation with her did more to improve my French than all my conversations with God. She was a square woman with a broad face beneath her wimple. A patch of white hairs sprouted from a mole on her cheek. I discovered she was shy, keeping mostly to herself at recreation time. One evening I walked over to where she sat, alone near the Grotto dedicated to the recent miracles of Our Lady of Fatima.

Sister Matthias didn't hear me as I stood watching her making musical notations on a page. When she did look up, she was startled and covered the page with her hand.

"It's you, child." Relief in her voice told me she saw me as of little consequence, or at least, no threat.

"Sister what is it you write?"

"Nothing child. It's nothing."

I knew this was not nothing. I could see passion when it was before me, and this was Sister Matthias's passion. She created music in her head as I did with song.

"Will you teach me to read music?"

Thereafter, I would sit with her at recreation and learn to read and write music. It was another new language, and as I learned each symbol, I began to hear their associated sounds in my mind. Now my conversations with God and Sister Matthias often revolved around music, all spoken in French.

Most mornings I would sing at least one solo at Mass, and I found it soothed, like no prayer could. Sister Matthias told me it was God's way of helping me pray. I know some of the choir, and certainly some of the other postulants, thought I was getting special treatment. While no one treated me badly, I felt apart from them, only happy when I could be with Sister Matthias.

Friendships were not encouraged. We were expected to behave as one community with a kind of group harmony, like the bees in the convent apiary. Despite this, all the women in the convent had someone with whom they spent more time, having something in common, even if that commonality was disapproval. If it could be thought that an eighteen-year-old postulant, and a fifty-year-old nun could become friends then she was my only friend in the convent.

My nursing training began in September 1937. The Matron at the hospital complained I hadn't the advanced schooling required. If she had only known the truth about my education and why it was cut short. But Doctor Berger, the medical officer in charge of the training school said I was admitted, so that was the end of it. I overheard Matron saying it was because Father van den Gheyn had insisted, and from that comment I assumed that I received special treatment because I did Father's friend a favour by smuggling the documents. I didn't know what was in those documents, but I was glad I had done it.

Matron sniffed her disapproval every time she saw me, her tall angular frame stiff with censure. Some of the other trainee nurses picked-up on her dislike of me and would not speak with me either. Their dislike did not affect me too much for I didn't stay in the nurse's quarters with the other girls but had moved into a room in the convent near the hospital.

I missed Sister Matthias and wrote to her often, talking about music and asking questions to further my knowledge. My room in the convent was tiny, with enough room for a bed and a small bedside locker. When I studied or wrote letters, I would do so sitting cross legged on the bed, balancing my books, or writing paper on my knees. On the wall above my bed, hung a small crucifix. As I studied, I would look up at it occasionally, talking softly with Jesus about what I had read or what I thought about something that had happened in my day. Every morning after Mass I would collect my books and ride an old bicycle to my classes.

It was one morning, just as winter had arrived, that I met up again with Sister Marcellina. Except she was no longer Sister Marcellina. She was the Jewish boy from the Alley, or rather I should call him a man. One whom I was later to find had taken the name Marcel. He crossed the road in front of me, just outside the entrance to the Bergmann. I called out but he continued walking.

I called again, "Marcellina!"

He turned and walked swiftly to where I stood clutching my bicycle, and took me by the shoulders, kissing me soundly on both cheeks and then once more in the Belgian style.

I was taken aback at the contact but laughed when I saw his serious face. He looked so well, healthy, his green eyes shining with life. His flesh had filled out the hollows in his cheeks and his shoulders and chest were broad and muscled under his collarless shirt. He saw me staring and smiled a lopsided grin.

I looked away trying to cover my embarrassment by saying, "Aren't you cold?"

"Working keeps me warm. How are you Sister Ursula?" He looked at the books in the basket on my handlebars. "You are a nurse. That is a thing of pride, a worthy calling."

He was an orderly at the hospital. Another position that Father O'Bryan had pulled strings to secure. He walked with me to the classroom building and then kissed my cheeks again, this time with more decorum.

"Perhaps I will see you again tomorrow?" I said as he turned to leave.

"I'm always here at the same time, if I do this shift," he said.

I parked my bicycle and walked towards the classroom hugging my books to my chest. A feeling of happiness and excited anticipation raced through my veins.

Every morning after that I would ride my bicycle in haste to be sure I would be at the entrance in time to see him. We would walk together, talking about local gossip, sharing stories about the past. I discovered his name was really Joachim Steinberger, but his Belgian papers were in the name of Marcel D'Haen so now he was Marcel. I told him my name on my papers was Aurélie Avraham.

"How is it then that you are called Sister Ursula?

I explained how the nuns chose their names and that I had been given the name of Saint Ursula. He looked bewildered but said nothing more. After that he called me Aurélie, refusing to call me Sister.

Then his shift changed, and I no longer saw him every day. My mornings dragged through the hours until I could get back to my little room where I would write to Sister Matthias. I poured my sorrow out in my letter. Oh, of course, not explaining my malaise as missing Marcel, but telling her how much I missed singing. It must have struck a chord because after that I was asked to sing in the choir with the Sisters of Mercy of Jesus and Mary.

Sister Lidwina, the choir mistress, explained that she and Sister Matthias had known each other since childhood. The Sisters of Mercy's choir sang at the cathedral on Sundays and feast days so, she would only have me sing with them if I had the ability.

It was arranged that I would go to the cathedral the following afternoon after class, and try out. I was accepted.

She said I had raw talent, but I bawled like an undisciplined cat. I needed training. I didn't know what she meant, but nodded, accepting her verdict, and assuming I sang too loudly.

This I felt was justified because it was obviously what Sister Immaculata meant when she told me that empty vessels make most sound. I realised then that I would need to learn to sing more quietly, like so many of the other nuns'.

A few weeks later, I saw Marcel going through the hospital entrance, and I stood up on the bicycle peddles to ride faster, calling to him as I did.

He heard me and waited his face alight with amusement. Mine was red with exertion. I stopped out of breath, and adjusted my veil, which had slipped back on my head.

"You didn't tell me your shift was changing Marcel." I heard the petulance in my voice and tried to adjust the accusation. "I wondered where you were."

He didn't seem to notice. "My shifts change fortnightly. I am on days for two weeks, then I have nights for two weeks. On day shift I begin my shift now; on nights I begin my shift at 6 o'clock."

"Oh," was all I could think of to say as we walked together across the road.

"Why did you want to see me?"

I could feel my face becoming hot. Why did I want to see him? I cast around for something to say. "Because you are my friend."

His expression seemed startled and then courteously he said, "I am honoured to be your friend."

I added. "And there is something else I wished to ask you."

"Yes, of course, anything."

"I had a friend once. Her name was Anna Schmitt. I wondered if you are a relative." My eyes searched his face for recognition, but he shook his head.

"I had a cousin called Anna, but she was Anna Steinberger like me."

An idea began dawning in my mind. "What happened to her?"

"I don't know. I think she is dead like the rest of my family." His eyes darkened until the green faded to hazel as he spoke.

Excitedly I told him about Anna, about how much she looked like Marcel. I told him her secret, the one I had vowed never to reveal, but here I thought she could forgive me. I told him she was Jewish, that an aunt had hidden her when her parents were arrested. For the first time since I had known Marcel, hope flooded into his face. He grasped my arms looking into my eyes. "Where is she now?"

I saw the hope fade as I explained that she was gone, and I never knew where they took her. "Father O'Bryan will help. He will be able to find her. Write to him or go and see Father van den Gheyn."

He left me then, running back the way we had walked. I called after him, but he didn't stop.

8. The Spanish War 1938

Marcel did find out what had happened to Anna. It was January 1938 when Father van den Gheyn, through his extensive networks, finally received confirmation that she had left Germany with an aunt who had managed to get a visa for America. Who the aunt might be, was uncertain and Marcel held out hope it was his mother. Anna's mother had two sisters. One was Marcel's mother and no matter the likelihood, she too may have escaped. He was still trying to track down where she might be in America, but that at least some of his family had survived made him seem content.

Once more he expressed his gratitude, not only for saving his life but for being instrumental in him finding family. Yet, I had done nothing, and I didn't want his gratitude. I thought of the Jewish family on the train, imagining Anna like that little girl, in fear for her life. Had they been fleeing like Anna and her aunt just because they were Jewish? Or, like me, did they also hide something more criminal. Had Anna's parents been arrested like Marcel, just because they were Jewish Communists…like my parents were Catholic Communists? Was it possible to be Jewish or Catholic and a Communist?

Next time I saw him, I asked Marcel. He smiled and said, "Being Communist is a conviction. For me, being Jewish is

73

not optional." He also said he didn't know about being Catholic but being Jewish is much more than a belief in God. "It is belonging to a community, a tradition. Why are you interested my little Aurélie?"

Anna was safe, but so far away it felt no different to me than before. Unlike Marcel I never believed Anna dead, but I was used to her absence. It dawned on me that I lived in a very selfish world. I hardly ever thought about anyone else and how they lived. I knew very little about the Jewish people in my country and what they believed in or even what made them Jewish.

I still did not really understand Communism although I vowed to learn what it was, when I discovered it was what my parents believed. Yet, my entry into the convent had wiped those thoughts from my mind. I was wrapped up with the pursuit of study and my own survival after Father O'Bryan told me what entering the priesthood did to change his life. The chance of becoming a new person drove me, and I forgot all else but my own egotism.

Now I recognised my ignorance. What a child I must seem to Marcel who had suffered so much, and yet remained so kind and caring. I knew very little about anything other than my own internal turmoil, and I wanted to change, so that rather than treat me as a small child he would come to respect me as an equal.

At first Marcel was reticent, but when he saw how serious I was, he brought articles torn from newspapers on politics, and books on philosophy, on Judaism, and books on Communism. He would find the thinnest volumes so I could hide them with my nursing books, after I told him I could not be found reading them.

I began to see that far from my Führer being the father to our nation, he was a man who bought the loyalties of others through trickery; fooled them by pretending to be everything to every man. He bribed children with sweets, paid mothers to bear children and stay home. He gave people what they thought they wanted. Yes, he brought prosperity back to Germany giving its people pride and hope. Yet, this was not enough for him. He wanted more; more Germans, more land, but only for those of whom he approved. He only acted for those who were his folk. For those who were not, he treated them very badly or at least his Storm Troopers did, and he did not stop them. I compared the Führers views with that of Jesus and found his antithesis.

That was a revelation to me. How could a man I had been taught to think was benevolent and kindly, the saviour of Germany, be the opposite of Jesus? Jesus called to all, the sinners, and the beggars. He excluded no one. That is what I had heard from the nuns all my life. Yet here was our fearless leader excluding and damning those whom he called less than human, his own people, who had voted for him.

I began to wonder, why my country would not want people who had lived there for generations; people who were an integral part of its fabric. People like my parents, like Marcel and Anna. I had no answers, and my head rang with confusion until I was given another distraction.

Three things came one after the other. The first was when Sister Lidwina told me I was to have my voice trained by a professional. I was thrilled. Now I would learn to sing in a clear reedy voice or the whispered hush so many of the other nuns used. I would learn to modulate my voice rather than throwing it about, drowning everyone within hearing.

The man who attended the convent to hear me sing was none other than my beloved Sister Matthias's brother, Alain Danois. Mr. Danois was a tall thin man who had the most peculiar hair. It was lank and dull like burnt straw. I later found out it was died black and underneath, he was completely grey. His mannerisms were abrupt, almost to the point of rudeness but I didn't mind. His ways amused me, and I suspected his rudeness was a defence against some past hurt.

He asked me to sing scales as he played them on the piano. I sang, trying to modulate my voice. It came out all wrong like

75

a husky whisper, out of tune. One of his eyebrows rose up his forehead as he turned to Sister Lidwina.

"Sing properly child." She sounded cross. I couldn't understand what was wrong and I looked at her helplessly. "Sing like you usually sing," She commanded.

Did she want me to sing like an undisciplined cat?

Mr. Danois turned back and began playing the scales once more. Perhaps she wanted me to show the extent of my failings, so I gave my voice its full breath. Mr. Danois then played in another octave, and I followed, then another and another. He sped up the pace and I followed then he played the lowest octave, but my voice could not go that low and I coughed at the effort.

When I coughed, he shut the piano and got up. He didn't look at me. He just walked to Sister and shook her hand. Sister Lidwina was beaming, while I stood next to the piano wishing the floor would swallow me whole. I was to learn that my assumptions once again were all wrong, but that was later when I began my twice weekly classes with Mr. Danois.

The second thing that happened, was that I passed my exams and graduated to working on the wards, in practical application of what I had learned. My first rotation through the wards was with the elderly, some of whom had lost their words and no longer knew their families. It was very sad, but I often saw Marcel who worked in this section of medicine in the hospital.

Seeing him made my time there more pleasant. He was so kind and patient with these old and frail people. I tried to emulate his kindness and began to see that Marcel was a better person than I. He had so much compassion, I felt humbled by him. Every break and every moment before or after work I would seek him out. Until one day I overheard a conversation that disturbed me greatly.

Two nurses were in the sluice room. I was about to enter with a cloth covered bedpan when I heard my name mentioned. I stopped, bed pan held stiffly in my hand, my other hand pressed to the door, keeping it ajar. I knew eves-dropping was not the right thing to do but I could do nothing else. I had not the courage to walk in as they talked about me. Neither could I walk away as I needed to dispose of the bedpan and its contents.

I stood listening in an agony of indecision until one of them said, "It's not right, running after a man like that and her having taken her vows. Matron should report her to the convent. They'd soon have her out of here."

A cry escaped my lips at their unfairness. One of the nurses yanked open the door to find me standing there. She pushed past me saying, "Sneaking around again, listening where you're not wanted, Sister." She emphasised the word Sister as her friend walked out behind her.

As the friend passed, she turned and pushed me into the room. I stumbled. The contents of the bedpan slopped over its rim and splattered across the floor. I sagged in defeat as I took in the mess, wrinkling my nose at the sudden stench of disturbed excreta. I would have to clean it up quickly or I would be in more trouble from Matron.

The third thing to happen was, in my view, the most terrible. Marcel told me he was leaving. I cried out without thinking. "You can't go, you can't leave me here."

"What's wrong, my little dove?" He turned to me with surprise written across his face.

We were standing outside the hospital, I with my bike leaning against a rail, ready to go to my singing lessons at the cathedral; he in his orderly's coat. A wintry wind blew cold, damp flurries of snow about my ankles. Marcel never seemed to feel the cold and his coat was unbuttoned, revealing his open necked shirt below. I looked at the hollow indent at the base of his throat. My throat constricted at the thought of him leaving. He couldn't go. I would go with him if he went. I didn't care about leaving here. I would just follow him.

"Where are you going?" My voice sounded flat and lifeless, and I cleared it, trying to sound bright and cheerful.

"To the Spanish War; I will enlist to fight the Fascists."

He said it as if he was going to the bakery to buy bread, but he gazed into the distance as if he was already far away. Then he said, "Hitler has troops in Spain, helping Franco. The Spanish Republic needs all the help they can get. Already the Nationalist Fascists have taken more than half of Spain."

His eyes were alive with fervour as he turned back to me. "Don't you see Aurélie? The Fascists will take over all of Europe if we don't stop them. Even now in Spain when they capture a town or city there are reprisals. They kill everyone, teachers, children, those who do not fight, they kill; those who do not agree with their politics, they kill." He stroked his hand down my veil and I shivered at his touch. "The Spanish insurgents use the Luftwaffe to bomb cities and towns, killing innocent women and children. If we do not fight them, who will? Soon Europe will be ablaze with Fascist flames, Hitler, Franco, Mussolini. We are all in danger my little Aurélie. It is every right-thinking man's duty to fight this evil. We are late to the fight, but better late than never."

"Who is we?" I asked in a small voice, afraid I would never see Marcel again. Afraid he was taking someone with him, someone who meant more to him than me.

"What?" He seemed puzzled by my question. "We are my brothers." He lowered his voice. "You know my beliefs my dove. It is men, who like me will band together to rid this earth of Fascists. I go with my comrades."

"When will you go?"

"We leave tonight."

"No!" I threw myself against him, burying my face in his chest as I clung to his coat lapels. I didn't care who saw me. "Take me with you."

He laughed then, and I felt the blood sizzle in my ears at the sound.

"I cannot take you little one. Even if you can fly like a bird on your bicycle, I cannot take a girl to war. You belong here. You are a healer. That is the noblest profession to which one

78

can aspire. You will heal those who cannot heal themselves. This is your calling in life. Mine is to go to war."

"No, I can't do it if you are not here, I won't." I almost stamped my foot but stopped myself in time. I was so angry with him. I stood stiffly, clutching his coat. How dare he treat me like a child?

"I will come back again, you'll see little Aurélie." He peeled my fingers from his coat and held both my hands in his warmth. "I will be back, victorious, and you will be a nurse, and I will see you all grown-up. You will have changed your veil from white to black. We will be friends forever, for you have given me my life and my only surviving family, and I am always in your debt." He kissed the back of each hand, and then he dropped them, walking away and out of my life.

I went back to the convent and threw myself onto my bed. I stared at the crucifix on the wall, but I had no will to speak with God. I turned my face to the wall, pressing my forehead against its cool plaster.

There was a knock at my door. One of the postulates had been sent to find me. I had missed my singing lesson. I sat on my bed and told her I was sick. As I spoke tears ran unchecked down my cheeks. I could not stop them, and I did not understand the depth of my unhappiness.

She left the room, running in a manner that if it were in the hospital would bring a rebuke from Matron. I was glad it was Sister Lidwina who came to my room and not one of the other nuns, whom I did not know so well.

I told her about Marcel and how he was going far away to Spain to be killed and I could not stop him.

She looked perplexed. "Who is Marcel?"

I forgot they didn't know who I was. To tell them I was crying over an orderly at the hospital would bring about the censure the two nurses in the sluice room hoped for. I lied then, calling Marcel my brother, before burying my face in my hands as a fresh surge of tears flooded my eyes.

She sat on my bed beside me, which was strictly forbidden to us postulates and put her arm around my shoulders. "There, there," she soothed. "Pray, and God will bring your brother home safe to you, if it is His will."

Although guilt stricken over my lie, it served me well in the days to come as I was called into the Mother Superiors office and asked to account for my actions. I had been seen in close embrace with an orderly at the hospital. I was lucky Sister Lidwina backed me up, explaining about my brother going to war with much greater conviction than I felt I could do, given such deception.

I could not stop crying and the nuns became worried. I was given a week off my training to commune with God and restore my equilibrium, praying for my brother. The nuns set up a Novena for him and every time I heard my lie repeated on their lips as they prayed for my brother Marcel, guilt flooded my face so I was sure they must see the truth. I prayed that God would forgive my lie and in His infinite mercy that he would still hear the nuns Novena for Marcel, even though he was a Jew and a Communist and didn't believe in God.

I wrote to Marcel, care of an address he had left for me, telling him about my lie, and begging him to stay safe, for Anna's sake if not mine. He never wrote back.

It was shortly after my birthday and three weeks after Marcel's departure that I was moved into the new oncology ward. It was the beginning of my realisation that nursing was not my vocation.

9. BRUSSELS, AUTUMN 1939

Torrential rain left muddy puddles on the pavements through which we navigated our way to The Brussels Club. Our shared bedsit wasn't far, not far enough to waste money on a bus or tram fare. While waiting for my house mate Madeleine to catch up I looked down at my shoes. The black satin was ruined. It would be impossible to get the mud stains out. Hopefully, no one would notice under the spotlights.

I sighed and called for her to hurry as I turned into the alley leading to the back of the club. I walked cautiously, expecting to have to barge my way through the crush of fans waiting at the back door. We were lucky tonight, it was still early, and only three were gathered, waiting in the pool of light that illuminated the backstage door. They looked up expectantly as I arrived, but then turned away in disappointment.

Madeleine caught up with me, panting with exertion. She grabbed my arm, "Wait, stop—Aurélie."

I stopped; not that I had much choice. Her grip on my arm stopped me moving ahead unless I was going to haul her along like I was some old cart horse. She regained her breath and turned her big, white-toothed smile on the fans. It worked immediately as it always did.

I watched her with them as she signed their autograph books. Hair fell down her back like a black silk curtain, obsidian eyes flashed in the sepia streetlight, charming them further. They had no idea who she was, but they didn't care. She was beautiful and exotic, her creamy skin like milky coffee, glowed in the light. Such beauty surely must belong to someone famous.

Then a car turned into the alley and Madeleine was forgotten. The fans were there for their hero, the jazz king, Robert Fontaine, and this they hoped was him arriving. But again, they were disappointed. The car drove by.

I walked to the backdoor, "Come on, Madeleine."

She ignored me. I couldn't believe it. It wasn't enough that it worked once, now she wanted to milk it. I said in my most firm voice, "Come along Maalatee, we'll be late."

She flashed a look of venom at me as she hurried to catch up. "Don't call me that!" She hissed.

"Why not; it's your name isn't it?" I grinned. It worked every time.

"I should never have told you my real name. You can't be trusted." She sulked.

When I first met Madeleine, we were both looking for a place to live. I hadn't known her five minutes before I heard her life story. She told me about growing up in her parent's restaurant in Antwerp, washing dishes, peeling vegetables, baking bread until she was old enough to wait on tables, her hair always smelling of onions, garlic, and fish. As soon as she could, she escaped to the glamour of show business. Dancing and taking off her garments bit by bit, she worked her way into theatres and clubs in Bruges, Antwerp, and Gent before arriving in Brussels where she once more reinvented herself.

She was experienced in show business, and all I had ever done was to sing in a convent choir, but I didn't tell Madeleine much about me, except that I was once a nurse and had changed my mind halfway through my training. The smell of people dying, the relentless decay, the suppurating wounds, the pain as tumours consumed healthy tissue. Revolutionary treatments in radium, the surgeon's knife, nothing stopped its relentless march. I couldn't bear it.

I told her I thought being a nurse and getting into nursing training at the prestigious Brugmann Oncology Ward of the Hospital was my dream, but the reality gave me nightmares. I began to see disease everywhere, in my dreams and in my waking hours. I could smell its distinctive curse, omnipresent even on a clear summer's day. I began to wonder what the point of living was, when at any time something so insidious, so hopeless, so voracious could quietly begin to consume you. I was not a saint like Marcel, always so kind and considerate of others. I was revolted.

I never mentioned Marcel to Madelaine. He had been gone more than a year, almost two, and I missed him. Thankfully, she was not a curious person, much preferring to talk about herself. She hated stories about sick people she said one day, apologising for not wanting to hear about my nursing career. Neither did I tell her about the convent. That betrayal, I buried deep with the guilt I still felt over walking away from the nuns.

We entered through the stage door into the dimly lit passage at the back of the club. The man at the door closed it against the gathering fans. Already they were increasing in number as opening time drew nearer. We took off our coats, hanging them on the hooks near the door.

I hated being rushed before I went on stage. I needed to sit in quiet contemplation for a moment getting myself into the right frame of mind. Unless I was singing, I preferred to remain in the background.

Madeleine was my opposite in everything. She chain-smoked relentlessly. She drank gin martinis. She flirted with everyone, chatting, and throwing her hands about in dramatic emphasis. Madeleine never had to worry about her voice going wobbly—just her legs. She was a dancer. A scantily dressed dancer who became gradually more scantily dressed as her act progressed, throwing articles of clothing to the audience who whistled and stomped when she sashayed onto the stage. I sometimes thought it was only Madeleine that many of the patrons came to see. No one seemed to mind if Madeleine was wobbly on her legs, she just grinned becoming saucier as the audience cheered.

When Mr. Danois, my singing teacher, heard I was leaving the convent, he suggested I try out at the club where he worked.

"It's a job," he said, "Until you get on your feet."

I was hired, and Mr. Danois said I should call him Alain. Despite no one paying him any longer, Alain continued with my voice training lessons, thrice weekly. Instead of the music room at the cathedral, we would meet in the club. It was a different place in the morning, its glamour hiding from the harsh light of day. Dust motes and stillness hung around us as we practiced scales, ignoring the smell of stale cigarette smoke and alcohol.

The first time we met in the morning, Alain stood erect as I walked into the room. His thin hips were cocked one higher than the other, and he smoothed his thinning hair flat against the porcelain skin of his scalp. His vertically lined face looked sorrowful as he explained that I should be singing classics—opera, with my voice, but he would teach me jazz because that was what the club was—a jazz club.

He taught me jazz, but we always began with voice exercises and scales. He would make me sing an aria before we began with the jazz. He taught me different pronunciations depending on whether the song was jazz or opera. It was like learning two languages simultaneously but eventually I got the hang of it.

He told me one day I would sing opera. He had written to someone he knew, and I should view this as just a fill in job. I didn't care. Jazz was king in my book and while opera was fun, any singing was fun, but I was consumed by the rebellion of jazz. To me it was the antithesis of the decorum by which I had been indoctrinated—it was my own revolution, safe and yet emotionally liberating.

Tonight, I was to try out two new American numbers we had been practicing, *Blue Moon* and *Summertime*. I so wanted to impress that great American king-of-swing Robert Fontaine.

I always tried to be early to work. Madeleine was always late but with enough nagging from me we would usually arrive in good time. Only Alain seemed to care if I was on time or not. There were always plenty of other girls willing to take my place and more willing to take care of the club owner, Monsieur Lallier, with his fat, seeking fingers. He would stare at me while fiddling with the buttons of a waistcoat that ridged rind-like over his rotund stomach. It was Alain whom I had to thank for Monsieur Lallier leaving me alone. I don't know what power he had over Monsieur Lallier, but he seemed to be the only one who wielded any influence, and the other staff were all terrified of him.

Alain saw me as I came out of the corridor. He tutted his tongue at the state of my muddy shoes, and his eyes rolled at my baggy stockings rumpled around my ankles.

"You should have worn a full-length skirt. I told you yesterday. You have to make a special impression tonight."

"But Alain, the hem would have dragged in the mud. Anyway, no one will see my feet and ankles on stage."

I straightened the scarlet and black pleated bolero, which had looked so smart when I shrugged it on earlier this evening. Now it was a sad limp affair, infused with the damp night air.

Alain clicked his fingers at a wardrobe maid nearby. "Give the jacket to her and go sponge the mud from your shoes. There is plenty of time."

He turned to walk away but remembering something, he turned back. His face took on a coy look. "And my dear," He grinned, his face folding into a mass of lines. I had never seen his true smile and it shocked me. Sometimes he lifted the corners of his lips, but the smile never extended beyond his mouth. Now he was positively smirking, sounding almost flirtatious.

"There is a rather delightful, if dishevelled looking gentleman waiting for you."

"Who?"

I wasn't expecting anyone. I had a few suitors, but none were serious, and it would have been unusual for Alain to let any of them in before opening time.

"Sorry to disappoint darling, but he says he is your brother. What could I do but pour him a drink? So dark and dashing, so dangerous looking." Alain shivered and licked his lips in bizarre parody.

Shocked, I watched the man for whom I harboured so much respect. This was a side of Alain I only suspected existed but never saw.

He continued, "I didn't believe the relative thing at all, but he speaks perfect Spanish and I have such a weakness for Spanish men."

I walked towards the bar, bewildered, until I saw a brooding silhouette nursing a glass of golden liquid, ignoring the barman shining glasses behind the bar, ignoring the bustle of waitresses as they readied tables and chairs for opening.

Rigo, the barman, winked at me as I came towards him.

"Marcel?" I asked cautiously, not believing the evidence of my eyes. I had not seen him since he walked away from the hospital almost two years ago.

The change in him was astonishing. His face had aged, with grim lines around his mouth and eyes. His thick, curly, dark hair had turned grey at the temples. He wasn't yet thirty, but he looked ten years older. Marcel stood up and I threw my arms around him.

"Thank God you are alive. I thought I had lost you. What happened? You never wrote."

I stood back, mostly because he needed a bath, but also to look into his eyes. They were cloudy with grief and despair, deep as a stormy sea in the dim lighting of the club bar.

He grasped my arm, "Aurélie, I need to talk to you." He glanced around. "In private."

I took him to my dressing room, a grand name for an alcove, but where I hoped no one would disturb us.

Marcel said, "You have to leave. I have found a place for you as a translator for the English, but they think you are a nurse. They won't want a nightclub singer. You will have to pretend. There is talk that we will be next. We must go—you must go."

"What are you talking about Marcel?"

"Don't call me that. I have a new name. I am Eduardo now. I have Spanish papers, but I am an exile. We lost Aurélie, we lost." He took my face in both his hands. "The Fascists are taking over everywhere. Russia has made a pact of peace with Hitler, but we have lost in Germany, in Italy, in Spain, in Austria, Czechoslovakia, now Poland. Our only hope is England and France. I am going to France. I will join up to fight the bastards, no matter what Stalin says, but you must leave. Get to England. I have friends who will help us."

"But Marc... Eduardo we don't need to leave. This is a neutral country. Here, you will be safe."

"Nowhere in Europe is safe, mi cara. Even now the Führer plots to invade the Netherlands, Belgium, France. He will not be stopped until he has the whole of Europe trampled under his boot, in lust for land and power."

His eyes wore a crazed look, and I was frightened. I watched his mouth as he said, "For me I must go, I have no choice. If the Nazis come, I will be captured again, arrested, killed. Your papers say you are Belgian, but they will not save you. We must leave but we have little time."

He took my chin in his hand. "You must be ready. My friend leaves tomorrow, and I promised him a linguist to translate for his family, and a nurse to care for the old grandmother. They travel through France to Calais; there you can get on the ship to England with them."

I couldn't take in what Marcel was suggesting, but I felt bulldozed by his urgency. "I have no visa for England. How can I get a visa so quickly?"

"He is connected. It will be all right."

I looked at him sulkily. "Who is he? How do you know you can trust him?"

"Trust me, mi cara, as I once trusted you."

His face softened and his eyes took on a dreamy look as his hands stroked my arm. It was as if he was stroking a cat, impersonal and absent. I shivered, but my mulishness dissipated under his stroking. I gazed into his eyes. I would never leave him. He only had to say, and I would go with him to the ends of the earth. I remained mute with sudden shyness as he continued.

"You never let me down. You gave up everything for me, a person of whom you knew nothing. I will never let you down and neither will my comrade. He is another reason I am alive today. We were together in Spain. But now England and France have declared war, and he must leave, get his family away, before it is too late. We must go too, now, while we can."

I heard footsteps and Alain hissed at me, an annoyed look on his face when he saw me standing close to Marcel, his hands on my arms. My ironed bolero swung from Alain's crooked finger. "Aurélie you are on in five minutes, hurry."

"Marcel--Eduardo, I have to go. Wait for me, we will talk after I have finished. Don't disappear again. I couldn't bear it. Wait and hear me sing. I will sing for you." I smiled to let him know I wasn't serious, but it was without conviction because it was half of the truth. I loved Marcel, Eduardo, Joachim, whatever he called himself, but it was a secret hidden love that I did not have the courage to tell him about. I loved him since first seeing him safe, washed and fed in St Boniface's cloisters with his glass green eyes fixed in concentration, looking at me so like my beloved Anna.

Madeleine pushed in front of Alain and sashayed up to inspect Marcel. "Mon chéri, oh lã lã." She slid her arm through Marcel's and pressed her breast against his side. "Where have you been hiding this delicious man?" She ran her fingers down his arm and gazed at his mouth in a cross-eyed dreamy way.

I felt hot fury burning my throat at her confident possession of him, but before my red face gave me away, I turned to take my ironed bolero from Alain's outstretched hand. The sequined beading glittered around the bodice, its red linen matching my burning cheeks and the red band around the hem of my black skirt. The outfit could be considered Spanish. Was it a premonition or coincidence? Would Marcel even notice?

He was gazing at the voluptuous woman holding his arm as a starving person would a feast. At that moment, I hated her.

"Aurélie, you have not cleaned your shoes or pulled up your stockings. Come, come, now. We have little time," Alain fretted.

I saw Marcel or Eduardo smiling, amused at this elderly man fussing over me like a nurse maid. He hadn't moved from Madeleine's embrace.

"I will be happy to wait for you in the bar." He held onto Madeleine's hand, still linked through the crook of his arm, and walked out.

I turned my back on them, trying to focus on my performance ahead, choking back jealousy.

As I stood in the wings waiting to walk onto the stage, I heard the opening to Wagner's *Aria for Elizabeth*. I craned my neck to see why Alain played this piece. I thought we had agreed to *Summertime,* but I knew this aria. Alain had made me practice it. It was an odd choice for the jazz club but what choice did I have. I went with the music, walking onto the stage, the lights in my eyes and the wave-crashing sounds of applause washing over me. I was immediately transported into another realm. I forgot Marcel, forgot Madeleine, forgot Alain, and forgot the change of agenda. It was the music, the song, my breath. There was nothing else.

I finished the piece, and Alain surprised me again, this time leading me into *Mon cœur s'ouvre à ta voix* from the opera, Samson, and Delilah. It suited my mood and passion, and I poured my broken soul into the song. Then it was over, and I bowed. The audience stood up, clapping, and calling for more.

I turned to walk off stage, but Alain began playing the opening bars of *Blue Moon*. Was I hallucinating? Had I made a mistake entering the stage too early. Perhaps I sang Wagner when someone else was supposed to be singing, but surely they would have told me. Maybe they had. I had not been listening to anything when Alain spoke to me. My head was filled with Marcel.

Dutifully I turned to the audience, and the sad timber of the song caught in my throat. Marcel didn't love me. If he did, he would not have been so happy to have Madeleine's arms around him. Then I was angry, and my blood boiled. I was wasting my time mooning over someone who hardly noticed I was a woman.

I anticipated Alain launching into *Summertime* and I didn't care any longer. I sang with an abandoned fury as tears jostled and spilled from my voice. All I wanted now was to leave, cry somewhere private and alone. I had loved Marcel for the last two long lonely years in which time I rarely saw him, and not at all since he went to fight the Fascists in Spain, but still I hoped. Now all hope was gone, and I knew in a flash of intuition Marcel wasn't interested in me, not like that anyway. I would not give up singing, not for him or for anyone. If he wanted to leave and go to France or England he should. I was staying.

Once I was finished my performance and was back in my alcove, I wiped off the makeup, searching in the mirror for signs of hurt, but my face was a mask of cold cream. When

Alain walked up behind me with a man I had not seen before, I barely gave him a cursory glance, just nodding slightly at his introduction.

I was expecting that at any moment, Marcel would reappear. I would tell him he should go, but he should go to England if he were going, take my place and go to England if he would not stay in Belgium. France was with England, and both had declared war, confident they could hold off the Germans with the French border fortifications. Yet, I sensed Marcel would not be safe if he went to fight in France. Despite what he said, Belgium was a neutral country, and we could stay here safely. But if he stayed, could I stand seeing him every day if he didn't love me. It would curdle my heart.

"Aurélie, you are not listening." Alain scolded me. "Monsieur Copeau has come all the way from Paris to meet you."

I turned away from my distraction, appalled at my rudeness. "Monsieur, I am so sorry. I was expecting someone else. Please forgive me."

He stepped forward, taking my hand. "Mademoiselle, you have the voice of an angel." His serious face furrowed between the eyebrows, as he bowed as if to kiss my hand but stopped short, his dark eyes searching mine.

Such old-fashioned gallantry made me smile, and I was a little flattered at his exaggerated attention, despite my face still being covered in smears of cold cream. Then it dawned on me. This man was Louis Copeau. Pressure on my chest made it hard for me to breathe. This was why Alain changed my repertoire so abruptly. This was Alain's dream, not the sleazy clubs in the back streets of Brussels. This was The Louis Copeau, producer of Opera in Paris.

He left his card, telling me to call him if I was in Paris. He was so relaxed as if I went to Paris regularly and should call on such a person. I hardly knew what to answer as he once more bowed low over my hand and withdrew. Alain followed; his thumb held up behind his back. This was it. Robert

Fontaine was due on stage, but I didn't care anymore. Louis Copeau wanted me in Paris.

I was still looking at the gaping space where Louis Copeau had stood moments before when Marcel walked in.

"You'll need to hurry," he said. "Just one suitcase nothing more." I noticed the crimson smudge on his cheek, another on his neck. "I have my friend's car outside. I can take you home to pack and then we must go."

He assumed, he always assumed. He would make the order and I would follow. That is the way it was before, but this time he assumed too much. I returned to my chair to resume cleaning my face.

"Did you like it?" I asked watching his reflection in the grainy mirror.

"Like what?" His face took on a look of perplexity at my question.

"Like my performance, my singing, my vo-i-ce." I made the last word into three syllables with frustration at his obtuse puzzlement.

He shrugged, "Ah, you know me, mi cara. I am not one for music, but I am sure you have a wonderful voice. Better that you are a nurse though—all that muck on your pretty face." He shuddered. He looked out into the passageway. I supposed he was looking for Madeleine and I bit back a sarcastic comment referring to her alley-cat morals. Then with urgency in his voice he said, "Can you hurry Aurélie, we need to get out of here. There are several Gestapo agents out there in your audience."

"Gestapo! Marcel you are not in Germany. You are in Belgium. There are no Gestapo here."

"Don't be so naive Aurélie—Gestapo spies are everywhere."

I gave up. This was not the conversation I wanted. "Marcel." I held out my hand in conciliation. He walked towards me, and I took his hands in mine. "Marcel, I am not

going to England with you. I am staying here. I have an offer
to go to Paris."

"Paris! Are you crazy?" His eyes blazed with a fanaticism
I had not noticed before. "The Nazis will stomp all over Paris
as soon as they take Belgium. My dove, you don't
understand."

I held up my hand to stop him. "No Marcel, you don't
understand. I am not going with you." My voice was harsh. I
stopped myself. "I'm so sorry. You must understand that I am
not afraid of the Nazis as you are. These are Germans, they are
my people."

His face dropped. "You forget, these are my people too
and look what they did to me and others like me, anyone they
don't like. You have Belgium papers, but they are counterfeit
remember that. Also, the name on them is Aurélie Avraham, a
name that could easily have Jewish heritage. When they come,
thinking they are your people will not stop them, no matter
how much you protest. The Nazis are brutes."

"I don't like what they are doing but I am not afraid of
them. They will not hurt me but you—they will hurt you." I
nodded, convinced of my reasoning. "You must go to
England. I will stay here in Belgium until I know it is safe
then I will go to Paris. Marcel," I said his name sadly in
farewell. My voice choked and I stood up to hug him. "Go
Marcel, go and I will see you again one day. Maybe in another
two years when you have finished fighting another war, for
another country that is not your own." That was spiteful and I
tried to lighten it saying, "Next time I see you, you will have
English papers and an English name."

"I don't want to leave you here. You will be safer coming
with me."

"No Marcel. Go now before your Gestapo ghosts find you
here." I smiled at him to show I was teasing.

Alain appeared at the doorway. "What are you two talking
about? Gestapo ghosts." He shook his head.

Marcel kissed me lightly on the cheeks, holding me to him as he whispered in my ear. "If you need to find me Aurélie, find Doctor Luc Sardou, he works at the Arc la Bataille, in Paris. He will know how to get a message to me. Remember Sardou."

He pulled on his cap and ducked past Alain. With a small bow he once again disappeared from my life.

In the end I didn't go to Paris. I kept putting it off, too comfortable in my life at the club. Besides, Monsieur Copeau had offered me nothing. Madeleine said he probably did that for all the pretty girls he met who had stars in their eyes. She was the one who reminded me that he hadn't offered me a job in Paris, just said I should call him. She said she wouldn't be so silly as to fall for that old line. I didn't tell her that it never occurred to me that he was anything other than serious. I decided it was my own pride that had allowed me to believe for a minute that he thought I was good enough to sing in the Palais Garnier. I told myself I was lucky to have a good job singing and a good friend in Madeleine.

The days turned to weeks and the weeks to months. I was safe in Belgium. France was at war with my country even though France's Maginot line made the German army hesitate. In the meantime, soldiers from Britain and France, on leave from the border regions, enjoyed our shows, sitting alongside Gestapo agents who watched them more than the show. They made such a noise, whistling and calling for more, more, every time I was on stage. I was becoming popular, and it was a heady feeling. I didn't want to give it up on the slim chance that Monsieur Copeau would even remember he had given me his card. This was neutrality, and naively I believed it would hold.

Then in May 1940, only eight months after I had last seen Marcel, it all changed. The German army mobilised towards the Low Countries and Belgium. The club emptied and soldiers in trucks headed east. The British and French had marched into Belgium to help stop the German invasion.

Rumours were everywhere. German planes began dropping leaflets, then bombs, and then paratroopers. Monsieur Lallier closed the club.

Madeleine said we would go to her parents. I had no other options. Without an income from the club, I could not stay in Brussels. We packed our bags and found a bus. It was heading for Gent, but Madeleine said it didn't matter as we could find a bus from Gent to Antwerp easily. She was intent on getting out of Brussels.

The wireless said there was fierce fighting near Liege. I couldn't believe it. Even now I did not believe Germany would invade a neutral country. Then the Luftwaffe bombed towns and villages, driving people from their homes. Refugees were now just another tool in the German arsenal against the Allies.

That was the tangled snarl of refugees that met our bus as we fled Brussels. Small towns and villages had emptied, with the townsfolk clogging the roads. They had salvaged what they could, and now walked with household or farm items tied on their backs, or pushed before them on carts, or sometimes in prams. Some lucky few had cars, piled high with household items. Troops, heading towards the front, pushed against the human tide, adding to the chaos, and our journey was slow.

Outside a small village, an overturned cattle truck stopped traffic altogether. The bus driver got down to see if he could find a safe path around the mayhem. Most of the passengers also alighted, while our driver went to speak with the driver of the overturned cattle truck.

Madelaine said she would find a telephone in the village to let her parents know we were coming. The noise of terrified cattle was horrifying, and I walked away and up an embankment, to sit among the wildflowers and wait in the warm sunshine, watching the flow of humanity milling about on the road. I didn't hear the drone of planes above the noise of the cattle, until it was too late.

10. Fleeing Belgium

The sky was a fathomless blue, pink streaks of evening cloud floating by, as I lay on my back on the embankment. From horizon to horizon, the only mar was a curl of oily black smoke. There was no sound, not the cattle, not a bird, not even the sound of men shouting, nor the rumbling of farm carts disturbed the silence. Was I dead?

Then my ears popped, and the noise assaulted me like a physical blow. Horses screamed, cattle hollered, a maniacal shriek split the air as bombs fell and burst into roaring flames. Planes whined and machine guns rattled out a rain of destruction. White-hot casings cascaded to the earth.

In the village buildings burned—their broken masonry a jagged toothed rictus through the inferno, the smell assailing my nostrils, burning flesh, burning wood, burning cattle, burning oil, everything burning, oily smoke obscuring the road ahead.

A groan came from my left and I turned my head. A woman lay next to a child. The child's lifeless eyes were fixed on the aeroplanes in the distance sky as they returned to finish their work. The Luftwaffe's black and white emblems were stark on their wings. I whispered, "Why are you trying to kill us? We are just civilians not soldiers."

I could see the man in the plane as he lined up with the road. His machine guns hammered, licking up dust spurts behind fleeing heels. Bodies crumpled under the fiendish hail. Vehicles burst into flames in roadside ditches. The overturned cattle truck burned and its surviving bovine occupants thrashed and screamed.

A truckload of wounded soldiers, Belgian boys with hairless cheeks, was blown in an instant from this hell. The hot whoosh of air rushed across the ground and scalded my body with its fiendish caress. A lone soldier stood in the road firing his gun at the planes before he crumpled like a rag doll, face buried in the road.

I couldn't move, and everything was happening in a kind of slow motion. All around was nightmare; cursing, praying, the noise of bombs, the crackling of flames, groaning people, screaming horses. Words jumbled in my head as I confused prayers. "Mary, Mother of God, Jesus keep us from evil, help us, save us." But my lips didn't move, and I knew God was not here.

Then cheering came from the relative cover of a tree copse. I saw the varied coloured roundels of Allied insignia racing towards the black crosses. A Stuka's tail spat smoke and spiralled out of control. Then the explosion. A great plume of smoke rose to join the deepening haze from the burning town as Spitfires chased away the Stukas.

I remained unmoving for minutes, perhaps hours, afraid to think, afraid to acknowledge what had happened. They were my people, these killers, and I didn't know what to make of it or how to defend it. They were trying to kill me. I was a woman not a soldier. I wanted to howl, I am only twenty years old, and too young to die. Why are you trying to kill us, unarmed civilians, women, and children, defenceless against your bombs and bullets? So too were the soldiers...It was better not to think about it, to remain in a mental state of limbo between life and death. Someone, an old woman I think, leaned over me. I blinked at her.

"She's not dead," she announced to someone outside of my vision. Was she disappointed?

I sat up and examined my body. My stockings were shreds, flapping at the ends of the threads still attached, my dress was ragged and torn. I pulled a flap of material over my thighs as I searched the area for Madeleine. I couldn't see her, but it was hard to focus.

The bus we vacated before the bombs began falling, was on its side, flames still licking the parts as yet unconsumed. The refugees who had blocked the road as the bus approached, now crept out of ditches, from under vehicles, although some didn't move, flung out carelessly across the road. People searched for their things, dazed as they piled possessions back into overturned carts, prams, cars anything that remained whole. A soldier walked with purpose to every screaming horse and shot each in the head.

People once more began to stream past, faces passive in helplessness and shock. Babies and children shared prams pushed by their mothers and sisters. Fathers and sons righted carts, or piled possessions back on trucks. Mourners held lifeless bodies, keening for their dead. Cars, some with mattresses strapped to their rooves, began to nose their way through the crowds and around bodies. Mothers stepped fearfully, watching the treacherous sky, clutching children's hands, and in the distance, I could hear the boom of field artillery.

A convoy of trucks and other vehicles came into view, more soldiers heading for the front, pushing against the fleeing surge of humanity. People moved to the side of the road, no longer cheering as they passed, instead sullen like me, despairing that the soldiers might stop this madness. At once, confusion rose in me as I thought of the Belgian soldiers and against whom they were defending. Whose side was I on? No, I can't think of these things. I must think of survival.

A girl, my age or younger, walked behind a cart. She held her arm, her face screwed against barely checked pain. I could see from where I was sitting that her arm was broken, a distal radius fracture. I could fix broken limbs. I couldn't stop the slaughter, but I could set a bone, and if I saved lives, I might, in a small way, atone for the destruction wrought by my own people.

I stood up and gestured to her. The man pushing the cart stopped, looking at me suspiciously.

"I can help," I said. "I am a nurse." I didn't hesitate over the lie because I could help and being a nurse would instil confidence and hope.

A little later, while setting the girl's arm with a rudimentary splint, Madeleine found me. Her hair singed, her dress scorched, her cheeks smudged, but she threw her arms around me crying with relief that I was alive.

I looked up at the sounds of new rumblings from another convoy as it picked its way carefully through the flames and debris. They were ambulances from the front. I went back to what I was doing. If they stopped, I would get bandages from them and other medical supplies to help.

They didn't stop though. Most of the refugees had moved on and there was plenty of room for the ambulances to pass. I tied a knot in the makeshift bandage as a car pulled up.

A man called over. "I say! Are you a nurse?"

His English voice sounded strange in that place, the rounded tones succulent and rich. I rolled the vowels sounds around in my head, mentally mimicking his style, ignoring him as I concentrated on the tonal nuance and my patients arm.

Madeleine rushed over to the car, speaking with him as I farewelled the man and his daughter, watching them walk down the road, leaving their homes, their livelihoods, their loved ones—for what? I didn't even know what this war was about or why we were fighting—fighting these people who were kind and caring and didn't ask us to invade their country.

Madeleine's voice penetrated my thoughts, calling me to hurry. She always wanted me to hurry, but why? Or was it me who always wanted her to hurry? I couldn't remember.

She stood impatiently by the car, hands on hips as the officer opened the door. She had managed to get us a lift with the Englishman.

"My bag!"

Madeleine bustled me into the car. "Never mind your bag, it is ash by now. We'll find things we need."

We hadn't driven twenty kilometres when I saw the tented hospital. Outside ambulances pulled up, dispatching stretchers, and walking wounded. The captain, whose name I didn't catch, hustled us towards a large barn. He introduced me to an English nurse, a matron as it turned out. He spoke too quickly for me to fully understand what he was saying but I understood many of the words. He was offering her an extra set of hands to help with the wounded, now pouring into the hospital.

The English nurse smiled, nodding at him as she took in my ragged and filthy clothing and stockings. As he turned his back and hurried away, her smile faded, and brusquely she ordered an orderly to take Madeleine to the camp kitchens to help. Then she indicated I should go with her.

She walked away, and I followed, wearily hypnotised by the pneumatic pumping of her flat heeled shoes. Abruptly, she turned to me, but my reflexes were slow, and we collided, which caused her a degree of dismay.

She demanded, "Do you have your papers?"

I thought she wanted my Belgian identification papers, my passport, which had been lost with my bag. Worriedly I shook my head, I could feel my eyes wide, dry, and gritty but at that moment I was too tired to fear her.

Her mouth formed a thin line. "Where did you do your training then? I can't let unqualified people into the wards, willy-nilly. Next the Captain will have every stray bit of riff raff palmed off on me."

I didn't really know what she was saying but it dawned on me that she was more concerned about my nursing credentials than my nationality. With relief I told her I had trained at the Brugmann Hospital. I tried to say I had only done two years of the three years expected to qualify, but my words became jumbled. My tiredness and limited English skills made it difficult to articulate clearly what I was trying to say. I could tell she was no longer listening as she called a passing nurse to take me off to find something clean and decent to wear.

Once changed into a uniform that was a little too baggy and a little too short for my frame, I followed the nurse self-consciously. The nurse, who introduced herself as Guilly, was sympathetic and kind in an efficient no-nonsense way. It was like one of the nuns from the orphanage had taken charge again. As I followed her back to the barn, she told me we were on duty at a casualty clearing station that she called CCS, but it didn't prepare me for the horror I found upon entering.

Orderlies carried stretcher after stretcher, dumping men on any surface they could find as quickly as they could, then they left to pick up another load of mutilated men, sacrificed for this, this... this what? I could not formulate the words. I who was light-headed with tiredness and hunger, stood frozen within a scene from Dante.

"Sister, over here!" Guilly yanked me from my dream with her command. Two orderlies laid down a stretcher. The orderly closest to Guilly, his nose bent as if once broken and his eyes bloodshot with exhaustion, laid down another man.

He nodded at one of the two stretchered men. "This one's near stiff. That one's a-thigh. More on their way; a femur and two skulls."

I could not follow the meaning of his words.

Guilly noticed my bemusement and laughed. "You'll soon get used to them," she said. "Our job is to sort and categorise the seriousness of the wounds."

"Triage." I said nodding.

Dawn broke before we were relieved. All night I worked alongside Guilly and other doctors and nurses in a mechanised stupor. I remained stoically upright, ignoring my tiredness, pain, hunger, and discomfort as a minor atonement for the sins of my countrymen.

As the night coalesced into morning, my view of the patients changed. The pitifully wounded men became merely the next task in front of me, inanimate objects, all blood, some screaming, some in catatonic silence, others braced against silent tears and yet others groaning and calling for their mothers, some soundless as death closed in. To me they became a category of seriousness to be stabilised and moved on as quickly as possible. And behind it all, battle's deadly orchestra played, distant artillery and machine guns, whistling bombs and aftershocks, rattling trolleys and glass, vehicle gears grinding through mud and planes droning overhead.

Once we were relieved, I followed Guilly to the canteen for food. I was hungry but craved sleep more. I knew I must eat but longed to put my head down—anywhere. As we reached the canteen, we overheard an orderly saying we were moving out, evacuating the hospital. The front was moving closer, the Jerries were on us.

I was afraid to ask who the Jerries were although I could guess. I kept silent, watching Guilly for direction, nodding and doing what I was told, walking in whatever direction I was pointed in, trying to keep upright and look competent and Belgian. I stayed close to Guilly, following her like the filial imprinting of a gosling, afraid to let her out of my sight in the confusing mass of bustling humanity. I had not seen Madeleine since we parted the night before.

When all the patients were loaded on the trucks, we set off in convoy. At one point I had been handed a mug of tea, milky and sweet. I wasn't used to drinking tea with milk and sugar, but it tasted like nectar as I gulped at the lukewarm liquid. I was sure Madeleine would be on one of the trucks and we would catch up later. All we could do now was get out of there. The shelling sounded close and if we stayed, we would be overrun. My mind shied away from the word, Jerry.

I clutched the rail of the truck as we bounced along roads choked with bombed vehicles and refugees. We moved so slowly I felt I could walk faster than the trucks were moving. My eyes closed and I dosed fitfully, jerking upright when sleep began to topple me. Eventually we arrived at a train station where we loaded the patients onto a hospital train.

When the patients were settled, I sat down where I was in a corner of the corridor intersection between carriages. I awoke sometime later. Someone had put a blanket under my head as I slept. I was stiff and sore, I supposed from the fall I had from the blast the day before, but I was alive and being taken away from the fighting.

There was nothing of which I could complain except the ants of uncertainty and guilt that gnawed at my mind. I had an overwhelming urge to confess my origin. Then the train stopped and stayed immobile. I didn't understand why. We were so close to the French border why couldn't it move a few kilometres to get out of Belgium where the fighting was.

I said to Guilly, "We will be safe in France. The French are prepared. They are not like the Belgians who never expected this. In France we will be safe, safe from fighting and bombs—they have defences."

Guilly shook her head. "Jerry will be in France in a heartbeat unless we hold them off at Sedan. The blighters tricked us. While we were busy chasing through Belgium, they were sneaking through the Ardennes. Jolly shifty I think, but what can one expect?" She saw the alarm in my face because her tone softened. "We are just waiting for coal; it was due last night but something's up. Don't worry it'll get here, and we'll be off as soon as anything. You'll see."

I couldn't believe it. In the middle of a war, we had run out of fuel for the train, and Guilly and the others were so calm, treating this like a village picnic, except there wasn't any food. I was so hungry I wanted to cry. I was tired and sore and hungry, and we had run out of fuel, and everyone sat around as if everything would be all right. These people were crazy.

I wandered off down the corridors looking for Madeleine. We should leave the train and walk. After all these people were British army, they had to remain in this waiting nightmare. Madeleine and I did not. We could join the refugees and walk to France.

Getting from one end of the train to the other wasn't easy. Patients wanted attention, water mostly, but some just wanted to chat.

A soldier standing at the end of the next carriage said, "Catch a breather, Sister." He offered me a cigarette, but I shook my head.

He placed the cigarette in his mouth, grinning at me as he did. His arm was in a sling, and he held the box of matches out to me. I took the box from him and carefully lit a match, which immediately went out. He laughed and the blood surged into my face.

My hand shook so much that he held my hand with his good hand while I used my other hand to strike another match. This time the flame held, and he bent towards it, his eyes holding mine until the final moment when he held his cigarette to the flame. His hand holding mine was warm and his grip firm. I pulled my hand away. He smiled and blew smoke-rings at the ceiling.

I hurried on, not trusting myself to speak. He would ask me questions, wanting to know things about me that I didn't want to tell him. One lie leads to another and another until my whole existence seemed a fabrication so fragile it was ready to collapse at the slightest miss step. I pretended not to understand the others I passed. When some of them tried French, I spoke back to them in Dutch. They didn't know how bad my pronunciation was, and it was better than my English. That was until I met the captain again.

"I say, you do look the part now." He gestured to the borrowed uniform and smiled at me kindly, his eyes crinkling, the finely grained skin around them fanning outwards as if he had spent his life looking into a far-off sun. He was polite enough not to mention the ill-fit. "How are you—Matron looking after you? I hear you worked like a Trojan last night. Good for you."

I looked at him blankly not understanding everything he said. Without thinking I mimicked his voice, his accent, the rolled vowels, and clipped ending to his words.

"Have you seen my friend Madeleine?"

He looked taken aback and said, "Your English is jolly good. My apologies, I assumed yesterday from what Madeleine said that your English wasn't up to much. Then of course you hardly said a word. I suppose that's understandable in the circumstances. Actually, you sound like a native from my neck of the woods."

I stood stiffly, unsure how to respond. The seconds stretched out as I racked my limited English vocabulary for something to say. He stepped in again saving me from saying anything.

"I say, I am jolly rude, you asked where your friend was, didn't you? She's in the next carriage. Took over the kitchens, jolly good cook, not that we have much, but she turned bully beef into an edible stew for the patients—those with appetites anyway."

Food! The saliva spurted from under my tongue at its mention. I nodded my thanks to the captain and squeezed past him. In the next carriage, Madeleine stood in the centre of a kitchen with a group of soldiers around her. She was chatting and smoking a cigarette, her hands flailing about animatedly as she blew long streams of smoke into the air.

She spoke in rapid English to her admirers. Her hair was caught up in a scarf tied at the top of her head. She had on a pair of men's trousers, pulled into her tiny waist by a belt into which a baggy shirt was tucked. The top buttons of the shirt were undone to reveal more cleavage than I thought could have been proper.

When she saw me at the carriage entrance, she exclaimed, "There you are! I've been looking for you everywhere. We are just about to fuel up and head off." She hugged me. "The captain says we are going to Calais. Isn't it exciting?"

How could she think any of this was exciting? I said, "What about your parents?"

"Pooff!" She flung her hand backwards in a gesture of dismissal. "They will be fine. They have a restaurant, and everyone has to eat, even Jerry."

11. FRANCE, MAY 1940

It was dusk by the time we arrived at our billet, a French Convent with the Archangel Gabriel standing guard at the entrance. His arms were folded across his breast. His wings were outstretched to greet us as our little convoy drove up. It was a relief to feel safe.

Surely a convent with such a great red cross painted on the ground outside its gate would be safe. I glanced across the surrounding countryside, flat as far as the eye could see. Flat and vacant but for neat green lines of potatoes. Only the occasional tree interspersed the orderly fields.

At least we didn't have to worry about the patients anymore. Orders had changed and we had vacated the ambulance train as it took on a new crew, heading for a hospital in Dieppe in readiness for evacuation of the wounded. Instead of travelling with the train, we were to set up a new casualty clearing station, and the Abbey was commandeered for our use, including barns and outhouses.

Admittance was slow in the first days, with a soldier who came down with measles our sole patient. After a day of leisure, eating potato cakes, sleeping in army cots, and bathing in hot water, we all felt better, and I began to pay more attention to my fellow travellers. Guilly, whom I still followed everywhere, told me her name was Helen Guilford. She was nicknamed Guilly at school and it stuck. It was an odd name and I struggled to get my tongue around it.

On day two, a group of us sat under a tree in the Abbey gardens. I leaned against the trunk feeling its smooth skin against my back. The nurses talked of home, their men, their families, familiar places. I listened carefully, my eyes closed trying to imagine what England was like, trying to remember the new words I heard, storing them away in memory for later examination.

Guilly sat in the grass next to me talking about her home in England. I opened one eye at the changed timber of her voice. A dreamy look of contentment settled across her face as she spoke about her family. I felt such envy I thought my heart would burst. How it must feel to have such a family. She talked about her parents and her brother George.

"He's a pilot in the RAF, protecting the skies for us." She pointed above her head.

I looked up expecting to see him flying about, looking down on us.

George was Guilly's hero, younger than her by two years and it was clear how much she doted on him. He was the best flyer to graduate from his class. He was the best at school, the best at cricket and it seemed the best at everything. A small smile crept to my lips as I listened to her expound his abilities.

One of the other nurses said, "Give it a rest Guilly. Nobody is that much of a paragon—do you have a picture?"

Immediately Guilly went to her bag and withdrew a rather creased picture of a young man in uniform. "It was taken when he joined up," she said proudly.

The women crowded round to have a look. I saw a dark-haired man with freckles across his nose, in an RAF uniform, his eyes laughing, his smile proud. He looked like Guilly.

"He's a corker!" One of the nurses said crudely.

I examined Guilly's face to see if she would be insulted, but instead she laughed and stroked the picture flat. "He is rather, isn't he?"

Sister Bertram looked up, pushing her round framed glasses closer to her snubbed nose. She winked at the others. "You can introduce him to me if you like Guilly. I'll show him a good time."

Now Guilly looked offended while the others laughed. I was mystified. Yet, as my English improved, I began to pick up the nuances of conversation. The slang and double entendre allowed them to say things otherwise forbidden by the manners of their culture. I had used jazz in the same way to overcome my inhibitions and I understood immediately. I recalled when I had first heard them calling me 'sister,' thinking they must somehow know I had once been in the convent, but it was just the name the English gave nurses.

Sister Bertram said, "Come on Sister Avraham tell us a story. What did you do before this bloody war began?"

I hesitated, wondering how much I should tell them and then I thought of Madeleine. She would tell everyone where we worked and wouldn't care for their opinion. I decided honesty was my only option and sat forward, my breathing a little ragged. "I was a singer in a nightclub in Brussels." I watched their faces, to see how they would respond.

Guilly looked curious. "I thought you worked at the Brugmann."

I nodded. "I did, but I left there last year."

Sister Bertram said, "Do you know, I think that Matron said that the MO once worked at the Brugmann, did some training or something? Apparently, he has a soft spot for the place."

I hadn't known. My English became muddled, and my face went red as I imagined him finding out I wasn't qualified.

"Who cares about the jolly old Brugmann, Sister Avraham said she was a singer. That's much more important. We can have a concert. What kind of singing, Sister Avraham?"

"All kinds, mostly jazz."

"Brilliant. Now we need a piano player. I saw a piano in the nuns' parlour."

"You'd better get their permission before you go scavenging it." Another nurse laughed.

The measles patient who was recuperating said he could play the piano. The Abbess was a little more cautious but was eventually persuaded to let us use the piano and allowed it to be moved to the barn for the occasion. The word went out and the whole village turned out for the performance.

I felt relaxed and happy as we prepared. The measles patient whose name turned out to be James Holland was a great improviser, and as we practice that afternoon, I laughed for the first time since fleeing Brussels.

But that night I thought we would be thrown out of the unit. I wanted to kill Madeleine for her brazenness. James was playing and I sang while the medical staff, nuns and villagers stood around watching. I signalled for them to dance as James launched into the introduction bars of *Night and Day*.

The captain, our chief medical officer or MO as the sisters called him, gallantly bowed to Matron requesting the dance. She declined, shaking her head, mouth pursed looking a little scandalised. Madeleine walked up to the captain and wound her hand into his as she led him to the cleared area of the barn. The empty cots, waiting for patients, looked on like silent sentinels as they danced.

Shameless hussy! I could see Matron's mind working. I hadn't told anyone Madeleine was a dancer. It was her story to tell. The MO seemed a little taken aback by her movements as she lithely moulded herself in his arms. Madeleine didn't care about social niceties. With her head thrown back she laughed up into the MO's bewitched face. Her hair hung loose down her back in a curtain of dark silk, her mouth red and challenging and her eyes flashing in the dim lantern-lit barn. She demanded everyone have fun and one by one she hauled farmer, officer and orderly alike into the cleared area of the barn to dance with her. The party was in full swing, and life tonight felt almost normal.

Since we had arrived Madeleine had made herself busy, busier than I. She made friends with the farmers and most of the nuns, charming them as only Madeleine at her most outrageous could do. She somehow made everyone laugh even over the most mundane things. She lifted our spirits. Because of her we had flour to make bread, we had cheese and eggs and potatoes, milk, and cabbage. We lived like aristocracy. I could almost forget where we were, what we left behind, believing we were safe now in France.

It didn't last. Next morning, we heard the drone of planes overhead. The now familiar whine woke me at dawn. I raced to the door where I watched them fly over cows grazing peacefully in fields. Then bombs began dropping one after another as I watched on in horror.

Soon smudges of black smoke curled up from a village burning in the distance. A little while later a convoy of trucks rolled past. Then the news came that the German army had broken through and had the Allies on the run.

It was only a week since I had fled Brussels and once again the fiercest fighting was less than 30 kilometres from us. I could hear the guns as ambulances arrived with their cargo of carnage. The shame of my deception washed over me as I saw the broken maimed bodies. Boys as young as I and younger, screamed in agony or sobbed for their mothers, but some just wanted a smoke, or water, always something they couldn't have. Some didn't move.

As I worked, I worried incessantly over what I should do. These people, these English, Belgian, and French people were my friends, kind, considerate, funny, and odd and they accepted me. I worked side by side with the other Sisters, harder than anyone in an attempt to undo the terrible punishment the soldiers went through at the hands of the German army.

I told myself that these men were soldiers, also fighting, both sides as bad as each other. If it weren't French men or English men or Belgian men it would be German men being cared for, German wounded. But these were just boys. I was driven on by guilt and shame, trying in my mind to justify and defend, but always coming back to the same point. Germany had started this. Why? I was German, but I didn't want war.

Neither did I want to be a nurse. I wanted to sing and have fun and be loved. I wanted to keep running away to where I would be safe, and at that moment, it seemed like the only safe place was England. My mind flashed back to Marcel. I should have gone when he told me. I hoped he had gone and had not remained in France to fight what seemed now to be a lost battle.

Yet, if I told the British who I was they would immediately see me as the enemy. I imagined the look on their faces, the look of betrayal. I couldn't do it. I couldn't say anything, but guilt consumed me. Why did we believe in that man when he had brought us to this? I had believed in him also, trusted him as he returned Germany to prosperity, believed his speech-making about the wrongness of the Armistice agreement, how it was designed to destroy the German people. Maybe it was, but could I justify this response, and at what cost?

Shamed and guilt ridden, I worked around the clock until I dropped with exhaustion, terrified I would be left behind when the British moved on. Should I ask the nuns if I could stay with them. I would be safe perhaps although I didn't have papers. I imagined when the Germans came, they would ask for papers, they always did, and I didn't have any. My fake passport had gone up in flames with the bus. What would happen to me? I couldn't fall all over them claiming them as my countrymen without papers.

I couldn't ask the nuns for papers without letting on who I really was. I thought of the kind nuns at Leuven, who had helped Marcel and me when we reached Belgium after that terrifying train journey. Their convent was behind the KW line where the Belgian soldiers along with the British tried to hold back the German Army. Now it was overrun.

I held on to hope, treasonous I suppose some might call it, that the Allies would be able to repel the German Army. It was a forlorn hope. The French had relied so heavily on the unassailable Maginot Line, they were unprepared for the ferocity and speed by which the Germans broke through at the Ardennes. My Führer was spreading his tentacles swift and wide with frightening efficiency.

The next morning a bomb fell on the painted Red Cross outside the gate, an irony that escaped most of us at the time because of the righteous indignation expressed by Guilly. The conflagration consumed the once welcoming Archangel Gabriel and burned the fruit trees that lined the driveway. I saw it as a message. We had cowered in the Abby basement in fear of more bombs. This may have been a stray dropped randomly, but that did not allay my fears. It meant nowhere was safe.

When I voiced my fear, Guilly said, "Well, this isn't afternoon tea in the drawing-room."

We remained lucky. Planes flew over us every morning without further incident. The nuns said that the bomb was intended for the railway lines nearby, but clearly, despite their calm, they were worried too. I overheard the Abbess asking the Captain if he thought the British and French armies could hold back the Germans.

Cheerfully he patted her arm and told her not to worry. He was always so positive, but doubt seeped into my mind. Eventually I plucked up the courage and asked Guilly what would happen to me with no papers. She listened carefully as I explained how they had burned in the bombed bus. She took me to see Matron who in turn sent me to the MO.

Captain Willoughby, as I found out he was named, looked stern as his brow furrowed in concentrated concern. "Yes, I remember the bus," he said, as I told him how I had lost everything I possessed. "You and Madeleine have served us well, we can't just abandon you, but we mustn't give up hope yet. Our boys will push old Jerry back from whence he came, just see if they don't. We'll have you back home in no time. Where did you say you trained, the Brugmann? They'll be delighted to have you back, I am sure. I did a short stint there myself just after the official opening in '23. I was still a wet trainee, but my father served in Belgium during the last bash and had made some lasting friendships. He recommended I spend time in the country. I remember they had just started the nursing school; you would have been well trained. Who would have thought we'd be back at it again, eh?"

He shook his head as if the whole issue were incomprehensible, and I struggled to follow as he seemed to jump from one thought to the next. I remained silent, hoping he would tell me something I could hold onto, but it appeared he had said all he was going to say on the subject.

He eyed me kindly. "Is there anything else, Sister?"

For a moment I was nonplussed, then I wanted to shout at him. He hadn't answered my question. What was I to do? I wanted to know what to expect so I could plan for it. I needed to know definitively—were they going to abandon us when things got too bad. Would they leave France and leave Madeleine and me behind in this God-forsaken place? Instead, I bowed my head and walked from his office. Deep in my soul I knew that I was on my own. I had always been on my own. I went in search of Madeleine, she needed to know. We should plan what to do, where to go, how to get away from this madness.

Madeleine laughed when I told her. "He's not leaving me to my own devices." She said emphatically. "He can't get enough of me."

I stared in amazement. "You are sleeping with him?"

"Of course, I'm sleeping with him. What did you think, although I must admit, there's not a lot of sleeping taking place? He's a randy devil, don't be fooled by his delicate demeanour."

The next morning, we received orders to evacuate as things were becoming too dangerous and the battle front was closing in. Our patients were taken to the ambulance train headed for the hospital in Dieppe. Later we heard Dieppe had been heavily bombed and Calais was on fire. I wondered what happened to our last hospital train. Did it get out safely?

We waited for orders at Arras. Food was running out and casualties were mounting. Many of the wounded arrived screaming, raw, bloody flesh raked ragged by shrapnel. I administered morphine, dug bullets from mangled flesh, attended to broken and missing limbs, cut away gangrenous flesh, and there was always blood, so much blood. I thought the stench would remain in my nostrils forever.

We loaded soldiers onto the train, their broken and injured bodies taking up every niche. Those who were able, sat back-to-back crammed into every conceivable space. When we could we tended civilians, setting broken bones, staunching, and bandaging wounds, but as the train pulled out from the station we climbed into the back of ambulances and left them behind.

I watched those poor refugees recede into the distance. The children, grubby with smeared ash from the many burning buildings, gaping after us. Mothers pleading with us to take the children. Fathers angry at their own helplessness. I might be one of them soon, left behind to face an army who was even now getting nearer. I tried not to dwell on much, except to focus on the task in front of me.

I was squashed into the back of an ambulance with five other sisters. Madeleine was still on the train with Matron and the MO, her lover, and I with Guilly. I was more determined than ever that I would not re-join the milling, terrified, and vulnerable refugees.

Our ambulance convoy was diverted to Bailleul to help evacuate the wounded. On the way there we drove through

Armentieres. As dark descended we crested a small rise in the flat plains, and I looked out to see the land behind us in flames. We drove into Bailleul in silence, entering streets where windows gaped, their jagged edges of broken glass like shark jaws. Ragged curtains flapped in the breeze. Crumbling masonry exposed family rooms like an open doll's house and everywhere buildings burned.

We dodged from place to place, taking cover from the bombs while we tended the wounded wherever they were sheltering, in cinemas or churches. Whenever we found a moment's respite, we scavenged food, but it was scarce. I thought we had removed the last soldiers from the hospital to the ambulances until I discovered a ward with half a dozen men.

A sister from a different unit said they were too ill and couldn't be moved. We argued; she from compassion for sustaining their lives even if they became prisoners; I from fear and a sense of urgency to be gone from that place. Or perhaps I was afraid that I would succumb to martyrdom and volunteer to stay with them, both options rushed through my thoughts. I ran back to the ambulance, a coward to the end.

The last run for the coast was slow. The rain made fields boggy, and water sat in pools in roadside ditches. Everywhere roads were choked with refugees fleeing the fighting and the bombs. A truck load of French soldiers, heading towards the battle front, passed and we gave way by pulling off to the side of the road, our wheels spinning in mud.

Broken wagon wheels, furniture, wheelbarrows, and farm machinery was piled high, blocking streets into villages. Rolls of barbed wire barricaded roads. Most bridges were blown-up, to hold up the advancing tanks, and our little convoy of ambulances moved with a lurching tortoise slowness.

As we approached the coast, I could see the columns of black oily smoke rising into the slate sky. Bombed oil repositories, Guilly guessed. Refugees walked or drove in both directions, some fleeing the advancing enemy, some fleeing the bombs dropping on their villages and homes.

I watched as we passed one group of refugees as they met another group, gesturing, shouting, and I imagined each telling the other that it was too dangerous to go in the direction they headed. At least I knew where we were heading although I was by now resigned to the possibility that we would not get there.

I stopped worrying about becoming a refugee myself and instead worried that we would not remain alive long enough to get our casualties to the coast. I wanted them to live. I didn't want to have their lives on my conscience also. They had faces, names. I couldn't deal with it.

I recited bits of prayers in my head. The holy words popped and looped in synchrony with the lurching rhythm of the ambulance motor, as our convoy snaked past craters and smoking ruins. The other five nursing sisters appeared so calm; one gazing silently at her hands folded neatly in her lap, another snatching a moment of sleep, some looking calmly out the window as the ambulance bumped its way to our destination. There was no conversation, but neither was there any sense of panic in their faces.

I fought to keep my own dread from rising. It was a volcano bubbling under the surface, pulsating and ready to explode. There was a sense of absolute terror, more so than that which I felt during the bombing and machine gun attack outside Brussels. I think if anyone of the other sisters had shown the slightest bit of fear on their faces, I would have lost control. Instead, I forced my trepidation down into the tightly packed coil, smouldering in my gut.

When we arrived at Dunkerque, orders came to get the wounded to the docks for loading onto ships. On the way, wailing sirens told us of the arrival of more bombers. The ambulances with the seriously wounded crouched under arches or under building awnings, all hugging walls. They stopped where they could and where possible, orderlies and sisters helped the walking wounded to shelter. Our ambulance driver pulled up and barked at us to move, and we scrambled to find shelter.

The RAF once more came to the rescue and air battles split the air in Armageddon ferocity. I scrambled for a railway carriage, helping a patient with a broken femur get down beneath it, skinning my knee and wondering if railway carriages would be safe or if they would be a target. It was too late to find anywhere else. Above us, fighters machinegunned each other in dog fights, swooping and turning, the ejected bullet casings bouncing like hot metal raindrops on the ground around us.

I lay next to my patient as the world exploded, debris flying, choking dust, my face buried in my hands. I should pray but I couldn't think of any words that would act a protective talisman. My body was board-stiff, pressed into the dirt, hoping the earth would absorb me. The stench of burning oil in my nostrils.

I heard the wail of the all-clear. I was still alive as was my broken femur patient who thanked me very politely for saving him. His face was a mask of agony as I helped him out. He lurched forward on his cast, and I struggled to hold him upright.

He looked stricken at his action, the pain clearly excruciating, but he apologised for his weight on me. He was in such pain, I felt I should be the one asking for forgiveness for not being able to help him more. We hobbled back to the ambulance, which was miraculously no less intact than when we took shelter.

We eventually found our camp hospital in a basement. More casualties came in every minute and confusion had us running in circles. The basement wasn't a real hospital and things weren't methodical enough to follow commands. Yet orders were barked,

"Get this man to theatre... get this man blankets."

But we didn't know where the operating theatres were or the supplies. We milled about pretending an efficiency we simply didn't have, while we tended our patients, scrounged for food, all the while praying the next raid would not get us.

The last raid had targeted the harbor and struck our ship, which now lay burning and broken, blocking access to the docks, the dead floating face down in oily waters. Two days we waited for new orders; nerves stretched as tight as my vocal cords attempting to hit the 3rd F above middle C. The bombing was relentless, there was no food and I worked in fury trying to be everywhere at once, but always keeping Guilly in my sights. If I lost her, what would become of me?

At last, we were told we were to go to the beaches at Bray Dunes. Ships would be arriving that night to take the wounded away and we should be ready with our patients. I worked in a fever of anxiety all day waiting for the call. When it came, I sat next to Guilly in the back of the ambulance, not speaking, not asking if I could go with them, just determined that I would be on that ship wherever it went, so long as it was out of this hell.

The beaches held hundreds, no thousands, of men in snaking lines of desperation. Tender after tender picked them up taking them to ships. More men staggered out of the forest and onto the dunes, desperate, many wounded.

Darkness fell and still the lines of men moved slowly into the sea. The smoke from the burning oil tanks blackened the sky and then it began to rain. Some of the nurses cheered with the men. Cloud and rain would hamper the bombing and strafing, they said. Bad weather might also hamper the boats, but I kept my dismal thoughts to myself. Praying that when the German planes came back, they wouldn't realise we were to the east, hiding in the dunes.

We worked in silence, loading patient after patient into boats to take to the ship. I prayed the fog would remain. How else could we defend against that kind of slaughter falling from the air? The dark waters swirled around our legs, the clammy bump of dead bodies and other unrecognised body parts nudged us, begging us not to be left forgotten on those benighted shores.

I slipped and staggered, my arms flailing as I tried to right myself. A wave knocked me off balance further and I slipped under the oily cold water. Panic filled me as I thrashed about trying to find my feet. I couldn't swim. I felt something clutching at my hair and I panicked more.

The yank of pain in my scalp as I was hauled upright, was from Guilly, who clutched my bedraggled body to her. "I thought we'd lost you," she cried, letting me go as suddenly as she hugged me. "Come on, we have more to load."

It was almost dawn by the time we were hauled onto the ship. The fog persisted, and the bombers didn't spot us, and the machine guns stayed silent. The waters around us showed evidence of previous attempts to load ships or perhaps it was just the grizzly flotsam of bombed ships in harbor, I couldn't tell.

People were lined on deck. "Packed in like sardines," I heard a sailor say and wondered at the strange reference but tucked it away for later examination.

Yet intuitively I understood. I too felt like a fish, shivering with the cold in my wet uniform, until someone found a blanket and wrapped me in it. My teeth chattered uncontrollably. I think it was from shock more than cold, but I couldn't be sure.

Guilly watched me with concern, but was completely calm as she made me sit, while she and the other nurses made our patients as comfortable as possible. I didn't want to let her out of my sight, so I followed her, determined to do my share of the work.

It was that which she explained to her parents when they extended their invitation for me to stay with them. She told them how brave and selfless I was. How despite my own losses my concern was only for saving the lives of so many of their boys. If only she had known my real motivation…

Guilt and betrayal at my deception again threatened to swamp me, and I was driven to confess, but I bit back my words. I never told her that it was fear that drove me on; fear that I would lose her, and that I would be left behind on that God forsaken beach or worse sent back to Belgium. I would never let them know about my German heritage, ever— or so I thought.

12. SURREY 1941

Spring had arrived, and I sat relishing the pale shafts of sunlight piercing the tall windows of the Guildford's breakfast room, made cheerful with vases of daffodils.

"My goodness, the bishop has completely lost his mind!"

"What is it Mother?"

"Here, read this darling."

Guilly took the proffered newspaper from her mother, surreptitiously rolling her eyes at me before she read the article. Her elbow rested on the table as she scanned the lines. She held a piece of toast between thumb and forefinger, suspended above the paper as she frowned in contemplation. I expected the thickly slathered jam to slide off the toast and plop onto the newspaper. But she righted it at the last minute.

"He does rather blow off, but I'm sure a lot of people will agree with the sentiments although only a brave man would point out anything so obvious. I doubt if this will win him any brownie points with his congregation. What do you think Aurélie?"

She pushed the folded newspaper across the table towards me, nudging it along, using a crooked little finger of the hand that held the toast. I watched in alarm as the jam slid to the other side of her toast. Finally, she raised the toast to her mouth and took a bite with a brittle crunch that showed cook had managed to get the toast just right, according to Lady Guilford's exacting standards.

I read the words, and distracted by my own worries, struggled to take in the context. I focused and reread the article. The bishop made a good point. Night bombing was cruel, but he missed the bigger point, war was brutal. What could I say to an English Bishop? Would he consider the bombs the British dropped on the people of the Ruhr, in retribution last year, barbaric?

The whole war was senselessness, but I would never say anything to upset either Guilly or Lady Guilford who had both been so kind to me--an enemy of their people, even though they were both unaware of my heritage.

I recognised my people were responsible. We the German people believed the lies. We saw him as our saviour as we battled to survive the crippling debts that were punishment for the last war. We had feted and worshiped a madman. We handed him power beyond wisdom, and we reaped now that which was sown. It wasn't fair, we were duped and now this mayhem; a war few wanted against these people, our cousins. This maniac had made me their foe. I never asked for it and I didn't want it now. Instead, thrust upon me now was a terrible moral dilemma.

It would have been better for me if I had remained in Belgium. At least then I would not have the choice I had now. Did I want to be an enemy of this country, or traitor to my own? That was my quandary as a paperless refugee in England, harboured by these wonderful women who took me in and allowed me to share their beautiful home. All I wanted was to please them. I owed them both so much. I am not sure what I would have done if Guilly hadn't suggested I go home with her after arriving in Dover. Now, the last thing I wanted was to say something to contradict or upset either of them. I pushed the newspaper back towards Lady Guilford.

"I think all bombing is bad really, not just night bombing; war is wicked but what can one do but defend oneself?"

Guilly smiled at me, amused by my perfected accent. She said, "Less than a year in Blighty and you speak like an old Roedeanian darling, Honneur aulx dignes and all that."

I shrugged, but as I looked into her eyes, I once more saw the bombs falling, and the terror of Dunkerque. My dreams haunt me nightly. I relive the moment when I stumbled and fell beneath the oily waters, disoriented, and terrified.

Guilly's eyes softened in sympathy, knowing that I remembered, and she intervened. "Mother, Aurélie is right. Bombing is barbaric but not a subject for the breakfast table."

Lady Guilford sniffed and picked up the paper, shaking it out as if to shake out the small rebuke from her daughter. Guilly gazed placidly out the French windows to the garden beyond.

How was I going to break the news to these wonderful women? I knew they would be curious, and I hated having to lie to them. Hated to leave them and the comforts they shared so generously with me, a stranger only eight months before. They had become family, the only one I knew. Now instead I was to go back, back into the hell hole that I had taken such desperate risks to escape, but I had no choice.

Sir Giles, Guilly's father, was responsible for my dilemma and in an indirect way, for my current predicament. Sir Giles told me they would understand, it would be all right, and I was doing it for the country. I hadn't said anything about whose country, but then he already knew.

It was because of him that I had met David Asquith again. It was because of Giles that I hadn't remained incognito, a Belgian girl, interpreter, and one-time nurse. It was because of David I became who I am now, a traitor to my country, an agent for the British. It was David's fault, but Giles led me to him. So indirectly it was Giles fault and I wanted to blame him for my forced lies to his wife and daughter.

He promised Lady Guilford and Guilly would understand that I would be engaged in vital war work. He said they would know not to ask any more questions. He said they would all be proud of me. It was Sir Giles who came up with my alibi, saying I should tell people that I had been transferred to Liverpool's Mill Road Hospital, to nurse the injured. He said, I should say that the hospital needed my linguistic skills for those foreign sailors, Allied wounded, and Axis prisoners, who were hospitalised there.

That was the story I was to tell them after breakfast before I packed my meagre possessions. I would promise to visit on my next leave, and I would write, of course. It wouldn't be for long and it was such a good opportunity to do my bit for the war effort, etcetera, etcetera.

I felt more treacherous telling these women that lie than I did becoming a traitor to my own country. I knew I would never write. I knew I would never see either of them again. I was going but I wouldn't be back I was sure of it, and the pain I felt at leaving caused my throat to constrict.

I was officially a traitor, but it didn't seem real to me. It wasn't of my doing. It was happening to someone else. I was just afraid, deeply, darkly afraid but without choice. The entire course of my life was dictated to me by others. I was a puppet pushed and pulled hither and thither by barely visible strings, held by barely visible puppet masters. It was the war, or so they said. In war one obeys but obeys whom? I am a traitor, and I will be taken out blindfolded and shot in Germany, or if I double-cross the British, I will be hung in England. I could choose.

It was all explained to me throughout these past months while I was bullied, harassed, trained, and scolded by sergeants expecting perfection. It happened while Guilly and her mother lived with the illusion that I was a translator for the Belgium Government in exile, travelling the country to translate for officials who could not understand one another.

It was all rubbish. Instead, I was taken from stately home to stately home, from barrack to barrack to barrack, from Devon to Bedford to Wales to Scotland, hidden in remote moors or tranquil countryside. Living in stables or hastily built Nissan huts. Sometimes, my bed was made of straw, and mice ran over my body. One morning I awoke and stared straight into the Stygian depth of a rat's eyes. It was sitting on its haunches examining me.

Sometimes I awoke in a four poster, the dust from hanging drapes, centuries without washing, causing my eyes to water and my nose to run. Mostly I slept in an army camp cot in a Nissan hut. I say slept, but many nights I tossed and turned in a light doze as I obsessed over ways to overpower and kill my instructors.

While I learned brute force, I was not strong enough or big enough to easily throw a large male assailant over my back. Instead, I found jabbing an elbow into a face and then bringing my knee up hard into the groin, more effective. I also learned to throw my assailant off balance by thrusting the heel of my palm up under a jaw or nose.

I learned how to clean, load, and fire rifles and pistols. My fingers became more dextrous, and stronger, as I rapidly forced 303 shells into a spring loaded magazine, overcoming the resistance until I could do it blindfolded.

I became a master at disguise, not just of myself but of small amounts of explosive neatly laid along the side of a train track. I left booby traps in corridors and doorways, cunningly camouflaged to be invisible to the unsuspecting enemy's casual glance.

I knew how to decode messages, how to read maps, how to intercept communications. I learned how to build and use a crystal wireless. I learned how to drop from an aeroplane with just a khaki balloon of silk between me and oblivion, a skill that would soon be put into practice. I learned how to blow-up or derail trains. I learned how to kill silently only using my hands or a handy piece of wire.

Mostly, I learned about endurance, but the thing that played on my mind was not killing but being killed. For they explained in graphic detail what we could expect if anyone of us was caught, especially me, a traitor to my own country. I learned how I would surely die, bullets riffling through my flesh, my expected life span weeks, months if I were lucky, not the years I had always expected. I was afraid, so afraid. I didn't want to die. I didn't want to go back across the channel to that horror. I wanted to stay with Guilly and her brother George.

I had finally met the paragon George. He was so cheerful he dragged me out of my shyness. His nose would wrinkle as he smiled. His freckles made an otherwise perfectly symmetrical square face look friendly. He was so much like Guilly I wanted to shelter in his arms.

When he pulled me close and gave me a long lingering kiss behind the Rhododendron bushes in the Guilford's garden, I felt I could easily fall in love with such a man. We were never given a chance. He wasn't home more than a few days before being called back to his unit. It was then I found out he was engaged. I cried, but not for long. My training changed all that.

Instead, my instructors told me that I would know my life, and I would know my death if I were caught. And I know for certain that I will be shot in France. The Nazis will take me out and stand me in front of a wall. I will be blind folded. Soldiers will line up in front of me. An order will be given, and my body will feel the hot bullets punch into my buttery flesh. They will rip and tear as they spiral through my innards, and as they exit they will explode, creating cavernous holes in my body.

I will fall to my knees, unable to remain upright as my life force ebbs away, and I will wonder what it was all about and why it had to be me. Then things will darken, and I will remember no more, my eyes glazed and wide but unseeing as they stare into a wintery sun.

They told me this detail, as they told me the other details of what I should do. They carefully shaped my thinking, moulding me as their instrument through fear and horror and longing. They turned my people into monsters. Explaining this was not a war with the German people, this was a war to stop the anti-Christ himself. One who made prisoners and slaves of the German people.

In grave voices they told me about the atrocities committed by the Nazis. In explicit detail they explained it all because they were not sure I could be relied on not to turn double agent. They showed me photos of a woman near Arras, where I had been not days before the German army broke through. The German soldiers, high on the drug Pervitin, crucified the woman to her barn door; her breasts hacked off, multiple daggers through her belly, blood shadowing the insides of her thighs.

Vomit surged in my throat when they held that photo in front of my eyes, but they held my chin forcing me to look at it, to absorb it into my soul, to remember each tiny detail. I screwed my eyes shut but it was too late. That one small glance snapped the image as an indelible memory. They told me it was the men of the SS-Panzer-Division Totenkopf who were responsible, the Death's Head Brigade!

An image of Lothar flashed into my mind as I remembered the death's head insignia on his cap. I didn't believe them, but they saw I remembered and prodded at my guilt. I protested. The German people I knew would not do this. This was the work of devils.

They showed me photos of the broken bodies of children lying uncared for, untidily strewn across the dirt, dolls thrown out with the blast of bombs, little arms, and legs askew, bodies punctured by machine gun bullets, charred, and blackened.

"Who took these photos," I asked?

There was no answer. Then they showed me the photos of the Abbey where we stayed. Where I had sung for the nurses, the nuns, and the farmers, where Madeleine had danced with the captain. The Abbey that had fed and sheltered us. The Abbey that even Arch-Angel Gabriel could not save. The photos showed its fire ravaged buildings, its burned and mangled gardens in which pits were dug, pits lined with the bodies of the kind, dead nuns, gunned down where they lay. These are the images that haunt me now.

These were not the deeds of soldiers fighting an honourable and just war. These were barbarians who must be stopped and brought to justice—these were people of evil, the death squadrons of the devil himself, spewing forth the pestilence of the apocalypse.

I began to hate my own people. I became confused, identifying with my enemy, my jailers, my teachers, reviling and rejecting my own. Confusion, dissonance, and nightmares, brought me willing and pliable to instructions, working hard for praise, a stroke of the arm, human kindness, and warmth. I craved and I excelled, and then they told me about Madeleine.

Madeleine had stayed behind in France rejecting her opportunity to escape, so that she could find me because I had no papers, and I would need her to vouch for me. Madeleine, strong and sensible funny Madeleine, who they said was raped and brutalised in the same way as the woman crucified to the barn door. They didn't have photos, but they had intelligence.

Intelligence—what a strange word for something so ugly, so evil. I cried then. I cried for myself, my loss, my horror. I cried for my friend, thinking I brought bad luck to everyone I befriended, and I vowed vengeance but that was then.

Now, I sat in this bright morning-room with the cut daffodils flaunting their sunny cheer in the centre of the table. I sat eating toast that crunched even when slathered with revolting carrot jam, which Lady Guilford said we had to eat because it was patriotic. I sat looking at the crumbs on the white damask tablecloth, wondering when to begin my own line of lies to these wonderful women. I had to tell them soon.

I tried to persuade Sir Giles to tell them, but he shook his head, his jowls wobbling slightly as he said, "Better coming from you my girl, more believable, besides, they won't thank you if you don't give them a chance to fuss over you before you go."

It was Sir Giles Guilford, who in trying to help me when I first arrived with no papers, caused my grief. It was because of his connections and his friends that my origins were uncovered.

It began when he took me to London to see a friend of his who was something in some Ministry. His friend promised to contact the Belgian government in exile and see what could be done about a passport and a visa. I needed papers or I couldn't work. For months I lived in fear that the Belgian Government would deny I was one of theirs. How much could they know? What records would they have access to in exile?

I lived on the charity and kindness of the Guilford's, but despite their generosity I felt I needed to make my own way and so I needed papers to get a job. Then the bombing began in earnest. It was as though the Führer had decided to bomb Britain into annihilation. We watched the Luftwaffe with their Dorniers, Heinkels, and Junkers going over the house day and night, occasionally releasing their bombs over the countryside but mostly heading for London, Sheffield, or Birmingham. We watched as barrage balloons went up, and then exploded into helium flames in reaction to the Messerschmitt's guns.

For weeks I would board the train daily with Sir Giles to go to London. If the train lines were bombed, we would drive if he had petrol, or I would climb aboard buses or beg lifts. I would navigate damaged city streets, making my way from sandbagged office to sandbagged office. The pavements were broken with piles of rubble and glass, craters, and gap-toothed hollows where buildings had collapsed under bombs.

I would find my way to desk after desk until people began to smile in acknowledgement of my persistence, cheerfully saying, "No news today I am afraid, Aurélie."

Until one day in October 1940 things changed. Instead of bidding me farewell at the station, Sir Giles said he knew another fellow who may be able to help me. Someone from his old college, he said. We crossed from the Trafalgar Street Station walking past great sentinel lions, along unfamiliar streets. We called in at Fortnum and Mason for Sir Giles to send a hamper to his son at Biggin Hill, who celebrated his 21st birthday. I remembered then I had turned 21 somewhere in France, but I had not marked the occasion.

Then we went on to an undamaged building in Baker Street. The entrance was down a flight of sandbagged stairs. Sir Giles and I were shown into the ante room of an office recently relocated to the building's basement. Stark white walls had been painted hurriedly, still showing the cellar-brickwork beneath. We sat on upright wooden chairs that reminded me of the school room.

I nervously picked the skin at the edge of my nails, watching dust motes hanging listlessly in the week rays of sunshine that found their way through gaps in the boarded windows, high on the walls.

Eventually a woman took us through to another make-shift office where she asked us to wait, offering tea, "No sugar or milk, I'm afraid."

She said it as if in apology, but the tone of her voice was automatic as if it was quite the usual thing to have no sugar or milk for the tea. She didn't wait to see us both shake our heads. She was clearly used to people saying no to tea without sugar or milk in this unlikely hollow.

It was here I met the man who was to be my new puppet master. My shock at meeting him rendered me mute. The crooked toothed smile, the fair hair, no longer flopping in his eyes, but now cut short and close to his head. I looked in disbelief at the man who entered the room, smiling, suited in English flannel and tweed, his hand outstretched to Sir Giles who was smiling into the face of Herr Asquith, Father O'Bryan's friend.

I learned later that Lieutenant-Colonel David Asquith studied for his undergraduate degree at Cambridge University where Sir Giles once tutored. At that moment of our meeting, he was still Father O'Bryan's friend in Munich, and I could not understand why he was here or why we were meeting him this day.

"Hello again Miss Magdalena or should I call you Miss Aurélie?" He mocked me cheerfully. "I hope I find you well after what seems to have become a rather amazing journey for the little orphaned girl from Berlin. I must say I didn't at first realise who it was that Giles asked me to help but then the penny dropped. It was a while ago now wasn't it? I must say you've grown up since we last met." He looked me in the eye as he said it. "I have been hearing a lot about you from various sources, not least my good friend Sir Giles." He nodded in Giles direction. "It seems you are a very resourceful woman." He paused, and his gaze took on a thoughtful expression. "But what kind of woman? That's what I need to know." Then his tone became brisk. "Please have a seat, both of you. I have already explained to Sir Giles, the great service you did for our country a few years ago. Would you like some tea, I am sure Judy can muster something although no sugar or milk I'm afraid, we are still trying to organise?"

I looked at Sir Giles who studied his fingernails and I felt an overwhelming sense of betrayal that I didn't understand. Betrayed by Sir Giles who brought me here and betrayal by a man I met only briefly but who turned me into a criminal smuggler, using my desire to help Marcel to his advantage.

He used my naivety and his association with my parents to make me trust him and he sent me from my own homeland. He used Father O'Bryan to bribe me with study in Belgium, something only he could arrange. He knew about me. He knew who I was and what I had done. Who knew what else he learned from his friend Father O'Bryan to whom I made my confession? He certainly knew I was a liar, and a German. I began shaking. Sir Giles knew he harboured a German woman in his house, an imposter and he had said nothing, despite knowing that Aurélie the Belgian refugee, the nurse, and friend of his daughter, was a fraud.

It was I who was the betrayer, the liar, the cheat. I hung my head looking at my feet as an intense feeling of fear and regret swept over me. I would be locked up in a prison camp for Germans. I thought of Guilly and her mother. How angry they would be with me when they discovered that I lied, abusing their hospitality. I glanced at Sir Giles, but his kind face hadn't altered. He knew all along, yet he still treated me with courtesy. I began to feel hope.

That was when it all began, only months ago, and now I was here, fully trained, a saboteur and treacherous SOE agent sitting at a breakfast table, building the courage to tell these two good women that I was leaving them shortly.

I would lie to them again. I would tell them I was off on another noble mission. I would explain with conviction born of training rather than truth, how my Belgian nursing qualifications had been accepted. At last, I had found a job nursing. I would be nursing wounded British sailors. It meant leaving them to go and live in Liverpool I lied, but I would see them again in a few months. In reality, I wanted to cry and beg them to let me stay here, safe with them. Instead, I let them fuss.

After breakfast I changed into my new Territorial Force Nursing Service uniform. Checking myself in the mirror, I adjusted the cap, different from the one I had worn as a novice, but affixed with yet another white veil. It struck me then that white was for purity. How ironic. I draped the grey-blue cape about my shoulders. Its scarlet facings more suited the way I felt about myself. Within hours I would have to change again, and then board the plane hiding in a hanger in Bedford, and I would be on my way to France. The one and only thing that I looked forward to, was singing again.

I saw David Asquith a lot in the beginning and lost my fear of him. He grilled me about my time in Brussels, looking interested when I told him about leaving the convent and nursing, to pursue a career in singing. I saw his interest and felt vindicated at my choice. Brashly I boasted that I had been offered a part in a Parisian opera by none other than Monsieur Copeau. I wanted David to know I had some talent; that I wasn't just the silly little girl he met in Munich who was destitute and alone. I wanted to brag that I had made something of myself despite him. I never needed his interventions.

I got a different reaction entirely. He leaned forward eagerly and said, "Copeau! Not Louis Copeau?"

I was puzzled and immediately nervous at my exaggeration. Why, when I told lies, was I always found out? One would think I would have learned by now, but instead my need to see respect in his face, not merely some secret amusement at my expense, propelled me into further exaggeration, only to be caught out.

"You know him?" I gasped in disbelief. How was it that these people all knew each other?

"If it is the Louis Copeau I know, we were at Cambridge together. How very convenient—your knowing Louis. Well, my dear, we shall be taking up his offer and you had better ensure you're in fine voice for the occasion."

That was when I began taking classes with a teacher from The Royal Opera. They took place after my day in the classroom or in field training or jumping from barn rooves into muddy fields to practice my landings. There was nothing David couldn't arrange.

"It's the war my dear," he said. "Everything must be done to win this. We can't afford to lose, you see. It would be the end of our Empire and we can't have that."

As it turned out, when I left the Guilford's I was to wait two days in Bedfordshire and then fly to somewhere near Falmouth where we waited another day for the weather to improve. I was dressed as a French woman by this time. My Territorial Force nursing service uniform handed in by way of exchange for new French clothes.

The clothes were authentic, French-made right down to the shoes and socks I was issued. The delay was a small stay of execution that caused me more anxiety than if I had gone immediately. By the time I boarded the plane I was eager to do so. Anything was better than the inactivity of waiting. My imagination played havoc as I dreamed-up things more terrible than reality. Anything was better than the unknown.

It was a moonlit night, and I could make out the Brittany coastline, a dark shape edged by silvery sea. The Halifax droned--too noisily--into enemy territory. My ears throbbed with the aeroplane's clatter; certain it would alert every person in the countryside below. Then, as we lost altitude searching for the drop zone, it began to drizzle.

The pilot indicated we should turn back.

I shook my head and shouted, "What's a little rain?"

By tomorrow I would no longer have the courage to do this. I didn't care at that moment if I died in the jump, at least I would not have to endure the agony of my own fear any longer. I moved to what had once been a bomb bay and checked my position, sitting with my legs dangling, waiting for the green signal before I pushed myself through the gap.

The wind rushed past and for a fleeting moment I fell through the air before the shoot opened, but it was all so familiar even in the dark and drizzle. I reached for the toggles, pulling them down to my eye level, checking the grey green mushroom of silk that opened above me. I twisted my body to face into the wind in order to land. I could see nothing but dark shadows below. Clamping my knees tight and a little bent, my arms tucked in and my chin on my chest as I had been taught, I anticipated the ground more than saw it. Seconds later, I lay on the sodden ground looking into the drizzling dark night. A dog barked in the distance. Dark figures materialised around me.

A man bent over me and said, "Violetta?"

"Oui." I replied. Who else might he be expecting to fall out of the sky?

They helped me remove my backpack and chute, which they bundled up and thrust into a potato sack. I hurried behind the three men across fields until we came to a dark farmhouse.

I was lucky they explained as they poured me a brandy and sat me in front of the stove to dry myself. Just this morning Germans were in the village but had moved on. I sent up a quiet prayer of thanks. If I had arrived earlier as was planned, I might have been caught. The next day they took me to a country railway siding where I met Lucien.

13. OCCUPIED FRANCE

At Rennes, Lucien and I changed trains. He handed me into the carriage courteously as if I were precious cargo. We were in love and to be married or that was the story for our journey to Paris. I would rather he was my brother, but his black eyes darkened as he said it was not possible because the papers showed our names were different.

My name had changed. Aurélie Avraham sounded too Jewish. David Asquith had asked me what name I might like to adopt, making sure it was French. I had chosen Madeleine, in memory of my friend whom I had abandoned. Having her stage name would forever remind me of my selfishness. David had chosen my surname and my papers showed I was Madeleine Chaumont, born in the now destroyed border town of Charleville-Mezieres. Its proximity to Belgium would, he said, account for any queries that might arise from a lapse in Parisian accent.

The train we boarded was full of German soldiers, polite young men who looked a little bemused at being here. One of them stood to vacate his seat for me, and I found it difficult to reconcile these men with the brutality I had witnessed. These were just ordinary German boys with good manners.

It wasn't until we reached Paris and alighted from the train that I was asked for my papers. Lucien gave the Gendarme both sets of papers and our pass. The Gendarme gave them hardly more than a cursory glance then nodded and we walked out of the station into sunlit Parisian streets. Only then did I release my breath.

Despite my anxiety I looked about me with interest. I was in Paris, and it was like there was no war. Nothing was in ruins and all around me life seemed normal except for soldiers everywhere. Great red, white, and black banners hung from buildings, which might have seemed strange for the Parisians but reminded me of Berlin. We walked along the street in silence, me tagging a half pace behind Lucien's stocky frame.

He would stop every now and again for me to catch up. "Stop gawking." He scolded. "People will see you are a foreigner. Act like a Parisian."

"Yes, of course." I berated myself silently, everything seemed so normal I was lulled into complacency.

Not even far-away London was this untouched by war, and yet here there was little evidence of conquest except for soldiers of occupation. I gazed down at the pavement, reflecting on my training and how it needed to become me, and I it. I was no longer Magdalena or Aurélie and I was well trained in the language and the Parisian idiom and expression, trained in my thinking, yet just for a moment I forgot.

One lapse can kill you; my instructor had repeated ad nauseum.

I pulled myself together, glanced at Lucien with distain, and walked off in front of him, my skirt sashaying around my knees. He strode to catch up, grinning as he slid his hand around my waist and pulled me to him. I stiffened.

"Relax Madeleine. You are doing well my beautiful fiancée. Kiss me, there are soldiers watching."

I leaned into him, suddenly afraid. His kiss was passionate, not the chaste lip touching experience I expected. When he allowed me up for breath he was grinning and said, "I will have to do that again very soon."

I had been taken for a fool. "There are no soldiers watching are there?"

He laughed again and taking my hand we walked on down the street. No one watched us although the streets were full of people. Bicycles and cars and pedestrians were everywhere. Pavement cafes with their little round tables were full of patrons. German soldiers sat among the Parisians as if they had been doing it all their lives, and only once or twice I saw distain for the occupiers on a Parisian's face.

Signs of war-imposed shortages were few although clearly there was a shortage of petrol. A peculiar car, modified with a wood burning combustion contraption strapped to its rear, passed us billowing smoke. Cycles pulling carts were everywhere, as were horse drawn carts. Lucien haled a velo-taxi as he called the bicycle powered vehicle, to take us to the Place de l' Opéra in the 9th arrondissement. We arrived and went in through a back entrance to the administration rooms.

My heart beat so rapidly I was afraid it would burst from my chest. Lucien said Monsieur Copeau was expecting me, but I wasn't sure if he would remember me, despite what I had told David Asquith. At that time David had flicked his hand up saying he would make all the arrangements, and yet I hadn't known what that meant. What if Monsieur Copeau only thought of a dalliance if I were to visit Paris. What if he didn't think I was good enough to sing in his opera? What if he had forgotten ever meeting me?

A woman arrived and asked Lucien to take a seat before she ushered me through to Monsieur Copeau's lavish office. I did not give David enough credit for his organisational ability. Monsieur Copeau greeted me cordially as if it were all arranged. I was to be part of a chorus of his current show *die Fledermaus*. I couldn't believe my luck. This was an opera I knew.

"An approved production by the occupying administration," he told me with a wry smile. Monsieur Copeau asked the woman, his secretary, to show me around and introduce me to Madame Ménard who was the Opera costumier.

The tour left me breathless and worried. How could I sing in such a grand place. It was beyond my wildest dreams of what Opera might look like. The stage was vast. The stairs of white marble and a red and green marble balustrade led to the foyer with its painted ceiling. It was beyond grand. It was intimidating, but perhaps that was what a Napoleon III style warranted.

The secretary handed me over to Madam, a stylish woman in her mid-thirties, with black wavy hair and black eyes. Her small hands, which measured and prodded me, reminded me of claws, so strong was the grip of her fingers. She told me to wait until she finished and then she would take me to a house where she had arranged a room for my board.

Lucien had gone, but he left a message that he would come to see me soon. How would he find me? I was to discover that this was a well-connected group of people, all once associated with the University--la Sorbonne, which was the centre of a rising resistance to the occupiers.

I left the Palais Garnier through the front entrance with Madame Ménard. Across the square was a large building with new signage, Nazi flags and sentry boxes.

Madame Ménard muttered, "The Boche have commandeered the building as their command centre. Why they had to choose here...?" She shrugged.

The house Madame Ménard took me to, turned out to be a tiny corner terrace, in a row of almost identical houses behind a low hedge, all with a small strip of garden in the front.

The two women in the house, Eva, and Marie, were both dancers with Ballet de l' Opéra national de Paris. I was to share the house with them. Previously there had been a third woman but Madame Ménard said, Clotilde had gone home to her parents.

I shook hands with Eva and Marie who were both pretty, wiry, and strong. Eva's hair was the colour of copper, and Marie's was a dark curly mass that she could never quite seem to pin down neatly.

I worried about living with two women of whom I knew almost nothing, thinking they might uncover something that would give me away, but the truth was they were not in the least interested in me.

As soon as Madame Ménard opened her bag and brought out bread, I was forgotten. The two women fell upon it as if they were starving, which I was to discover later was true, and would be my fate also in the months to come, for there was a great shortage of food in the country. Later Lucien told me that even those who were indifferent once, now hated the Boche.

"They may be polite now they are in Paris, but they have stolen our pride, our food, and our country. They will pay!"

Outside of work I had little contact with anyone except Madame Ménard to whose house I would go for costume fittings. Occasionally, I would see Lucien, but always briefly. Each morning I went to rehearsal at the Palais Garnier. In the afternoons we played matinees, and at night we put on shows where the audience were mostly German officers and their wives, or mistresses.

A fortnight passed before Madam Ménard, gave me a slim case of music sheets, and asked me to deliver them to a friend I was to meet in a café. Until then, I had no idea she was involved, but it turned out Madame Ménard owned a wireless, which was used by London to send and receive messages.

Visiting her house for fittings, was the perfect cover although I began to think the best thing about those visits was that she always had food supplied by her brother, a farmer somewhere outside of Paris. At times I thought her food might be all that would keep me alive. I did not have the networks and families by which others sustained themselves, and there was nothing in the shops. Yet, I feared for Madame Ménard because having a wireless was an extremely dangerous thing. It was the quickest way for agents to be caught but Madame said she was careful. I hoped for her sake she was right.

After I had lived in Paris for a month, two things happened simultaneously. The first was that I went to work one day to find the person playing Adele, Rosalinde's maid in the production, was taken off the listing. She was Jewish and Jewish people could not perform in the theatre. I was astonished but I remembered the situation in Germany before I left. The same thing happened there.

The second amazing and most unexpected thing was that I was chosen to play Adele. I found out that I was to try out for the part when I was in the dressing room. I had heard about the Jewish girl being banned and I was in a dark mood. It wasn't fair. War should not interfere in the arts. Singers were not soldiers.

I was just stepping into my costume for rehearsals when Madame Ménard came in, "Non, non, non, she said, "take that off." She prodded and squeezed me into Adele's costume and pushed me out onto the stage for an urgently convened audition.

As I listen to Monsieur Copeau explain what he wanted me to do, I blessed Alain for training my voice, and for the first time I was grateful to Gertrud for teaching me how to perform Adele's *Laughing Song*. She may have stolen my papers and deserted me, but thanks to her I was given the part.

After that, my other role also changed. I was no longer asked to play messenger for Madame Ménard. I was too valuable. Instead, I was given two other tasks. First, I was to make contact with someone called Jean Moulin, who was holed up somewhere in the Bouches-du-Rhône and organise for him to get to London. If there was any man de Gaulle needed to bridge the ideological divide between the Gaullists, Anarchists, and the Communists it was Moulin. Secondly, I was to make friends with a German officer, Oberstleutnant von Winterfeldt. No one said why.

I wasn't sure how I was to go about doing either of these things, but it turned out the first was easier than the second. I merely asked Lucien to get a message to Monsieur Moulin for me. Lucien was suspicious as he was suspicious of all socialists and Communists but when I told him it was a direct request of his hero de Gaulle, he set to the task with dedication.

The second task was harder and in the end, I asked Lucien also. It took him two days to find out where the officer liked to go in his leisure hours. Surprisingly, it was a jazz club where often a well-known quintet played.

Lucien said he would introduce me to a man who worked there, a musician, one of the band members called Armand who played bass. All I was to do, once I was accepted as a singer, was to seek out someone to introduce me to the officer London wanted me to befriend. It needed to be someone acceptable, who could make the introduction without it seeming contrived.

Meeting German officers became easy as my fame in the opera grew. From being a completely unknown chorus girl to becoming the famous maid Adele changed everything, and bouquets began to arrive at my dressing rooms with cards asking me if I would take supper with an admirer. I didn't know how I could sort out one from the other or which I should accept. In the end fate made the decision for me.

A young officer Lieutenant Friedrich Kerschner was the most persistent. He came night after night to see me in performance, each night sending flowers and notes of admiration begging me to accompany him to supper after the show. I contacted London with his information, and they said, go. So, one evening after the show I invited him to my dressing room to thank him for all his flowers and good wishes.

As soon as I met Friedrich, I knew he was from one of the old families. His conservative views and old-fashioned manners marked him as one of those with money. On our first date he took me to the Ritz, and I knew my assessment was right.

Before he picked me up, he told me to dress in my finest for he wanted to show me off. I am not sure to whom I was to be shown but it seemed as we walked into the Ritz, it was not me he was showing off but himself. I was merely an adornment for his ego.

He was not in any way interested in me, but he was interested in the fact that I was an opera singer and that I was attractive enough to be seen with him in public. I soon discovered that although I as a person was of no interest, he was interested in the way I behaved, in the way I walked or the way I wore my hair and the suitability of my clothes. Thanks to London and Madame Ménard my clothes were stylish.

They were clothes suitable for an up-and-coming opera singer but with everything so difficult to get in Paris, people made do. Yet, for Friedrich my best wasn't quite up to his standards. His criticisms weren't overt, but they were there in the way he noted that we would have to change this or that.

"My dear Madeleine," he said. "I will have to see what I can do to arrange something of better quality—something more appropriate for you to wear when you are with me."

My blood curdled and I struggled through dinner, drinking too much champagne to avoid shouting at him. Who was this man to take such a proprietary attitude towards me? If I wasn't good enough, why did he want to take me out in the first place. I fumed, but reminded myself, he was a means to an end. It didn't help, and by the end of the evening, I complained of a headache, and he took me home although I still had not accomplished what I set out to do.

That night for the first time in Paris, I went to bed with a belly full of food and wine, but still no further in my quest to meet the man who was my assignment. How was I to manipulate such an introduction?

I asked Louis Copeau if I could sing at the club on my nights off.

I might persuade Friedrich to come to the club. That way, I would be able to stage-manage an introduction, if both men happened to be there on the same night.

Louis frowned and played with the pen on his desk "Why Madeleine? Here you have all the singing you want. You are becoming so popular. Why would you sing there? That place, well it has a certain reputation, you understand?"

I smiled. It was such a quaint thing to say, so old fashioned like something I imagined one's father saying. "I will only sing good songs. Nothing raunchy and just the odd number with fellow musicians, that's all."

"You will be careful won't you Madeleine?" Louis's face creased with concern.

What did he mean be careful? What did he think I was doing there--walking into some kind of bagnio? I had not been to the club, but I was assured it was just a jazz venue and restaurant, nothing more. Why would I need to be careful?

Neither could I tell his why I needed to sing there. Instead, I told him I loved jazz and I missed it. He knew I used to sing jazz at the club in Brussels and it was true, I did miss it. Although I didn't tell him I was to have little choice in the songs chosen.

I would receive a song with the words and music delivered to the club. The delivery purportedly from me, and I would sing it on the night instructed. I supposed there was to be some transmission of messages, but I didn't ask. I just prayed that I would be at least a little familiar with the songs chosen. I didn't want to go there and make a fool of myself.

I was also curious that the club was the venue preferred by this mysterious officer, Oberstleutnant von Winterfeldt. The Nazis didn't approve of jazz although French jazz was still tolerated, and so long as American songs were disguised as French songs all would be well.

Lucien took me to the club one morning. It was a three-story white building at the end of the Rue Pierre Fontaine, just across the Place Blanche from the Moulin Rouge. The white building was draped in the familiar flags displaying Nazi insignia, indicating they had made this their venue. Another surprise.

It wasn't opened when Lucien and I arrived but when we walked in, memories of the Brussels club flooded my mind, and the smell of stale cigarettes and the odour of old spilt alcohol made me choke with nostalgia. The blackout curtains were still drawn despite the sunshine outside and a single stark light without a shade illuminated the gloomy upstairs room.

Lucien introduced me to Armand whose hair straggled in greasy lank locks past his jaw, a cigarette hanging from his lips. He smoked incessantly, dragging, and puffing with quick jerks. With his free hand he fiddled constantly, grabbing anything within his reach, a glass, a bottle opener, a cork mat, a box of matches, it didn't matter.

Lucien left me with Armand who walked over to a bar and poured me champagne. It was ten o'clock in the morning, but I took a sip and surprise made me look up at him.

"It's good?"

"It's delicious," I said. Although my experience with champagne was limited, I could tell this was a good wine.

He smiled, waving his hand for me to follow him as he walked me down to a cellar full of champagne. "My family's. Better we sell it here than it is looted."

Then Armand began what seemed to my puzzlement to be a lesson in the finer points of making good champagne. He made me taste and savour the liquid every time he explained a part of the process. If it were a bottle from inferior stock, he would make me spit out the wine. If it were from his family's wine, I could swallow it. Two hours passed, while he instructed, but he also told me stories.

He told me he was from a place near Épernay; how his father had brought the wine in a truck to him when the Boche came. All his father had ever wanted was for Armand to stay on the farm. He hated the idea that Armand was a musician who had no interest in farming. Now his father needed him to sell the stuff to the German's, at least those few with money to spend. For once Armand was of use to his father.

Bemused by all the wine and information it dawned on me that Armand was asking me to help. "How can I help Armand? I can only sing."

"Ah but Madeleine if you understand champagne, you can demand the best. That way when the Boche want to buy you a drink you can tell the good stuff from the bad. They will not be able to fool you and you can insist on only good wine. If they offer you a drink, then you must insist on wine from Épernay. Never ever waste your time drinking inferior wine. Life's too short." He grinned and puffed out more smoke.

I began to think Lucien had not explained himself very well to Armand and I asked. "You know I am here because I want to sing occasionally, don't you Armand?"

"Sure." He said, waving his hand to clear the pall of smoke that hung over us. "But quid pro quo, ma chérie."

So, if I wanted to sing here with these men, I would have to sell Armand's champagne. If Friedrich thought this was the best of the best, he would have to have it, and it would be easy to convince him. "I think I can help you Armand, but I can't guarantee anything, all right?"

"Sure, sure." He grinned at me again puffing furiously at his cigarette. "So how does it work then?"

"What do you mean?"

"How can it work that you sing here?" He shrugged his shoulders as if the question were not important.

"I am not sure. How does it usually work?"

He blew air sharply between his teeth. "People come and then we jam, but we know them, they are friends, and we know their ways. "You--an opera singer, how can you jam.

147

We will have to practice sometime—what songs can you sing, besides opera."

"I can sing jazz." I said a little put out by Armand's casual dismissal of my ability.

"Sure, anyone can sing jazz, but can you sing so they want to listen?"

"I'll show you."

"Not now. Wait until the Gypsy gets here. He'll decide."

"Have more wine." He poured more of the exquisite champagne into his glass and held the bottle over mine, but I put my hand on top of the glass.

"No, I can't drink any more. I won't be able to ride my bicycle home."

He laughed again and lit another cigarette from the stump of his last one.

14. PARIS

I arrived late at the club. It was Thursday night, and the tables were booked to capacity, but I had only just finished at the Opera. I surveyed the place I had sung in several times over the past few weeks. This was certainly a German hang out, and they had made it their own, the cloak room full of coats, shelves stacked with peaked caps, insignia announcing this was a place where the non-commissioned did not set foot.

"Mademoiselle Chaumont you are late." Friedrich stood aside to let me pass, and then his hand pressed into the small of my back as he guided me possessively through the warren of tables. "Come, I will introduce you to my superior officer."

Interspersed among tables of officers were civilians. French men and women, music lovers, sat together in groups, some fraternised with the enemy, but first this was a place for music but not just any music. Here people collaborated or resisted, conspired, and played. It was all one, but jazz was everything.

Red and white banners with the familiar hooked black cross blocked any views from the windows. Not that it mattered; blackouts meant one could not see out anyway.

What a sight it must have been in its heyday with the red lights of the Moulin Rouge lighting the square opposite. I wished I could have been there before all this. If only I had agreed to take up the offer when Monsieur Copeau first asked. Now the Moulin Rouge remained dark like the rest of Paris, the frosted streets shrouded by gently falling snow, vacated by cold revellers seeking warmth, and the darkness concealing all from English bombers.

The men at the table stood-up as we approached and Friedrich brought his heels together, dropping his hand from my back as he introduced me to the mysterious officer.

"Oberstleutnant may I present the lovely Madeleine Chaumont." He turned to me; his puppy brown eyes formal as he bowed slightly. "Mademoiselle my superior, Oberstleutnant von Winterfeldt, who has insisted upon meeting you."

It was a gallant lie as it was I who arranged the meeting; I hoped subtly, but perhaps so subtly that Friedrich really thought it was as he said.

The Oberstleutnant stepped forward. "Mademoiselle it is my very great pleasure. I have been fortunate indeed to meet with you. You have the voice of a colourful flower."

A colourful flower, how odd, but his French was agonisingly precise, mangling the melody of the sentiment he tried to convey as he hesitated between each word. Yet, his gaze was penetrating as if he was trying to see into my soul. A muscle jumped in his closely shaven jaw, and I decided his contradictions were the result of nerves.

"You have heard me sing Oberstleutnant?" I replied in German, smiling gently to help ease what I supposed, might be nervousness in the face of my growing fame. To wield such power made me feel dizzy as I saw him trembling like a rabbit in the spotlight of borrowed glamour. It was only later I found out I was mistaken.

He looked taken aback, then relief lightened his serious face, a smile softened his angular features, folding the skin in curves at the corner of his finely sculpted lips. "Fräulein, I am impressed. Where did you learn to speak German so well?" He paused and then said, "Ah my manners; time enough for that later. Please..." He pulled out a chair, one hand summoning a waiter with a quick click of his fingers.

"Champagne Fräulein?"

Friedrich was dismissed. As the Oberstleutnant turned his back, a dark look flashed across Friedrich's face, but I doubted if the Oberstleutnant even noticed. Men of privilege seldom see the effects they have on the people they command.

Across a small dance floor, the quintet played on a raised platform; gypsy jazz adapted for German tastes, with Nazi approved lyrics. I brushed back an imagined strand of hair and Armand bowed slightly towards me. It was enough. I would not sing tonight.

I turned lightly to focus my attention on my companion. By some unseen command, the other officers had also vacated the table, leaving the Oberstleutnant and me alone in the crowded room. The Oberstleutnant spoke quietly to a waiter who came back a few moments later with a bottle of champagne.

The wine's crispness and bead told me that here was a truly fine vintage, aged en tirage. This was better than Armand's wine. Only the best for my officer. He must be an important man. Or perhaps he was just a man of refined taste. I hoped not, for it's harder to betray those one likes.

"Fräulein, your health." He raised his glass, grey shadowed eyes catching the low light as he watched me across the glass rim. "I am not usually much of an opera fan—but you are outstanding. I saw you earlier tonight at the Opera Garnier. I once went to see *La Traviata*. Have you played it? You would play Violetta so well."

I became very still, my eyes fixed on the band across the room as a chill ran through me. What did this man know? Was it just coincidence that he used my code name? I tried to think of something witty to divert his attention and turned to examine him, casually relaxed in his chair. I was reminded of a leopard waiting for its prey. My mind went blank, and I took another sip of wine.

He spoke again as if there was no interlude. "I heard about you, and now I know everything I heard was true, a beauty, a voice and, I see also a clever brain."

He smiled again; his eyes fixed on mine as though he was reading my soul. The blood rose in my cheeks. I felt short of breath, and I took yet another sip of champagne to cover my confusion. If I weren't careful I would get tipsy. My first breakthrough and I fell to pieces like a schoolgirl—a terrified blushing stupid schoolgirl.

"Oberstleutnant..."

"Please, my dear call me Dietrich."

"Dietrich." I bowed my head in acknowledgment, forgetting what I was about to say. I really must get some control. I should be aloof, playing hard to get, sharp. Instead, I improvised saying lamely, "You don't like opera?"

He laughed. It was a chilling thing, his laugh. It made me shiver as I listened to the throaty, self-depreciating chuckle. In it there was a confidence born of absolute certainty in his achievement, his authority, his right to exist. He was a man born to command.

The nervousness he'd displayed earlier was gone. Perhaps I imagined it, perhaps his tenseness never existed. I had learned to take adoration as my due and expected every man to tremble before me. Perhaps I was misguided by my own conceit.

He fiddled with the white damask linen napkin that lay discarded next to his glass. "I have a secret Madeleine; may I call you Madeleine? I can see we will become friends you and I, very good friends." His eyes lingered on my lips.

I was breathless and it wasn't mere coquetry. "A secret?"

"Yes Madeleine, I must confess, I am a jazz fan. The classics are wonderful but jazz, what can I say—I love jazz and this place is my haven. The opera is all right, as is the cabaret." He rotated his index finger in the direction of the Moulin Rouge across the street. "But it's jazz that quickens my blood." His eyes captured mine as if in embrace before he said, "It's the pure rebellion in it. Yes, even when it conforms to good German rules as this does." He nodded in the direction of the band. His interrogation followed so quickly I almost didn't notice. "Will you sing more of your American songs tonight?"

He must have seen the exchange between Armand and me, missing nothing. I had underestimated him. He knew jazz too, even the difference between French and American compositions that I thought I had been so carefully disguising since I had taken to singing in this club. I would not be able to fool this man easily.

My hands felt sweaty, but staying close to the truth, I said, "No, I don't want to sing tonight." I smiled up at him flashing a look from beneath my lashes. "Tomorrow I must sing a matinee and a night performance. After that I sing at Le Montecristo for Monsieur Bedaux, so I must save my voice."

"I didn't know you were to sing at that party."

Ha! I exulted internally—you are not that well informed. I regained my equilibrium with the knowledge that he wasn't all powerful.

He smiled. "I will be there also."

I sagged--my triumph short lived. "You know Monsieur Bedaux?"

"Indeed, he is a good friend to us. I shall look forward to seeing you tomorrow night then. You might sing a request for me?"

I stumbled over my words saying, "I'm not sure Monsieur, my producer, would be happy with that."

"Monsieur?"

"Yes, Monsieur Copeau."

"Louis Copeau?" He seemed more interested than I expected.

I was out of my depth with this man. He was controlled, intelligent, worldly, and while I could see he was fascinated and attracted to me, he was not a fool in puppy dog love like the others, like poor Friedrich whom I flattered and used to get me this introduction. I was astounded he knew Monsieur Copeau's Christian name.

"Do you know him?"

"I think I might." He gazed across the room as if he were thinking. "I attended university with a Louis Copeau, or rather he was finishing when I began, but we attended the same music club. I remember him well." He looked keenly back at me.

I had hooked him, but I was afraid. There was more to this man than this war.

A disturbance at the door redirected his attention. Three men entered and the hub of voices in the room immediately ceased as people watched the Geheime Staatspolizei trio, shrug off coats dusted with snow from the coldest May in many years. God had surely turned His back on France when German secret police could brazenly walk into a French jazz club.

My Oberstleutnant sighed. "Come Mademoiselle the evening is ruined. I will escort you home."

Twenty minutes later, Dietrich held out his hand for me to alight from his warm staff car. We were outside the little terraced house I shared with Marie and Eva. From the corner of my eye, I saw a shadow slouched against the wall. Lucien lurked behind the hedge waiting for me. He must have a message. I hoped Dietrich had not seen him, but if he had, he gave no sign.

Eva and Marie were not yet home judging from the darkened silence of the house, but it was early, and like most performers, night was their daytime. It was mine too and I didn't want to be home. I was hungry and there was no food in the house.

Few people had food in their houses these days. It was a luxury only the Boche could afford. I winced at the term that I now used like a Parisian. Here only six weeks and I was already calling the German soldiers blockheads. What did it say about me? I could not afford such thoughts; they had me spinning in moral circles.

Yet my stomach growled with hunger just like any other Parisian. The unseasonably cold weather destroyed crops and the German Army commandeered any surviving harvest. I had expected the Oberstleutnant would buy me dinner, but I was disappointed. He walked me to my door, bowed slightly saying goodnight before returning briskly to his car.

It wasn't me playing hard to get, it was him. I watched him go before stepping into the small hallway and taking off my coat. Minutes later I went through the house to the kitchen door, unbolting it to let Lucien in.

"Lucien you take foolish risks." I chided in a whisper. "What if he saw you?"

"What if he did? What's he to you Madeleine my love."

"Stop Lucien. You know this is not possible."

He sighed throwing himself onto a sagging sofa. "I'm so tired Madeleine, and so hungry. Do you have food?"

I shook my head. "I don't think there is anything." I looked in the cupboard. "Ah, two turnips."

I threw the wizened vegetables to Lucien, and made coffee, a disgusting brew of barley and chicory with saccharine for sugar. As he devoured the turnips, I clutched my coffee cup to warm my hands. It was awful, but it was hot and filled my belly and for that I was grateful. I sipped patiently. One could not rush Lucien.

He took a gulp of his coffee before he said, "Was that him?" He jerked his head in the direction of the road where Dietrich had stopped his car.

"You have news Lucien?"

He picked at the fraying thread of stitches holding his boot sole to the leather upper. "Merde, next I will have no shoes to wear. I need shoes Madeleine; how can a man fight for his country with no shoes? Tell them I need shoes! Shoes and meat, in the next drop. Men cannot fight with Trinitrotoluene alone."

"Tell me what you have for me or is it a secret?" Sarcasm edged my impatience.

He looked up, mildly surprised, and said, "Moulin has agreed to meet, but de Gaulle is wasting his time." Lucien shrugged. "I know these red devils. They don't want to join with the rest of us. They sit on the sidelines while Russia is in league with the madman. Few of them are French enough to go against Stalin's decree to resist the Fritz bastards. Although they are fools to think they won't soon draw the attention of that lunatic in Berlin. His boots will tromp all over them, and then we will see who will fight. When the war ends, they want France for the Communists but if they join with de Gaulle, they won't be able to take it. They will never swear allegiance to de Gaulle." He put his hands on his knees, pushing himself upright. "I must go now unless you will relent and share your bed with a weary saboteur ma chérie." He walked towards me, a half-smile on his face, his eyes underscored by the deep dark circles of malnutrition and tiredness but still willing to chase his passions.

"No Lucien. Don't."

He sighed again. "I must starve for all things... Oh, I remember, you might want to tell them also that tomorrow the Boche will arrest foreign Jews. They will take them to a camp near Orleans called Beaune-la- Rolande."

After Lucien left, I stood in the hallway contemplating his message. What did he mean, tomorrow they would arrest all Jews? Should I pass the message on now? If I left it until tomorrow it would be too late. I had to go now or how would they be warned in time? What could they do? I hesitated. I would speak with Madame Ménard. She would know what to do, and besides, I needed to pass on the message about Moulin.

I shrugged back into my damp coat and let myself out the house. Snow fell, deadening my footsteps and slushing beneath my boots as I formulated the message.

Madame Ménard lived in a basement near the Palais Garnier. Her husband, who had been with the French army was missing, presumed dead. He was actually alive, but she never admitted it, always wearing widow's black. Monsieur Ménard was in London with de Gaulle's government having escaped, as I had, from Dunkerque. I suspected she protected herself from both Nazi interest and neighbourhood gossip by pretending he was dead although it hadn't stopped her taking a lover.

Madame Ménard was rumoured to be Monsieur Copeau's lover. I didn't know if she was or wasn't, and besides, I had suspected Monsieur Copeau of a preference for his own gender, but I did not share this idea with anyone else.

How was it, everyone seemed to know Monsieur Copeau? When I said Copeau's name in London, David and Sir Giles had looked at each other, and in unison asked, Louis Copeau? And this evening the Oberstleutnant said the same thing. Either it was a very common name, or they all attended the same university together. Was it a bizarre coincidence or was it something more?

I didn't know, but Monsieur Copeau was always charming to me, if a little distant. I suppose he was a busy man. I was lucky he still wanted me to sing for him. I was lucky he had returned after initially fleeing when the German Army bore down on Paris. It seemed he fled south as we fled north, I and Madeleine.

Madeleine my poor, poor Madeleine, so loyal and brave, tortured to death by the Death's Head battalion, and lost to me forever. I had never deserved her loyalty. It had never occurred to me to stay and try to find her. I had assumed I was the only one in peril, gave no thought to others behind me; those poor souls whose photos my instructors had forced me to see. The ones like Madelaine, tortured, raped, fighting, and dying. My only thought was to flee, to escape and to save myself.

I had convinced myself that I could make it up to Madeleine by finding her killers and avenging her death. How foolish I had been, imagining that by adopting her name, I would remain focussed on revenge. How naive! I was never driven by noble ideas of vengeance, just guilt, fear, and cowardice, but it keeps me alive.

I was so lost in recriminations, I did not hear the car that pulled up beside me until a voice said, "Madeleine what are you doing out here? You will catch your death."

"Dietrich!" Guilt flooded my face. "Dietrich." What was I to say? I settled for a half truth. "I am going to my friend's house, I'm hungry." I blurted out the last lament without thinking and cursed myself as the words left my mouth. When this man was about, I seemed to lose all judgment.

All he did was laugh, before saying, "Where are my manners?" He stepped out and standing aside, held the door in invitation.

"I returned, hoping to persuade you to accompany me to dinner, for as soon as I left you, I found myself wishing you were still with me. Is that wrong of me?"

I don't know what possessed me, but I said, "You are too late now. I have another appointment."

"Ah, perhaps he will understand."

"You will have to wait your turn." What was wrong with me? I expected to see a frown at my rudeness but instead he laughed again.

"Well Mademoiselle let me at least be your chauffeur. Then I shall leave you to go about your business."

I thought of the food I would miss and looked longingly at the warm car. "Perhaps I can accompany you after I speak to my friend."

He was watching me in that way that made me forget who I was and what I was supposed to be doing.

A small muscle jumped in the smooth angle of his jaw. "Then, allow me to drive you to your friend's house and once you are finished, we can dine at Fouquet's."

To spurn his offer would look churlish. It would make him at least curious if not suspicious. I would have to be bold. "I am going to my costumier for a fitting for Monsieur Bedaux's soiree at Montecristo.

When we arrived at Madame Ménard's building, I got out the car and walked across the road feeling his eyes following me. It made me lightheaded with fear as I knocked on her door. I had foolishly placed her in danger. So impetuous! I heard Sister Immaculata's voice in my head. That's always been your problem Magdalena.

15. UNDONE

I had been looking for Marcel since I arrived in France. Not, I admit, immediately I arrived. My first mission was to find my way around a foreign city, but I had asked Lucien to find Marcel with the Communists.

He glared at me with suspicion. "Who is this Communist? I think you have too much to do with these people. First it is Moulin now this new one. What, am I to be asked all the time to take messages to these people? You English, pah!"

"No Lucien, this is different. It is someone I know. Not business. I ask only as a favour."

"Hah! What is he to you?"

"He's a friend, just a friend and Jewish so I fear for him. I fear he will be captured and put in Beaune-la- Rolande."

Lucien nodded, for a moment thoughtful, his mouth turned down at the corners. "Yes, if he is in Paris, it is likely. Already they have rounded up many and will continue until none are left. What's your friend's name? I will put out the word, but I promise nothing."

I hesitated for I did not know what name he would now use. I didn't know if he was Marcel from Belgium, or Joachim from Munich, or perhaps Eduardo from Spain. I gambled.

"He is Spanish, exiled by Franco his name is Eduardo."

"What else?"

"Pardon?"

"What's his family name?"

"I don't know."

"I thought he was a friend." He sighed exasperated. "A description then."

"Dark hair, as tall as you but slighter in build. Green eyes, around thirty."

"A Jew, a Communist, a Spaniard called Eduardo with green eyes. What's that thing you English say, *autant chercher une aiguille dans une botte de foin*?"

"Looking for a needle in a haystack."

"It is possible someone will know." He shrugged. "Come my beautiful Madeleine what do I get in return."

"Oh Lucien, stop. You know I cannot."

I am sure he did not bother to look far, and I did not want to push him in fear of arousing his jealousy or suspicion. So, I prayed Marcel would be safe, and focused on my mission.

Throughout the rest of May, I continued to see Dietrich. It was the easiest job I ever had, and a pleasure for he was good company. He knew I was always hungry and plied me with food which I accepted like a grateful puppy. Once I began seeing him, all my stage door German suitors fell away and only flowers from Dietrich arrived although he seldom came to the Opera himself. When I asked him why he never came to see me he looked at me with that half-amused smile and stroked my cheek. "I have seen you. I came the night we met don't you remember?"

"But you have not been again."

"No, because you are playing the same opera."

"Others come often."

"Are you pleased, for they come to watch you; you know? The entire Wehrmacht is in love with you."

I made a disparaging sound in my throat. "I don't care, but they come even though they see the same opera every night.

Yet you do not come, but you have stopped them waiting at the stage door."

"Do you wish to be bothered by such men?"

"What such men? They are men like you?"

His face changed and a look of anger flashed in his eyes. "Not all are such as me."

"What? They are German soldiers. They are just like you?" I was teasing him, but I went too far and shrank back at his anger.

"The Waffen-SS are not soldiers. They are political thugs, and the Palais Garnier is crawling with their lice. I prefer my own place and perhaps the club for they seldom go there."

I shrank back at his anger. It was true. Most of the men in my audience were Schutzstaffel officers, rather than Wehrmacht officers, but could one still make that distinction now Germany was at war?

After that argument with Dietrich there were once more men lined up at the stage door and flowers filled my dressing room. I wished I had not said anything, for the peace I experienced when Dietrich made sure I was not bothered by fans, was lost. Until one night no flowers came, and only one man remained to see me. He wore a high ranking Geheime Staatspolizei uniform, and did not wait at the stage door, but came to my dressing room.

I wiped the pancake from my face and scowled at his intrusion. Why had no one stopped him from coming backstage. I spoke sharply that he should wait.

"Ah Magdalena or should I call you Madeleine, surely this is no way to speak with your Papi."

My breath stopped, and my heart rose into my throat as if it would escape the confines of mortality. I swung around to face Karl. Terror broke from every pore. I could say nothing; do nothing, just stare but my mind raced. He would expose my secret and I would be undone. Then rage replaced fear as he softly shut the door behind him and stood over me, hat in hand twirling as he examined my face and body; his gaze resting on my breasts, barely covered by my under-shift.

"Clean your face." He said walking to a chair to sit down. "Then you may greet me properly."

Slowly I swung around to face the mirror and picked up the wad of cotton I was using to wipe my face. My mind shrieked uselessly. How can I get out of this, what will I say? How can I make sure he says nothing to anyone about my background? But what can he know, only that I am German not French as everyone here thinks? That is not so bad. I have reinvented myself for art, nothing more. That's all he will know.

I regained control and said, "Karl, you surprised me. I didn't know you were in Paris."

"And you my Magdalena. When everyone raved about the Arian beauty at the opera with the voice of an angel, I cared little for such time-wasting activity, but when I found von Winterfeldt was interested I knew I must meet this Lorelei of the theatre."

Pretending calm, I continued cleaning my face saying, "I don't think his interest lasts, as you can see one minute all men are banned from my door, but now no longer and I know not why. Yet, you are here. We should talk of you, not von Winterfeldt."

I saw his eyes hooded and sceptical gazing at me in the mirror, and I picked up a towel to bury my face. There is only so much time one can spend cleaning off make-up. I wanted desperately to know what had happened to my daughter, but if I asked would he use it against me? Laying the towel aside I stood up and walked towards him, my hand held out in greeting.

"How is our daughter?"

He remained sitting, his arms resting on the chair, ignoring my question, and acting as if my hand was not there.

"Do you still love me Magdalena?"

I stopped cold and contemplated killing him. My mind was racing for a solution, but I must play this out, so I laughed as if self-conscious. "Karl, I was a child. I have grown beyond love now, but you were my first and that is always special, no? I was very hurt when you left me, but I understand your need for a child. I hope she is well." For a moment sadness swamped me, but I pulled myself together and said, "Now I have recovered from my loss..." I shrugged. "I have all I want. I'm famous, with men at my feet. I have given away childish games." I turned back to dress. "Champagne Karl? I can call for champagne or we can go out to find it. Where is your favourite place to go in Paris?"

I was supposed to meet Dietrich, but he would have to wait. I didn't know what to do. I was between the devil and hell's fire. "Although I can't stay long as I have a prior date."

"You have changed Magdalena, and I have no time for champagne, nor do I bed whores. It is not you I want but von Winterfeldt. If you want to continue your new career and maintain your new identity you will bring him to me."

With my dress half-way over my head I froze, what did he mean? I said lightly, "Well you are in luck because he is my date tonight, and I go to meet him at the club. Come with me."

"Don't take me for a fool Magdalena or try to play games with me. You know who I am, and you will do exactly as you are told or return to Germany disgraced, perhaps imprisoned, if I decide to place you into Schutzhaft—protective custody.

Despite my resolve I gasped. "Why? I have done nothing except sing."

"You left Germany without my permission or your papers, therefore you left illegally."

I swung on him then. "You abandoned me and stole my daughter!" Hurt welled up buoyed by a sense of injustice, but immediately I pulled myself back together. "I had no papers." My voice was sullen.

"Yes, you sold them. I suppose to pay your way here. You ran away from your duty and sold the papers you had stolen from me your rightful guardian, to a whore on the streets of Berlin."

"Gertrud!"

"I understand that was the whore's name."

"Where is she?"

He shrugged. "I do not concern myself with street whores. But I am your father, and you belong to me Magdalena. You will do as I say, or you know what will happen."

I shrunk back defeated, and my voice shook. "What do you want me to do?"

"You are to continue seeing von Winterfeldt. I will be back, and you will tell me all the places you go, to whom you speak and everything he says. Do you understand?"

That night Dietrich sensed something was wrong and I could not shake off my apprehension. He took me for a late supper to his hotel, the Lutetia, where he said we would be undisturbed. My nerves were strung to breaking point and I began to get a headache, but I tried to smile and go along with him. I was hungry and if I went home, I would have nothing to eat.

It was the first time I had been to the Lutetia with him, and I went with a sense of fatalism knowing this was the next thing he wanted from me. I could not play coy now but what was I to do? As we sat at dinner, I ate little, for every mouthful felt like it would choke me. My thoughts kept returning to how I might kill Karl.

Dietrich placed his hand on mine and smiled. "What bothers you? You know you are safe with me, and I will never take advantage of you, but here we can relax, eat and then if you so wish I can take you home."

I shrugged and tried to smile back. After all, what was one place or another? What was one puppet master or another? I was much more afraid of Karl than I ever could be of David Asquith, and I was not at all afraid of Dietrich. I would be fed and that was the most important thing. Besides, in a place full of Germans, I might uncover some useful information, but for whom?

After dinner, we sat in the lounge sipping brandy and listening to the resident quartet. They stopped playing and the cellist came to our table. He leaned over and said something to Dietrich that I did not catch. Dietrich laughed and said, "Perhaps not tonight."

The man turned to me and said, "You would like to hear him play, would you not Mademoiselle?"

"Play?"

"Yes, play. This man is a musician of very fine calibre—piano, violin, saxophone, guitar, whatever instrument he is given, he can play."

I searched the cellist's face, then turned to Dietrich. "You didn't tell me." I knew he liked music, but he never let on that he was a musician. I shook my head in amazement. "You never said."

"No, he is too modest." The cellist smiled at me and shrugged. Then he spoke to Dietrich. "But you will play now and impress further the young lady?" He turned back to me. "I have had the pleasure to hear you sing mademoiselle. I know you will not fail to be impressed by the talent of a fellow musician. In this place, at this time, that's all we are—musicians, nothing more."

Dietrich shrugged. His customary detachment was replaced by an eager kind of humility that made him look boyish.

"Do you mind?" he asked.

I could see he was itching to get onto the stage with the others.

"Just one," he said. "I will play my favourite for you."

I settled back to watch. Who would have thought such strict military bearing would harbor such poetry. He disappeared behind the curtains coming back with a saxophone. He loosened his collar and rolled his head as if limbering up, then nodding to the others, he brought the saxophone to his lips.

The wild sounds of *Tin Roof Blues* filled the room. The other guests stopped and turned to watch and as the tempo picked up, their feet began tapping. I was astonished. I didn't think such music would be permitted in a German stronghold.

He played several more tunes. Then he walked over and took my hand. "Sing with me Madeleine." He led me to the microphone. The lounge began to fill with German men, smoking, their sleeves rolled up, their collars loosened and their bodies swaying to the music.

This was truly a surprise. My only experience with German soldiers was at the Barracks at Dachau and in the public bars, restaurants, and theatres of Paris. In my head was an image of a different kind of person. Here I did not see frowns or hear words like Negermusik.

I sang, *The Man I Love,* and they loved it despite its English words. Here were music lovers, lovers of jazz and swing and the strictures of elsewhere did not apply. I was taken aback and re-evaluated my view of German soldiers. They could not all be seen in the same light as Karl and Lothar and his contemporaries.

That night I let him lead me to his bed un-protesting. He closed the door of his room and took me in his arms, so tenderly as if I was porcelain. I shivered and he backed away looking into my eyes as my teeth chattered.

"Shall I stop?"

I shook my head.

He took his time, stroking my inner arms, kissing my palms and the insides of my wrist. He took off each article of clothing I wore, disrobing me until I lay naked on his bed. He gazed upon me as an artist surveying his work, his eyes dark with desire. He was the first man I had been intimate with since Karl, and maybe Lothar, although if Lothar did more to me than kiss me, I could not remember it. The experience with Dietrich could not have been more different.

Afterwards he leaned over, kissing me again looking into my eyes with his so serious. When he smiled, lines crinkled and radiated from the corner of his eyes. I traced them with my fingers. A pulse beat in the hollow at the base of his neck and a muscle in his jaw jumped. I could not tell what he thought but suddenly I couldn't bear my deception and buried my face against his chest.

He tilted my head to look into my face, now wet with tears of self-pity and fear.

"Madeleine what is it?" He got up and brought me a clean hanky, wiping my eyes as he held me. "There's something wrong, tell me. Is it what we did? I knew it was too soon. You were not ready. I am a fool, forgive me Madeleine."

Shaking my head, I made up my mind I would tell him about Karl. He should know the Gestapo were interested in him although I could not understand why. As far as I could tell he was a senior administrative officer whose sin was drinking champagne and playing jazz. And sleeping with a spy, but neither he nor Karl knew that, or I would not still be here.

What story could I conjure. If I told Dietrich, I risked him exposing me, but if I did not I was in more trouble for I could not play this game three ways. I would be caught. I just had to hope Dietrich was the lesser of the evils and would keep quiet about what I told him.

Then my Belgian name gave me an idea. After all it was in his interests to know, but what if he gave me in as a Jew? I didn't think he would because he didn't seem to harbor the same prejudice as others. I saw him talking and laughing with one of the musicians at the club who was Jewish, and he often sat with the Gypsy talking about music.

"Dietrich..."

"What is it Madeleine."

"My name is not Madeleine."

"It's not?" He became very still.

I hurried on. "I am a Belgian refugee, and my name is Aurélie Avraham." I saw a flicker in his eyes. He already knew. Oh God what else did he know but I bluffed on. "I had a visitor tonight in my dressing room."

He smiled teasing, "Well last time we spoke you made it clear you were not happy with me barring men from calling on you. Now one does, and you are upset, but why the name Madelaine?"

"No... you don't understand this man was Gestapo."

His face stilled, his mouth set in a grim line, but he waited for me to speak.

I picked at a thread at the seam of the sheet. "He wants me to spy on you."

Strong hands gripped my arms, hurting me and I jerked back. His grip relaxed. "Tell me everything Madeleine."

"Will you promise you won't expose me Dietrich? I am frightened but what he said is not true. He said I was a Jew and if I do not tell him everything you say and where we go, he will deport me to work in Germany. I am not a Jew, Dietrich, but I am afraid. Why is he interested in you?"

Dietrich had now sat back and was examining my face speculatively, but I could not read his expression. He seemed to have become very calm like he was unconcerned by my confession, and it made me nervous, almost as if he did not believe me. This was not the way a person should act on hearing this information.

"What is the name of this Gestapo officer Madeleine?"

"Karl Hoffermann."

An eyebrow went up a little and the nerve jumped in his jaw but otherwise his gaze didn't waver from my face.

"And what is it he has instructed you to do."

"I must report everything you do to him."

"Where and when?"

"I don't know. He didn't say." Tears ran down my cheeks. Fear and self-pity consumed me. All I wanted to do was sing. I wasn't cut out for this game. Suddenly I had an overwhelming urge to tell Dietrich everything and have him hold me in his warm embrace. I felt safe with him like I never felt before, but

I bit back the urge, my hands making tight fists against such folly.

Then he smiled again and pulled me to him. "My little Madeleine, it will be fine. The Gestapo are paranoid and merely mean to find out if my administration is involved in the black market, they know my fondness for champagne. We will devise something for you to tell them that will keep them happy. Come dry your eyes. In the meantime, tell him anything you please, I will leave that to your discretion. I have nothing to hide."

"You won't say anything about my name?"

"Madelaine Chaumont is a beautiful name and suits its owner so well." He smiled.

It was then I knew there was something else he wasn't telling me.

It wasn't long before I had a real lesson in what it meant to be Jewish in occupied France. It was a night in June, when they took Madame Ménard. I thought it was I who had compromised her, but it seemed that was not the problem. Instead, her part-Jewish heritage was.

No one was safe and no one raised a protest, no one demanded to know what was going to happen to the people they took. There were rumours of course, rumours of camps that did atrocious things, things I could hardly believe of my people.

All the Jewish people rounded up on the streets or in their houses were taken, and we just let them go, fearful that the eyes of the occupiers would turn on us—them. I wasn't sure if I was an 'us' or a 'them' or anything, anymore. I just wanted to get through each day and survive.

I asked Dietrich for the truth, but he just stared at me sadly. Then he said, I shouldn't believe such ugly stories. I was also grateful to him for he got Madame Ménard back to the theatre. I was terrified they would find her wireless, but all they wanted was the Jews and they had no idea of her other role.

Then a friend of Monsieur Copeau's, who was with the Italian Opera company, arranged for our company to join the Italians for a performance in Madrid at the revitalised Madrid Royal Conservatory. Louis decided Madame Ménard must leave France, and Spain was her way out. Once more I turned to Dietrich. He arranged travel permits for us, including for Madame Ménard.

Sometimes I forgot Dietrich was not my lover but my assignment. It was hard because he never acted towards me with anything but consideration and affection, teasing me about my love of American swing and always making sure I had some gossip to give Karl.

Karl never came to my dressing room again but sent an errand boy to interrogate me. I was glad I did not have to report to Karl, for I am not sure I would have been able to act quite so well in front of him, as I did in front of his officer.

Dietrich told me Karl was too important to worry about me and he was amazed he had spoken to me himself that first time. I knew then that knowing Karl's name made Dietrich both believe and become suspicious of me. The ridiculous thing was that I trusted Dietrich. I constantly reminded myself that saving a Jew was one thing for him to do for me, but I had to be careful I did not allow him to see more of who I was.

It was a difficult balancing act, but foolishly I believed I was managing it. Unwisely also, I did not tell London about Karl in case they made me leave. I did not want to leave the opera or Dietrich and convinced myself that between Karl and Dietrich, each would protect me for their peculiar purposes. Given their antipathy towards each other I knew they were unlikely to communicate, cross referencing their knowledge of me.

16. SPAIN

Spain was a favourite place for Germans to vacation and although at one point, we thought Spain would enter the war in support of Germany, it seemed that Franco preferred to stay out of it. Perhaps because his country was still reeling from the recent civil war.

Would Dietrich come to Spain while we were there? He didn't, and strangely I felt a little disappointed. I thought he would miss me, but I was mistaken. As it turned out it was just as well. It would have been a little difficult to explain why a British Embassy official visited me at my hotel.

The man from the Embassy was tall, in his early thirties, but stooped, and was so serious he might be mistaken for a more elderly man. Before he sat, he fussed with his trouser creases, and I almost expected him to place a handkerchief on the chair, but he had taken it out to clean his eyeglasses. Once seated, he fidgeted with his tie, and then his shirt cuffs as if the confinement of clothing were irksome. His hair was dark and thinning in the front making his forehead appear enormous.

He saw me glance at it and smoothed his hand self-consciously across his head.

"I am sorry I did not catch your name."

"Henry Moffatt." He said shortly.

I rolled his name around my mouth, savouring its sound and said to him, "You have the name of an explorer."

He looked startled. "What do you mean?"

"Isn't Moffatt the name of a great explorer of the African jungles." I asked, remembering a name I had heard once that was similar. "You are a figure from history."

Poor man lit up, thrilled at the notion that I saw him as such a romantic figure. I was glad to give his ego a boost. He looked like it didn't happen very often. Then he seemed to remember his purpose and his manner changed abruptly. Niceties were forgotten in a debriefing as harsh as any interrogation I had experienced during my training in England. The questions were mainly about Dietrich, what he thought of things, what his attitude was, what his job was.

I found that despite my close relationship with Dietrich over the last weeks, I knew almost nothing about the man. I began to feel like I failed in my assignment saying, I didn't know, to question after question. I said I thought he did something in the administration of the German occupiers in Paris and was involved in the black market somehow, but I wasn't sure what or how. I explained he was friendly with some very unlikely people from Nazi sympathisers to gypsy musicians.

Then Henry frightened me completely, asking me in the mildest manner I had heard him use since the interview began. "Are you a German spy, Miss Avraham— a double agent?"

I was caught off guard. They knew about my reports to the Gestapo. How? Who was spying on me?

"No! Why do you ask this?" I sat rigid, my nails gouging into the palms of my hands.

We know you're playing a double game. You have been playing with the Gestapo.

"No. It is not like that."

To my horror and shame, tears bubbled from my eyes, and I could not stop them. I was a failure, no good at this stupid role. I was a singer not a spy. What did they think, these people who coerced me into doing something for them, something I did not want and for which I had no talent? I was not made of the stuff of deception. Then I remembered all the deceptions in which I had engaged, and once more blood surged to my neck. Who was I? I no longer knew.

Henry watched my struggle. He used me, this mild-mannered man with his thinning hair and round glasses that sat on cherubic cheeks; used me, and manipulated me, trying to catch me out. I pressed my lips together. I must be careful. I could not trust any of them. Not the British, not Henry Moffatt, not David Asquith, not Dietrich von Winterfeldt, not Lucien, not any of them. They were all intent upon using me for their own ends. I would say no more. Henry was trying to trap me.

Henry said again, "Miss Avraham why are you talking to the Gestapo."

Snivelling I said, "I have no choice." Haltingly, I told Henry how Karl found me and threatened me and how I told Dietrich. My eyes fixed on his face as I said, "But they know nothing about this. They think me a foolish girl. Karl knows my German background, but Dietrich thinks I am a Belgian Jew."

Too late I realised had been an idiot telling him I was German. I had no idea how much he knew, but his gaze didn't waiver.

"Why did you not report this to London?"

I had no answer and stared at my clenched fists. Quietly I said, "I'm frightened, I don't want to do this anymore."

"Why did you tell von Winterfeldt about the Gestapo and not London? I only ask because if you are not in league with him then I must tell you, he is using you."

My eyes flew to Henry's face. What did he mean? Henry saw my bewilderment.

"You must know von Winterfeldt is Abwehr, German Intelligence and you are either in league with him or he is using you. We are sure he knows you are Violetta. Which is it? Are you his agent or his prey?"

"Damn you. Damn you all to hell." Tear sprang from my eyes. I didn't know what possessed me. One minute I was frightened and confused then I was so angry, and I didn't even know why or what caused my anger. It was the injustice of being accused of being a double agent I supposed, or my stupidity. I hadn't guessed Dietrich was also a spy, but at that moment I realised that despite his tenderness, I was just an assignment to him.

A memory flashed through my mind of Friedrich saying that Dietrich arranged our meeting. I thought I had done it, but it was Dietrich, not me. He was playing me. All along he used me. I remembered the flicker in his eye when I told him I was Aurélie Avraham. He knew already, of that I was certain.

I was a sobbing mess as Henry looked on in consternation. I knew I let Dietrich under my skin but what did they expect of me. They wanted me close to him. I supposed it was the strain, but it didn't augur well for my ability to withstand interrogation.

Henry offered me his handkerchief. I took it, snuffling as I tried to regain some control. I was a traitor for these people, spying on my own country and yet here they were again, accusing me unjustly of turning against them. If I had, who could blame me—a German woman such as I am, sleeping with a man they called enemy, but I could not.

The pressures of the last few months, living a double life—a triple life, an agent for the British, a German born woman pretending to be English or Belgium or French. A woman made to sleep with a man fifteen years my senior, no matter how nice he was, and report on it to the Gestapo, was all too much to bear. How could they expect this of me? I did not have the ability or experience. I will be shot.

"I don't want to go back to Paris," I said. "I'm scared."

"There, there, chin up." Henry got up as I dried my eyes on his now sodden handkerchief. His attitude was calm as he picked up the telephone, ordering tea to my room. Hanging up the phone he walked over and opened the door into the corridor. Another man, older and shorter than Henry walked into the room. Henry didn't introduce him but called him Sir.

The English think everything is fixed with a cup of tea, and it's true, I thought as the sweet, milky liquid calmed me. The man called Sir waited, watching me sniff, handing me a clean handkerchief when he saw the wet rag that had been Henry's clean handkerchief. Henry excused himself from the room.

When the man began speaking, I was mesmerised by his accent, a soothing Scottish brogue that caught my imagination. He spoke as if he knew me, and it gave me time to gather my tattered self-control around me. He told me Guilly, and Lady Guilford were well, and Sir Giles sent his love.

Once I was calm, he broached the real purpose of the meeting. It was done so delicately, asking soft questions about Dietrich's likes and dislikes and what we did together. He said he didn't want to know anything intimate, but he was interested in the things we had in common and the places we went.

So lulled by his soothing tone was I that I found myself engaged and eagerly telling him as much as I could, although that wasn't much. Whenever I asked Dietrich a question, the conversation would take another direction altogether. It began to dawn on me that Dietrich was using me all along. I was the one being manipulated, not him.

It was a sobering thought as memories crowded into my mind of places we frequented. I saw his teasing smile, his quiet humour. I heard his voice as he held me in his arms as we danced in one nightclub after another. I heard the endearments, his breath on my ear as he whispered some outrageous piece of gossip about some other officer in the room, who liked young men, who visited which brothel, and then he would look into my eyes to watch the shocked expression with amusement as we danced. I thought of him playing with my fingers, his long pianist fingers touching me. He had strung me along, played me like the proverbial cat with a mouse. I was a silly naive and arrogant little mouse. My face flushed with shame.

The man continued talking, unconcerned with the turmoil of my thoughts. He seemed familiar with many of the venues in Paris and talked with nostalgia as if he wished he could go to them also. Then when I was thoroughly lulled into an accepting torpor, he asked if I thought Dietrich might be in love with me.

I jerked upright, slopping tea in my saucer. I thought Dietrich liked me but love; that was different. Real love seemed almost a myth to me. I doubted anyone had ever loved me, let alone someone like Dietrich.

"My experience with love has made me an unbeliever. It is a concept that doesn't exist."

He simply smiled and looked at his hands. Then he said he wanted me to try to turn Dietrich to our cause, intimating that Dietrich was already working against the Nazis, and as I knew, was under Gestapo surveillance. He wanted me to manipulate Dietrich into loving me and get him to defect.

As if I could! I hadn't even recognised the game he was playing with me all along. I didn't let Sir know what I was thinking but instead asked him how I could do that without compromising my position.

"You are resourceful my dear. I am sure you will find a way."

And then he stood up to go, shaking my hand and saying how much they appreciated my contribution and how sorry he was for upsetting me with the interrogation by Henry Moffatt.

Then I was certain. "You know something more than you are telling me."

"We know we can count on you, my dear."

"Please, I don't want to go back. I'll be shot. If he already knows, it is just a matter of time."

"You underestimate the power you have over him Madeleine. You will be fine, I promise."

I returned to Paris, excessively vigilant and scarcely able to eat or sleep. Now that I knew Dietrich knew who I was, how could I continue in the way we had been before? How long before he had what he needed and handed me over to the Gestapo.

A week passed and then another and I could not fathom what Dietrich wanted from me. If he was using me as a source, he was not very focused. Instead, he was attentive and caring, but never pressed me for information or tried to get me to say or do things I did not want to. Neither could I think of a way of broaching my assignment and I was as jumpy as a frog. I shuddered as I lay sleepless in bed at night imagining the feel of the bullets ripping through my flesh.

I really was a coward but not only that I was also inept. Every time I tried to broach the subject words stuck in my throat. I couldn't turn Dietrich and I couldn't look for Marcel. I hadn't even managed to meet one of the Deaths' Head Brigade to extract revenge for Madeleine's death, as I had vowed. And my fantasy of killing Karl was just that and no more.

All I wanted to do was get away from them all, run and hide and be safe. But where? It was then I made up my mind I would find Marcel and ask him to help me. Perhaps he would be able to think of something or find me somewhere to hide. He, of all the people in the world, was the only one I thought I could trust. He and Anna, they were my family.

17. SARDOU

It was hot for October--so hot. Truly the weather this year was topsy-turvy. The sun beat down on my neck as I walked along the street to the charitable hospital where I was told Dr Sardou worked. My heels beat a tattoo on the cobbled street, and I matched my stride to the syncopated rhythm in my head. My stomach flipped over, turning to liquid as I remembered last night at the Hotel Lutetia with Dietrich. I was beginning to believe that I might be succeeding in making him love me.

My arrival at the hospital brought me from my daydream. I opened glass doors, walking into a reception, cooler than the sun-baked streets, and asked for the Doctor.

A receptionist nodded at me. "Doctor Sardou? Yes, he works here but he is not on shift now." The woman glanced at a clock on the wall. "He may be in soon, in half an hour. You can leave a message if you like." She examined me curiously. "I know you, don't I." She asked seeming a little embarrassed by her boldness.

I shook my head.

"Yes, yes, you are an opera singer at the Palais Garnier, aren't you?"

I inclined my head slightly in acknowledgement. It was the only problem with my role, this constant celebrity. I loved the singing, but not what went with it although I couldn't deny its advantages.

I did not relish going back out into the heatwave that had over-taken Paris even this late in the year, weather that could not make up its mind, but I was also irritated by her rambling on about her passion for opera.

Perspiration trickled down my spine as I willed her to stop talking. I practiced my kind smile on her, my distant, disinterested but gentle smile that Eva called condescending. It was either that or I would scream with frustration. Nodding in accord as though I was listening, I let my mind drift, and her voice retreated to a mumbling in the background.

I thanked fortune that I had finally found the man. It had taken months visiting every hospital I could find until I eventually found him in this backwater with the lunatics. It was very different from the Arc la Bataille where Marcel had told me to find him.

So lost in thought was I that I didn't realise the woman behind reception had stopped talking and was looking at me strangely.

"Are you all right?" She asked, concern crinkling her forehead.

"Yes, I'm sorry--the heat." How rude I must appear.

She smiled saying, "It's terrible and the lack of food with the stress of living like this makes a person distracted. One can't concentrate for a minute. Dr Sardou told me that. Would you like a seat, a drink of water perhaps? It's so hot today, you will be worn out."

The door opened and a man walked in, holding the door while he surveyed the room. He was broad shouldered and handsome, his brown hair too long to be fashionable, his tie loosened with the top buttons of his shirt undone.

"Luc!" The receptionist breathed. "Shut the door, you will let in the heat."

The man was immediately contrite and turned to shut the door.

She's in love with him. A flare of something flickered into life and died again as quickly, and I recognised my old enemy, envy.

She said, "Mademoiselle, I am sorry I do not know your name, except I should because you are famous, I saw you sing at the Le Montecristo. It was my birthday, May...Oh but you must forgive my rudeness. I forget myself. This is Dr Sardou."

Fifteen minutes later, sitting in a small office I explained in a gush of disconnected phrases that I was looking for Marcel, who gave me the Doctor's name when we were in Brussels. My voice was peevish with veiled complaint at how difficult it was to track him down in this out of the way hospital for lunatics.

"They are not lunatics Mademoiselle; they are psychiatric patients in need of care and consideration, as do we all. Only the Nazis think otherwise."

How dare he equate me with a Nazi. I almost hated his sanctimonious superiority at that moment, and in my defence I became haughty and distant, hoping he would immediately apologise for his rudeness to me. I was a famous opera singer, and he was, he was...My dress stuck to my legs with sweaty indignity and all I wanted was to get out of that little room and away from the man with the most uncompromised moral compass I had come across since I met Father O'Bryan. His decency was a slap in the face to my shallowness, but I needed to know if he had heard from Marcel.

"Excuse me. I mean psychiatric hospital." I said it sarcastically but as I did, I knew I was in the wrong and he had been right to correct me although the knowledge didn't help my mood. I wanted to blame him, to wipe that morally superior, but oh so sexy, look of concern from his face.

"Marcel said you worked at the Arc la Bataille." It was an accusation.

He countered with his own complaint. "I did, but I also expected to see you, a long time before now."

I got up. "Sorry to waste your time."

"But Mademoiselle you do not yet have your answer. Please sit down and I will see if I can get you what you want." He shut the door behind him leaving me alone.

I sat down, bemused by my reaction to him. The heat had addled my senses, perhaps it was fear or a longing for the clean safety of domesticity. Instead, I was beset by my lack of morality, for one moment imagining I was superior to this man, who gave his life and energy to causes above his own.

No wonder the receptionist was in love with him. Had I met him before, my life would have been so different. I might be now living in a small house with children playing at my feet, making his dinner, gazing outside to a tidy garden as I waited for him to come home from work.

I sighed. That kind of life was never intended for me. God places us where he wants us. But if there is no God then who or why...? Better not to think about it. I waited for five minutes and was becoming suspicious at the delay. All I wanted was to know where Marcel was. I was contemplating leaving when he came back again.

He stood in front of me, a frown puckering his forehead. In his hands was a small box and a piece of paper. His eyes were light with the intensity of a summer sky, the pulse in his throat beat steadily in a damp hollow between the cleft of his unbuttoned collar. He said, "I have first to ask you something. May I?"

I nodded cautiously, my suspicion heightened but all he did was glance at the piece of paper in his hand and ask, "What was the name of your best friend when you were a child?"

He looked up at me expectantly.

I breathed, "Anna." And as I said her name her face rose before me as a vision, her wide mouth laughing as she danced about on skinny legs, teasing me for my ignorance. I felt flushed and faint with heat and the memory of my loss.

"Mademoiselle, are you all right? It's this blasted heat." He turned hurriedly, laying the paper and the box on the desk as he strode to a small basin, turning the tap to get me a glass of water. He held my head while I drank, a tender gesture I am sure he used for all patients, but his hand burned against my neck.

"I'm fine now, thank you. Yes, it is the heat, I am unused to it." I stood. "Thank you for your time."

"But I haven't finished." Dr Sardou looked worried. "If you are quite well now I will continue." He picked up the paper again, glancing at it before saying, "I am to tell you, she is well and together with Eduardo in America. He requests you join them." He paused, then said, "He left me with some things of yours, in this box. I was to be sure first it was really you."

I had stopped listening. Anna was with Marcel in America! I couldn't believe it. Was Dr Sardou lying? I held out my hand for the paper, but he took my hand instead, feeling my pulse.

I felt uncomfortable with my hand clasped in his, but all he said was, "Your pulse is racing, perhaps you should rest a minute."

I jerked my hand away. "Thank you Doctor, may I have the paper and the box."

He said, "Of course."

I stood up. "I am fine I will not disturb you any further."

"If you insist." He picked up the paper, carefully folding it along the lines already creased, and placed it on top of the box, handing both to me. "Marcel said you are a friend to our cause. There is something you might do in exchange, a message…"

"No." I grabbed the box and paper and wrenched open his door.

I felt his eyes on me as I walked the length of the corridor, trying not to turn around to look at him one last time. I knew there was more to this man's story, but I could not afford to ask. I left the hospital, knowing that I had been unforgivably rude. All he asked was a quid pro quo, something in exchange for the package, but intuition warned me of danger.

I had been ungrateful but what more must I sacrifice? Anger rose in my throat and then resignation. This was my life. This was war—and each small decision I had ever made had led me inexorably into the hands of my puppet masters. What if I refused their bidding and went back into the hospital, back to Dr Sardou, to his honest blue gaze to find out what he might want of me, for I was sure he was also like Marcel, like my birth father, Communist resistance and I couldn't afford to get mixed up in that also.

Yet possibly it was all the effect of my frenzied imagination. I blamed the heat for my behaviour, and it wasn't until I sat in the little velo-taxi that I looked inside the box. It held a Spanish passport in the name of Aurelia Valdez. My face looked back at me from the photo. Where did he get this? A slip of paper fell from the pages of the passport onto my lap. On it was a poste restante address in New York, America.

My hands trembled as I flicked through the pages of the passport, scanning the paper Dr Sardou gave me but there was nothing else. I leaned back in the Velo. Anna was with Marcel in America. They are safe. The two people I loved most in the world are safe. I had to go to them, but I knew this decision was not one I would be allowed to make.

18. VIOLETTA

I sat huddled in a blanket; my legs curled under me for warmth. Snow lay thick on the ground outside in the cold December afternoon. There was no longer any fuel for heating, not even Dietrich could get any for me although thanks to him we survived reasonably well, given the widespread starvation that gripped France in that desolate winter.

"Madeleine you must leave." Dietrich strode back and forth
across the tiny space of the sitting room. "They took the dossier of your activities to Hoffermann's office. I have seen it myself. They are suspicious and their suspicions are focused on you, but they must convince the Gestapo. It is only Hoffermann who protects you now. Once he sees the file, things will change and before long you will be brought in for questioning."

"Such foolishness. They would suspect their mothers." I hoped to steer Dietrich away from his focus on my activities. "Anyway, I am to sing at the Tuileries Gardens again this Sunday. French songs with a German band, isn't that civilised? The Gestapo love me, they don't want to hurt me, and you will look after me Dietrich."

He stopped pacing and a fierce expression consumed his face. "I won't be able to. They will ship you to Germany under the Night and Fog decree and I will not be able to help you. Madeleine if you remain here, I can no longer protect you." He kneeled before me and buried his face in my lap. "My love, I couldn't bear it if something happened to you."

I looked down at the back of his beautifully shaped head. He's a handsome man for one in his thirties. I stroked his neck feeling the corded strength as I traced my fingers down to his broad shoulders, then back up to touch the bristly hairs at his nape with my thumb. I said, "Anyway what is an administrator doing in the offices of the Geheime Staatspolizei? I thought you despised them?"

I looked at him innocently, keeping up the pretence that he was just an administrator, a civil servant in occupied Paris. This was my last opportunity to do what I was sent to do. This was Dietrich at his most vulnerable. Then I would leave before the Gestapo got me. He was right, it was only a matter of time, and the reason I had been free to move about was because of his protection and because Karl knew who I really was and used me. Karl knew I could not be the British agent Violetta as the Abwehr believed. Bizarrely, Karl's distain of me had been my protection until now.

I was careful with my wording. "Come away with me Dietrich. We can go to Spain. You can leave this behind and start a new life. I know your heart is not in this war, you have the soul of a musician not a soldier. I know how you despise what some of your people are doing."

Then he shocked me as he grasped my arms, so his fingers dug into my flesh. His face was wild as he said, "We can stop the games now Madeleine, I know you are a British agent. I know you work for SOE; you and Louis are both working for David Asquith. I know you are Violetta. What I don't know is why Hoffermann protects you."

I was more astonished at his use of Louis and David's names than admitting he knew I was Violetta. I never suspected Monsieur Copeau of being SOE. How stupid I am. How could I have not seen it, but then aside from our contacts we weren't told who else was out there in case we were caught and tortured for names. Dietrich's voice sounded hurt and angry as he grasped my arms.

"You think me a fool Madeleine. Yes, I know Louis. I also know David Asquith and Giles Guilford. I was at Cambridge with them sixteen years ago, Giles was our Tutor. They didn't tell you that, did they? I know they want me to turn traitor and they use you to do it. I knew before you told me that your name is Aurélie Avraham, a Belgian Jew. I also know you pass messages through your terrorist contacts mostly Lucien Rochelle and formerly Madame Ménard. You wanted to meet me, I also wished to meet you, remember—but I didn't think it would come to this. I didn't intend to fall in love."

I tried to keep my face expressionless asking in a small voice, "Lucien?" I was shaking now so much that my teeth began chattering. He continued as if he could see through my lies, to my soul. I couldn't believe he admitted it. He set me up from the beginning. He knew all along and he arranged the meeting.

"Yes, my dear I know who he is. The only reason you were still alive when I met you was that I planned to turn you into an agent, one who we could have used against the British, and until now this is what my office believes I am doing."

I could not contain my shock. He said he was turning me into his agent. He was turning me into a double agent for the Germans. I wanted to laugh then. I could feel the urge pushing at the edge of my sanity as the absurdity of the situation struck me. I hung my head so he wouldn't see my face.

"My superiors are not satisfied with my progress. They need to know who is behind the increased attacks against the Wehrmacht. They suspect you are playing me for a fool and demand I step up the intelligence or they will take you in and talk to you themselves, and Madeleine, we both know what that means."

"Dietrich you are hurting me." I jerked my wrists from his hands, my mind in a swirl of panic.

"I have seen your passport Madeleine, the Spanish passport. You should use it before they come.

I shouted. "You've been through my things!"

He shrugged, ignoring my fury. "You've been through mine."

It was true but I had found nothing. He was better at this than me.

"What is Karl Hoffermann to you Madeleine? I don't understand why he doesn't have you arrested. It cannot be just the stories about me that you feed him surely."

I shrugged watchfully as he stared at me puzzled.

"My man tells me he insists you are not Violetta. We know you are British SOE, yet Hoffermann insists you are not. How is it you fool him? You do not cover your tracks that well for a spy, my dear. What is it that he knows about you that I do not know? Tell me Madeleine. I can't protect you against the Gestapo. When he sees the Abwehr dossier, it will convince Hoffermann, and they will come and arrest you. It is a matter of hours not days. I can help you--get you a travel permit, train tickets—anything, but you have to go, leave France."

A clattering noise stopped us. Holding my breath, I turned in fear to Dietrich. Had he brought the Gestapo here with him? I heard whispered giggling. It was Eva and Marie home. Dietrich didn't move.

"Go!" I hissed. Never before had he remained here with me when they were home. I needed time to think.

He stood his ground and again grasped my wrists. "Madeleine if you won't think of yourself, think of your friends. Can you not see what danger you are putting these two women in? Their association with you makes them a target also."

"No, it's not true!"

The two women walked into the room, surprise bringing Eva to a stop while Marie bumped into her.

"We didn't know you had company Madeleine." Eva sniffed her disapproval at his uniform as she tried to tidy escaping tendrils of coppery hair.

Marie began giggling again. They were both drunk. I could see Eva swaying as she stood staring at Dietrich, trying to maintain an aloof hostility on her face. Her smudged lipstick was evidence of recent passion.

Dietrich took my arm and pulled me from the couch. "Ladies," He nodded, as he marched me past their befuddled faces towards my bedroom. He pulled an overnight bag from under my bed and began going through my wardrobe. His frustration at the fripperies of fashion was clear as he sucked his teeth, discarding one item after another. Eventually he pulled out some walking boots and a severe woollen skirt and jacket.

"Change into the skirt and jacket and sensible shoes. You can take some underwear, and a change of blouse but you should travel light."

I sat passively on the bed. He was ordering me about like one of his subordinates whom he could command as he willed, but I didn't know if I could trust him. Why would he try to save me if he thought I was Violetta? Was this a ruse, another of his manipulations?

I tried once more. "Dietrich, come with me, please."

"What, so you can turn me against my own?" His voice was harsh. "Madeleine, I don't like what is happening. I don't want this war to continue any more than the next one. Some of my best friends are British, you—you know I love you. I would do anything for you."

He loved me. I couldn't believe it. All this time I had been trying to make him love me and now he finally said it and I didn't believe him. "Then come with me."

"No Madeleine." He looked into my eyes, and I looked away. I heard his sigh. "If I thought that you loved me, and we had a future together I would go with you, but you don't. I am an assignment to you."

"No! That's not true."

"I'm not a fool, but I am content that I at least had some of your love. Now my duty lies elsewhere but first I will see you safe."

There was a timid knocking on the bedroom door as Eva poked her head around, taking in the disarray and the suitcase.

"You are going somewhere?" She shook her head as if to clear the distraction, and then made a gesture with her hand as if urgently summoning me to a private conference. I followed her out the door where she whispered, "Lucien is here at the back door. What's he doing in here?" She jerked her thumb towards my bedroom.

"It's a long story Eva, I'll tell you later." I walked through the house to the kitchen.

Lucien looked worse than the last time I saw him. He was filthy with black smudges across his face and his collar.

"What are you doing here Lucien?"

"Madeleine, they are coming--you must leave now."

I looked at him blankly wondering how he knew.

"Now Madeleine! They are on their way; their car is stopped not blocks away as they await reinforcement. I overheard them."

"She's going."

I spun around as Dietrich came up behind me.

Lucien stared at him, and then he looked to me with accusation and betrayal written across his face.

"No Lucien."

Dietrich interrupted. "There is no time now. You take Madeleine with you. There is a cafe near to the Hotel Lutetia. Someone will be waiting for you. It may take me a while, but I will get there. I can distract them, but you must hurry." He handed me the thick woollen clothes, walking shoes, stockings, and my coat. "We don't have much time, quickly change Madeleine. I will collect a few more things while you dress."

"Who are you to give orders? Madeleine, he is not to be trusted." Lucien's eyes didn't leave Dietrich as he spoke.

Dietrich rounded on him, his eyes flashing dangerously in the dim light, voice low with intent. "Lucien if you do what I tell you we can get her away, if you play stupid ego games, we are all lost. You may not like it but for this moment we are on the same side." He added as an afterthought. "Just for this moment and not again. If she is in the Abwehrstelle, they will not look for her there. They will look for her at the university or one of your hang outs."

He turned to me. "Please Madeleine."

I nodded. My mind was cleared, and it galvanised me from my lethargy. "Yes. Lucien we can trust his word. I will change."

I pushed past Eva and Marie, who both crowded into the corridor watching in an alcoholic infused bewilderment.

Dietrich turned to them saying, "Ladies if you wish to stay safe you will do exactly as I tell you. Do you understand?"

Minutes later we left as they arrived, three black Mercedes Benz rolling quietly to a halt outside the house. Dietrich walked out to meet them as they alighted, pulling their greatcoats up against the cold. I could hear him talking and saw him pointing to the house, saying, "She's bolted."

Lucien pulled me along as I stumbled over cobbles in the laneway behind the house, my eyes stretched tight with fear, failure and choking loss closing my throat.

It took us two hours to get the few kilometres to the cafe. Lucien knew the back alleys well, but it was slow going hugging the shadows to keep out of sight. He was wisely cautious. I was impatient thinking he was being overly wary, but I said nothing. My track record showed I wasn't very good at assessing danger.

There were few people out on the cold dark streets even though it wasn't yet curfew, and there was little time to delay. It was more dangerous for us being caught out after 9pm. Anyone out after curfew would be an obvious target. I worried about Dietrich. Would he convince them? Or would he be in danger because of me.

Eventually we arrived at the cafe and stood sheltering in its dark shadows, debating whether we should go inside or wait exposed in the street. A man in civilian clothes came out and stood on the steps, looking both ways along the street. He walked towards us and said, "Mademoiselle Madeleine?"

I peered at him, trying to see if this was a trap but Lucien was now committed, and said, "Yes, this is she."

The man walked closer and embraced me. I remained stiff with surprise, but it was a friendly greeting as if from an old friend. He took my arm leading us into the cafe and ordered coffee. We sat down to wait.

There were quite a few people in the cafe, all German soldiers. I stared at the door, picking at the skin around my nails, with a sick feeling in my stomach. Fear mixed with euphoric triumph because Dietrich said he loved me, and I told myself I had succeeded in a game I thought was beyond my capability. I was also terrified that he would betray me, and I would be caught by the Gestapo. I glanced across the table at Lucien who looked like he was trying to make himself invisible. Then a tearing blast of a distant explosion rattled the windows.

The men in the cafe stood as one, their training masking their thoughts and feelings. Efficiency and purpose took over. They grabbed guns, caps, and coats as they rushed outside. The cold air swirled into the cafe through the open door as they left.

The waiter walked to the door peering outside then closed it softly, turning to us with a shrug. Our coffee came, real coffee. Only we three and the staff remained in the cafe, the man who met us blew gently into his coffee, unconcerned as if the blast had not happened.

"What is it?" I touched his arm to get his attention.

He shrugged. "Probably terrorists--Communists I would think. Now Russia has betrayed us, Stalin's bandits will try to destroy Paris, turn it to rubble. They have no respect nor appreciation of beauty. Don't worry. They won't get far. We have the best men. They won't get away with much more of their terror before they are caught, but we are perfectly safe in here."

I glanced at Lucien who shrugged. Clearly, he thought the story plausible. We sat in silence drinking our coffee. Thirty minutes passed and my agitation increased, marked off by each minute that ticked around the clock on the wall. It showed eight thirty and we did not have long before curfew. Then the cafe door opened, and Dietrich walked in. The man with us stood, and bowing to me slightly, he said, "Mademoiselle." Then he picked up his coat and left and Dietrich sat down in the seat he vacated. The waiter walked towards us, but he waved him away.

Dietrich pushed a package across to Lucien. "You must go; keep away from the river. They will be scouring its banks for bandits. There is a clean shirt and papers for you and a pass across the frontier to the southern zone. You are going to visit your sick Grandmother at Limoges. You will need to get to Gare d'Austerlitz in the morning, the train leaves at ten. You must hurry and get off the streets now before curfew. They will place roadblocks soon. The explosion was across the river at 84 Avenue Foch."

A smile played at the corner of his mouth and our eyes met. Everyone knew that was the headquarters of the Gestapo. He glanced again at Lucien. "Clean your face, it has smudges, and it will draw attention."

Lucien wiped his face with one of the café's clean white napkins leaving dark smudges soiling the starched linen.

Dietrich stood up, placing some money on the table for our coffee. It was far more than coffee should cost and I saw the gleam in the waiter's eye as he bowed. Another of Dietrich's spies I thought uncharitably, forgetting momentarily the danger of my situation.

We followed him outside. His car was parked at the curb, and he held the door for me as Lucien scurried away. Dietrich looked around briefly before getting into the driver's seat and releasing the foot break.

"Where are we going?" I asked the question not really expecting a reply, but I wanted him to look at me. His set face, jaw clenched in determination, frightened me. But he didn't speak. He didn't even look at me as he drove through the dark streets. A muscle jumped in his cheek but otherwise his face remained stony. There was a black smudge along his jaw line. I raised my hand to wipe it and he jerked his head away in suspicion. I hated the way that look made me feel.

"You talk about Lucien cleaning his face, what about you? What is this black stuff?"

He glanced in the rear-view mirror but in the dim light could see nothing. He pulled his handkerchief from his pocket. "Clean it." He angled his chin towards me as he kept his eyes on the road ahead, the narrow beams from the semi-blacked out lamps casting little illumination.

A suspicion began forming in my mind. Did Dietrich set the explosive in Avenue Foch's headquarters? Is that how he knew they would first search the banks of the Seine?

"It was you!"

His face remained a mask, and he said, "We are nearly at the station. You will go to Bayonne, then on to Hendaye and across the Santiago Bridge over the Bidasoa River to Irun. There is a British diplomatic mission at Bilbao. With your Spanish passport you will be able to cross as a Spanish person returning home. You must remember the country is Franco's now. Do not let them think you have Republican sympathies. You will need to think of a good cover story for why you have been in France in case you are asked but it is unlikely. Get rid of any French papers you have. You don't want to be returned to France by the Spanish police. Can you speak Spanish?

I shook my head, "Just a little. Will you not come with me?" My voice was small?

He was so cold, and business like in his arrangements. "I have your suitcase and handbag in the boot. I took the liberty of placing a purse with Spanish pesetas in your handbag for when you cross the border. I have also put the Spanish passport and other effects along with the return portion of a train ticket. I must say the Spanish passport is good quality. I would almost believe it to be the genuine article."

Nodding miserably, I was close to tears as he issued instructions. We pulled into the Gare Montparnasse, avoiding the throng of bicycles and a bus, as travellers hurried to beat curfew. Dietrich parked the car and turned to me, looking into my eyes, his darkening with emotion. He raised his hand tracing the outline of my face as if he wanted to embed its shape in memory. Then abruptly he turned away, switching off the ignition and got out of the car, retrieving my suitcase and handbag from the boot.

He opened my door, holding his hand out to help me alight. We gazed at each other as moments passed. I willed him to kiss me once more but instead, he took his scarf from his neck and draped it about my neck, proprietarily adjusting my coat and hat as if I were a schoolchild. He summoned a porter who took my suitcase.

Dietrich tucked my hand into the crook of his arm. We walked along the pavement and into the imposing station entrance. Soldiers saluted him, a Gendarme stood aside, pedestrians looked at the ground and stepped aside, making way, bobbing their heads in subjugated fear. He led me to a train waiting at the platform, and as I stepped into the carriage a whistle blew as if it had been waiting only for me to arrive.

I leaned out the window. "Dietrich." I held out my hand in supplication as the train lurched forward.

He remained tall and erect with his face neutral. His arms hung loosely by his sides, relaxed and in command as he watched me leave. His hand did not lift to wave as I retreated into the cold night.

19. MADRID

I was alone in the luxurious surrounding of the first-class compartment. I held his scarf against my cheek inhaling the lingering smell of him, his cologne, his soap, just him. Loneliness swamped me. He was most likely married anyway. I never asked. He was right, he was an assignment that was all. It was fear that heightened my sense of longing for him now, nothing more. I had lost my protector and now I was alone, but I could manage without him.

I tried to sleep but it was fitful, full of ghosts from the past. I awoke at every stop, scarcely breathing as I waited for someone to hammer on my compartment door and arrest me. Lying rigid, I strained for the sound of footfalls coming to my carriage, until with a gasp the train's breaks released, and it jerked into motion once more, rattling along until the next stop.

Its steam whistle sounded at inexplicable intervals and three times guards banged on my door asking for my papers. Each time I spoke in French until the puzzled look of a German soldier would have me switch to German. It was something for which they were so grateful, they treated me with great courtesy. If it were a French official, I would speak French eliciting a contented harrumph. Silently I thanked the

197

nuns at school for their attention to my gift for mimicry and language.

I reached Hendaye without real incident. There I was to change trains because of the rail gauge difference between France and Spain. Dietrich had not mentioned that, and I wished I had previously travelled by rail instead of flying to Madrid. At least then I would know what to expect.

At Hendaye I waited for hours for a train to Bilbao, sitting on the platform with countless others, mostly peasants, who shared their bread with me. I was eaten up with an ache and a strange kind of jitteriness. Here was the test. My Spanish accent was poor and trying to brush up while speaking with the peasants at the station didn't help, for I was in a first-class compartment and clearly not a peasant. Therefore, I did not seek to mimic their accents. Mostly I remained silent, nodding thanks, and limiting my conversation. Mine was a schoolgirl's Spanish, good enough to pick my way through a novel but not good enough to be taken for a Spanish native.

In my mind I began making up an elaborate story about leaving Spain with my parents as a child. By the time the train arrived it was late and as I boarded, Spanish officials asked for my passport. I prayed they would not want to engage me in conversation. As it turned out there was little to worry about as they merely glanced at my passport and bid me welcome home before passing on to the next passenger. I threw myself onto the seat in my compartment, knowing the train would get to Bilbao too late, and the consulate would be closed.

At Bilbao I found a ticket office and with some of the pesetas Dietrich gave me I bought a ticket to Madrid. I began to feel more confident. No one pointed a finger at me and shouted imposter. I would get away with my disguise as a Spanish woman despite my limited language skill.

My head ached as I leaned my feverish forehead against the cold glass of the train window looking out at a moonlit Spanish countryside. Lights shining out from every building, showed my arrival in a country that was not worried about war and aerial bombings, although there were plenty of signs of the recent civil war, with broken or pock marked buildings and deep shell holes. Exhausted after the last days of vigilance I lay down and slept through the night.

We arrived in Madrid at the start of the business day. Outside the station, the teeming concourse deafened me. Buses, horse-drawn carts, and donkeys vied for space on the street. Cars and lorries belched black smoke, while people shouted, and pedestrians barely escaped being run over in the melee. I tried to get my bearings. Which way was the British Embassy? Nothing was familiar. I thought my short journey to Madrid with the opera might have given me some landmark I could recognise but there was nothing.

Eventually I plucked up the courage to ask a passer-by, who I was sure was not an official. He pointed down the long boulevard ahead reeling off directions that I did not fully understand. I thanked him, nodding vigorously and began walking along the pavement clutching my suitcase with its meagre contents.

I walked, what seemed to be, halfway across Madrid until needing to rest, I stopped at a pavement cafe and ordered rolls and coffee for breakfast. A mournful waiter told me I was on the right route for the Embassy. At least it would be open for business once I eventually arrived. I scowled at the ridges on my palm caused by the handle of my suitcase, ruefully aware that I should have taken a taxi, but I was unsure how much it would cost or if I had enough money.

I was glad of the boots Dietrich had insisted I wear, and for the woollen suit, for a northeast wind blew across the city. I finished my breakfast and got up to lug my suitcase the long final kilometres to the Embassy. The scurrying clouds had looked like it might rain, but the sun eventually broke through and rose in the sky, bathing the buildings in light and burning off the last of the morning mist.

By the time I arrived at the Embassy the winter sun blazed overhead in what was now a clear sky. My woollen suit stuck to me as I stood outside the building staring at its Spanish facade. Through the entrance I could see the arched cloister surrounding a courtyard, with an expanse of lawn along one side. No one challenged me, and no one asked me for papers.

For a moment I imagined Henry Moffatt's face as he saw me walk into his office. This time it would be I who was unannounced. I didn't tell London I was fleeing my post. I hadn't time, but then what could they say—that I must remain? I thought not. I imagined being welcomed. Perhaps sitting down to real English tea once again with Henry and the man I only knew as Sir. I imagined commenting on how nice it was to all meet again, being very English.

I was already discarding the Parisian facade to don my British persona. I would be nicer to Henry Moffatt. I would apologise for shouting at him last time we met. They would give me papers and a ticket to England where I would see Guilly again and my ordeal would be over.

Reality dragged me from my daydream as I was stopped by a Spanish policeman at the entrance. He asked me my business and for my papers. I hadn't prepared anything to say. I hadn't made up a story to get by, thinking I was free in Spain. I had forgotten to be careful about constructing my fables, only thinking of getting out of France. I gawped for what seemed like minutes at the man who looked back at me with eternal patience, as if I were a simpleton who must be humoured.

Eventually I said, "I am here to see Mr. Henry Moffatt."

"You have an appointment?"

"Yes." I lied, thinking Henry would see me. I said it with more conviction than I felt.

"Papers," he demanded. I fumbled for my Spanish passport. He took his time examining it, suspicion aroused by the solitary stamp leaving France and one on entry to Spain. "Wait here," he commanded, turning to disappear with my passport.

I didn't wait. I had made it to Spain, but I was not safe. What if Henry was no longer here? I had entered the country illegally on a forged passport. The Spanish locked foreigners like me in camps. If one were lucky, the British Embassy would eventually come to the rescue but only for subjects with British nationality. What would they do to me?

If the Spanish thought me French they would send me back. If I claimed to be British and the Embassy did not claim me, I was done for. The Spanish would hand me over to German police in occupied France. I walked away. My steps quickening in case the policeman returned. I walked to a group of trees across the road, standing with a trunk between me and the Embassy, peering around its girth to see what the policeman would do when he returned.

When he came back, he had a uniformed consulate guard with him. The guard looked about, speaking rapidly to the policeman. The policeman pointed to where I had been standing. The guard threw-up his hands in a gesture of exasperation and walked back inside. After what seemed an age the guard came out again accompanied by another man.

With relief, I saw the familiar tall, stooped figure. His round glasses caught the sunlight and flared briefly as he turned. I walked out from behind the tree just as the guard gestured at the policeman. Henry looked about himself pushing his glasses higher on his nose. He turned to walk back inside.

I ran across the road calling his name.

A vehicle screeched to a standstill; its bumper skewered to the pavement as it tried to avoid me. The driver shouted obscenities, but I rushed onwards to a disconcerted Henry Moffatt. I wanted to hug him. Seeing him standing there with his pink forehead glistening in the bright sunlight, was like a blessing.

"Miss Chaumont! What are you doing here?"

"Oh Henry, I'll tell you everything, but can I have a cup of tea first?"

We sat in his office waiting for the tea to arrive. He listened in silence as I told him the story although I was circumspect about how much I said, leaving out the role Dietrich played in my escape. I am not sure why, but I felt a sense of secrecy about him.

I knew I succeeded in doing what the British wanted of me, but stubbornly I felt Dietrich did it for me personally, not for them or for any war effort or any country. He did it from decency and because he loved me, and I didn't want to repay that by giving them leverage to blackmail him into doing something he wouldn't otherwise do. So, I kept quiet.

"Henry mopped his brow with his large hanky and said, "I will need to contact London for instructions. In the meantime, you will have to stay here, out of sight. The city is crawling with Gestapo agents, and it wouldn't do if you were abducted and whisked back to France. The Embassy is a bit crowded I'm afraid. We have all sorts awaiting repatriation. In the interim I will provide you with some writing equipment. You can write it all down. London will need a report as soon as possible. I don't suppose you type, do you?"

I watched him arrange things, feeling a wash of intense pleasure at his steadfastness. "Oh, Henry, I am so glad you are here. I'm so sorry about the way I shouted at you last time we met. I was scared I think, but it doesn't excuse my rudeness."

He blushed, his pink face turning a shade deeper. He peered through his thick round lenses. "It's quite all right you know. What you are doing for us is jolly good. What you have done, well jolly brave."

I didn't think I had done anything much at all. I had failed in my task, the most important assignment I had been given. All I had done really was pass messages between people and sing songs with unknown messages contained in their words. I was hardly a success at being a spy, and I certainly wasn't brave.

Besides, I let the side down by being discovered and getting my emotions entangled with one who was their enemy, even if clearly, he was not mine. If I worked harder, perhaps more deliberately, I could have turned Dietrich, and he would be here with me now. I pushed the discomforting thoughts away returning to mimic the spirit I imagined Henry expected.

"Yes, quite." I said ending the conversation, busying myself with pouring tea. I was pulling on my disguise as a stalwart English woman, mimicking Guilly. Dear Guilly, she would be someone of whom Henry could approve.

My stay at the Embassy seemed interminable. The place was crowded with refugees and escapees. We were camped in various accommodations in the grounds of the Embassy. There were soldiers, those unlucky ones who had been left behind at the great retreat of the British Expeditionary Forces eighteen months ago.

All this time, they had been left to dodge and hide and make their way through war zones and occupied territory until they reached Madrid. They were left behind while I got away. Left to make their way from farm to farm, trusting in people, hiding, being hidden, helped by brave people who despised the common enemy, my countrymen.

There were also a half dozen British civilians who were trapped and had fled before the invading army, some became separated from wives and children, some were trying to get back to wives and children, some wives and children had lost their husbands and fathers. There were pilots who had been shot down, bailing out of burning aeroplanes, surviving while others died in flames or were captured.

These were the lucky ones who had escaped detection. Their survival weighed heavily as they remembered friends who had not been as lucky. I heard stories of how they placed their trust in strangers who helped them escape, climbing over the high Pyrenees through impossible conditions. Now they were holed up here, some cheerful, some withdrawn, some without papers and some without hope, but all waiting for the Embassy to get them home.

I listened humbly to stories of heroism, of Dutch and French women and young children bravely leading British pilots through German patrolled prohibited zones. I heard of astonishing feats of endurance as men and women climbed the rugged mountain range, of altitude sickness, of hunger, of frostbite, bravado, and fear. I had done nothing in comparison with these people.

I also heard horror tales and rumours of imprisonment, of work camps, of death camps, of mass executions, until I excused myself from the conversation. I could not take the anguish, the guilt by association, the atrocities committed on defenceless people, children. Towns had been wiped out, whole villages executed for harbouring fugitives, brave men and women risked and gave their lives for others, finding safe passage through German occupied territory.

I maintained my fiction. I was Belgian to the core, once again Aurélie Avraham who may have once had a Jewish ancestor, but I really didn't know much about that. I was now a good Christian girl who wore white ankle socks and second-hand clothing that had been donated to the Embassy, and I helped where I could.

A few nights before Christmas, the Ambassador and his wife held a Christmas party for their numerous guests. I told Henry, I would sing if he could find someone to play an instrument. One of the pilots could play the piano. Another one, a Canadian, played the saxophone. I pushed away memories of Dietrich playing the saxophone. He was my past now. I must bury him there.

I am not sure where Henry found a saxophone, but I had good company that night as we made our way through my entire jazz repertoire. For the first time I tried scat singing, not knowing many of the words to the newer tunes the Canadian introduced. Others sang too and someone recited some stirring poetry about another war. It was a poem of loyalty and courage where everyone died.

The room fell silent as the poem progressed. It was about a charge of cavalry so futile I could not comprehend its point. I listened to the words, *all in the valley of death, rode the six hundred.* I saw the charge as it forged through a barrage of Russian guns. I imagined the overwhelming odds against them as they were cut down, man and horse. I imagined the carnage, the shrieking horses and blood and wondered at the futility of such heroism.

Theirs not to reason why, theirs but to do and die.

I wanted to weep at its pointless gallantry.

Storm'd at with shot and shell, Boldly they rode and well, Into the jaws of Death, Into the mouth of Hell.

The memory of the roadside slaughter in Belgium rose in my mind, and I saw again the bodies jerking as machine guns ripped through flesh. I heard the fire maelstroms in Dunkerque, saw the rattling rain of casings, heard again the noise of fire consuming buildings. Smelt the burning flesh and felt the oily water closing above my head.

The poem ended and the speaker fell silent. Not a whisper disturbed the air as each one of us relived memories.

Then a voice rose in song and was joined by other voices. *"There'll always be an England."* They sang. More voices strengthened the chorus until the piano could barely be heard.

I listen carefully to the unfamiliar words, trying to memorise them and noted the sadness rising in my chest at the senselessness of our countries fighting each other. What purpose could it possibly achieve? Taking the tension out of the room, someone else began to cite what I understood to be a nursery rhyme.

There was a crooked man, and he walked a crooked mile, He found a crooked sixpence against a crooked stile; He bought a crooked cat, which caught a crooked mouse, And they all lived together in a little crooked house.

The rhyme was me, my life. It was never a crooked man but a crooked girl who lived in a crooked house.

Trying to distract myself from my own misery I drank the sherry which had been provided by the ambassador's wife. It was my first taste of the sweet Spanish wine, and it eased my aching soul as I stood watching the party swirl about me.

It was a strange Christmas party. The saxophone player and the English pilot came over to talk to me. The sandy haired Canadian sax player, his name was Howard Newton, was called Newt by his friends. He laughed so hard at my puzzlement at being called after a lizard, it broke the spell of my melancholy.

He explained a Newt wasn't a lizard it was a type of water salamander. That didn't help my understanding at all until the tall English pilot, Michael, or Micky as his friends called him explained that Newt was an abbreviation of his surname, which until then I had not known. I turned away as Henry put on a record.

In shock I walked over to him, looking at him questioningly.

"What are you doing Henry?"

"It's the aria from *La Traviata* by Verdi. I love it." He blushed and took off the record. "Perhaps this one is more suitable. Vera Lynn, have you heard it? It's called *A Nightingale sang in Berkeley Square*. It's the latest thing." His cherubic cheeks pushed his glasses up his face. "The thing about the song is that there are no nightingales in Berkeley Square." He laughed, "Ironic isn't it?" He peered at me with myopic intensity.

I wasn't sure what he was trying to say but decided I didn't want to know. I moved away while the song played, listening carefully to the words about two lovers meeting. Despite that small piece of strangeness, the night was wonderful. I almost forgot the sense of loneliness and longing I had left behind with Dietrich.

Over the next days, to pass the time we played cards, watched the occasional cinema show and I typed report after report for Henry, despite it being Christmas. I had little else to do. On New Year's Eve, Micky the pilot piano player left with a group of his compatriots, and I felt sad to see them go. He left his address begging me to write. Against my better judgement I promised I would.

A few days later, Newt left with another group, their bus bound for Gibraltar and a ship back to England. He promised to look me up if I gave him an address. I told him I didn't know where I would be. I didn't tell him about the Guildford's. I did not want any more entanglements with soldiers or pilots or anyone.

Finally, my turn came. Henry said he was to accompany me, for he was due leave in England. I was glad to have his company on the long journey across Southern Spain, for I was the only woman in a coach load of airmen and soldiers.

Two days it took for us to cross that vast stretch of Spain. The scenery breathtaking as we drove across the mountains. Clouds swirled in deep valleys. Rocky outcrops contrasted silvery against the drab olive and lush greens as mountains gave way to rolling hills and plains. We passed places where the earth was laid bare, showing rocky soil that somehow gave sustenance to kilometres of crops and fruit trees. Trenches and bombed villages reminding us that the country had been shattered by civil war. Yet, it was a land full of beauty, texture, and colour in the brilliant Iberian sunlight.

We stayed overnight in Cordoba, where we were free to go out at night for the first time since I had been with the Embassy. My fear of discovery and capture were subdued by the beauty and hospitality of the place. The brightly lit streets thronged with placid families, strolling in the cool clear evening air. Henry escorted me to dinner, laughing at my greediness, asking how one who ate so much, could remain so slim.

He didn't know the frugality of my life in Paris, couldn't know the hardship endure by famine as the German army hungrily consumed everything, while they sent French people's food to the German troops, who were also starving on the Russian front. They took so much food that animals starved, and farmers no longer had seed left to plant.

Henry had no idea. He thought of me as glamorous and exciting, but he didn't know who I was, or what it is to want. I threw back Fino to cleanse my palate and my mind. I would not spoil this evening with anger at his ignorance. I drank too much, and Henry's head began to swim out of focus. I leaned on him going back to our hotel and he kissed me, gently at first and then more insistently.

My drunken state craved the warmth and touch of another human being. Momentarily, I forgot who and where I was and leaned into his embrace. As I did Dietrich's face materialised in my mind. I jerked back from him, my eyes teary and wide.

Henry looked immediately contrite and began apologising, declaring his love and shame at taking advantage. The Fino and food rose together in my throat, and I threw up in a ditch.

The following morning, I awoke with a pounding head, my tongue stuck to the roof of my mouth. At breakfast Henry ordered coffee and rolls, insisting food would help. He wanted to talk about that kiss, but I told him it wasn't a good idea. It wouldn't be professional. He said he understood and immediately retreated to his former correct politeness, my friend and colleague once more. I was relieved. I didn't want to hurt him.

That evening we arrived at the Spanish border near the town of La Linea. A long line of low buildings crossed the entrance to the border. We alighted from the coaches and were escorted into one of the buildings where Henry left me for a moment to speak with someone. The others in our coach were directed through another door. I was left alone in the room with its closed counters and dusty windows wondering if I was in Spanish or British territory.

A Spanish cleaner came in with a mop and bucket. I sat in a chair far enough out of his way while he mopped. He swirled the mop around in circles, in what looked to me to create more mess than it cleaned. Watching him warily I noticed he mopped closer and closer to where I sat until he was next to me.

He stopped mopping and glanced around the room then in a low voice, he said, "Signorina Aurélie?"

I remain stony faced wondering who he was, who had sent him, what he knew. My mind raced, my Spanish passport was in the name of Aurelia Valdez my temporary British papers were in the name of Aurélie Avraham. I was not sure which he used Aurelia or Aurélie. Did it matter? Should I pretend I was someone else? How likely was it he would know my name unless he knew more than just my name?

When in doubt stick as close to the truth as is possible, I heard my instructor saying, but without giving anything away. The more lies you tell the harder it is to remember them and keep from tripping yourself up. For what seemed like minutes nothing moved in the room. He waited for my answer.

Eventually, I said simply, "Yes."

He nodded, taking a crumpled envelope from his overall pocket, and handed it to me. Then he picked up his bucket, all pretence at mopping vanished as he walked towards the door.

"Wait!" My heart was thumping so hard it caused my throat to constrict.

He let himself out the door shutting it quietly behind him. I contemplated running after him but at that moment Henry reappeared with another man. I stuffed the envelope into my pocket and stood up. Henry looked at the floor still wet from the pretence at mopping. He raised his eyebrows but otherwise said nothing as he introduced me to a tall, lean man with wavy dark hair and a finely pointed moustache, who he introduced as Bartholomew Wrexham, an officer from Passport Control, Immigration Services. I knew he was not from Immigration. I was to be managed and interviewed by SIS, Britain's intelligence service.

Mr. Wrexham shook my hand, holding it in both of his as he said, "My friends call me Rex." His dark eyes glistened like deep oily pools, and he gazed at me for minutes longer than what I thought was necessary. Still holding my hand, he then led me through another door down a corridor. We passed the others who had been our companions on the coach from Madrid. They sat on hard benches waiting listlessly for someone to interview them. Britain needed all the intelligence it could get.

20. GIBRALTAR

At ten o'clock the next morning I sat across the desk from Rex, his moustache freshly waxed, and gleaming with importance, the windowpane behind him brilliant with Mediterranean light. Outside the sea glittered, and the huge Rock rose, like a giant gunsight aimed across the Straits towards North Africa.

"Let me be clear about this," Rex said. "Your report states that Lucien Rochelle warned you the Gestapo were on their way to arrest you. Do I understand that correctly?"

"Yes."

"And Lucien helped you get to the train station and purchase your ticket for Spain?"

"Yes."

"And you were not intercepted by anyone, not even at the station?"

"Yes, I mean no."

"Which is it, yes or no?"

"No one accosted me at the station."

"They just let you buy a ticket to Spain?" Rex struggled to keep the incredulity from his voice.

I knew I should elaborate on my lies further, but I was feeling nauseous. Perhaps from the breakfast I had tried to eat an hour earlier.

"I told you, I have a Spanish passport."

"Yes, conveniently given to you by a member of the Communist French resistance."

"That's right. I am sorry but I am feeling unwell. I stood up. "Where is the bathroom?"

Something in my face must have alerted Rex to the seriousness of my request because he hastened to show me out the door and down the passage to the women's public lavatories. As I leaned over the basin splashing cool water on my feverish face I began retching. A thin drool clung to my lips, and I cleaned my mouth, feeling decidedly unwell. I glanced at the mirror and saw my normally pale face seemed even more drained of colour, but my eyes were rimmed with pink. I dried my face, and then dabbled at the water marks splattered down the front of my dress, before I returned to the office in which Rex waited patiently, a concerned look crossing his face as I entered.

"I say are you all right to continue. Are you ill, you look terribly pale?" He pulled out my chair so that I could be seated again.

"I'm not feeling very well, and I have written all of this in my reports. Remember I was a celebrity--people knew me in the streets."

I regretted saying that as soon as the words left my mouth. My celebrity was as a French woman who would not have held a Spanish passport, but Rex continued writing something in his notebook and seemed not to notice. I wanted to escape from him, to go and sit alone in the bedroom I was allocated in the Bristol Hotel, which had been commandeered by the Royal Air Force.

I needed privacy, to re-read the letter burning against my skin under the protection of my waist band. It was too much effort to say more, and I lapsed into silence.

"Righty ho, we'll call it a day then and continue when you feel a bit better. Will you be well enough for the reception tonight at Government House. Everybody will be there. I could pick you up at say seven. I would be delighted to show you off in what passes for society in these parts, mostly men I am afraid. The civilians are all off in Jamaica and such places—safety for the duration you know."

"Thank you, Rex, I appreciate your offer, but the Group Captain has already arranged my escort. I am sure I shall be well later, just something I ate. I shall see you tonight then, and tomorrow we can continue our discussions." I smiled at him in what I hoped was a friendly way, but I feared it was more a grimace.

"Let me organise a car to take you back to your hotel."

"Thank you but I need the walk. It'll do me good."

My heart lifted as I stepped out into the warm winter Mediterranean sunshine, redolent with the smell of salt air and seaweed. I didn't much care where I walked so long as I could remain in the sun, and away from any intelligence grilling. I wasn't feeling up to the creativity and imagination I required to craft my lies and half-truths.

Instead of returning to my hotel, I walked along steep narrow roads towards the Alameda Gardens where I was told, bands played on Sundays, and where monkeys lived. If one could ever be alone in a garrison town of thirty thousand homesick men, this was it. Few women remained in Gibraltar, other than nurses and the Spanish women workers who came across the border daily from La Linea de la Conception.

Yet, it seemed that every step I took was watched by a dozen curious eyes and every passing truck was packed with shirtless wolf whistling soldiers, white with rock dust from drilling defence passages throughout the narrow peninsular. To avoid them I found myself scrambling through alternative routes along steep paths, rather than the main road, until I reached the Alameda.

213

In the relative privacy of the gardens, I found a bench where I sat for a minute surveying my surroundings, looking for hidden watchers. It was unlikely, but I had to be cautious despite my craving for the content of the letter. Eventually I pulled it from my waist band, unfolding the thin sheets of blue paper carefully, smoothing the pages.

My Darling

If this finds you, I know you are safe and for now that is all I can hope. I have taken a foolish risk writing this but since you left, I have mooned about like a lovesick schoolboy. I should not have let you go. I should have gone with you. We could have compromised, but then I remind myself that my feelings are not your feelings, and I straighten my spine vowing to focus my attention on what I should, my work.

That too becomes insane, and I find it increasingly difficult to rationalise what I do or the point of it all. Twice I have found myself on the streets outside the house of our mutual acquaintance, but both times my nerve fails me, and I find I cannot go ahead with any of it. I am stuck between the abyss and the inferno and my heart breaks for want of you.

Your smudged-faced friend is well, settled in nicely with his grandmother whose health and vigour improves daily. Your house mates mourn your absence although they have immediately filled your vacancy with a new mate from the same stables. I have found them some coal in this terrible winter for we are all cold and I have promised it to them for their stoicism.

I am sorry for the cryptic nature of my communications, and I cannot say more although my lack of dedication to my duty has earned me a reprimand for which I must pay with the blue chasm of despair, only a small space between me and my love as I bid Paris farewell.

Bon voyage my love.

Yours.

I ran my finger across the last line as I stared vacantly at the letter, my thoughts in turmoil. A longing enveloped me as I felt his presence almost tangibly, his scent, the smooth cool skin of his cheek as it pressed against mine, his strong arms and long elegant fingers playing absently with the edges of my sleeve.

Tears welled in my eyes. I shook my head, why was I feeling like this? I must be coming down with a cold. I re-read the last paragraph unsure what it meant although it was obvious, he was leaving Paris, but why was he in trouble? Because of me? Had they found out? No, it wasn't possible for if they knew he would be shot, a traitor. What is the blue chasm of despair--only a small space between us?

A rustling noise made me look up, immediately vigilant, my fingers folding the paper as I looked around for the source of the disturbance. A troupe of monkeys came out from the bushes heading for a small goldfish pond. They bowed to drink, their hands clasping the bank edges, their eyes alert. I watched in amazement, a smile spreading across my face as I saw a mother with her baby looking in my direction.

I flinched as a voice behind me said, "They're interesting characters, aren't they?"

I stiffened. How long had the man been standing in the bushes behind me?

He stepped out very slowly not wishing to spook the monkeys and said, "I love these creatures. Sorry I startled you, but I come up here to watch them whenever I can." He held out his hand. "I'm Stephen Mulbray. I was studying to be a veterinarian but now, oh well you can see, I'm one of the fly boys in the same hotel as you." He pointed to his sleeve insignia. "You would not have seen me, although I noticed you last night when those secret agent types brought you in. Escapee, aren't you? Jolly good show, I must say." He glanced at my face. "I've shocked you. There are no secrets in this neck of the woods you know. War or not, everybody knows everything there is to know about a newcomer, especially a girl and especially one as pretty as you."

He folded his lanky frame onto the bench next to me. "Let me tell you a bit about the Barbary Apes. They are Macaques actually, from North Africa originally. They say the Moors brought them over. It would have had to be a human who brought them; they couldn't have swum could they although it's not so far. I am sure I could almost swim across, if I had a mind. The Strait is only about fifteen miles across." He paused, "They are now the property of His Majesty under the care of Captain Fitzgerald. I'll introduce you if you like. He's a good fellow, loves his apes, gets a bit cross when I call them apes though; tells me in no uncertain terms, that they are definitely not apes." He paused and then said, "I say, I am blathering on rather aren't I. Please forgive me, nerves I suppose, pretty girls and all that. Please speak, it's the only way I will shut up."

I smiled at him, hoping his curiosity would not extend to the letter on my lap. "It's nice to meet you Stephen Mulbray. I am Aurélie Avraham, and you are right, I have only recently arrived. I am Belgian and I am a singer, recently escaped from France and happily, waiting to travel to England as soon as I am able. I have never before seen monkeys, not real monkeys, only pictures."

"Really, not even in a zoo? Oh, my manners, sorry." He held out his hand. "Miss Avraham it's very nice to meet you. Now that you have seen the monkeys may I buy you a cup of tea?"

He stood up and held out his arm.

I discreetly tucked the letter back into my waist band before taking his arm, while he chattered on about the other animals and birds of Gibraltar and something called the Barbary partridge

His words washed over me as we walked to a small café. It overlooked the impossibly blue Bay of Gibraltar towards Algeciras in Spain.

After tea he walked me back to our hotel, apologising for the uncouth behaviour of the men passing. "It's the army and navy, an airman would never be so impolite."

I could tell he was revelling in the fame he was earning in this town of love starved men. At the hotel, he asked if he could take me to some club that night and looked crushed when I explained I was to go to the Governor's House reception with the Group Captain.

His demeanour changed immediately. "Oh gosh, I am sorry I didn't know you were spoken for. I will mind my manners from here on—completely."

I watched him walk away and I was mystified. I still had a lot to learn about how the English mind worked. I went up to my room craving a long hot bath.

The evening reception allowed only one sherry before dinner. I felt I would need more than one sherry if I were to get through the entire evening. The Group Captain, a married man with four children back in England, was a gentlemanly soul with his ready smile, and pink nose. I could tell he was a popular man, both with his men and with the hierarchy, as he whisked me around the room, introducing me to one lot of people after another.

My head spun with names and faces and my poor attempt at making small talk with people with whom I had little in common.

"How was it my dear…must have been hell."

"Well, you're safe now."

"Oh yes, I know Sir Giles well, went to school with the blighter."

I nodded and smiled until I thought my face would crack. All I craved was peace and solitude and somewhere to sit down. After a while, having dispensed with their duty, the group of men soon forgot me and spoke over my head. Relieved to be ignored for the moment, I concentrated on remaining upright.

There was no sensation as I fell to the floor. When my eyes fluttered open, a glass of water was pushed against my teeth. A sea of creased faces hovered above me. I must have fainted, something I had never done in my life before now. I scrambled to get to my feet, straightening my skirt, mortified by such a display in front of all these people. "Sorry I don't know what came over me."

Someone held my elbow. "Are you sure you are all right?"

A large woman bowled her way through the throng. "Make way now, clear a space. You sir, get her a chair, and for God's sake give the girl some air. There's nothing more to see here. Some privacy, please gentlemen."

The men moved away immediately, turning their backs to walk to the other side of the room. In a way it made my embarrassment more acute.

The woman grabbed the glass. "Here dear drink some water. Perhaps it's the heat. Stuffy as hell, in this room. Do you suffer low blood pressure, or is it something else?"

I drank the water and felt better. "I just need some air. I am sorry to cause such a fuss."

"It will give us all something interesting to talk about. It's not every day these officers have a pretty girl swooning at their feet."

She laughed so loudly and with such authority I wanted to sink into her shadow. "Do you feel well enough to stand? I'll organise an ambulance to take you to the hospital for overnight observation. We don't want you managing to escape Jerry, only to wind up with some ghastly disease."

"Please, I'm fine now. There is no need."

"Nonsense, besides, I can't abide all this small talk, and this gives me just the excuse to escape. I'll have a word with the CO."

She left me sitting alone in the middle of the room with the other guests pretending I didn't exist, and me willing the floor to open and swallow me. I didn't dare move in case I drew attention.

The woman bustled back and began to fuss over me.

"Really I'm fine." I protested. "So silly of me but honestly I feel right as rain."

Matron, who I was to discover this kind woman was, would have none of it and bundled me into an ambulance, climbing aboard herself as we left the party with even fewer women than before.

The next morning, I sat on the broad veranda of the Colonial Hospital rugged-up against the cool morning sea breeze, waiting for the doctor to do his rounds. I felt a little nauseous again but nothing that required this level of fuss. I was probably coming down with a cold.

I began to resent the kind intentions of the staff who would not let me leave until doctor had seen me. I had a private room, only because I could not be billeted with all the other patients in the wards because they were all men. It was a grand room with soaring ceilings that opened onto an arched balcony, facing the Bay of Gibraltar where white caps played on indigo waves in the cold wind, but it was lonely despite the kindness I had received.

Strangers sent flowers and fruit and notes of dismay at my being taken unwell, hoping I would be up and about soon. I had a note from Rex who said that Henry had departed for England. He was sorry he was unable to see me before he left, but he had told Rex how well I could sing. Rex asked if I would consider singing on Sunday, if I was well enough, at the winter gardens.

Unused to such sympathy, I felt almost smothered by it, and yet the morning was barely half gone. I opened yet another note, this time from Stephen the RAF pilot I had met the day before.

Dear beautiful girl (I don't know how to spell your name), but I do know you would have been better coming out with me last night. At least I wouldn't have put you in hospital. That's something only the Brass can manage. May I visit you? Please say yes.

Best wishes, Stephen the monkey watcher.

I laughed aloud. They really were the kindest and most decent people I had met in a long time.

An entourage of medical staff entered my room.

"Ha, there you are my dear, come inside at once. You will catch your death of cold out in that gale."

I smiled at the same woman from the night before, her brusque manner concealing warm compassion. She was dressed in her Matron's uniform, and she bundled me back to bed just as the doctor arrived.

I froze, as if someone had slapped me.

He turned, in a comical double take to stare at me. "My God, it's you, Aurélie Avraham. You survived!"

I remained speechless at his affront. How could he greet me so warmly, after his callous disregard for Madeleine. He had left my friend behind to her terrible fate, while he escaped to England.

"Get her into bed. She's had a shock."

"No! I am not an invalid." I pushed away the helping hands. "What happened to Madeleine?" I said it with all the venom I could muster. I wanted to hurt him, and I didn't care about the people watching.

He looked contrite. "I am so sorry. If we had known, we would have made sure you were on the train with us. I can see how angry you are, and of course you have a right to be, but we thought you would make it through with the ambulances. We only made it by the skin of our teeth. We made inquiries, but there was no news. I must admit, I feared the worst, but Madeleine swore your life was charmed, and by Jove, it seems she was right. Here you are, hale and hearty I hope, although that's what I'm here for isn't it?"

He turned to Matron. "Matron please allow me to introduce a great heroine of this war, Sister Avraham. She and I were with the BEF in May 40 at the great rout." I saw Matron purse her lips at his reference to the British retreat being called the great rout, but he continued unabashed.

"Sister Avraham was an absolute brick, worked twice as hard as anybody trying to save lives, but we became separated." He looked back at me. "I guess you have been hiding out since. Was it the resistance who got you out? Gosh what a story you'll have to tell when you see Madeleine again."

His broad smile, his jovial demeanour--none of it was right. I couldn't take in what he said and standing there made me feel woozy again. I swayed and Matron caught me and tucked me back into bed. The grey tunnel of my vision cleared, and I sat up again despite Matron's protests.

"Where is Madeleine?"

"She's in England." His smile had gone, and he looked concerned. "She's with my mother in Kent, and our son Marcus, who will be a year-old next month. We got away at Saint Nazaire on one of the hospital ships, and were married soon after, given the circumstances." He actually blushed.

I couldn't believe what I was hearing. Madeleine was alive! They had lied to me. All this time I had mourned her, blaming myself for her fate, thinking I was a coward in not staying to look for her, like they said she had done for me. I couldn't believe they had told me so many lies. What else had they lied about? I didn't know what to do, what to say to this man whose face was beaming. I needed time to think. He was in love with Madeleine, and they had a son. I should be rejoicing. I tried to smile back at him.

"I'm so glad all is well Captain, and I am so glad Madeleine is well. I was afraid..."

Matron said, "Major dear."

"What?"

Willoughby smiled. "Promotion--probably undeserved but not to be refused, what?"

I lay back on my pillow, emotionally drained, but I needed to speak with Captain, or rather Major Willoughby without this audience about us.

It was like a signal, for immediately I lay back, the interlude was over and medical efficiency took over as Major became Dr Willoughby. When he had finished prodding and poking me, listening to my heart beating, looking at my tongue, and smelling my breath, he turned to Matron. "Matron, can you clear everyone out, I'd like a word alone with Miss Avraham if you don't mind. We have a bit of catching up to do."

"Of course, Major, but what about the other patients?"

"I won't be long; they can wait a few minutes."

When everyone had left the room, he pulled a hard-backed wooden chair closer to the bed and sat down. "We have a lot to catch up on, you and I, don't we?" I stared at him wordlessly. He nodded as if coming to an agreement with himself. "Look Aurélie, may I call you that?" I said nothing, and he fiddled with his stethoscope for seconds before clearing his throat. "I don't know what's happened to you in the past months, but I am sure you have had an ordeal. We will have to spend some leisure time together just to fill each other in with the details and Madeleine will want you to stay with us when you get home."

I wished he would get to the point but still I said nothing, not wanting to distract him from his purpose. He straightened his shoulders as if to take a step into territory he would rather avoid, which made me nervous.

"What is it?"

"From a medical point of view, you're fine."

I let out a whoosh of air. I had not realised I was holding my breath fearing some ghastly diagnosis. I had heard a person had recently recuperated from smallpox in this hospital.

"However, from a social standpoint you may be in a bit of bother." His gaze slid away.

I blinked. What was he talking about? My voice croaked. "I don't understand. What's wrong with me?"

"I would have thought you would have figured it out by now, being a nurse."

"Major, tell me what's wrong."

"You are expecting, my dear."

"I beg your pardon?" What did he mean expecting, expecting what? Then it dawned on me. I lay still gazing at him, his kind grey blue eyes crinkling the thin skin around his eyes. Madeleine was lucky, she was safe and well looked after by the love of this man.

He patted my hand. "Do you want to tell me about it? I will have to tell Matron, and it will get out. Nothing is sacred on this Rock. Everyone knows everyone else's business before they do, especially about something like this. What do you want me to do?"

My brain raced. He thought I had been raped or had a lover, and he wanted a story concocted for him to put out and save my reputation. He didn't want to tell a lie, so he wanted me to tell him something that I would be happy to have bandied about. I was at a loss. It never occurred to me. Pregnant! A warm glow suffused me as I thought of Dietrich. I wished I could tell him. He would be so happy.

Willoughby cleared his throat. Then my predicament broke through my fog. An unmarried woman having a child was no light consideration, the scandal would be difficult. Could I invent a husband? It came to me instantly, after all I had a passport in the name of Aurelia Valdez, I could have a husband with the name of Valdez who... what? I needed time to make up a story, one that would satisfy Rex and the people in London. I had to have time.

"Major..."

"Call me Michael, Aurélie. Please, we have been through too much to stand on formality."

"Michael, I need time." I hoped he would catch on.

He understood immediately, standing up saying loudly, "We'll need to do some tests before we are sure of our prognosis, and I think you will need to stay here for another day just for observation, Miss Avraham."

"Valdez now Michael."

"Pardon?"

"Mrs. Valdez now, I will tell you all about it tomorrow, and Michael, thank you."

He squeezed my hand and walked to the door, stopping to wink at me before he walked out, saying, "My goodness, Madeleine will be thrilled."

He closed the door quietly behind him leaving me alone with my chaotic emotions, a seesaw of elation, fear, and worry. What could I do? I needed a fictional but plausible husband, one whom I married in secret—why? I would have to tell London why I had withheld the information? Where was my husband now? Dead he must be dead—how?

A few days later I explained my situation to Rex when Michael eventually allowed visitors to see me. The fictitious back story I invented followed truth and fiction in equal parts and went something like this. Miguel Valdez was a friend and comrade of my Jewish friend Marcel. They fought Franco in the Spanish war. Miguel was an outcast, one of the many Spanish Republican refugees living in France since they lost their battle against their own home-grown Fascist Nationalists. When the German army invaded France, Miguel and the other Spanish refugees took up with the early French resistance. Marcel and Miguel were in the same brotherhood of Communists who became active once Russia threw in their lot with the allies, and it was Marcel who introduced me to Miguel. We married in secret.

"Why hadn't I told London?" Rex wanted to know.

"I didn't see what business London had in my personal life. Besides as a Spanish national by marriage, it would have been likely that London would have abandoned me."

"Nonsense," said Rex but I noted the suggestion struck a chord.

"I did what they asked me, I never revealed my sources, but surely they did not think that all the information I passed to them came from Lucien?"

"Of course."

I watched him wryly. Of course? What did that mean. I didn't tell Rex that Lucien hated the Communists almost more than he hated the German invaders. Instead, I told Rex it was Miguel who managed to get me on the train, boldly dressed as a German officer, once he knew that the Gestapo were on to me. No one had stopped us, why would they, a famous opera singer with her German Officer beau. Rex believed that too, so I elaborated further. It was Miguel and his men who had set off the bombs at number 84 Avenue Foch.

Oh, how I enjoyed the lies I told him that day, thinking all the while of the lies they had told me about Madeleine. It was petty and harmless or so I thought, but it gave me some satisfaction. The look on his face when I told him about blowing up the Gestapo headquarters was priceless. No longer did I agonise over the omissions I had made in my previous reports. I had been faithful in all I had done, except for protecting Dietrich from their blackmail, and I did not regret that one bit, for the father of the child I carried hidden safely in my womb.

Rex became agitated. "You say your husband set off the bombs at the Gestapo headquarters?" He had a look of what I interpreted as incredulousness on his face.

I became afraid, something was wrong. I had gone too far with my story telling. Rex looked grave as he put down his pencil and notebook. He rose from his chair and walked across the room, gazing out the window to the sea beyond.

Fear ate away my triumph. "What is it?" What did Rex know-why had he stopped believing me? He knew something. Oh, why hadn't I kept to my script? Now they would know I had lied, and they would think I had turned renegade. I was in trouble, I knew it.

His brown eyes glistened, and his wavy hair flopped over his right eyebrow, but his tone was mournful as he said, "I am so sorry to tell you, but I think your husband may be dead."

"What?" I had not expected this. "What do you mean? He's not dead. I left him at the station; he said he would follow me..." I bit my lip. I could not keep embellishing the story. I would be caught out. I should listen more and talk less.

"We had word that all the Communists involved in the plot to blow up the Gestapo Headquarters were rounded up and shot before they managed to do any damage. The Gestapo got to them before they managed to lay the explosives. They were infiltrated and very little damage occurred, or that is my understanding, but all the conspirators were shot without exception."

What was he talking about? I heard the explosion myself. It happened before I got on the train, not afterwards. His eyes dropped from mine, and then it dawned on me he was telling me my husband was dead and I should react as if I cared. But it was preposterous, I had made up the story.

It was Dietrich who had set the explosive and he was not shot. Who? Then I knew, Dietrich had set false information about it being a Communist plot. An image of Dr Sardou filled my mind, and I hid my face in my hands. How terrible. Had the Gestapo rounded up innocent people and shot them? Surely Dietrich would not have engineered such a terrible thing to cover his own tracks.

Rex saw my expression and misreading my horror, he walked over to me hurriedly. "I am so sorry Aurélie, I beg your pardon, I should call you Mrs. Valdez, but please accept my condolences."

I lowered my eyes and sniffed softly as if crying, and then wiping my eyes I looked up at him. "Please keep calling me Aurélie for we are friends now, you and I, and thank you for telling me about my husband. I would like to be alone for a while if that is all right."

"Certainly." He hastened to pick up his pencil and pad and withdrew, closing the door softly behind him.

I lay on my bed staring at the ceiling, trying to make sense of it all, wishing I knew what had really happened. Had Communists been shot for the explosions? Surely Dietrich would not have done that. No, I could not believe it! My thoughts turned back to Rex. At least he had believed the fiction about my marriage, and I cannot mourn over people whom I do not know. But perhaps I did know one, if they were Communists, Luc Sardou. No that wasn't likely.

Still, one minute I was a newlywed, next minute a widow. I should have to wear black now. That would keep the grasping intentions of the hungry hordes at bay whilst I remained on this tiny piece of British soil. All in all, it was working out, at least for me although not for those in the wake of the destruction I was leaving behind. I just needed to get a berth on a ship, and I would be out of there and on to England and all would be fine, somehow. But the death of the Communists dragged at my conscience.

The door opened. It was Michael. "May I come in Aurélie?"

"Of course, Michael please I am bereft; I have just been informed my husband has been shot by the Gestapo."

Michael looked shocked before he saw the smile on my face. He sighed, "Well, I am very sorry for your loss Mrs. Valdez, but I have good news for you. Our tests have come back, and you are in the clear, not a single illness, just a little matter of baby Valdez. Congratulations. Do you want to leave the hospital, or would you prefer to stay on for a few days? We are running half empty at the moment, so I am sure there will be no one screaming for your bed just yet. Would you like me to arrange it?"

"I would be so grateful Michael. I am not yet able to face going back to the hotel. I know I shall be treated as though I am made of porcelain, and I can't bear it. Just a few more days and perhaps soon, I will hear if I have managed to get a berth on a ship, or better yet a flight on one of the RAF planes going home."

"Consider it done. I'll tell Matron. Were you serious about your husband being shot by the Gestapo, by the way? That sounds rather serious."

I crossed my fingers and said, "He apparently tried to blow up their Parisian headquarters. He's a hero of the resistance Michael. I will need to be alone for a while to grieve."

Michael shook his head sorrowfully, but didn't want to know the truth, so he bought the story. At least he could state factually that this was what I had told him.

"I have the day off on Sunday. Perhaps if you feel up to it, I can take you for a drive to see the sights and then a spot of lunch somewhere? What do you say? It might do you good to get a little sun and fresh air. You are far too pasty."

"Whatever the doctor orders, Michael." He left the room in search of Matron.

True to his word, the whole of Gibraltar soon knew the mysterious Miss Aurélie Avraham was in fact the grieving widow of a hero in the French resistance.

"Dreadful he had died in such a terrible manner but for such a valiant cause." They said, "It was such a miracle that he had managed to smuggle his wife out of the country before she too was caught and shot."

There was also some rumour about Miss Avraham, or Mrs Valdez and some great service to Britain, nursing or resistance work, people said behind held-up hands, but of course, loose lips and all that. Well, she was a jolly plucky young lady and he a brave man, even if a Communist. No more to be said.

A few days later another letter from Stephen arrived, apologising once more for his behaviour, which was completely out of line considering everything, and he hoped I would forgive him. Poor Stephen.

After my Sunday excursion with Michael, I walked into my room, worn out by a day of sightseeing, climbing, and walking. I only had a few more nights in the hospital and I would be back to my hotel. It was such a shame. How quickly I could change my mind from wanting to leave that first morning until now. It wasn't just the privacy I was afforded. I had actually enjoyed my stay, imagining this is what a holiday might be like. Despite the activity on the Rock there was no bombing, no fighting, not even a damaged ship had come into the harbor while I had been there.

If this were war, it was the kind of war I could tolerate although I knew it couldn't last and I was right. That night I was awoken by an explosion from what seemed to be the north of the hospital, in the direction of the Spanish boarder at La Linea.

I lay in bed listening to the sirens as vehicles raced in the direction of the landing strip. It was a small explosion, and I convinced myself that it was just gas bottles exploding by accident rather than an act of war.

I turned over to go back to sleep. I was more tired this time than during my last pregnancy, one I had not mentioned to Michael. He had the good grace not to mention it to me although I was sure he must know.

A small scraping sound caused my eyes to fly open and I felt more than heard someone in my room. Then a hand closed around my mouth. I struggled in terror but was held fast by strong arms, and then a familiar voice.

"Hush my love, stay still so I can kiss you."

"Dietrich!" What had he risked being here?

He relinquished me and propped a wooden chair under the door handle.

"You can say you locked it when you heard the explosion," he whispered as he once more gathered me in his arms. "How I have longed for this moment."

I remained stiff as he murmured into my hair. "When I heard you were in hospital, I had to come."

"How did you know?" Fearful of his reply I pulled away from him. The night was so dark I could barely make him out and lit the small lamp next to my bed.

He stroked my hair and said, "You really are not much good as a spy my dear. You must know we have agents all around you. There are Spanish Falange in our pay from Campo de Gibraltar who come across daily. Even the Gestapo hang out in cafes across the bay at Algeciras watching every movement through their telescopes. They know who you are, Madeleine Chaumont. Even though the file on you was burnt to ash in the explosion at Foch Avenue, they are still convinced you are Violetta and one day their surveillance will pay off. They will see you walking in the street. You must be careful, for if the Gestapo find you here, they will send an assassin. If I can get to you, so can they."

Fear curdled my stomach. "Did you do the bombing tonight?"

"No." His mouth turned down ruefully. "I knew about it and took advantage, but they think I am safely in Tangiers. Remember my darling I told you I had been posted to Tangiers. I watch and report on the shipping that comes and goes. It is my punishment for letting you slip through our fingers, but no one comments when I take the boat out for a spot of recreational fishing. No one cares much what I do. I am no longer central to strategy."

I crinkled my nose; I could not remember him saying anything about Tangiers or anything of that sort. Then I knew what he meant; Tangiers was across the Straits of Gibraltar, the blue chasm of despair—only a small space between us? How could I have been so dense? "Dietrich did you blame the Communists for causing the Foch Avenue explosions?"

"What?" He sat back on the bed, and then illumination lightened his face. "So, the British bought the story. The Gestapo are still looking for the culprits, but they would not want to own their own weakness or failure. Making up a suitable fiction and spreading it widely saves their ego."

I was a fool. Every word I uttered to this man gave him more intelligence about what the British knew. What a stupid spy I was, but of all my puppet masters he was the one I trusted, and I threw caution to the wind. My eyes teary I said, "I am having a baby Dietrich that is why I am here. I fainted, so stupid..."

He stroked my hair until I stopped crying. Did he really care? And then I did the most foolish thing of all. I told him my real name and where I was from. I recounted my adoption and Karl's abuse, explaining about my stolen baby and why Karl had not believed I could be Violetta because he already knew who I was. I knew Karl was after Dietrich, although I didn't know why, but he should know to defend himself.

I blame the pregnancy, the hormones flooding my body, but he was the only man I trusted in the world at that moment. I began crying in earnest as I begged him to find my child and keep her safe.

He wiped the tears from my cheeks, "We trade in lies and secrets my love. It is our job but not to each other, never to each other."

He left then and I felt as if my heart would break. I walked out to the balcony looking into the night until the cold February light suffused the sky and I returned to my bed. I was horrified at the recollection of my irrational revelation. It wasn't until long afterwards that I came to know it was my confession that finally turned him.

21. BAKER STREET LONDON 1942

David Asquith sat at his desk fiddling with his pen as he frowned in concentration at the document before him. Shafts of weak winter sunlight illuminated his short blond hair. I had a flash back to Father O'Bryan's sitting room, wondering then why he didn't cut the hair that flopped constantly in his eyes. What a foolish young girl I had been. What an irrational woman I had become. I waited for him to absorb my report before him.

The ship that carried me from Gibraltar to England took weeks, sailing a good way out into the Atlantic before heading north with its convoy, around the northern tip of Ireland and into the Clyde River. As soon as we berthed, I rang Guilly telling her I was coming home. She was subdued when I rang.

"Oh, Aurélie I am so glad you received my letter. Come home quickly. It will do mother and father such a world of good to see you again. We are all so worried about George."

All this of course was news to me, and I had no idea what had happened to George, neither did I receive a letter but all I said was, "I'll be home soon."

It wasn't until later David gave me a slew of letters and told me that George was missing in action.

Now sitting in this office, I asked if they had any further word on George although I imagine Sir Giles would already know everything there was to know. I wouldn't put it past him to keep the news from his own family. The man was obsessively correct and obedient to the rules, regardless of his own wife's anguish at the knowledge that her only son might have died in an inferno when his plane was shot down. Yet perhaps he was unhurt and managed to parachute to safety, or perhaps he was already on his way across the Pyrenees. Extraordinary tales of survival were possible. I had seen that in Madrid, and I fervently hoped it might be so for George.

David looked up, "Your story is extraordinary," he said. "You're lucky to have got away. The nation owes you a debt of gratitude Miss Avraham."

"Mrs. Valdez." I corrected, relief that they believed my story rushing across my shoulders. I had already been grilled, but I thought David might be more sceptical than Rex, but it seemed I would get away with it. Or perhaps it just suited them to go along with it. Who could know the minds of the British secret service?

"Oh yes, my apologies, of course, Mrs. Valdez and you are, ah hem, are..."

"Expecting, David," I said.

"Hem, yes indeed. May I offer my congratulations although it does cause rather a problem?"

"Why?" The look on his face seemed almost regretful. "What problem?"

"Well, you are a married woman now, about to have a child. This means we will lose one of our best operatives abroad, if a rather unconventional operative."

"No—I can still work. Lots of women are recruited to work here with children. And look," I stood up smoothing my dress against my form. "I hardly show at all."

The blood rose into his face making the tips of his ears glow pink. I had forgotten to act like an English lady. I quickly resumed my seat, smoothing my skirt, and saying, "I want to go back and look for George Guilford. I could help the lines of escape, become a courier or something in the southern zone. No one knows me there and the Germans don't yet occupy Vichy France. I heard stories, I'm certain I could do it."

"Yes, I am sure you could. It would be an excellent job for you, and I am sure you would succeed admirably, but the fact that you are um, ha, expecting rather puts the dampener on that little adventure I am afraid. It wouldn't be seemly."

"But..."

He held up his hand. "Mrs. Valdez you have done enough, we are extremely grateful. You have provided invaluable information but now you are due time off. Have your baby, and then we shall see. Besides the Gestapo seem to have wind of who you are, so it's best if you lie low here awhile. Perhaps we can find something here for you to do, something equally valuable, after your confinement."

"David, what's happened to George?"

He raised a eyebrow. "Why, he's missing in action, shot down somewhere between Hull and Lübeck, in the North Sea, I understand. We don't hold out much hope Aurélie. The Red Cross hasn't turned up anything yet and if he came down in the North Sea he wouldn't last long in this weather."

My heart sank. He wasn't one of the lucky ones who would be found by kind people and hidden, handed from safe house to safe house, until he could get to Spain. This was real. Missing in action meant they just hadn't found his body yet, nor would they in the North Sea. My heart ached for the Guilford's. I could understand why Sir Giles had not told his wife where George had gone down.

"How awful," I said quietly.

"Of course, you can't repeat this to anyone, you understand."

"Yes, I understand." I looked at my fingers, while the irregular ticking of an erratic wall clock disrupted the quiet, and David scratched something on the paper in front of him.

"David, why did you and Sir Giles lie to me?"

"I beg your pardon?" He looked up, seeming dismayed by my abrupt question. "What do you mean, lied to you?"

"You told me Madeleine stayed in France to look for me. You knew she was here, married to Major Willoughby. Yet you deliberately lied, making me think she had died the most horrible death and it was my fault. Why?"

It was David's turn to look at his hands, shifting uncomfortably in his chair. "We didn't know then who she was, not for sure, not when you came to us. We found her eventually. We had to verify your story, but we told you before we knew. We based our assumptions on a hypothesis of what could have happened—before we found her, you understand."

"No, I don't understand. You had me anyway. If I hadn't worked for you, you would have exposed me to Lady Guilford and Guilly. I couldn't bear that, not to lose another family who had taken me in with such love and kindness. You would have put me in an internment camp, an enemy alien. You didn't need to lie to me about Madeleine also."

"We had to be sure."

"Sure of what?" My voice went up in decibel. "That I would not return to serve that maniac in Berlin? One who has done this to me, deceived me, deceived my people. You believed that I would flee back to the land of my birth, a place where I was rejected, with no family to care for me. You thought I would go back to serve a man who encourages his officers to abuse children in the name of Lebensborn; to a place full of bombs and killing. A place that hated Anna and Joachim for their heritage. A place in which I had no one and nothing."

Anger made long pent-up words tumble out, tripping over each other in their haste to be heard. I wiped my mouth where angry spit had accumulated in its corners. "You knew me there; you knew my life there, and yet you still lied. Couldn't you see I would have done what you asked without that?"

Tears flooded my eyes, spilling over my cheeks as the long-checked dam of fear, loneliness and longing overwhelmed me.

Immediately he arose and came around to my side of the desk. Patting my shoulder, he offered me his handkerchief. "There—there..." was all he managed. His embarrassment at my emotional outburst drying my tears more effectively than his sympathy.

I blew my nose, holding out his hanky to return it.

"No, no, you may keep it, my dear."

"Sorry." I sniffed.

"Don't mention it--probably your delicate condition." He returned to his chair.

I tried to control the new spurt of fury at his patronising tone. "I'm going back to Weybridge, to the Guilford's but I need a story for my condition. I can't tell them about my husband, Miguel Valdez. How could I have met such a man when I have been in Liverpool all this time? You will have to concoct an alibi for my condition."

He looked taken aback. "Yes quite." He tapped his pencil on the desk, silent for long minutes. Then looked up and said, "Do you want to remain Valdez, or would you like a nice English name. A husband missing in action—oh no, perhaps not appropriate in the circumstances. A sailor from one of the boats. You nursed him after his ship was torpedoed."

"So, where is he now?" My sarcastic tone was lost on David in full flight of creative deceit.

"He'll need to be deceased. Too much trouble if he isn't. A deceased sailor will give you a small pension as well. Yes," he said warming to his theme. "A nice young lad, orphaned like you. No other family, dying from his wounds. You married him from pity." He looked at my face. "No? Oh well, perhaps he got better and went off to become torpedoed again. This time he bought it."

He was grinning at me and then I knew for sure he hadn't bought the Valdez story. I wondered what he really believed.

"You're very romantic David." I said dryly. "My poor husband. What's his name? What's his rank and what ship was he serving on."

"Hem. It'll need to be an unlucky ship, torpedoed twice in the time you have been nursing in Liverpool." He frowned briefly. "No, wait, I have it. He was a doctor at Mill Road when you got there. He was hurt when the hospital was bombed last May, you nursed him at the..."

"The hospital was bombed! No one told me the hospital I was supposed to be working at was bombed. Where have I been all this time?"

"Ah, yes rather an oversight."

"What else is an oversight. Surely, I would have communicated with Guilly about this. Anyway, I would need to be an elephant if I were still pregnant."

"Well perhaps but..."

"Come on David. You'll have to do better than this. Look here's the story. I met up with an old acquaintance from the Brugmann Hospital in Brussels where I trained. We fell in love and married but because of the war we didn't want to make a fuss, so kept the marriage a secret." I saw Luc Sardou's face and thought of safe domesticity.

"That will be difficult."

"Why?"

"Because we will need the collaboration of the Belgian Government in exile to get the right papers for you to remain here, outside our protection. Too many people involved."

I sat back in my chair biting my lip. It was easier to make up fictitious stories in German occupied Europe than it was here although perhaps not for the Germans themselves. It was only easier if one was living outside any law, then no one could check the stories.

"All right, back to our sailor."

"No." David looked thoughtful. "I have an idea. I think he should be a colonial. That way we don't have to deal with relatives—at least none here, not in the immediate future. One of the Rhodesias perhaps. Someone of good British stock; an RAF man. We have a number of flying schools training pilots in Salisbury, in Southern Rhodesia. That'll do it. He would have been newly arrived from a flying school in Salisbury, coming over to join our RAF boys. Wounded on the troop carrier coming over here—a stray bomb, I think. Not too much damage—one of the Union Castle line, but of course that's classified. Nursed back to health, by you of course, then later shot down over... Malta, I think. The Luftwaffe and the Regia Aeronautica have Malta under siege and it's one of the most dangerous places to fly in and out, so quite believable. It will give you something in common with the terrible grief the Guilford's must be suffering." He leaned back in his chair, apparently pleased with the fiction he was tying together.

"That's a little insensitive don't you think David, particularly in the face of George having been shot down and reported as missing in action."

A frown creased his brow. "We'll have to keep the fiction up in the face of Sir Giles's bereavement of course." He tapped his teeth with his pen as he thought. "You haven't yet heard that the fellow's been shot down. Perhaps he's still alive and —yes, it should come in a telegram over the next few weeks. When you tell them you are married, he will be still alive, and you can promise them they will meet him on his next leave. How's that. I'll tell Sir Giles that you met the fellow in Gib. That way he'll understand why the fiction of meeting in Liverpool. Can't have the rest of the family knowing you were in Gibraltar, can we? I'll get the papers organised. No one's ever heard of Southern Rhodesia, but we have quite a few of their boys in various units. I know, we'll call him Ashley Farnworth, I once knew a chap by that name. Good fellow. Dead years ago, of course. I'll see to it Mrs. Farnworth. The Colonial Office will be in touch. Please accept my deepest commiserations, for your impending loss." He smiled at me conspiratorially.

Could he not see the insensitive paradox of his fiction as he created it in front of a woman whom, he thought had lost her real husband little more than two months ago to a Gestapo firing squad? But then his callous disregard for my own supposed bereavement might mean he suspected the child was Dietrich's. After all he must realise, I was sleeping with my assignment. Yet his ability to create such a fiction for his own colleague, when Sir Giles had so recently lost his own son, also horrified me. This then was the world of spies, so lost in deception and fantasy that we lost sight of the real world. Was Dietrich like this? Did I know him well enough? Was I like that? Something fluttered in my stomach.

When the telegram arrived at the Guilford's three weeks later, Lady Guilford took to her bed. It was just too much for her coming so soon on top of her own loss. My guilt at the hurt I was causing drowned me in remorse, and I withdrew from the family, too stricken to lie to them further. I couldn't stand it, rubbing salt into raw wounds, it was cruel.

Once again, I wanted to scream the truth, and I blamed David Asquith. He was the master puppeteer who had caused so much grief, but I knew that would make it worse not only for me but also for them. I had to uphold my end of the bargain. I played the grief-stricken widow wrapping my guilt in silence. I thought of all the other women in Britain and Germany and Holland and France and Russia and America and all the other places in the world, as they too received the news that their husbands were never coming home, and I was racked with guilt.

I couldn't stand the responsibility any longer and eventually I rang Madeleine asking if I could visit. I made my excuses to the Guilford's and went to stay with her. When I arrived, she greeted me with joy, calling me her sister as she introduced me to Michael's mother. Of course, Michael had told them both about finding me, he said through colleagues although he was warned to say nothing of Gibraltar, and he didn't ask further questions. I told Madelaine the tale that Guilly knew and said nothing about the rest.

As I walked into their tiny house, the smell of roses and cinnamon flooded my senses. Marcus, her beautiful little boy, so serious with his golden skin and jet hair, was the darling of his grandmother's heart as he followed her around on unsteady legs.

The garden was a triumph of vegetables and flowers. Round beds, surrounded by white stones, were overflowing with a jumble of the mixed plants. Cabbages vied with carrots and leaks and potatoes and onions. Roses bloomed proudly above, and runner beans looped between thorny bushes.

Madeleine explained the compromise between her need for food, and Michael's mother's need for roses. I felt envious as I watched her, so happy with Michael's mother and Marcus in their little house. Their familiarity belying the vast separation of cultures. With the vegetables in the garden and hens in a small pen out the back under an old Bay tree, Madeleine created delicious eastern cuisine out of the little that could be found.

I had been there a few weeks when Guilly phoned. It was towards the end of March 1942, and I had just turned 23, a birthday I kept to myself. On the phone Guilly's voice was tight with choked back tears as she told me that a stray bomb had fallen on Weymouth. Guilly had been on night shift at the hospital when it happened. The blast had killed both Sir Giles and Lady Guilford in their home.

I promised I would be back on the next available train. I looked around at the tranquil surrounds, at the contentment of Madeleine and Mrs. Willoughby, with an almost physically overwhelming nostalgia. Why, oh why, couldn't my life be like this?

I made up my mind. I couldn't stay in England. I was a jinx, and I couldn't stand the tragedy of this war any longer. I would leave before harm befell Madeleine's family. She was so happy. They seemed to want for nothing, and their happiness only heightened my loneliness, guilt, and the crazy notion that if I stayed, I would bring disaster to them.

I said goodbye to Madeleine and Mrs. Willoughby, bending my ungainly body to stoop and hug little Marcus. He laid his ear on the small bump of my belly, patting it with his little hand, his glowing face smiling up at me in joy and amazement as he felt the baby move.

On the train heading back to Weybridge and Guilly, I began making plans to leave England. Somehow, I would get to America. I would go to Marcel and Anna. I would leave all this behind me to begin a new life with my child. No more lies I promised myself, at least Anna and Marcel/Joachim knew who I really was.

22. DEATH, LOSS, AND LEAVING

We stood by the graves of Sir Giles and Lady Guilford. Slashes of dark mud contrasted vividly with the surrounding green grass. The flowers on the newly turned soil were bruised by the heavy rainfall that fell steadily. My borrowed mackintosh and galoshes kept me relatively dry in the downpour.

The Vicar and the other guests, including soldiers and spies like David Asquith, took their leave of Guilly, who stood dry eyed under her umbrella. There were so many people who wanted to make their condolences, I thought we should stand there forever, and I was feeling faint.

It had stopped raining and now they were all gone, only we remained at the graveside, staring at the graves as if Guilly could not walk away. My tiredness made me bilious and weak, and I was finding it difficult to remain upright.

Eventually Guilly said, "Aurélie, I'm leaving. I can't bear it anymore."

I nodded. "Where will you go?"

She turned to me then, her face a crumpled agony. "I have to leave you understand, please say you do. I can't stay here any longer. I can't stand the death and destruction. I just can't. I have no one left now, like you I suppose. We have no one left but each other and you have your little one to look forward to, but I have nothing. Come with me Aurélie. Come with me to Africa. You can go to your husband's family in Rhodesia, and I can go on to Zanzibar. We can go together you and me, sail across the sea to a place that doesn't rain bombs in the night, please Aurélie."

I took her hand. "The war is everywhere."

A vision of Gibraltar and Spain arose where no bombs fell, but for how long? Like me, she was now an orphan, but how much worse was it to lose one's whole family when one is conscious of it.

She continued, "I am studying for my midwifery exams so that I can apply to go out to Africa with the Colonial Office. It means I will have to resign my commission, but they have assured me they will be glad to have me.

"Doing what?"

Training midwives in Zanzibar. I will head up the nursing unit. It's part of a campaign to improve conditions in the colonies. Please Aurélie, it's rather daunting to think of going to Africa by myself but you—you almost belong. You have family there."

"They won't let me go." I said dully. "I have no passport no visa. I don't know his family. I am a stranger to them; they won't want me." My voice was flat, drained of life, the effort of speaking, telling lies, was too much. I remained standing with effort. The need to support my friend kept me upright but I wanted to lie down, even here in the mud—just lie down and sleep.

"That doesn't matter, you will get to know them. As his wife you will be entitled to a British passport. They will love you and they will want their grandchild near them. I know. If only George had married his fiancée and had a child. I am sure it would have helped."

I thought of the Guilford's house blasted into dust and rubble. It was just as well he did not, or it would be another

243

death to bear. If Guilly hadn't been on duty at the hospital she might have gone too and I... I couldn't stand thinking about it.

"We must look to the future," I said for want of anything else, for I could hear Lady Guilford's voice in my head saying just these words. But I asked myself, what future? It would never end, this war. We are doomed to go on and on until there is no one left to fight, just bones and ash in a drizzling grey world. I fell silent, swaying over the graves with dizziness and fatigue.

She explained her plan and at one point I wanted to shout at her that my husband and his family were all fiction, but I remained silent. All my energy was required to remain standing.

Then an excruciating pain shot through me. I fell to my knees in the mud, catching the edge of Guilly's handbag as I went.

"Aurélie, Aurélie what is it?" She knelt beside me, then looked around, shouting, "Help, someone please."

But there was no one about to hear us alone in the cemetery.

"Tell me Aurélie tell me what's happening?" The nurse took hold of Guilly as she pushed my wet hair back from my eyes.

"The baby's coming." I said through teeth gritted in pain.

"Can you walk?"

I managed to push myself onto all fours in the mud, but could go no further, panting with the pain that came wave upon wave. It was too soon!

"I'll get help, wait here, will you be all right? Stupid question! I'll get help."

I tried to nod but the pain took all my will to remain as I was and not curl up in a ball in the mud. I heard Guilly running across the grass shouting for help and later I heard people running towards me.

I was lifted and carried and then I remember nothing more until I awoke in a clean hospital bed. The mud was gone, and the sun shone through the windows at the end of the ward. Lining the walls were beds filled with the wives of service personnel, some nursing babies, some asleep. The smell of Lysol and carbolic mixed with the smell of nappies and breast milk, hung in the air.

I called out but my voice came out in a croak. I cleared it and tried again and instantly a nursing Sister came to my bedside.

"You're awake at last." She smiled, her Irish brogue lilting like music in my ears. "I'll fetch Guilly from next door. She said we were to call her the moment you woke." She turned to go.

I held out my hand. "Wait please, my baby?"

Her face straightened into the professional mask we all wore when bad news was to be given. She said, "Guilly would like to explain. She won't be long."

That was when I knew. I knew my baby was dead; dead with all the rest, in this poor, dark, ash laden world that God had abandoned. It felt like I too was dead. It was just that no one had thought to tell me. If I wasn't, I wanted to be. I wanted oblivion. I couldn't take anymore. I lost everyone I loved, and I deserved it. It was my punishment for all the lies I had told, all the deaths I had on my conscience.

Guilly came and explained my tiny baby boy had never had a chance. A problem with the placenta. He had been stillborn but had been dead before my contractions began in an attempt to expel him.

I lay in bed, unaware of the passing hours. Day turned to night and night to day as people came and went. Then David arrived. In my grief-crazed mind I decided that it was he who was responsible. I struck out. I had killed my child, and I blamed David. I spoke to him, or rather spat at him in anger as I hauled myself upright in bed. All the sorrow and loss bubbled-up like lava.

I wasn't so far gone that I didn't realise that I was in a ward full of other women. In a voice pitched low with icy intent I hissed at him that he had the blood of my baby on his head. "You think you fool everyone with your mild-mannered look, your golden hair and reassuring smile, but I know you. Yes, I do, you are guilty. You are an evil despicable puppet master who thinks he can just jerk a string and make me dance. Well, no more. I will do no more."

Exhausted by the surge of emotion I laid back against my pillows feeling bilious and already embarrassed by my outburst. I knew it was unfair, but I still blamed him for it. Defensively, I avoided looking at him. I would not apologise.

He hovered at my bedside, while I refused to face him, but I felt his gaze as it seemed to go on forever.

He pulled a chair closer and sat down. "My condolences Mrs. Farnworth." He spoke loudly as if keeping up the fiction.

It was a slap, a rebuke while he maintained the stiff upper lip, ignoring my bad manners, pretending the meeting was merely a normal visit at a sick bed.

Silence stretched to minutes until he broke it, his voice soft as if talking to an invalid. "Aurélie, I am truly sorry for your loss, but we need you. You must get well."

"No! I want a passport and a visa to go and live in America. I will not do anything more for you."

Once more the silence stretched out before me, until I turned my head to see if he was still seated next to my bed. He was gazing at me in the way one does when one does not really see, his eyes distant as if I were merely an object in his way. He looked tired. Dark smudges underscored his mild eyes, and his normally clean-shaven jaw was studded with glinting golden stubble. Heaving himself to his feet, he sighed as he put his hand in his pocket, pulling out a small bar of chocolate. When I didn't take it, he placed it carefully on the locker next to my bed.

"I'll come back another time when you are feeling better. Please Aurélie believe I never wanted this to happen. I know how it feels and I would never wish it on anyone. Get well and come back to us." He patted the bed cover next to my arm and turning, he walked away his shoulders slumped.

It was later when Guilly came to visit that she told me that some years ago David's wife had miscarried. She became so depressed she had taken her own life. I was mortified that my own misery had caused such pain in another. I saw the look on his face now for what it was, such sorrow and such helplessness. I was a selfish, despicable person and I did not deserve happiness. I gave Guilly the chocolate bar, lying again about not liking chocolate. It was a such luxury item; I did not think I deserved it.

Three weeks passed and I was staying with Guilly in her tiny flat when David came back to see me again. Guilly was still talking of going to Africa. I let her words wash over me, letting her think I would go with her as soon as I could arrange a passport and heard from my fictitious in-laws.

She checked the mail daily, excited by the thoughts of a new adventure. I couldn't muster the energy to tell her she was wasting her time and I let her believe. I know it was wrong but if I told her I wasn't going she would leave me, and I would be alone again. I wanted the fiction. I wanted to pretend.

It was an afternoon in late April when David arrived unannounced. Guilly was still at the hospital as I opened the door to his knock. I was relieved to see him, to apologise. He sat down in the sitting room. His frame seemed almost too large for the small space. The light filtered through the windows making the room seem dull and lifeless. He held his hat between his knees, turning it around and around as he listened to my garbled words of apology.

Finally, he nodded and said, "It's behind us, but Aurélie, the war is not finished." He leaned forward. "We can finish it sooner, together, working as one. We can finish it."

"Why David? I'm not that important. There is nothing more I can do. The Gestapo know who I am. I can't go back, they'll find me."

"We don't need you to go back but we do need you Aurélie. I can't tell you anything at the moment, but I need you to come with me. You will have to pack an overnight bag. You'll be back tomorrow."

"Why can't I stay here and get the train into the city?"

"The place we need you is not in London."

"I will have to tell Guilly?"

"What will you have to tell me?" Guilly walked into the room, holding sprays of apple blossom in the crook of her arm, and a box of chocolates in her hand. She glanced at me then looked at David. "David what's going on? What do you want with Aurélie? Why are you here?"

"Good evening Helen. It's good to see you again. I hope you won't think me too rude if I have to tell you to mind your own business." He grinned at her, stripping the offense from his words. "You are looking amazingly well." He took her by the shoulders and kissed her cheek. "All I can tell you, is that Aurélie here is a linguist and we need a linguist. It's for the war effort you know. I'll have her back safely tomorrow. It's just a quick job."

"But she is going to Africa with me."

To his credit, he didn't miss a beat, but I saw a slight lift of his eyebrow. "You're not going tomorrow, are you?"

"I am just waiting for my exam results, and Aurélie wants to visit her late husband's family. She's just waiting for a passport."

"I am surprised you would consider it, but your plans will have to be carried out without Aurélie. The country needs her."

"What? To do a bit of translation. What a lot of bosh! You have lots of people to translate for you. Oh, I know, I know, you and Daddy...I can't ask, can't say anything. Mum's the word and all that. I am just so sick of it." She took a breath. "But whatever it is, someone else also wants to see Aurélie."

His hands, still resting on her shoulders, tightened. "Who? What do you mean someone else?"

"David let go of me." Guilly shrugged off his hands and laid the flowers and chocolates on the table, before taking off her coat and hat, and hanging them on the hat stand. "I mean nothing. It was just a man. He asked me if this was where the lovely Aurélie Avraham lived." She turned to me. "These are for you darling, what a dish but good heavens--where he found such chocolates, I have no idea. He obviously doesn't know that you don't like chocolate, or that you are a married woman, or rather a widow." Guilly's smile was sad. "Don't worry I didn't tell him anything. I thought I should ask you if you were ready to be bothered by suitors before I said anything encouraging."

"But you took the flowers?" David looked at me, alarm written across his face. "Is it a suitor Aurélie?"

"Why shouldn't it be? Aurélie is an attractive woman."

They both stared at me as if I might know something.

I shook my head. I couldn't think who it could be. "What did he look like?"

Guilly thought for a moment. "I don't really know. The light wasn't good, and he had a hat on, but he was tall and had a nice, clean shaven square jaw. I really didn't get a good look, although I did tick him off for loitering on our doorstep. I must have embarrassed him for he thrust the flowers and chocolates at me and dashed down the steps…Ah…He had an accent…American or Canadian."

"It might be one of the boys I nursed," It could be someone I had met in Gibraltar or Madrid. "It's possibly Howard Newton. I met…nursed him in…Liverpool. He's Canadian and he said he would look me up."

David exhaled. It sounded like relief. "Right, Aurélie pack an overnight bag. You need to come with me now."

"Hold on David, you can't go ordering Aurélie about like that."

"It's all right Guilly. I need to go with him. I'm sorry, but I'll be back tomorrow." I walked over to hug her. "Go to Africa. You can do it. You don't need me to get you there. I can come out to visit you or I will see you when you are home on your next leave." I said it, knowing it would never happen, but she needed to believe it or else she would never find the courage to go. I had been holding her back long enough. I was selfish. "It will be all right." I tried to smile brightly as if this was an everyday thing, but a wave of something--longing perhaps--swept over me, making me shiver. "David, can Guilly come with us?"

"What are you talking about Aurélie? I don't want to go anywhere with you. Or rather I do but not this cloak and dagger stuff. Good gracious, I am beginning to realise I don't know half of what you get up to." She laughed at herself. "I sound just like my mother...Go on dear. You go off with David and play his silly games. I'll be fine. I'll wait until I hear from you before I make any more plans. Perhaps when you get back tomorrow your passport will have arrived."

She rolled her eyes at what she had assumed was the passport office delay, and guilt surged at my deception.

I fled from the room to pack. Not that I had much. It would take minutes to throw the few items I owned into a bag, collect my hat, coat, and scarf, Dietrich's scarf, and leave with David on another journey into the unknown.

Ten minutes later, I kissed Guilly saying, "I'll be back in no time." Wondering if it was true or if it was David's way of keeping things secret. I followed him out the door.

Guilly ran after us and called, "Wait, your flowers, your chocolates…"

I turned at the top of the stairs and looked back at Guilly fondly. "You have them. I don't really like the smell of apple blossom anyway."

23. La Belle Hélène

It was almost dark when we got into David's car. He must be pretty special, being able to drive everywhere when no one else could get petrol. I remembered Paris, and the Gestapo. They always had fuel. It seemed spies and secret police were exempt from enduring the hardships the rest of us mortals suffered. Immediately the thought popped into my mind I felt mean and small. It wasn't fair. David was presumably on His Majesty's business although that seemed like a grand thing in which to include myself.

I had to stop seeing David as being to blame for my life's woes. He was just doing his job as I was to do mine, whatever it was, but I knew he used me. He used me in Munich to get those documents away, although I did it willingly. To me it had been a side issue, a bargain to get Joachim away. What would have happened to me had I remained. Would the alternative have been worse? Would I now be the plaything of men like Lothar or would I have remained a servant of the Highland House. Both seemed like poor options.

I sat in silence as we drove through darkening streets, wondering about Joachim and Anna. What did they now call themselves? Was Joachim still Eduardo or did he have another alias? Was he married and what about Anna, what was she doing? I shifted in my seat.

"David, if I do this for you, and do it well, will you get me a passport and a visa for America?"

David frowned; his concentration taken up by the darkening road ahead. "What's in America Aurélie? He glanced at the scarf. It's Harvard isn't it? Why do you want to go there?"

I hadn't known about the scarf. It was odd but I had no time to think about that now. "You remember Munich…the Jewish boy?"

"Of course."

"He invited me to stay with his family."

"I thought you were heading off to Africa." A smile lifted the corner of his mouth. "Didn't I hear something about in-laws and passports." He arched his eyebrow again, mocking me.

"Don't be mean David. Guilly doesn't know. It seems natural to her for me to want to meet my in-laws. What else could I say?"

"Yes, sorry I didn't mean to tease but it did take me by surprise. You should warn me about these things you know."

"Don't change the subject. You haven't answered my question."

"What question was that?"

"David! Will I be able to get a British passport?"

"Ah, mm. Yes, I see, well I am not sure but let's get this thing done, then we'll see, eh. Don't be in too much haste to depart these shores Aurélie. America is not as good as people make out."

"Have you been there?"

"Well no, but several of my contemporaries went to America to do postgraduate studies at Harvard. You may recall, I did my postgraduate studies at the Humboldt University." He smiled. "It was why I ended up going back so often. If I hadn't we would never have met."

I turned to look out the window. Wet beads of drizzle scurried across the glass pane, and it dawned on me that David had been in British intelligence since his university days. That was why he went to university in Berlin. His area of expertise was Germany, which was why he was my handler. To him this was just business as usual, the handler and his asset. The war had just ramped up his role, but I was tired of being used for his purposes. I would find the right moment, and then I would hold him to ransom. He would get me a passport if it were the last thing he did.

After a couple of hours, we pulled into a country home. I had no idea where we were. Somewhere near Bedford, judging from the direction we took, but without signage it was hard to know, unless you knew the country well, and I did not. From the road, a mass of dark shrubbery obscured the house. Tall silent trees overhung the long-rutted driveway, which opened into a wide parking area in front of a large house with a Georgian façade, a white pillared portico, and dormer windows. Three other cars were already there.

We alighted from the car and David took my small bag as he ushered me up the steps to the front entrance. I expected someone to open the door for us, but no one came. David opened it with a small push of his foot, and we walked into a gloomy hallway in which stood a hall table with a mass of cut flowers in a vase. I smelled apple blossom, among other scents, and wrinkled my nose. It must be the season. I thought of Guilly and wondered if she would go without me to Africa.

David shut the door carefully behind me, closing off the light to the outside, for despite the halls gloomy interior the smallest light could be a signal, a beacon to planes flying high above us. David stalked across the hall, his heels ringing in the silence. Large double doors on the other side of the entrance hall were closed, but a slither of light shone along their base. This time David knocked, and we waited.

The door was opened by a large man, his head devoid of hair, his eyebrows bushy, and his nose fleshy and beaked. He had a fat cigar clamped in his mouth and a glass of something that looked like whisky clutched in a ham-like fist.

"Ah, Davey, good fellow. You've brought the girl." His eyes travelled slowly up and down my body as he examined every inch of me.

I could hear the blues in his accent as my mind mimicked its tone.

I saw David flinch at the name Davey, but he said, "Colonel I would like to introduce you to Mrs. Aurélie Farnworth."

"Yup, she's a looker ok and sings like an angel I hear. Know any American songs sweetheart?"

I glanced from this giant to David for some clue. Surely David hadn't brought me here under such secrecy to sing to Americans.

"Come on in. I'm forgetting my manners keeping you standing here at the door. What can I get for you to drink sweetheart? It's a miserable night out there, but that's nothing unusual to you Brits, hey Davey boy?"

I walked into the room. Lamps illuminated two chesterfield sofas and other miscellaneous chairs and tables. A fire flickered in the hearth, a surprisingly warm and welcoming sight in the damp weather. Three other men stood as I entered. The colonel introduced me as Au-rae-ly. The other three men were introduced by their Christian names, nothing more.

"Well Au-rae-ly, this here is Hank, short for Henry." He indicated the other man, "and this here is, William short for Bill."

I flashed a querying look at the colonel until I saw he had a big grin on his face. He was teasing me, laughing at his own joke, or perhaps mocking William for not wishing to be called by some abbreviation of his name. I wasn't sure which. I turned my attention to the third man, who the colonel called simply, "James our host."

Hank and William, dwarfed by their colonel, looked as if they had come out of the same seed pod, short, stocky with black slicked-back regulation hair, and dark suits. Both looked uncomfortable standing next to their huge colonel.

James our host, reminded me in a way of Alain. A pang of longing ran through me at the memory. He had refused to leave Brussels with us on the bus, saying his place was there as he needed to look after Monsieur Lallier and the club. I heard his voice in my head as I pleaded with him to come with us, but all he said was, Cherie even a conquering army needs some entertainment, non? Was he still entertaining German soldiers? I hoped so for at least then he would be alive.

James was much less overtly theatrical in his manner. He was also a good few years younger that Alain, but one could see something of the theatre in his manner. Perhaps it was his hair, dyed black in the same way and worn long on his collar.

The evening was a curious affair. I sat sipping gin while the men drank whisky. Not that I was given a choice, for according to the colonel, gin was a woman's drink. I did not complain although it burned my throat, but it also warmed and relaxed me as I took tiny sips, just wetting my lips so as not to gasp at its fire. No one was in a hurry to tell me why I was there.

The men soon relaxed back into the armchairs, drinks in hand. They forgot about me and appeared to take up a previous conversation, arguing about baseball versus cricket, two games that were a mystery to me.

The colonel leaned forward making his point aggressively with language like, "A pansy game for sissies."

The room was warm and the fire mesmerizing as the searing spirit on my lips soothed my agitation. Closing my eyes, I leaned back into the comfortable wing-backed chair near the fire, their murmuring voices reduced to a background lullaby.

A loud rap on the door startled me from my soporific state and I sat upright as the colonel strode to the door. Surely this must be the reason I was here. Two men entered, and I sat struck rigid, wondering what kind of trick this could be. The first man looked about the room until his eyes settled on me. With three strides he reached my chair, kneeling beside me, gazing into my eyes.

He smiled. "You wear my scarf." His grey eyes were dark with what seemed to be sadness.

"Dietrich." Without thinking I touched his cheek.

I pulled my hand back, my fingers covering my mouth. I couldn't believe it was him. This must be some trick. David and the colonel were watching me silently as if waiting to see what I would do. I turned back to Dietrich. I was the deer caught in the spotlight, and I waited for the bullet.

Instead, he stood up, grasping my hands as he pulled me to my feet. "Aurélie my love, I am sorry—I am so sorry about the baby."

It was as though to him there was no audience, but I remained wary.

He pulled me to him, his strong arms crushing me to his chest. "Perhaps a moment alone gentlemen." It sounded more like a command than a request, and his English was perfect, with only the slightest trace of an accent.

Throats cleared and the men turned their backs to walk away to the far side of the room. I pulled back to look at him. Who was this man, a German spy in the middle of England, in a house full of English and American warriors?

"Dietrich what... how... why are you here?" My voice wavered and my mind thrashed about for an explanation.

"I came for you. They told me you were in the hospital, gravely ill, but you are better now?"

"No." I shook my head in disbelief.

He sighed. "But I was coming anyway. The madman goes too far, and I am on shifting ground. I have no choice but to trade with the British and the Americans although I do not fully trust them, perhaps with the exception of Asquith."

"Shifting ground." I repeated dumbly. "What do you mean Dietrich?"

"Hoffermann is convinced I am in league with the British..."

The colonel interrupted. "All right, that's enough time for you love birds. You've seen her and held her in your arms like you said, now it's time for your end of the bargain."

Dietrich looked wryly at the colonel. Turning back to me, his hands framed my face. He leaned in and kissed me, whispering, "I love you—stay safe and I will find you again...one day."

The kiss lingered on my lips long after he and the others had left the room, and his words looped in my head. What did it mean? What was shifting ground? Did Karl suspect him because of me? What was he trading? I stared at the space he had vacated, feeling terribly alone, and vulnerable.

James took my arm, interrupting my dream-like state. "You won't have had dinner yet Aurélie." Gently he tucked my hand into the crook of his arm as if he could sense how I felt. He began walking me to the door. "Come we will find you something to eat? There's sure to be something in the kitchen. Then when we've eaten, I can show you to your room. All the servants have been given the night off I'm afraid and there's just us, so we'll have to make do."

James escorted me along hallways and through doorways until we came to the kitchen, where he pulled out a chair, and sat me at a big wooden table. He stood with his hips cocked like Alain, his hand held to his cheek as he surveyed me, his eyes soft and kind in the bright kitchen light.

"Hmm, you look more like a champagne girl than a gin girl, am I right? I may just have a bottle left over in the cellar. Perhaps while no one is looking we could drink the evidence between us. What do you say?" He was trying to cheer me up. "I do apologise for the trip to the nether regions of the house, but I like to come here when no one is about. It feels a little naughty, don't you think?"

He disappeared through another doorway leaving me to wonder what he meant by being naughty sitting in a kitchen. A few moments later he reappeared with a tray, on which was a bottle of "37 Clos des Goises, some bread, butter, and cheese. "Not much to eat I'm afraid but given the circumstances."

My mouth watered. I hadn't had cheese for so long. He laid a plate and a butter knife down next to me, and then took a seat opposite, cutting the rustic loaf into thick wedges, knifing a slice to lift and lay on my plate.

While he buttered his bread, he said. "You know, I once heard you sing. He laughed at my startled face. It was a few days before Chamberlain gave Herr Hitler the ultimatum to get out of Poland. I remember the timing because I had to cut my holiday short. Dear father, he was insistent I fly home immediately. Bloody Hitler ruined everything."

He took a sip of his wine, looking at me carefully over the top of his glass. I could see he was trying to distract me from brooding, and I was grateful and intrigued by his revelation. He took a breath as he laid his knife aside. "I did go back a few months later you know, with the BEF. I understand you and I departed those shores in the same embarrassing manner."

I hiccoughed. James was in that battle against the German bewegungskrieg, or what the British press called blitzkrieg, across Belgium and France. He was at Dunkerque. I could feel my eyes stretched tight as I waited for him to tell me more.

"We have much in common, you and I, don't we Aurélie?" He picked up the cheese knife and then as an aside he said, "So much for Belgian neutrality. I wonder if Sweden will hold out now Norway's gone, but we won't talk about that, will we? Look, eat something." He waved the cheese knife at the food. "Let me cut you a piece of cheese."

I took the proffered cheese and put it down on my plate. I wanted him to continue his story. Food was a distraction and could wait as far as I was concerned. "You saw me sing, in Brussels?"

"Oh yes, you sang at some steamy club in the centre of the city."

I found my breathing becoming shallow. I couldn't believe him. This was more of a coincidence than was possible. Surely! It must be some kind of new trick they were up to. I watched his face. It looked sympathetic and then without warning he took my breath away completely. "Yes. I was with Louis, you remember Louis Copeau?"

He picked up the bottle of wine on the table and looked at it as if it might give him a clue to the next words he should say. I was holding my breath, afraid to breathe in case I disturbed his train of thought.

"I must admit we went there as a bit of a lark. Louis said some bloke had been writing, nagging him to come, and as he was in Brussels anyway, we may as well call in. We were the old boys reliving their misspent youth, if you see what I mean. Well, it was a bit of a seedy joint wasn't it?" He looked at me apologetically. "I recall the stripper had a rather amazing reputation."

He was talking about Madeleine, and I recoiled at the word stripper. She had been an exotic dancer, not a stripper although now I thought about it there wasn't much difference.

He chuckled and busied himself with his bread and butter. "We couldn't believe our ears when you came on stage. Louis immediately put down his drink and sat goggle eyed watching you. It wasn't just your looks either. Your voice. Well, it's an amazing gift isn't it? It was so out of place in that sordid joint, the whole room hushed as you began singing. I thought Louis would weep. Then you launched into jazz. Louis sat back and said it was amazing, such range, such versatility. He could barely contain himself until you had finished, rushing off to find you in your dressing room. Then afterwards all he talked about for days was you. He hoped you would go to Paris and take up his offer. You were a cut above that was certain." He paused for a moment as if thinking about something. Then he looked up at me saying, "Look if you need a job singing in

England, I'm your man. I have some very good contacts in the West End."

I brushed the distraction aside. "You know Louis Copeau?" It was all I could think of.

"Of course." James sliced a hunk of cheese and laid it on his bread. "I've known Louis since university. We were at Cambridge together you know."

I couldn't believe it. This was some kind of bazaar ritual. All these men, on both sides of the war, all from different countries, all at one university together. He raised the bread and cheese to his mouth.

With my most venomous tone I said, "Did the colonel and Hank and William attend Cambridge too?"

James took the bread away from his mouth and laid it down on his plate. "Good lord no. What on earth makes you ask that?"

I dipped my head and took a sip of the champagne. Thanks to Armand, I could tell this was quality. It tasted exquisite. I decided not to say more, bewildered by the customs of these people. I could not work out anymore what was true and what was a trick. Who was James and was he sincere, or was this merely another ruse to get me to do something for which I was unprepared? Gulping my wine, I nibbled at the cheese James had sliced for me and vowed to do nothing more for these people, who had manipulated me from the very beginning.

The next morning David came back from wherever he had been the night before. We ate breakfast with James, bacon and eggs, a luxury I never saw in London. James grinned at my amazement, saying, "It pays to farm but don't get me wrong, this is not an everyday occurrence, not at all. It's a special occasion. You are worth a little contraband. It's not every day I have such a pretty girl as my guest." He looked at me gravely. "How's the head?" We had drunk the whole bottle the night before and then moved on to a whisky night cap. "I always think that the mark of good champagne leaves one clear headed the next day, what do you think?"

He was right. My head was clear, and I felt almost light-headed. The sun shone in a porcelain blue sky. The rain of yesterday had gone. I ate bacon and two eggs with relish, drinking real coffee and freshly squeezed orange juice. I had not felt so wonderful for a long time and my vow to move on and no longer work for these men lingered in my mind. I didn't delve too deeply into my lifted mood and put it down to good champagne and good food.

"The Americans brought the coffee and the oranges." James had noticed the pleasure on my face as I sipped one then the other, savouring the contrast of warm bitter and cool sweet. It had been a long time since I felt so happy and carefree.

Driving back to London along the Bedford Road didn't diminish my joy as the sunlight sparkled on the countryside. It seemed washed clean by the rain with drops of dew still gleaming on grass stems. I turned to look at David, driving with his usual concentration. It now occurred to me that my suspicions about David knowing I lied about my husband Valdez was correct after all. What lay behind him letting me get away with it? Not that I cared at this point. I was simply curious.

"David," I asked, "How is it that Dietrich is in England? What was last night about?"

David's face became still, shut off like stone. We drove in silence for a while and then I asked him again. "David you haven't answered me."

He pulled over to the hard shoulder of the road and stopped the car. "Listen Aurélie, this is not a game. You can't talk about this stuff—not even to ask questions, not even here with me in the privacy of the car. You signed the Official Secrets Act and this is one of those things we just don't discuss. You must not mention his name again. Do you hear? I'll tell you one thing and one only. You failed your mission. Yes, you did manage to turn him eventually, but you were not supposed to fall in love with him. How can we trust you now?

He has turned, but it's on his terms. That in my book is a failure."

His words were like a slap to a hysteric; monotone, serious and threatening at the same time. I sank into silence at his reprimand and said in a small voice, hardly above a mutter. "I am not in love with him."

He rounded on me then, his voice harsh. "You think we are fools. Why did you lie about a fictitious husband helping you escape France, getting you out of Paris? It would have been near impossible without German complicity!" His voice was bitter. I had never seen him so angry, his lip quivered with rage as he said, "You lied to me and now you want me to trust you again. You want me to trust you with more information. How do I know you are not playing a double game—you and he both?"

"Please, you're hurting me."

David looked down to his hands on my wrists and pulled away, seemingly taken aback by his own actions.

"David please, I am not... I do not love Dietrich." Inside I recoiled as I said it, but quickly quashed doubt before it grew. "I am not double crossing you; I promise. I lied because I didn't want you to know who the baby's father was. I was ashamed, that's why I lied about a husband. Please David you must believe me. Dietrich doesn't know me as you think he does. He..."

But David didn't let me finish. "He knows you better than you know yourself. He has known about you from the beginning, manipulated and played us off one by one for his own ends. You do know he's married of course." David saw the look on my face and pushed his advantage home. "Oh yes my dear, he was engaged to some Prussian Princess way back when we were at university, had been since they were children, an arrangement between two houses until the Weimar Constitution in 1919 declared you German's all equal. He probably has a dozen children running around his little Schloss in Brandenburg."

"Don't, please David, stop."

"Why shouldn't I? This stuff is not a state secret. His marriage is on the record. I must ask him about his children. Although who knows what lies he is prepared to tell. I am still not sure that he is not a German plant. Anyway, he's the American's problem now, thank God. You know he's a member of the Battalion Brandenburg, one of Canaris's men. If he is a plant, thousands of people could die, and I will hold you personally responsible. You know what that means? You know what happens to spies and double agents!"

I nodded, chastised. I thought again of my training, of their warnings about being caught, of standing in front of a firing squad. But this is England. Here I will hang by the neck until I am dead. The nightmares I had before, now visited me again in broad daylight.

Then I thought of all the innocent people dying, bombs dropping, the blood and noise of the slaughter. I saw London in ruins, buildings now no more than rubble. There were great holes where people had once lived, and children played. Now they were dead—gone, ash blowing in the wind. It wasn't like Paris. Here the bombs had taken a heavy toll on the city, and I understood Guilly's desire to leave it behind.

There was no place for youthful silliness in this game. It was deadly serious. I shut down my feelings. I would not think of Dietrich. I turned my face to the window, as David started the car. He seemed a little nonplussed at his outburst.

In an attempt to mollify him, I said, "I'm sorry David. You're right of course. It's the sunshine and the champagne and the bacon and eggs, and James made me laugh so much. It made me forget for a minute. I won't do it again."

The rest of the way back to London I remained silent, watching the countryside as it passed, noticing more clouds building on the horizon. The rain would be back soon.

It was late morning when we pulled up on the street outside Guilly's flat. David carried my bag, despite my protests that I could carry it myself. He was gentlemanly to the end or perhaps he just didn't trust me to do that either. I fumbled under the door mat for the flat key, but it wasn't there. I lifted the whole mat up in puzzlement.

"Guilly must have forgotten to leave the key. I'll have to go to the hospital to get it. Can you give me a lift David?"

David nodded. "Are you sure she's not home?" He tried the handle and the door swung open.

"Gosh, she must be home. I thought she was working today." I walked into the flat. The apple blossom sprays were arranged in a vase on the dining table, and I wrinkled my nose at their faint perfume. "Guilly I'm back." I turned to take my bag from David. "I can manage now, unless you would like a cup of tea before you get back to the office."

"Yes, I have something to talk to you about so a cup of tea might be nice."

We were being excessively polite to each other after his angry outburst in the car.

I took my bag to the bedroom, leaving David in the sitting room. Guilly's bedroom door was shut, and I knocked gently. It was late for Guilly to be still in bed. I hoped she wasn't sick. There was a lot of flu around, but that didn't answer why she hadn't locked the door the night before. I would have to scold her about that. She wasn't in the country now. Her bedroom door swung open at my knock.

A nagging feeling that all was not well, nudged me into the room. It was still dark from the drawn blackout curtains. A shadowy hump in the bed showed me Guilly was still asleep. I laughed with relief. "Lazy bones," I said as I walked across the room to open the curtains. Mimicking her voice, I sang, "Wake up, wake up you sleepy head, rise up, rise up the sun is red…"

When she didn't move, I walked closer. I saw the stark look of her open, glassy eyes. There were traces of vomit at the corner of her mouth, a dried trickle clinging to her chin, and a pool on the sheet. Her unseeing gaze looked past me to the sunlit sky beyond the window.

I must have cried out and seconds later David rushed into the room.

"Dear God, no!"

He strode to the bed, placing his fingers at her neck. It was pointless for her eyes told it all. He looked around the room, spotting the opened box of chocolates next to her bed. "This was meant for you. Do not touch anything." He backed from the room. "Come out of there. She's gone and there is nothing we can do. This requires damage control. Aurélie!"

His sharp tone jerked me from my shock. I looked at him in horror. "We can't just leave her. We have to do something."

David walked over and taking my arm he marched me out the room. "That tea, Aurélie, you were making tea. You need to make tea." He marched me into the kitchen and filled the kettle and placed it on the hob. "Now can I trust you to make tea? I need to use the telephone."

I nodded obediently as I turned to occupy myself with tea making. I looked in the caddy, but there was only dust, fine tea dust left from our last ration. Why did we need tea anyway? I left the kettle on the hob and followed David to the sitting room. I had to know what he was planning. I stopped when I heard my name.

"It was clearly meant for Miss, Mrs...Farnworth. There was a man loitering yesterday, probably something in the chocolates. It's their modus operandi. I should have seen it coming. Sorry, yes sir, I'll see to it. Helen Guilford—Yes, Sir Giles daughter, a senior nursing sister with the rank of captain in the Queen Alexandra's Royal Army Nursing Corps. No, there's no one left." He paused. "I say, that's a bit off isn't it, sir... All right—it's an idea— no I don't have a better one. I'll see to it, but we'll need to get Aurélie out of London."

He stood with his back to me, his left hand on the back of his neck, his head bowed as he listened into the telephone receiver pressed against his ear. "Right, I'll see to it. *The London Times,* I think—in the personal column, that's what

Captain Guilford would do. Yes sir." He hung up the phone, turning to see me watching him.

This was meant for me. The kettle whistled, and I turned to attend to it, moving mechanically to remove it from the hob. Guilly had died and it was supposed to be me. It was the chocolates that were delivered by the man in the hat, my unknown admirer.

Except he wasn't an admirer, was he? He was an assassin and he killed Guilly instead of me. I couldn't believe it. Then a thought struck me. How sure were we that Guilly was dead? Perhaps she was merely ill. I would go back and check. David couldn't tell me what to do here, not now, not with Guilly alone and sick in her room.

I emptied the kettle down the sink, then after drying my hands, I went back to the bedroom. Guilly hadn't moved. I stepped closer reaching out to touch her. David grabbed me from behind. He held me tightly and dragged me from the room.

Fury was etched in every care worn line of his face. "Which bit of don't touch anything did you not understand? You are in danger Aurélie. Focus now. The police will be all over this place and we must make sure they find what they are looking for. Where are your papers?"

An hour later he led me from the flat, a suitcase of Guilly's clothes and personal effects in the car. I had nothing of my own, except Dietrich's scarf, which I had secreted around my waist, under my dress, and out of David's sight. My hat and coat remained in the hallway. I wore Guilly's coat, too short for me and too wide. I carried Guilly's handbag, wore Guilly's hat with a flowery silk scarf tied over it, and knotted under my chin, to hide my hair. My clothes hung in Guilly's wardrobe. My temporary resident papers, with Belgian refugee stamped in them giving me temporary residence in Britain, were stashed in her drawer. My fictitious marriage certificate, my baby's death certificate, my hairbrush and toothbrush were left behind in Guilly's dresser.

David said the police would be informed Guilly had taken her effects, and left for Africa, and that it was I who lay dead in that room. The small matter of our different heights, builds, and hair colour didn't seem to bother David. It was the notice in *The Times* with which he was most concerned.

"How would Helen word it," he wondered aloud?

I pointed out the inconsistency of his plan. "If Guilly had left the country how would she know I was dead? And how would she have placed the item in the classifieds?"

"Good point. Not that any of it matters. We don't need to convince anyone of anything except the people who want you dead. I'll make sure the police only find what we want them to find. Hmm, perhaps a story in the evening standard about the poor refugee murdered in her bed by a jealous lover, how does that sound."

"Do jealous lovers use poisoned chocolates?" Sarcasm covered my anger at his insensitivity.

"We don't want to panic the population now do we?"

He was only worried about spinning his propaganda. Tears spilled from my eyes. She was dead; my best friend was really dead. Everyone I loved died. It was my fault that Guilly was dead, I told her to take the flowers and chocolates.

Chocolates were such a luxury, and Guilly loved them. She would not have needed to be asked twice. Why didn't I see the trap? Why didn't I make Guilly throw them away with the flowers? Why didn't I make her go to Africa earlier? My throat constricted. It really was my fault; I kept her here waiting for me to get a passport and a letter— post that was never coming. More lies for my own selfish ends.

David stopped at a public phone to make a couple more calls and then we drove back to Bedfordshire, arriving in the mid-afternoon. So little time had passed and yet so much had happened since we had left this morning. This time a very old man opened the front door. He tottered down the steps towards us, as David pulled up in front of the house.

"Good evening sir." The man said in a surprisingly firm voice. "Mr James is expecting you in the withdrawing room and the young lady. Oh, and someone telephoned earlier. There is a message for you with Mr James. Do you have bags sir?"

"Don't worry, Masters, I can handle them."

"I wouldn't think of it, sir. Please go along in. You know where to go don't you? I shall place your bags in your rooms."

"Just one bag for, for... the young lady. I won't be staying."

"Very good, sir."

A frown flitted across the butler's face, perhaps disapproval, but it was so brief I could not read its meaning. We walked to the house, leaving Masters to care for my one small bag, which I could have carried quite easily myself.

James stood at a low sideboard pouring drinks into glasses, champagne for me and whisky for him and David. It was clear that there were two lifestyles in England. One belonged to James and his ilk and another to the rest. Was this why the Communists complained? I didn't care. James treated me so well I almost felt like I had come home. He never judged me but was unfailingly charming and polite. I didn't have to tell James my history. He accepted me as I was--whatever he thought that might be.

Instead, all he said as I re-entered the room of the night before was, "Well, well, I have managed to lure you back to me again so soon. What jolly good luck my dear?" He kissed me on the cheek. "It's been so long since these halls were decked with beauty, and I missed you as soon as you left. Now my dear, a toast?" He held up his glass and looked into my eyes. "To the return of our lovely Aurélie."

"Ah, no!" David coughed. "Aurélie is dead." David's voice was flat, as if he repeated a line from a script. "You will read about it in the newspapers tomorrow, murdered by a jealous lover, poor girl."

James raised an eyebrow at David then turned to me saying, "Well, a toast to the lovely... David please, do introduce me to your companion."

David's Adam's apple bobbed in his throat, his face became pale, and he examined the floor at his feet. When he eventually spoke, his voice was hesitant. "Ah, um, um James, I... that is..." He paced towards the window before turning back to face us. His usually calm eyes now looked stricken.

James had mild curiosity written across his face, but I didn't know what to make of David's obvious distress, until he blurted out.

"Oh, hells bells! Excuse me, Aurélie." He squared his shoulders and said, "James, I would like to introduce you to the Honourable Helen Guildford, daughter of the late Sir Giles and Lady Guilford."

I gasped at such disrespect. Dead only hours and already used for their purposes. I knew this was coming of course but being so introduced threw me. "No!" I cried out. You can't do this."

But James did not miss a beat and quickly spoke over my protests.

"Good heavens, the lovely Helena. Our very own Helena of Troy, pursued by princes, adored by the gods, I haven't seen you since you were so high." He indicated a height about his hips. "So very pleased to meet you again. Mm, let me see." He raised his eyes to the ceiling as if trying to recall some fact or other and then said, "Of course, la belle Hélène. Did you see Saint-Saëns opera in 1919? Oh but of course not, you would have been far too young."

He was giving me a persona from the opera that I could live with, and although my anger at David was hard to contain, I was grateful. James placed his hand on the small of my back, guiding me over to a seat before handing me a glass of champagne. "I heard about your harrowing escapades with the BEF in '40, well done and congratulations at your well-deserved award."

I wasn't sure if he was talking about my story or Helen's story, but I supposed it no longer mattered because we had been there together at the end, but I had no idea about any award. Then it struck me. He was blackmailing David into giving Guilly a commendation, a medal for her work at Dunkerque. It wasn't much but it would be a tribute to a woman who had given so much.

I nodded thinking it was the least they could do for Guilly. It didn't occur to me then, that as Guilly, I would be the one receiving the award. I only thought of her honour and her family, gone now, all dead. I realised James was still talking and I re-focussed my attention on what he was saying.

"It's a pleasure to have you under my roof. Come along, have a sip of this delicious vintage. Not as good as last night's drop but not bad, not at all bad. You will have to tell me all about your exploits over dinner."

His immediate acceptance of my new role and his mention of the Saint-Saëns opera had a funny effect on me. It steadied my nerves as if I truly were in an opera, on stage playing a part. Helen of Troy would be my part now as I pushed away the thought of poor dead Helen, Guilly, my friend.

James had managed to allow me a fantasy by which to compose myself and subsume my revulsion. He allowed me to repress my shock and anger under instant recognition that the show must go on. I could see James was a consummate performer. Where had he learned it?

"Now my dear Helena, we are to have guests for dinner, and you will need to withdraw to attend to your presentation."

I looked from James to David in bewilderment.

David stood up and said, "I must take my leave." His eyes were hard as if he blamed me for the subterfuge. "I will be in touch, but for the interim you will have to remain here. James will show you the ropes and make sure you are safe. Just do as he says and be a good girl."

"David…"

He saw the tears in my eyes, and softened, kissing me on the cheek saying, "It's been a long day. Take care of yourself Helen, and please understand I am sorry. It's the war you see; we all have to follow orders. James will introduce you to the Pee Wees. It may be a while before we see each other again."

24. Autumn Propaganda

It took me a while to accept my name was now Helen or
Helena as they all called me. David was right, James had
introduced me to the Pee Wees, or to use the proper name, the
Political Warfare Executive. I was now a Pee Wit. I told
myself that it didn't matter what odd names I was called or for
whom I worked. All that mattered was that I was once more
singing.

This time I was called upon to sing old favourite German
folk songs, popular French songs and American jazz, my
beloved jazz, with the resident Pee Wit band. It had been
almost ten months since I had last sung publicly, and I needed
to get my voice into training.

Tom was in charge. He had been kind to me, and it seemed
we were all misfits and oddities. I was not that unusual, for
Tom spoke fluent German having been born in Berlin like me,
but unlike me he wasn't ashamed. He didn't feel the guilt that
plagued me. Perhaps it was because he wasn't really German.
He was just born there. I had been introduced to Tom at
dinner, my first night back with James.

It was then I also discovered James had worked for the
BBC prior to this operation having been set up. The BBC
were still arguing about censorship, moral considerations, and

independence from Government, when James and others quietly slipped away to create the team of which I was now a part. Unlike David, James was not a spy, but a man engaged in propaganda and lies. There was not much difference between us.

Over dinner, Tom had asked me questions in German about Berlin, which I answered as frankly as I could. I really didn't have much knowledge of the city outside of Friedrichstadt and Mitte, where I had once lived with the Hoffermann's, because prior to that I had spent much of my time confined to the convent. I was vague about the Hoffermann's, only saying that I had been adopted by them and had run away to join the theatre. It was another lie, but I didn't see why I needed to lay bare my shame. As he questioned me about the theatre in Berlin, I repeated much of what I had learned from Gertrud, pretending a familiarity I did not own. It seemed to satisfy, and he asked me to go next day for a singing audition.

Before Tom arrived for dinner, James arranged for his mother's maid to come over and do my hair. He introduced her as Haddis. She was to cut and colour it with some vile smelling concoction she mixed in a glass bowl. I sat in front of a mirror and watched her smooth out a long strand of my hair. She placed the blades of scissors against it, and looked at me in the mirror, her hazel flecked eyes meeting my blue ones.

"It's not too late to change your mind," she said.

I shook my head and watched as the strand fell to the floor. It lay curled in a long loop, like hay falling from the harvester. I felt a momentary pang, but I had never before had short hair, and I was curious.

After she had finished, my hair was short, dark brown in colour, and was dressed in waves and rolls. Looking in the mirror I felt I was looking at a stranger. My skin, always pale, now looked stark by comparison with its dark cap of hair. Transparent lashes and brows disappeared against my skin making my face seem somehow naked and vulnerable. My eyes always blue now shone with a light intensity as if they were made of glass rather than the proper substance of eyes.

Haddis expertly flicked colour across my brows and lashes with pencil and brush, making my eyes appear enormous. Although I had done my make-up in the theatre, this needed more subtlety and it took a while to get the hang of doing it every day, getting the brows arched in just the right way without looking like a clown. I decided I looked quite odd, but that was then, now I was used to my new look. It was peculiar really because all the other girls, talked about lightening their hair with peroxide and some of them actually did it. I was not the only oddity in the group.

A few days after the dinner, Tom took me to a place he called the Rookery. I was asked to sing some songs. All were American songs, the real thing with uncensored words. He said we were broadcasting to the German navy, mostly the U-boats. The music was the hook for it turned out that jazz was very popular on the U-boats.

My fluent German was handy, and Tom said I would be called upon to read the news when the regular girl Rita, was not available. Messages were crafted to alarm and spread disquiet. Aside from the American songs everything was in German, of course because we were pretending to be a regular German wireless station. The news we broadcast was mostly accurate. At least, it was more accurate than what they would have received from a real German station.

We also beamed wireless broadcasts into France, containing coded messages. Even my songs included messages where words would be changed regularly for the benefit of the resistance. Would anyone who had heard me before, remember or recognise my voice? If they did, they would call me a collaborator, especially people like Eva and Marie, after seeing me with a German Officer. I tried to imagine what happened after I left but my thoughts would become maudlin or worse. I gave up thinking about the people

I had left behind and concentrated on the present, deciding that the likelihood of them listening or recognising me was slim.

Yet we knew the resistance listened, and it reminded me of my songs at the club. I liked to think that Lucien might be listening to me now. Would he recognise my voice? Would he still be alive? Could he survive now Germany had taken over Vichy and the whole southern zone?

Whatever else, I was singing again, and I was having fun, but others were not so lucky. In quiet moments, I berated myself for forgetting the reality of my situation, and that of others. All the while I could not forget my baby daughter, now almost six years old. I prayed nightly she might be safe, spared from bombs and barbarity, away from the fighting and from Nazi influence. I hoped, with Karl's rank, he might have found Frau Hoffermann and my daughter a place to live in a safe country area away from Berlin.

Otherwise, I was content, although I always feared it couldn't last. I had never been allowed to have fun without paying for it. Somehow, some day it would end, and a bill would be presented. I pushed those thoughts away, forgetting for long moments, enjoying my new friends and work. Then David came back and ruined it.

Ever since I had become Helen Guilford, I had also taken on Helen's commissioned rank, within the Queen Alexandra's Royal Army Nursing Corps, bestowed after Dunkerque. David explained that her/my transfer to the Intelligence Services was officially concluded, and rather than a nursing rank, I was now an army captain in the Political Warfare Executive. He pulled a wry face and said, I would have the responsibility of leading my team in a manner befitting a British officer.

My team! I had thought I was just a member of the group. No one had thought to tell me I was to be in charge of the musicians and singers. I was no longer just an agent with a British officer as my handler, I was now an officer. That must give David indigestion. Obviously, he didn't think me suitable material because he explained that I might wish to understand what this meant. Everyone would expect me to *behave* as a British officer. He gave me a manual which he told me to study. I wanted to laugh.

Then as realisation of my new madness as an imposter dawned, I became terrified. I studied the manual carefully. Yet, despite this rather significant oversight in planning my transition to Guilly, I loved my job, and the people I worked with were such a lot of fun, eccentric, strange, and just downright peculiar sometimes.

They valued me and treated me as one of them and no one cared that I didn't order them around but worked with them as equals. They valued my knowledge of streets in Berlin, giving authenticity to the stories they created. They valued my knowledge of Paris and applauded my voice and ability at mimicry.

I had never felt quite so much authentic camaraderie and although I studied the manual, I was never expected to behave like anything other than I was. I felt safe here with people who were rapidly becoming my people. I still didn't dare venture out much despite my new look with its short wavy dark hair. I was still afraid that someone would find me, like they had found me before in London.

Although most people in Britain didn't know about the unit, of the ones who did, many did not approve of the loose morality of propaganda. I didn't care. I was singing again and decided that was what I had been born to do. I was unconcerned with the low approval from certain members of the British Government who abhorred our tactics. They found the smutty innuendo about what the German soldiers' and sailors' wives and girlfriends got up to while their men were away, abhorrent. But it was our job to sow discontent. We did it they said, unfairly and I must say some of the stories we broadcast, even made me blush.

Our digs had once been the stables belonging to an Abbey, now requisitioned by the Pee Wee and I bunked in with all the women in our unit. I was happy for weeks, until on a bleak winter's day in mid-December the British Government condemned Germany for the mass extermination of Jewish people. Until then I thought the rumours were malicious gossip. I never believed the stories and did not want to believe them now, but the nagging feeling of guilt by association, persisted.

I threw myself into my work, doing as much as I could in atonement. We broadcast what small facts we gleaned about these atrocities, willing the German people to turn against this war, hoping the sailors in the U-boats would lose heart with such appalling stories that no one, other than a fiend, could condone.

The most difficult thing about our propaganda war was that we had to pretend we were on their side, a German station for German people. If they had guessed our origin and our purpose they would not have believed anything we told them. I had no difficulty because I really was on their side—the side of good German people, not the Nazi monsters. But not all adapted so easily as I. There was such hatred of all German people by this time, I was glad they thought me English.

We worked six days a week but always had at least one day off unless there was some kind of flap on somewhere. Most of the other girls went out on their days off. If they had homes nearby they would go to family or to relatives. Sometimes they would go to the pictures or to a dance. I went a few times to Bedford with some of the girls, but I was so afraid of being recognised that I didn't enjoy it at all. My obsession with the Gestapo assassins made me jittery and I decided it just wasn't worth it. There were so many people in Bedford, Americans, and British and other nations, the man with the hat from London might easily hide among them.

So, I stopped going into any of the towns or cities and often volunteered for extra duties on my days off. On such occasions, I was taken to a grand house a few miles from where we were at the Rookery and spent my Sundays in a hut with several others. I would be given a stack of documents to go through, translating intercepted letters, particularly those to German POWs in England. There were also notices, newspaper articles and sometimes official German communiqués.

Occasionally, I translated English to German for our leaflet drops or the fake German Newspapers we published. Some of the material received was merely propaganda, and we had to sort the fiction from fact, but much of the information I saw was from real communiqués and just needed translating to English.

Sometimes I would study aerial maps, marking things I recognised, or we would work with other intelligence reports to identify landmarks for what I guessed were bombing runs. I was fearful of seeing bombing scheduled for Friedrichstadt. I hoped the area had been spared, but there was no one I could ask. I thought of Dietrich. I should have asked him when I had a chance.

There was always more urgency here than with the Pee Wees, and more work than we could manage. I increased my volunteer time and was given a bicycle to commute the seven or so miles between the two places.

The Nissan hut I was assigned to was in the large grounds of the stately mansion and my crew weren't like the people at the Rookery. Instead, they were earnest and overworked, and there wasn't much laughter or teasing. I was relieved I didn't have to work there every day, although I was glad to give my weekends to the cause. Reading the German news and communiqués made me a little homesick and I wanted to know what was happening in my own country. Of course, I would not have admitted that to a soul.

I was going through these papers one Sunday afternoon. It was late and getting dark. The dinner break was starting, and my shift was over. My bicycle had no light, and I should get back to my billet in the stables before it got too dark. I was about to pack up when I saw his name, von Winterfeldt, in the heading of the page.

I stopped short, pulling the paper from the pile. Was it just a similar surname or was it him? I was in a quandary; the others were waiting for me to leave. Our shift was over, and we were vacating the hut. I hesitated, could I steal the document and bring it back later? No that would be a breach of the Secrets Act and I would be arrested. I could be accused of being a spy. I couldn't risk it.

I would have to go, leaving it behind. Someone else would translate it. Next time I came it would have disappeared into the vast filing system. This was my only chance. I quickly scanned the page, risking the wrath of the waiting men, one of whom was already walking back. I could hear his footfalls. I read as fast as I could, skipping over chunks looking for something relevant. I found it as the major arrived at my table.

"Did no one tell you Captain, all work, and no play, makes for a dull operative. There is dedication and dedication but keeping a man from his dinner does not count." He smiled at me to show he wasn't serious.

I tried to keep the horror from showing in my face, and mumbled an apology, getting up quickly, knocking a pile of files to the ground in shock induced clumsiness.

He bent to help me. "Is everything all right?"

I turned away as my eyes filled with tears. "I'm fine, just tired," I mumbled.

"Yes, we are all tired, the whole bloody country's tired but we have no choice. We must keep going because what's the alternative, right?" He placed the files back on the table and stepped back to let me walk in front of him.

I nodded my thanks and walked out the hut. "Good night." I said as I collected my bike from where it leaned at the side of the hut. It had turned cold and misty. Winter was just days away.

My teary eyes blurred as I rode along darkening country lanes. It couldn't be. It just couldn't be. Dietrich executed for attempting to assassinate Hitler. Why? I thought he was going to be taken to America with the American colonel. Instead, he must have gone back to Germany and been caught. Tears coursed down my cheeks, blinding me as I rode along familiar lanes.

The road was empty of vehicles at this late hour on a Sunday, and I didn't see the cow in the road until the last minute. I swerved and the cow dashed the same way. I tried to swerve the other way but clipped the cow with my front wheel. It bolted, leaving me and the bicycle in a mangled mess, in a puddle on the road.

I was very late getting back, hobbling, and drenched, grazed and bruised but in a better state than the bicycle. I would be in a great deal of trouble tomorrow for ruining government property. Or, at least, that's what David's officer's manual warned, but I didn't care.

I lay on my bed ignoring the other girls and their questions. I didn't go for dinner that night, nor did I get out of bed the next morning. I lay there wondering if a person might will themselves to death. I didn't want to live any more. Everyone I loved died. My daughter was probably dead too, just like mine and Dietrich's baby, and Guilly and all her family. Through the night the cold ate its way into my wet body, but I ignored it.

Later in the morning I was moved to a cottage hospital nearby. I was bathed and my grazes were dressed. Tests were conducted, but the doctors remain mystified. I lay staring at the ceiling with not the energy to speak even though I knew they needed me to say something. How could I tell them what ailed me when I did not really understand it myself?

In the afternoon David arrived with James. I hadn't seen either man for weeks. I was uncomfortable they had come. They sat by my bedside in silence for a while and then James took out a book and began reading. It was a book of Shakespeare sonnets. As he read, words began to penetrate my mind. Tears of regret and longing oozed from my closed eyes.

He stopped reading to sit on the bed, holding me close to his chest while I sobbed. He stroked my hair making small noises that soothed my distress until I began to hiccough. He found a glass of water and held my head as I drank, telling me what a good girl I was, so brave. I didn't feel brave, but his words made me feel better as he dried my cheeks with the bed sheet. He held my chin and I looked at him through swollen pink eyes.

"What's the matter Aurélie?" He said using my Belgian name rather than his usual Helena. I think it was a calculated tactic at intimacy and immediately my antennae went up. Something was wrong. He wanted me to tell them, but they already knew. That was why he read me love sonnets. They knew Dietrich was dead, why I was upset. Why did he ask me?

I lay back in my bed and said dully. "I fell off my bicycle and broke it. The manual says I will be punished for misuse of government property."

The startled incredulity in David's face was priceless. I had begun to realise they were testing me. David needed James's subterfuge to help test my resolve, but with James here I could not break my oath under the Official Secrets Act. If I had told David I knew Dietrich was dead, it would be a breach under that Act, but in my grief I had nearly succumbed. They really didn't trust me. After all this time I was still being tested. I needed to think. I stared at the ceiling.

"I'm tired. I'll be all right in a while, but I need to sleep. Thank you for coming to see me. Thank you for being kind." I smiled a wan smile, but it was all I could muster.

David stood up. "All right, old girl we'll see you back tomorrow then. Bright eyed and bushy tailed, hopefully."

I didn't understand what he meant by bushy tailed but it didn't matter. It was true that I was tired, and I did need to sleep. I would worry about what it all meant tomorrow.

I'm not sure if it was my intense misery that brought on the pneumonia or if it was the drenching I received after the antics with the cow. Whichever way around it was, I wasn't able to get out of bed again for weeks.

When my fever finally broke David was again my first visitor. He told me they had been worried about me. Was it true. Unlikely. I was becoming bitter and cynical. He told me I was to get my wish, to go to America when I was well. Now I was excited and wanted to get up at once, but I wasn't free, not yet.

It transpired I was being sent as a trainer, to Canada to a place David referred to as the Farm or Camp X. It was Military Camp 103, an SOE training outpost on the banks of Lake Ontario. He said a sea voyage and change in surroundings would do wonders for my health.

Secretly I thought they wanted me far away from Europe. They didn't know what I would do, now I knew Dietrich was dead, and they couldn't take any chances with me staying in England.

Then I discovered they had found a man skulking outside the hospital, looking for me. David said they had him in custody although he hadn't said much, yet! They had found my photo at his home, so they knew it was me he was after. I was still blonde with long hair in the picture but the fact that he knew I was in the hospital was worrying.

He was an Englishman who had belonged to Mosely's Fascists, and I am not sure if he could have done me any real harm, given my training, but I was in a weakened state. This was the real reason they were sending me to Canada. I assumed they had at first wondered if the man was my contact or my assassin. I suppose that was why the test, but more worryingly for me was that the Gestapo knew I was in the neighbourhood. But why pursue me?

David said not to worry. They would get it out of the man if it were through his last breath. Still, I couldn't understand it. I wasn't that important that the Nazis should waste their resources. Questions burned in my mind, but I longed to be gone. Somewhere safe.

25. NORTH ATLANTIC CROSSING 1943

The passenger liner towered above me, grey war paint muting its form against a dreary English sky filled with barrage balloons. The decks were already lined with troops, Americans and Canadians mostly, on their way home for rest and recuperation. Soldiers, airmen and sailors saluted me and self-consciously I returned their acknowledgement, feeling like a fraud with my new rank. Such formalities had mattered little at the Rookery.

The crossing was to follow a route not far below the edge of the Arctic Circle to the New World. This was where icebergs floated, their mass hidden below water, seeking unwary Titanics to destroy. This was where U-boats skulked alone or in packs like hungry wolves looking for vulnerable prey.

I heard a husband reassuring his wife the ship would be safe because we were travelling in convoy. I knew there was still danger, although we were gaining the upper hand in the battle for the Atlantic. Even now, British operators in Bedfordshire were checking the location of U-boats and I hoped they would tell the ship's captain. Although, that was never a certainty, depending on other strategic considerations, especially if it let Jerry know we had broken their code. How easily the term 'Jerry' came to me now.

By the time I reached my cabin, I was frozen to my marrow. Icy air filled my lungs and reminded me of earlier talk of bracing sea air being just what the doctor ordered. They could have no idea how cold it was.

I was lucky to have a cabin on the upper deck. Most of the internal cabin walls on the lower decks had been removed and installed with rows of bunks for the troops. It was only the officers and a few civilians who had any kind of privacy and even that was often shared. Although I had an officer rank, I reasoned I had a cabin to myself thanks to David pulling strings. I could hear his voice. *Can't have spies sharing sleeping quarters with the hoi polloi.*

On my final evening at the Abbey stables, the girls had thrown a farewell party, toasting my recovery and imminent departure. I hadn't had time to get to know them well, but I was sorry to leave. They had treated me like one of their own in the few months we had billeted together. The billet party was a combined affair for in a few days they would pack their belongings to move into new accommodation.

The promised Nissan huts were finally ready although I think our stables might have been cosier than the huts; bleak, cold and unwelcoming as they were with their single belching stove in the centre of the long tube. It would be too bad if you were allocated a bed at the furthermost end, for the warmth from the stove would never reach you.

I prevailed upon James to bestow some whisky and gin for the occasion. He hinted at being invited but it was just for the stable billet, and I was glad no one else could come. At the party we roasted potatoes and chestnuts in the fire, and someone managed to scrounge elderberry wine for which I developed an immediate liking, oblivious to its potency until the next day.

The next morning my head pounded as I boarded a train for London. I was to meet David, and he took me for dinner at the Savoy Hotel to celebrate my promotion to Major. He explained I would need the rank in my new role. I was mystified at how he could bend the system to his needs, but didn't argue, and he said it would mean more pay. He handed me a British passport in Guilly's name. To me it was more precious than gold and I opened it reverentially and stared at my photo. My details explained I was born on 26 April 1915, in Weybridge. I was now four years older than I really was.

I looked quizzically at David. "I am 28 years old."

He nodded. "Fraid so my dear."

I shook my head wondering if he remembered the last false passport he had organised for me. He was determined to make me old before my time.

He also handed me a brown paper parcel with several neatly folded Intelligence Corp uniforms, complete with service medals and Guilly's Royal Red Cross medal, along with the rank of Major. No one in the world gains promotions like I have, for doing absolutely nothing to deserve it. At least Guilly had deserved her captaincy as a senior nursing sister. It seemed that my promotion to major placed me at the level of a matron in the Queen Alexandra's Royal Army Nursing Corps. I who hadn't even finished my nursing training. It was another lie, I felt I could not sustain.

All evening David remained upbeat and expansive. We toasted the 8th Army who had taken Tripoli, and surprisingly, the Soviets who were gaining ground on the German army in Stalingrad. I smiled and clinked his glass, but I really didn't want to hear about war, not even that the tide was turning in the Allies favour. I didn't want to think about German men and boys freezing to death on the Eastern Front, waiting for supplies, frost turning their fingers and toes black.

I hated the madman who cared so little for our country that he threw men away at the impossible task of Russia in winter. Hadn't history taught us anything? Nor did I want to hear about besieged and starving Russians, their bravery, or their sorrow. Selfishly, I wanted only to live in the moment, to soak up the glamour and glitz of my surroundings, to escape from reality and carnage, cushioned in the Savoy's graceful embrace.

The following day I was off again, with David's warning, to keep a low profile for goodness sake, ringing in my ears. I was heading for Liverpool, finally to see the city where I was supposed to have been stationed while I was in Paris.

Waiting for the train was interminable, and to pass the time, I watched the moving throngs of people. Young women clung to their sweethearts, red lipped, wide eyed faces bravely hiding fear as they farewelled men, whom they knew they may never see again. By the time the train arrived, I was tired as I pushed my way with my bag through the throng.

I was not yet fully recovered although it had been two weeks since the fever broke, and I tired easily. But I soon straightened my shoulders when I saw men slumped on the platform, some asleep on their kit bags. They had more reason to be tired than me although I also knew that sleep could be an escape from horror, so long as it didn't invade one's dreams.

The train filled quickly with heaving, breathing, bodies occupying every conceivable space, reminding me of the hospital trains in France. Except here, there was no moaning, no screaming from the agony of wounds, so terrible I could scarcely conceive how I had managed to remain calm nursing them. I couldn't believe it was less than three years ago. It felt like a lifetime. It seemed like this war would never end. It would go on and on until there was no one remaining, only a world left to subside into dust.

The train trip took hours longer than it would in peace time, stopping all the time, sometimes for no apparent reason. By the time I boarded ship, I could barely keep my eyes open through the droning safety and survival instructions. I took the survival rations and personal preserver, which they insisted we keep to hand at all times, and only then could I go to my cabin. I fell into the bunk, unconscious.

The creaking motion of the ship wakened me in the early hours of the following morning. The ship was leaving. I threw on my coat, and grabbed Dietrich's scarf, tucking into my coat collar, to keep out the cold air. A tug pulled us out to sea as ghostly sailors flitted about their tasks and the quay receded into foggy gloom. The land either side of the Mersey was merely a dark silhouette against the horizon. Would I ever see England again? I returned to my cabin and slept, rocked by the ship's gentle movement.

As we headed towards Iceland it became colder and every morning, I walked the decks for exercise until I discovered there was a contingent of American Red Cross nurses on board. I went in search of them, introducing myself and explaining my story or rather, Guilly's story. I told them I was to engage in work with the British Colonial Office, and I was going out to take up a post in Africa. I almost believed it myself, so accomplished at lying had I become.

The Americans were friendly people, frank and easy going, accepting me into the group immediately. Best of all they knew all the new swing music and told me new words to songs by Glenn Miller and Benny Goodman. They talked as if they knew these people personally.

Not to be left out I said, "I once heard Glenn Miller play in concert. We weren't able to go inside the hall because it was only for American troops, but we sat outside listening and imagining."

No one was terribly impressed and one of the nurses, Laura Howard said, "It's an awful long way around to get to Africa via America honey?"

I shrugged. "It's the convoy system."

She offered me a cigarette.

"I don't smoke, thank you."

"How on earth do you know unless you try? You'll want to learn or how else can you smoulder for all those divine white hunters?"

287

Grinning, I took a cigarette and held it to the lighter flame.

"Suck don't blow honey," she said.

The acrid smoke curled into my lungs in a scorching lick, and I choked. They all laughed as if my coughing fit was the funniest thing. It was the first time I felt nauseous since boarding, and I had to go back to my cabin to lie down, but I was back the next day in time to hear about a concert they were planning. Happily, I offered to help, declining with exaggerated aversion the ever-present cigarette that was handed to me. I would never do that again.

It was agreed. I would be one of the three make-believe Andrew Sisters, singing *Boogie Woogie Bugle Boy from Company B* and *Don't Sit under the Apple Tree*. For a moment I remembered apple blossom and Guilly, but forced the image away, just thrilled with the part. I would be singing again, and I was never happier than when I sang. My role was to be the soprano, playing the part of Maxene, with Laura singing contralto for LaVerne, and Diane as mezzo-soprano for Patty.

The Americans were irreverent and had no time for British formality. Laura was from New York, exotic with black wavy hair and pillar box red lipstick. While she smoked incessantly, she feared no one, and spoke her mind in a way I envied. Diane was a paler version, from Boston, her manner reserved although she constantly apologised for Laura's brashness, saying, "Oh, Laura you are naughty," or 'don't mind Laura, Helena, she has a heart of gold under that wayward exterior."

With my exciting new friends, loneliness evaporated, and I threw myself into singing practice, spending my free time making props and costumes out of anything we could find. My health improved and I began to put some flesh onto my previously emaciated body. The pneumonia had caused me to lose so much weight my clothes had hung sack-like on me, and I was forced to use pins and tighten my belt a notch to hold up my skirt. But now the pins would soon be redundant and my cheeks, usually so pale, took on a glow, losing their dark hollows.

Several of the American and Canadian soldiers joined us enthusiastically. Those who could play an instrument, formed a band. The drummer was a Californian called Brian, who spoke such an odd mixture of slang I could never understand him. He seemed to find this amusing for he was always saying things that would leave me helplessly bemused. Then he would walk away with a smile on his face.

Some of the sailors asked to join in when they were off duty, so practice became patchy depending on their availability, but it didn't matter and whenever we could, we would get together and play through our repertoire. The most difficult thing was keeping the rest of the troops at bay until the appointed night of the concert.

There was always someone or another sneaking in to watch. The ship's recreation area was on the lowest deck. We asked for a volunteer guard and a dozen men immediately stepped forward. They took it in turns playing cards or chatting at the door while we practiced. The door guardians' self-appointed organiser was Major Daniel O'Hara, who fancied himself a comic and his exuberance was infectious.

We were to arrive in Reykjavik the next day and had been given permission to visit the town. Since the journey began I had not seen any signs of a convoy and realised we travelled alone after all. The ship's captain said we would pick up our convoy after Iceland although we weren't told much more than that.

Daniel gave us a daily bulletin of events on the ship, which I suspected was just speculation and gossip. As we steamed into Reykjavik harbor, the sky, sea, and land all merged in the cold afternoon light. Except for an orange glow of sun that occasionally seeped through the clouds on the horizon, the snow and ice-covered landscape seemed devoid of colour. A forty-knot wind blew, and the temperature was minus 10 degrees Celsius.

Daniel led an expedition to town, but the weather was so awful, I preferred to huddle in the ship's lounge drinking hot cocoa, a treat I had not previously experienced. The warmth of the ship's boilers kept the worst of the wind and cold at bay and only the hardiest souls ventured forth with Daniel to explore. When they returned they said they had heard that a wealthy Swiss Industrialist would board with his family, and a first-class suite had been reserved for them.

"We should send them an invitation to our concert," Laura said. "Diane, you have that smart writing paper your mother gave you. Now is the time to put it to good use."

Diane rolled her eyes. "How is it that every time you have a good idea it means work for me." She winked at me and smiled to take the sting out of her words.

I was grateful for that clue, for many times I would be left biting my lip in concern at the unfamiliar cultural banter, wondering if I had inadvertently caused offense. The wink was a nice way to know when they were joking or teasing.

The next day dawned crisp and cold but at least the wind had died. The sun, still weak on the horizon, casts its fingers of light across a clear sky, the colour of a robin's egg. I was disappointed we were leaving because without the thick clouds and blizzard conditions of the day before, Iceland was stunning. Too late, I wished I had gone the day before with the few brave ones who went to explore.

Iceland was another country that tried to remain neutral as the German army invaded Denmark. Yet, this time it wasn't the Germans, who disregarded a nation's sovereignty to ride rough shod over their neutrality. The British had simply walked in and taken over, arresting any Germans. They calmly brushed aside Icelander indignation with generous promises for the future, but in the interim, Iceland was a British colony for the duration. At least it had fallen without a bloody battle.

That night we sailed south-west into the northern Atlantic. I sat in my cabin thinking of the people I had met. Diane and Laura had not known each other prior to this war, and it is doubtful they would have met if it had not been the war that threw them together. It was the extreme circumstances that made fast friendships of unlikely associations.

I thought of Anna and Guilly, how quickly we formed a bond, how much a part of my life they were despite the short span of time we had together. It seemed I had known Anna all my life but in reality it was for less than a year. I had only known Marcel on and off for a few months, less for Madeleine, a little more for Guilly, and yet they were somehow a part of my fabric. Could one make such instant and enduring friendships in times of harmony and peace. War made strange bedfellows of us all.

A picture of Dietrich materialised in my mind. I tried to push it away as I always tried to push away thoughts of Dietrich. Lately I was having less and less success. His eyes haunted my sleep and found me at odd moments in the day. The more I pushed him away the more he seemed hell-bent on finding me, at least in memory. I couldn't bear to examine why, and preferred not to think about him at all, not wanting to dwell on the nature of his death. Had he been afraid or have regrets?

I was angry with him being so stupid as to be caught. It was an irrational thought as most spies were caught eventually, especially double agents. I had just been lucky, my role as spy was a light one, and I had never been required to go into Germany, and work in the teeth of the Nazi camp. Besides I was well protected, first by Dietrich, then by Karl and finally by British Intelligence, mostly David I acknowledged. I had never trusted him, but in that I was wrong. Although I also knew he protected me only as far as I was of use to the minutiae of the British agenda, whatever that was outside of winning the war.

Dietrich had also told me I could trust David. I should have listened more carefully. I squeezed my eyes against the rush of hot tears and paced the floor of my tiny cabin. I would never let them take me. I would kill myself or whoever was in my way if anyone even tried.

Why had he gone meekly to his death by firing squad. If I knew how to kill a person with my bare hands, Dietrich would know ten times better, although killing someone was easier to do in training than in real life. I thanked God I had never had to do it, and I wasn't sure if I could, despite the training and practice we were made to do. Why did he go back to Germany? What had the Americans made him do? Why hadn't he escaped, killed his guard, killed himself, anything but face a firing squad. I shuddered. It was my own living horror.

I needed to think of other things, happier things. Of James and the glint in his eye as he laughed at something I said. At David's cricket passion. Of Tom's knowledge of the theatre in Berlin, his head thrown back with laughter showing the gold fillings in his teeth. I turned my thoughts to my Pee Wits, the singers, and the technicians, but I could not banish Dietrich from my mind. His smile would come to me, lifting at the corner of his softly sculpted mouth, his eyes lit-up at secret amusement at the absurdity of this world and all its human folly.

Diane banged on my cabin door, calling for me to come outside. The cold air took my breath away as I followed her to the deck, pulling on my gloves, buttoning my coat, and pulling Dietrich's scarf up over my mouth.

The deck was slippery with ice as we stood with the others clutching the rails, watching the lights in a midnight blue sky as they swirled, and sashayed, showering bolts of blazing green across the great void. I watched in awe as tears froze on my lashes.

26. THE CONCERT

We decided the concert performance would take place the night before our arrival in Newfoundland, in two days' time. I prayed for the weather to hold but we were determined that the show would go on regardless. All fears of U-boats, bombs and icebergs were forgotten, or at least by those of us engaged in the concert. It was like any other theatre production I had ever been in, no matter the venue, no matter the quality. Last minute nerves had everyone running about jittery with preconcert apprehension.

When I arrived at the lounge, the usual guard was posted. Four soldiers were sitting on crates outside the doors playing a game of cards. They leapt up and saluted as I passed. The recreation space was stark with bare steel floors and exposed steel beams.

Diane confronted me, holding a broom in front of her like a weapon. "Where have you been Helena? Must I do all the work myself?"

Another one of the nurses, Patty-Jane, took pity at the sight of my stricken face, saying, "Don't mind Diane, she's snapping at everyone this morning. Apparently, Laura has disappeared and can't be found anywhere. Typical!" She rolled her eyes. "A moment of work to do and she vanishes."

Diane flew to defend her friend saying, "She works harder than anyone."

Patty-Jane laughed and with scorn in her voice said, "Yeah, well, where is she?"

Diane slumped, "I don't know." She turned to me. "I am sorry Helena. I shouldn't be so waspish, but I am so worried about her. I've searched the ship. She can't have fallen overboard, can she?"

I glanced at Patty-Jane, with her pixie-like face and white-blond curls. She rolled her eyes. Her accent was from the south like that of the American colonel I had met at James's house. I thought she was being a bit hard on Laura, who worked as diligently as anyone, and even though she pretended indifference, her work said otherwise.

I took the broom from Diane and began sweeping saying, "Don't worry, she'll turn up any minute you'll see."

Half an hour later Laura sauntered in. Her mouth was held in a barely suppressed smile as she waited patiently until Diane had finished scolding, and said, "Have you finished darling?" She exhaled smoke in long white tendrils. Her red mouth widened with barely concealed glee.

Diane threw up her hands in resignation and said, "So, are you going to tell?"

"You'll never guess who I met, and he's gorgeous."

"Who?" Diane asked dutifully.

"The Swiss gentleman of course. I went to invite him to the concert. Max Kaufmann," she said dreamily.

"Golly, so he really did come aboard at Reykjavik. What about his family, did you meet his family?" Diane asked. "He must be someone special to command a first-class suite."

"Or filthy rich," said Patty-Jane wryly. "He's probably one of those dreadful armaments dealers, selling arms to Germany so they can kill our boys. I certainly won't be mooning over him."

Diane snapped back. "No, he won't. The Swiss are neutral, and I know for a fact that they sell arms to America anyway."

Laura laughed. "You girls should hear yourselves. If they are neutral and selling arms to both sides, who can blame them; makes me wonder who the fools are in all this war-- those making money from it, or those valiantly giving their lives so the rest can make lots of dough. Anyway, isn't your father in armaments somehow Diane? But enough of that. All I know is that Mr. Kaufmann is an absolute gentleman. I saw no sign of family, only a dour private secretary who didn't speak and hardly looked at me. He gave me coffee. Real coffee!

"You had coffee in his suite? Oh, you didn't Laura. That is so risqué." Diane's face was scandalised.

"Why not? He said his secretary had just made it and it would have been churlish of him not to invite me to share it."

Diane changed the subject. "Well, is he coming to the concert?"

"He said he doesn't mix much socially, a little bit of a recluse, I think. Although I wouldn't have thought he was shy. I eventually got him to promise he would think about it."

"It's a bit weird travelling with a private secretary, a man of all things...Don't you think?" Patty-Jane couldn't maintain her scepticism in the face of such intrigue. "What I want to know is what was he doing boarding in Reykjavik to go to America?"

"Patty-Jane, you are so suspicious. Not everyone you meet is a spy." Said Diane.

"I didn't say he was a spy."

Diane said, "No, but you think there are spies and Communists under every bed."

"Well, if he's a spy he can stay under my bed anytime, or better yet, in it." Laura said.

I began to feel uncomfortable with their joking about spies and Communists and moved slowly away, sweeping the floor in concentrated focus. I didn't want to get dragged into a conversation I didn't want to join.

As I left, I heard Diane say, "Well tell us more. If he's not in armaments, what business is he in?"

Laura said, "You think I waste my time interrogating him about business. I have better things on my mind."

That evening Laura once again went to the stateroom suite before dinner. She came back smiling and singing. "I'm in love."

I looked on, envious of her happiness.

Diane cautioned, "Be careful won't you. You can't throw yourself at a man like that and not expect him to take advantage."

For the first time since I met Laura I saw her face turn pink. She rounded on Diane angrily. "A man like what Diane? You don't know him, he's not like that. He's a gentleman and what's more I think I have persuaded him to come to the concert. You better all do me proud girls. Sing like you've never sung before. I want to wow him."

The ship was crowded, but I had found a quiet place, up a flight of steps from the recreation area. It was a small space between the extra cargo crammed onto the quarter deck. I would lean on the rail and watch the sea. It was a form of meditation, a place to think, relax and rejuvenate before I went back to my maintained persona. Not that I found it particularly difficult, but preserving an image takes energy.

I was excited by the prospect of performing in front of a live audience again. Singing into a microphone and recording for wireless was all very well, but nothing beats performing in front of real live people. Somehow my performance always fed off them, growing proportionally with the size of the audience. When I was singing there was no façade, just the real me.

The next day, I skipped into the lounge where Laura and Diane were already hard at work. The room was decorated with pink and white paper, hung in great loops from the ceiling. It gave the place a festive air like being in the centre of a carnival. None of us owned fancy evening clothes so we decided to dress in uniforms, emulating the Andrews sisters in the film *Private Buckaroo*. We all wore our own skirts and shoes, but Laura and Diane had borrowed army jackets and caps. I had my own uniform, but I thought perhaps I should wear a similar American uniform, seeing I was playing an American singer.

The jacket I was given was far too big, but I didn't mind. I couldn't wait to get out there in front of my fellow passengers and sing. I stood between Laura and Diane for our final rehearsal. The band behind us was tuning their instruments. We decided on one last song to make sure everything was in order, and then we would disperse to rest and bathe, ready for tonight.

"Take off your scarf Helena. You can't go on with it. It's the wrong colour."

"Hey, that's a Harvard scarf isn't it?" Brian, the Californian drummer said. "I had a friend who went to Harvard, and he had one just like it. Where did you get it Helena? Got a beau you're not telling us about?"

I shook my head, bereft of an answer. I pulled the scarf off and felt the blood rising up my neck, under his curious gaze. I went behind the curtain and wrapped the scarf around my waist, so it was hidden from view. This served two purposes, one to hide the scarf and two, it bulked out my waist so my skirt would not fall down in the middle of our routine. I don't know why I wanted to wear the scarf, but it was becoming an obsession with me. I couldn't bring myself to take it off except to bathe. It was warm, I suppose.

"Helena, did you hear?" Laura called to me.

"Hear what?" I said smoothing my borrowed jacket over my skirt as I came from behind the curtain.

Laura as usual had a cigarette hanging from her mouth, her eyes squinting against the curling smoke as she picked at the pink and white paper, wrapped around the microphone stand.

"Mr Kaufmann is coming tonight."

Diane interrupted. "You mean, after you nagged him so ferociously, he agreed he might look in sometime during the performance."

"Come on girls," Brian beat a tattoo on his drum. "I ain't going to wait here all day, while you have a little gossip."

Laura put out her cigarette and we ran through our numbers, but it was mechanical. We all knew our parts well and were saving ourselves for tonight. A round of applause and a few whistles created a disturbance at the entry. A crowd had gathered and our so-called guard, who was supposed to be keeping people out, had instead joined them.

Laura laughed and bowed so I followed suit. Diane looked peeved and then smiled. Encouraged, the men came further into the room calling for more, but the band were packing up.

"Come back tonight and we'll give you more." Laura answered their pleas.

As I stepped down from the dais, Daniel was there offering me his hand. His eyes were serious for once as he looked hopefully at me. "Can I come as your beau tonight beautiful Helena?"

"Ease up Ace, I think you'll find you're too late," Brian said in his lazy drawl. He flashed a smile at me, his teeth perfect and white in his sun browned face. "Ain't that right baby doll?" He turned to Daniel saying, 'She has a beau already. A Harvard cat she's keeping quiet about."

Daniel looked stricken and said, "Is that true Helena? Do you have someone?"

I didn't want to hurt Daniel by refusing and I dithered about how to answer when I saw Diane and Laura arguing at the door. I glanced at Daniel's worried face, and cowardly to the last, I said, "Excuse me I have to see what Laura and Diane are up to."

I ducked my head and scurried over to where they stood, leaving Daniel none the wiser. It was mean, but I needed time to think. If I said I had a beau I would have to make up an accompanying story and then Laura, Diane and Patty-Jane would want to know why I hadn't mentioned him before. If I said I didn't have anyone that would only encourage Daniel. It was too complicated.

"You can't go up there again Laura. It's cheap." Diane's face had a pinched look as if she could use the force of her desperation to protect her friend from her own folly. "The man will think you are a, a, a.... oh I don't know but it's not done to chase a man like that, and certainly not to go to..."

The ship shuddered and I staggered against Diane who fell heavily against the doorway. We looked at each other in alarm, waiting for the noise of an explosion but none came. By this time people were surging to get out through the door. I felt a strong arm around my waist as I was almost carried through the door, up the stairs and along the corridor. Brian had me clasped close to him, pushing his way on deck.

The main deck was crowded with people, pointing, and talking as they watched a long low island of smooth white ice float by. Across its midriff were bands of blue from darkest midnight to transparent light. It was a beautiful sight to watch but deadly. We all knew that most of the ice was below the water line. It seemed, the captain had taken evasive action in time, turning the boat hard to starboard, and the iceberg floated by a quarter of a kilometre away, but even at this distance it was enormous.

I realised Brian's arm was still around me. His actions had prevented me being trampled in the rush, but I am not sure I was in enough danger to warrant this close confinement. I eased out from his grasp, moving to stand with a more appropriate gap between us, when I saw Daniel watching. He missed nothing and his face darkened as he watched Brian flash another of his broad smiles at me. Neither of them watched the iceberg. I walked away, just not strong enough to deal with this.

As I returned to my cabin, I saw the silhouette of a man standing at a window. His outline was indistinct against a dark internal background, but there was something familiar about it. I knew who he was when I saw Laura disappearing ahead of me in the direction of the Stateroom, her Swiss gentleman was waiting for her. At least she knew what she wanted. Again, I felt the familiar rush of envious yearning. Such a wasted emotion I scolded myself.

That night at the concert, I stood in the wings, and listened to the audience. They were a rowdy bunch, whistling, catcalling, and jeering as the forerunner acts finished, one by one. I was transported back to the Belgium Club before that terrible blitzkrieg.

From the wings, the crowd was an indistinct mass behind the glare of a bright spotlight. Ours was the last act, but the show was already a success and energy surged through my body. We walked on stage accompanied by the introductory riff of our song. A familiar surge of exhilaration rushed through me, and everything disappeared from my consciousness except the song, and its rhythm.

I was home, the place I was most comfortable, music cocooning me in its bewitching embrace. I lost time and track of the songs we sang. Too quickly it was over, and the crowd stood, hooting, and whistling, shouting more, more, more, stomping their feet, and clapping. Brian did a drum roll as we bowed and then I heard my name called.

"Helena, Helena we want Helena." It was Daniel leading the call, but others soon took it up.

Laura pushed me forward, and she and Diane took a step back, swaying in time to the applause. I hadn't anticipated this. I had nothing else prepared. Brian was tapping a rhythm quietly on his drums. I turned to the band member nearest me.

"Do you know *The man I love*?" I asked the pianist.

He nodded and I turned back to the pink and white paper-wrapped microphone. The room was silent except for the shuffle and breathing of so many bodies in the confined space.

I sang the words with all the pathos of my aching soul, pouring out my longing in a sound that even took me by surprise. Not a soul moved as I finished the song and then they erupted in applause. I couldn't contain my elation, turning to grin I included Laura and Diane and the band in the acclaim. We were a triumph.

They called for more, shouting encore, and I gave willingly, singing until my voice was hoarse. Eventually I called for a break. By now the party was in full swing. A drink was thrust into my hand, and I managed a quick gulp before I was picked up bodily and passed from person to person until, dishevelled I found myself at the exit. My borrowed jacket had been twisted in the melee and I took the opportunity to duck out, and up the stairs to my private space on the cargo deck to get some fresh air and adjust my clothing.

I straightened my jacket and skirt as I stood at the rails of the ship looking into a grey polar night. I patted my waist. My scarf! In a panic I lifted my jacket to see if it had slipped and caught in my skirt, but it was gone. I had to find it.

The dark shadow of a man stood between me and the stairs, his back to the dim blue blackout lighting. In the pale light I could make out the dark and light stripes of my scarf, held outstretched in his hand.

"Oh, thank you, thank you." I hurried towards him. "I was so worried I'd lost it."

"It must be important to you." He said in German. His voice was low and familiar. I squinted to see him better. Then ice coursed through my body.

"Hello Magdalena, or should I say Helena. You change your name so often, although this time I must admit, your disguise is quite effective. I would not have recognised you but for the voice. To think I nearly didn't attend the concert."

My breathing lost its regular rhythm. "Karl?" I looked around. Cargo lined a corridor to the stairwell. There was a bulkhead directly behind me and the ship's rails to my left. The only escape was either down the stairs or along a gangway, both of which were behind Karl.

"Not Karl, Magdalena. Rudolf Kaltenbrunner, private secretary to the Swiss industrialist Max Kauffmann, and a Swiss national."

"What are you doing here?"

He glanced at the cargo and back at me. "I think it is more interesting to know what you are doing here, my daughter."

It was like a slap. "I am not your daughter! Why can't you leave me alone? What have I ever done to you?"

He laughed and lit a cigarette. "You flatter yourself. I am not here for you, although it is a fortuitous surprise. Now you can pay for your treason." He inhaled and took a step closer, and I stepped away, my back to the bulkhead. His next words threw me. "But before you do you will tell me, where is von Winterfeldt?" He examined the scarf in his hand. "I remember he always wore this. How is it you have it in your possession I wonder, or is it just a coincidence you have the same type of scarf?

"It's mine. I bought it in London," I said.

"This I do not believe. Even I am not so ignorant that I do not know that this is from the American university von Winterfeldt attended. It seems you and he are still up to your old games. Where is he hiding?" He chuckled. "Imagine finding both Violetta and von Winterfeldt, Germany's two most notorious traitors. The Führer will bestow on me the German Order."

Oh my God, he knew more than I gave him credit! But he didn't know everything. He didn't know Dietrich's university was Cambridge in England. He appeared not to know Dietrich was dead. That was a surprise. I didn't have time to ponder this now. I needed to focus.

I tried bravado, playing for time. "So, if you were not looking for me then you are running away. I heard the rats had started bolting, now the war turns against the Nazis."

He scowled and I knew I had hit a cord. What did he really know and what had he guessed? Dietrich said my file was destroyed in the bomb blast, but then why did they come after me and try to kill me?

He leaned against one of the cargo containers and put his hand under his coat. A flash of insight made me think the cargo containers might have something to do with him. I said nonchalantly, "This cargo of Mr Kauffmann's, is it weapons?"

He laughed. "You are still a foolish girl. I never knew why the Abwehr gave Violetta such credit. Now I am certain they were fooled by von Winterfeldt. Even though you are both traitors to your fatherland, you are not very clever, either of you."

I saw a shadow move in the stairwell and began talking to distract Karl.

"I am just a singer trying to survive in a world you created, yet you have turned traitor to even that. You are nothing more than a coward, leaving your wife and my child behind in Germany to face the consequences of your actions, while you flee to safety. What is it that you do Karl? You know Germany is losing the war and have fled to save yourself. Is that it?"

His face darkened, but his voice remained passive. "You were always a foolish child. I am here in the service of my country; unlike you and the traitor you were bedding in Paris." He paused then said, "as it seems you are still." He stepped closer and I could go nowhere, trapped by the sea and the bulwark. Something glinted in his hand, a CZ vz 27 pistol, a favourite weapon of the Gestapo.

Karl spoke in English for the first time, and he was surprisingly good. I had never heard him speak any other language before. "Now we will walk quietly to Herr Kaufmann's suite. Should we meet anyone, we will tell them you have been invited to take champagne. Herr Kaufmann has a very good vintage."

I held my breath as Daniel stepped onto the deck. Even at this distance I could see his rage.

"So, this is what you Limey's get up too when no one's around!"

Karl hadn't moved, hadn't even looked around, but as Daniel came closer, he took two strides and grabbed me around my waist, spinning me around playfully as he thrust the pistol into my side. "Who is this man, my darling Helena? Is he bothering you?"

He was so close; I could smell the apple blossom pomade in his hair, and it made my knees buckle. My whole body shook, but his grip kept me upright.

The silence grew, my mind blank. If I yelled we would both die. I vacillated. Daniel stood hands on hips and glared. Karl maintained his casual stance but with a vice-like grip on me and an amused smile on his face.

Daniel gave up first. "I guess it's none of my business, but Major Guilford, don't think you'll be welcome on the American's deck again."

In despair, I watched Daniel leave. If I called out, Karl would kill him. No one would hear the shot from this deck, and no one would look for us here.

When Daniel's form had disappeared from view, Karl said, "Major! Why did the American call you Major, Magdalena? Have I caught myself a British commissioned officer? Do the British know who you are?" He chuckled. "You are full of surprises. But now you are even more valuable, and will be of great use to your Fatherland…and your father. Walk nicely to Herr Kaufmann's suite now and you may live for a while longer."

He loosened his grip, but the gun remained firmly pressed to into my side as he walked close behind, and a little to my right, his left hand on my left shoulder as if in comradery, but he was steering me.

We walked along the narrow gangway next to the stairs, and towards another set of stairs leading to what in normal times might be called the promenade deck where Kaufmann's suite was located. On the left of the staircase was a steel wall, on the right bannisters, and below another narrow gangway.

When we reached the base of the stairs, I heard my name, or rather Helena's, called. It distracted Karl long enough, and I spun around, jerking my elbow into his face. A bullet ricocheted off the steel wall above my head. I ducked around the corner and ran along a short corridor away from Karl.

Someone else had taken that last shot and it wasn't Karl. Neither was he following me. I stopped in an alcove. Footfalls sounded along the steel deck above my head. I crept back the way I had come.

Karl was crouched at the base of the stairs, his pistol directed at the gangway above. He was hidden from view to the upper deck and presumably waited for whomever fired that shot to descend the stairs. Clearly he was no longer concerned with me.

The footfalls above slowed. I could not see to whom they belonged, but I hoped it was Daniel come back to save me. He would need help or Karl would shoot him as he came down the stairs.

I unbuckled my belt, and with a glance up the still empty stairs, I ran swiftly and silently up behind Karl. I knew I only had a moment to act, for if he saw me he would shoot. If I couldn't manage to reach him and gain advantage, his weight and strength would throw me off his back in a second.

I leapt, looping my belt over his head, wrenching it hard, but Karl had already turned and grabbed my throat, bringing the pistol in line with my head. I deflected with my left arm all the while hanging onto the belt with my right, and kicked him hard between his legs.

He buckled and the gun flew out from his hand, but Karl was already recovering and pushed me towards the ship railing. I held on to the belt and tried to push back, but I was running out of strength. He was weakened from a lack of oxygen, or he would have had me, so I hung onto the belt for grim death. Then I felt the ship's railings at my back, his fingers pressed into my throat. I was losing consciousness, but before I passed out he would have me overboard. I determined to take him with me and yanked harder on the belt. His face darkened; rictus teeth bared.

A shadow loomed above both of us, and then Karl slumped. Someone had coshed him from behind. I let go of the belt and twisted beneath him, using all my remaining strength to heave him over the railing. Then I fell to the deck on my knees, gasping for air.

Brian glanced over the railings and said in his usual quiet drawl, "Man overboard." He knelt beside me. "Are you okay baby doll?"

Another man clattered down the stairs. It was Daniel, with a wild look on his face. He was clutching Dietrich's scarf.

He walked up to Brian. "What the hell! What did you do to her?"

Brian stood up. "Calm down Major O'Hara. She's fine. Fell down the stairs is all."

"Horseshit. Where's that man she was with?" Daniel looked about.

I stood up and said, "What man?" Then I ran to the rails and vomited into the dark churning water below. I wiped my mouth looking at the heaving sea. There was no sign of Karl.

I turned away, unable to process any emotion to Karl's death. I had killed a man. I had never killed before, or at least not directly, although my actions may have led to many deaths. Both Brian and Daniel were watching me.

Brian said, "Look Helena, Major Guilford, I don't know exactly what happened here, but neither you, nor Major O'Hara, can say anything.

"The hell you say." Daniel said.

"Major," Brian said turning on Daniel. "This is classified. I know you outrank me, but I am serious. I am on an operation for the Office of Strategic Services, tasked with following Kaufmann. He cannot know that anything has happened to his secretary. We all need to go back to the concert party and act like we never left."

"Kaufmann's secretary! That man Helena was with. What happened? Where is he?"

Brian said, "He jumped overboard. We no longer have him to worry about. Come on Major O'Hara, you saved Helena's life, and I don't know the whole story, but I expect you are addressing a woman who is about to be decorated as a British war heroine for outing a Nazi spy." He paused and grinned at Daniel. "If you hadn't come back and told me she was going to drink champagne with Kaufmann, she would probably be dead by now, so maybe you'll also get a commendation when I hand in my report."

Daniel looked stricken. "Kaufmann was dancing with Laura you see, so I knew you were not going to be drinking champagne with him, I asked Brian what he thought of it all. But I am really sorry for what I said to you back there. Jealous, I guess. I should have seen you were in distress."

"It's alright Daniel." I cleared my bruised throat. "It's all worked out. But Brian, shouldn't we report Kaufmann to the Captain."

Daniel said, "Why would we report Kaufmann? Did he know his secretary was a Nazi? We have to tell Laura!"

Brian said, "What part of classified don't you understand Major. You can tell no one anything, not even Laura. Have I made myself clear?" He shook his head. "Look, Kauffmann is a suspect and must remain in ignorance so I can find out who his contact is in America. It's better if we leave him to finish the job he's come for, then we can nab him."

"Jesus Christ. What about Laura?" Daniel looked panicked.

"Better Laura has her heart broken than the Nazis win the war, don't you think Major O'Hara. Look, just know he is part of one of the worst criminal gangs this earth ever spewed forth."

"A criminal?" Daniel was clutching at straws.

"A Nazi." Brian replied.

307

I tilted my head. Yes, that was exactly what the Nazi's were, criminals of the worst kind--on a massive and organised scale.

"What about Kaufmann's secretary?" Daniel asked. "You can't just make a man disappear and think no one will notice."

"That's true, but we three will know nothing about that. When Kaufmann finds he's missing, there'll be a search and they will conclude he fell overboard, which in a way, he did. Doesn't need to be suspicious so long as we were at the concert or with each other the whole time, okay?" Brian took my hand in both of his. "Now which of us fine chaps would you like to have been necking with in the dark?"

"It'll have to be me," Daniel said promptly. "You can't have a major necking with a captain."

"Didn't you just ask Patty-Jane for a spot on her dance card?" Brian said.

Daniel grimaced. "Hell. I did. She'll be wondering where I am."

How could they be so callous as to joke at this time. "I don't need to have been necking with anyone. I merely went out on deck for a breather after our performance."

"Pity," Brian grinned. "But baby-doll..."

Daniel intervened. "You will address her as Major, Captain."

"Okay, Major baby-doll, we need to talk. I'll need a report of what happened." He peered at my neck. "And you'll need to hide those bruises."

I put my left hand to my neck. Then I held out my right to Daniel. "Thank you for rescuing my scarf Daniel. I will need it now."

He looked at the scarf in his hand with surprise as if wondering how it had got there, then brought it over to me and draped it around my neck. I had a sudden flashback to the Paris station when Dietrich had made the same gesture. My eyes stung and I turned away.

Brian picked up Karl's pistol and threw it overboard. "Pity," he said, "it would have made a nice souvenir." I was horrified and walked ahead, back to the party.

Brian brought me a drink and stood next to me. We watched Daniel dance with Patty-Jane. Then I saw Kauffmann dancing with Laura, and I questioned how he and Karl were tied into all of this. I was seething with questions and fears.

I had killed Karl and it didn't for a minute concern me from a moral standpoint. In fact, I was relieved his stain was now wiped from the earth. The only thing was that his death left my daughter in Germany with Frau Hoffermann. Without Karl, they would have no privileges and no protection. That was when I decided, no matter the cost, I must return to Germany to find her.

Another thing puzzled me. How was it that Karl did not know about Dietrich's execution? He was supposed to have been a part of a plot to assassinate Hitler. That was not an event a senior member of the Gestapo would be ignorant of, no matter the lies and propaganda put out by the Nazis. But I knew all these questions would have to wait for answers.

I needed to find out more about Kaufmann and that cargo on the deck. I was convinced Karl was somehow concerned about it. I also needed to know more about Brian's role, not that I imagined he would tell me, but people let clues slip and I was good at turning fragments into plausible stories. I hitched up my skirt, which had slipped down my hips without a belt, and turned to Brian. "Can we talk?"

Brian glanced at me, saying nothing for minutes. Eventually he said, "Do you know what Kaufmann's secretary wanted from you?"

"Sorry Brian, I too must pull the classified line on you."

"Okay." Brian grinned. "I must say I did wonder how a nursing sister, even one of your Army Intelligence rank, learned to fight like the devil." His eyes held a questioning gleam. "Can you just give me something to put in my report?"

Now it was my turn to remain silent. How could I tell him any of it? Eventually, I said, "Just reference David Asquith, British Intelligence."

The sound of an exclamation interrupted the strained moment between us. Laura called out, "There you are Helena. Everyone's asking for you. Will you sing some more?"

"I shook my head. Too tired. I might head off to my cabin if you'll excuse me." I would not be able to sing for a while with my bruised throat, but all I said was, "Thanks for the drink, Brian. Night Laura."

Brian said, "I'll see you to your door Major."

Laura grinned, and I acquiesced. Kaufmann was an unknown quantity and I could not see him in the room. We walked in silence to my room, Brian's eyes flicking about, and alert. At my door he said, "Goodnight Major. I hope I will have the privilege to meet you again one day, maybe when the war is over."

I nodded and closed my door. When the war is over. I wanted to cry. The war will never be over. Tomorrow we would reach Newfoundland, and I would depart this ship, to fly in military transport to Lake Ontario to fulfill my duties at Military Camp 103.

When this godforsaken war was over, I vowed I would sing again: in New York, in Hollywood, London and Paris, and anywhere else that would have me. But first, I knew I would have to go back to Germany and find my daughter. Then, when this war is over I will find Anna and Joachim. When the war is over.

NEW YORK 1943

Fifth Avenue, Office of Strategic Services

The telling of my story had taken longer than I anticipated, and this was now my fifth interview. Throughout, the Brigadier General had made few comments, although he jotted down notes. Now, I had finished explaining my history as honestly as is possible with all the normal flaws of human recall, he sat back in his chair and gazed at me as if trying to read beyond what might be visible.

I recognised that in attempting to tell the unvarnished truth, I had exposed my incompetence as a spy, but there was little I could do about that. "You know the rest from my report about what happened on the crossing, but as you can see General, that is why I must go back. I don't claim to be brave, nor to have much by way of skill at the intelligence game. If anything, I think I might be blessed with luck as my friend Madelaine once said. I know I can do this, especially as the two German people, who knew of my real identity, and my sedition, are now both dead. My disguise will hold. The one thing I do have in my favour, is being at ease among my countrymen and women. Even in Paris I sometimes forgot I was living a double life. It is hard to pick out a suspicious

311

person when they are comfortable in their surroundings. Besides, I have friends who will help me. If Father O'Bryan is still in Munich, he will help. The nuns will also help me find my feet. All I need is a story that will explain my absence, but that part is simple. I have been thinking about what was in those crates Herr Kauffmann was transporting. While I know that is classified, there must be a way I could infiltrate whatever system he was using, if it still exists. It is just a matter of developing a strategy and a new story...That is a skill I do possess along with my ability at mimicry and to believe whatever lie I am currently living."

The Brigadier General stood up and said, "Wait here a moment." He walked out of the office, and I felt a tingle of anticipation. I know they will accept my proposal. It's just a matter of time, and I will return to Germany to find my daughter.

About the Author

Gillian Long has a PhD in literature and creative writing, and a background in publishing, psychology, politics, and executive leadership in both civil service and the not-for-profit sector. She has lived and worked in Africa, and Europe and now lives on a farm in the Australian Wet Tropics of Far North Queensland. Her previous novels, short stories, forthcoming titles, and other writing can be seen at https://gillianlong.wordpress.com

The 9th District.

Gillian Long

ISBN: 978-0-9945598-3-8

Set in North Queensland during the great depression when men's lives are cheap, immigrants are expendable, and a mysterious disease is sweeping through the cane fields, Mark Anders has had enough. He challenges the powerful sugar industry, and the fight becomes brutal.

The 9th District is based on real events in Far North Queensland, at a time when the 1930s global conflicts played out in the streets, farms, and in the sugar workers barracks of the small sugar towns. It is a story about one man's journey from rejection, to radicalisation, and finally to redemption through love.

Mark's ambition is to make enough money to buy a farm and become a member of the powerful Cane Growers Association. He soon discovers there is more to belonging to the ranks of this regional form of a landed gentry than mere land ownership and they will stop at nothing to destroy a Godless Bolshevik.

Greenwash

Gillian Long

ISBN 978-0-6455760-5-4

Set in Queensland this global conspiracy acts out through a local crime, and an environmental disaster as Dr Jack Fallon races against time to expose the truth before catastrophe destroys all he loves.

Jack is often accused of being a loner, but that suits his role as a mining engineer, who spends most of his time in the outback. His mother disappeared under strange circumstances when he was a child, and he took solace in the riches of the earth. But its geological structures are notoriously unstable and may yet take everything he now holds dear including Sophia, the woman he loves.

While Australia is recovering from a pandemic, fires, flooding, and shortages due to Putin's war, the Australian government is touting an economic recovery led by green gas. Green Synergy, the Australian agent of a global cabal, is the firm of choice leading the way. Increasing gas and oil exploration and extraction gives Jack the opening he needs to return to his home in Queensland, but he soon begins to doubt the wisdom of his choice.

Dying Days

Gillian Long

ISBN 978-0-9942671-1-5

Matt Reid, an ex-British Special Forces soldier, arrives in Australia in search of his biological father.

He meets Alan Fletcher, a retired war correspondent, whose story about the disappearance of a Rhodesian SAS soldier in 1980, sends Matt off to Zimbabwe on a mission to find the truth.

What he doesn't plan is to become a person of interest to a paranoid secret police or to uncover plots of treachery and revenge and a half century old family feud.

This is a story about discovering family, falling in love, and finding redemption.

The Trouble with Maggie

Gillian Long

ISBN 978-0-9942671-8-4

This is a modern tale of morality, longing, lust, and lies.

Maggie had everything she wanted; a wonderful husband and two gorgeous kids. Her life was perfect, until the fateful moment she ignored her dead grandmother's warning and her life changed forever.

Set in rural Australia, this story is about the trials of marriage; secrets, guilt, love, and temptation, but most of all, it is a story about Maggie's journey to redemption, while filled with heroism, hedonism, hankie-panki, and hocus-pocus.

Watershed

Gillian Long

ISBN 978-0-9942671-4-6

It's the end of the 2020s and Australia struggles under tyranny. The economy has collapsed as terrorism escalates.

Conscript Blake Lincoln returns from an endless Middle East war, wounded and a national hero. When he meets Charlotte, all he wants is to have his old life back.

Instead, he uncovers secrets that will blow the government apart.

Watershed is set in Brisbane, Sydney, and Canberra, and takes in the vast wilderness of Cape York, and the raw beauty of the Kimberly region.

It is a story about the insidiousness of political corruption, the dangers of social injustice, the fragility of democracy and the power of family, as one man prepares to abandon all he believes in to save the woman he loves.

www.ingramcontent.com/pod-product-compliance
Lightning Source LLC
Chambersburg PA
CBHW021453240626
47154CB00002B/348